08

P9-BJX-568

250

Wandering Star

SHOLOM ALEICHEM

Wandering Star

Translated by FRANCES BUTWIN

New York

CROWN PUBLISHERS, INC.

Wandering Star

Part I

1   "THE BIRD HAS FLOWN"

Early one Sunday morning, toward the end of summer, Leah, the Cantor's wife, awoke before anyone else, looked out the window, saw it was broad daylight, and exclaimed to herself, "A plague on me. Market-day and I'm still sleeping." Quickly she dressed, splashed cold water over her fingernails, swallowed down the morning prayer in one gulp, and snatching her basket, set off for the market place in such haste as though God knew what bargains lay in wait for her.

Outside the heat of the day smote her like a blast from an oven. Though it was early, the little Bessarabian town of Holeneshti already sweltered in the sun. At the market place Leah felt like a fish that has been tossed back into a cool stream. Here was no ordinary market. It was more like a fair. The peasants had brought to town their finest dairy products, vegetables and fruit—and everything a bargain! Huge melons and green cucumbers were practically given away. As for onions and garlic and other greens—no use asking. Leah bought everything, a little here and a little there, and soon her basket bulged. And then, at the last moment, the Lord sent her a bargain to crown all bargains—a mess of fish. Leah hadn't dreamed of shopping for fish, but they fell right into her lap. Actually, to call these fish was a presumption. Minnows, mere heads and tails—eat and spit—but the price! She'd be ashamed to tell anyone. Yes, this had been her lucky day at the market. Out of the single ruble she had brought with her there still remained a good bit of change.

Well, if that was the case, she must buy the Cantor a present—ten freshly laid eggs to make into ten eggnogs. "The High Holidays are coming and Israel must be in good voice. Did you ever hear such a thing? And some candy for Reizel. What a sweet tooth that child has."

Fondly she thought of her daughter. Then, lest the thought appear a boast before the Lord, she added under her breath, "May all the harm meant for her fall on my head."

And the Cantor's wife darted in and out of the booths and stalls, appraising, bargaining, choosing, until the rest of the ruble had melted like snow in her hands. Only then did she start for home.

Nearing the house, she heard a series of trills. *Mi-i-i bo-a-ash va-mi-i ba-maim.*

It was the familiar, beloved voice of her husband which had rung in her ears for so long and of which she never grew weary. Israel was preparing a new version of the *Rosh-Hashono* prayer. "And we will declare the might . . ." Her Israel was not one of those renowned cantors whose names had spread all over the world. But in his own town of Holeneshti he was renowned enough. You may be sure the town wouldn't exchange him for one of those new-fangled city cantors or let go of him for a million. But that was beside the point. If Israel the Cantor hadn't managed to teach on the side, they would never have made ends meet. Luckily, besides being a cantor, he was also a fine Biblical scholar and a master of the Holy Tongue, and the Lord had also blessed him with a talent for penmanship. He had a round dozen youngsters in his *cheder* from the best homes in town, Rapalovich's son among them. Two such sources of income were not to be sneezed at. Still, it often happened that both occupations didn't bring in enough to provide for the Sabbath. Never mind, they hadn't starved yet.

As she put down her heavy basket and wiped the sweat off her face, Leah wondered why her daughter Reizel didn't come running to meet her. Usually, when she came home from market, Reizel ran out of the door, her face shining and her long braids swinging behind her. "What did you bring me, Mother?" she would call, as she burrowed into the basket for sweets.

"Wait, wait," the mother would stop her. "The river isn't on fire. First we have to put on a pot of chicory for your father. Did you ever see such a thing?"

4

But today nobody ran out to meet her. The basket stood untouched where she had set it. Except for the Cantor's warbling, which now rose to a crescendo, the house was strangely quiet. Reizel must still be sleeping, thought Leah, and busied herself about the stove. As she worked, she muttered under her breath:

"May night's darkness descend on my head. The morning half gone and she's still in bed. There's a girl for you. Any minute the boys will begin to arrive and she'll be running around half-naked. She thinks she's a small child. Israel, Israel!" She raised her voice. "He doesn't hear me. Just listen how he's letting himself go this morning. Dear God in Heaven, a person would think he expects to have his pockets stuffed with gold for his singing. And, instead, Reizel goes around in broken shoes. May the harm intended for her come down on my head. How long will that girl sleep? I'll have to go wake her. Have you ever seen such a thing?"

And Leah went up to the curtain that divided the room in half, lifted a corner with the tips of her fingers, and peered in. She looked at the bed, then at the window, and remained standing stock-still. She felt as though a heavy millstone had turned over in her breast. She screamed to her husband. "Israel!"

He stopped in the middle of a high note.

"Leah, what is it?"

"Where's Reizel?"

"What do you mean, where's Reizel? Isn't she sleeping?"

Half an hour later the news had spread through the town. The Cantor's daughter had disappeared.

People began streaming through the house. "What's the news?" "Is she gone?" "Where did she go?" "How did it happen?" Questions and answers flew back and forth. The Cantor alone said nothing. He stood in the middle of the room like a stone image, staring at the people who came and went. People touched their foreheads with their fingers, meaning, "The poor man has gone out of his mind."

Leah didn't stay home. Followed by a crowd of other women, she ran distraught through the town, wringing her hands and crying, "Reizel, my daughter, my treasure." They looked into alleys and gardens, they combed the bank of the river, they crossed the bridge, they hunted through the cemetery. Reizel was nowhere to be found.

At last the women brought Leah home half-fainting with terror and grief. The house was overflowing with people. Someone had rolled up the curtain that divided the room, and Reizel's bed stood exposed to view. It hadn't been slept in, and the window was wide open. A couple of the town's wags winked at each other.

"So the bird has flown from its nest."

The good people of Holeneshti weren't above making a jest of another's misfortune.

In those days every little Jewish town, no matter how poor, boasted its own Croesus, known as Rothschild.

The Rothschild of Holeneshti was Ben Rapalovich.

To go into detail about the extent of his wealth is superfluous. Suffice it to say that every day of the week Rapalovich's table seated no less than twenty-odd souls. Aside from sons and daughters, sons-in-law and daughters-in-law, and grandchildren, all of them with well-nourished bodies, red cheeks, and fat jowls, there was his mother, an ancient crone whose head shook in a perpetual "No, no," the wet nurse, a good-looking young wench with rosy cheeks, and a certain young fellow, a distant relation, whom Rapalovich employed as his secretary and cashier.

At the head of the long board, like a king surveying his subjects, sat Ben Rapalovich himself, a typical Bessarabian Jew, with a comfortable paunch and an exuberant beard which refused to lie down like a proper beard but radiated in every direction from his dark, glistening face.

When the Rapaloviches sat down to a meal, their laughter and talk, the scraping of chairs, and the rattle of dishes and silver were deafening. But Rapalovich refused to be distracted by a small thing like noise. When he ate, he ate, and what went on around him was no concern of his. One thing at a time was his motto. He himself had little to say, but he didn't mind others talking. Only once in a long while, when the noise got really out of hand, he would pound on the table and shout, "Quiet, you bastards. Look down into your prayer books and attend to what you're reciting." Which meant, "Look into your plates and watch what you're eating."

For Ben Rapalovich spoke in a shrouded language of double meanings. To him a horse was a "fellow," money was "crockery," a wife was "an affliction," a son was a *"kaddish,"* a daughter was a "blister." Bread was "yarn," a house was "an attic," an alcove "a cell," and so on. An entire dictionary could have been compiled of his speech.

In the least conspicuous place at the table, among the little children,

6

sat his wife Beilka, a frail little woman, silent and unobtrusive. Each time you saw her you were struck with fresh wonder. How did this tiny crumb of a woman bring forth such a boisterous brood? And yet, as is often the case, this tiny woman carried on her frail shoulders the burden of the entire household. She was everywhere at once and her head ached for everyone. Long ago she had given up her position of honor to the aged grandmother. She seemed to have no wants or desires of her own. Her whole life was bound up in her children.

The old grandmother, whose head shook with palsy, seemed to have been created for the express purpose of reminding the others of the last stages of man. She had lost all her senses but one—a sharp eye. It was she who first noticed that the youngest of the brood, Leibel, was missing from the family board.

Her sharp eye scanned the long table and her voice quavered. "Where's Leibel today?"

Everyone hushed and looked around. It was true Leibel was missing. Though the Rapalovich clan was so large, it had never before happened that one of its members stayed away from a meal.

Peremptorily the head of the house issued a command.

"Let the young lamb be fetched from the pasture." Which meant, "Bring the boy home from *cheder*."

At once a messenger was dispatched to the home of Israel the Cantor.

The family was on its last course, fresh melons and hot chestnuts, when the messenger returned with the astounding news that Leibel hadn't appeared at *cheder* that day. And he added another bit of information. The Cantor's only daughter, Reizel, had vanished during the night, no one knew where.

It was as though a bombshell had exploded in their midst. Too shocked for speech, the family stared at each other in silence. If a thought had occurred to anyone, he kept it to himself. Only the old grandmother, accustomed to speaking her mind, said, "Take a look into the cash drawer. I could swear I saw Leibel prowling there last night."

Rapalovich shrugged. Old people had strange whims. Nevertheless, he nodded to the cashier and that worthy bestirred himself and went up to the cash drawer. He unlocked it and leaped back, shouting, "Master, the money is gone."

At these words, a cry was heard at the end of the table and a small figure crumpled down in a faint.

It was the silent, unobtrusive, frail little Beilka.

The town of Holeneshti seethed like a vat. Here was a scandal for you—two scandals rolled into one. A young couple had disappeared, and such an oddly assorted couple, the poor Cantor's daughter and the son of the wealthiest man in town.

Shopkeepers locked up their shops, teachers dismissed their pupils, workers laid down their tools, housewives forsook their pots and pans, the whole population poured out into the streets and overflowed the market place. Men, women, and children gathered in knots to air the scandal.

Rumors and conjectures began making the rounds. If one person reported something, a second capped it with something else; a third interrupted to say both storytellers were nothing but dumb oxen. Now the way he heard it. . . . But before he could begin, a fourth remarked that the third man knew less than the dead. Wait until he told them *his* story—a long, fanciful tale citing example and precedent for this and that detail. . . .

Then a newcomer joined the group, a red-headed fellow with dim eyes, and put forth a ridiculous query. "Listen, my friends, let me ask you a question. How does it happen that the two birds have flown on the same night that the Yiddish theater packed up and left town?"

"Listen to him, what's one thing got to do with the other?"

"It seems to me one thing has plenty to do with the other."

"Your brain's addled with the heat. Go jump in the river."

The crowd burst out laughing and the red-headed one put on an injured air.

"Cackle till you burst. If you're so wise, let me put another question to you. What were the actors doing last week at Israel the Cantor's house? If you don't believe they were there, take a walk to the Cantor's and ask him."

"And pour more salt on his wounds? Not us."

"Then stop babbling foolishness and let me tell you what the actors were doing there. It seems they found out the Cantor had a pretty daughter who could also sing, and knowing he was a poor man they asked him to let them take her into the theater and make an actress of her. Well, friends, is that to your taste?"

"It tastes good enough. But how do you account for Rapalovich's young son?"

"There you've got me. My head's been splitting all day trying to figure that out. Is it possible Rapalovich's son was in love with the girl? How could that young whippersnapper get into such a fix?

8

Should I say the Cantor put the girl up to something? We know Israel too well for that. Then was it his wife? There might be something in that. No telling what a woman will do."

"Hush, children, the Governor rides," called out one of the wags, pointing to the police chief who just then flew by in a shiny carriage hung with bells, and drawn by a pair of white horses which the crowd at once recognized as "Rapalovich's steeds." Next to the police chief huddled Yechiel the Musician, who had played for every performance of the Yiddish theater.

At sight of the carriage and horses and Yechiel's pale, frightened face, the stock of the red-headed one with the dim eyes soared sky-high. The listeners drew closer to him as he unfolded his story. Now his words not only had taste; they assumed the substance of truth.

With this clue to the disappearance of the young couple, let us leave the good people of Holeneshti to sharpen their wits on the new evidence, and turn back a short time to the day when the Yiddish theater arrived for its first visit since Holeneshti became a town and Bessarabia a province.

2   A STRANGER ARRIVES

Earlier that summer a stranger had arrived in Holeneshti. His appearance alone caused a mild stir. On his head was a battered derby, in his hands an imitation-leather suitcase. He was short and homely but his eyes were shrewd and his face was clean-shaven from top to bottom.

When the stranger announced that he had come to engage a hall for a Yiddish theater, the mild stir turned to an uproar. People came running from all over town to gape at him.

The inhabitants of Holeneshti had never seen a live actor. What was the theater? Did you eat it with a fork or a spoon? Did you sprinkle sugar or salt over it?

Sizing up the town and its inhabitants with one glance of his shrewd little eyes, the stranger pushed the derby back on his head, and said, in a curiously rasping voice, "I can see by the looks of things that our ancestor Adam never observed the Sabbath here."

9

A simple statement, it seems, yet it caused so much merriment, the stranger had to gape in his turn. When the guffaws had died down, he spoke again, this time earnestly.

"Friends, I've come a long way and my stomach is rumbling with hunger. Can anyone tell me where I can quiet its rumble?"

An ordinary request, you might think, and yet this, too, was received with high glee. The street rang with fresh peals of laughter.

The stranger appeared hurt at this levity. "I'm not joking. In plain words, where can I tie on the feed bag?"

That capped it. The crowd seemed to have been seized by a collective cramp. They doubled over and, holding their sides, rocked back and forth with unsuppressible laughter.

Within half an hour the whole town was repeating, "Where can I tie on the feed bag?"

"What a *schlimazl*," they chortled, and wiped the tears from their eyes.

The *schlimazl* presently found what he had been seeking, a hostelry that served food. Not a pretentious place, but it would do.

Having dispatched a juicy herring and washed it down with a glass of native wine, our worthy drew a cigarette from his breast pocket, lit it, and addressed himself to the landlady, a presentable woman of gipsy complexion named Necha. He began peppering her with questions. Where was her husband, or was she a widow? Or perhaps a divorcee? The landlady found it hard to keep a straight face, and turned away from the *schlimazl*. Whereupon the *schlimazl* slung his cane over his arm, tipped his worn derby over one eye, and, putting his hands in his pockets, went strolling through the town. As he walked, he kept his eyes peeled for a likely place to set up the theater.

He was not alone in his rambles. At his heels trotted a ragged but enthusiastic mob of small urchins, newly won devotees of the Yiddish theater. And at last the stranger stopped before a huge, empty structure covered with a tin roof, in a big courtyard which also stood empty.

"When God created the world in six days, He must have set this barn aside for the Yiddish theater," the stranger exclaimed, and walked into the yard.

It was Rapalovich's yard and barn he had stumbled upon.

Holeneshti didn't have to wait long for the Yiddish theater. As soon as the *schlimazl* had rented Rapalovich's barn, he dispatched the following letter:

10

My dear friend, Albert,

I am writing to report that I am now in Holeneshti, a town in Bessarabia, as big as a yawn but chock full of people who devour cornmeal mush and guzzle wine as though it were water, but they will run to the theater as though the devil were behind them. And I have hired a hall that would do London proud, and it has a stage so big you could ride a sleigh and a team of horses through it, with a tin roof so a drop of rain can't squeeze in. The owner of this theater is named Rapalovich. He is stuffed with money like a sack with grain, still he wanted a down payment but I told him to cool his heels the money I said would come in the mail any day. And I found a lodging place. I'm not bragging but I can't complain either the landlady is a juicy little morsel it's eat drink and enjoy yourself and everything on credit. Don't let the grass grow under your feet but send me the decorations and playbills and pawn everything and bring the company down. If you sit around on your ass any longer we'll all starve to death and to get an engagement here is as easy as eating a *rossel fleisch* is for Hotzmach, and speaking of Hotzmach tell him to stop making eyes at the prima donna he'd better take care of Ethel Dvora first and will you please be so kind as to go over to my lodging I left a briefcase with some censored plays under my bed and send me the playbills without fail and don't get into a huff because I am not sending a wire all I have to my name is twenty kopeks.

Your friend who sends kind greetings to everyone,

Sholom Meyer

In a few days Sholom Meyer received the following reply:

Honored friend, Sholom Meyer,

A curse on you, why did you have to borrow fifteen rubles from Braindele Kozak and tell her to charge it to my account do I have accounts with her you bastard you know how much we all love Braindele that tightwad the way she trembles over every groschen as for the decorations and props you mention in your letter either you're playing dumb or you've gone mad you know very well that the props have been pawned long ago and where will I get the money to get them out of hock when I can't get an engagement here for love or money and I won't throw my own savings down the drain to stuff other people's gizzards they were too hard to come by in the first place. Unless they all sign a contract as Jacob signed for Rachel without any mention of profits or shares everybody wants to be a full partner how do you like that? Hotzmach my partner too! He'll never live to see the day though he keeps threatening he will run off and start a company of his own let him run till he drops dead where will he get the props and the scripts

and who will support his cast may he rot ten feet under ground.
I am sending you the playbills and I want you to hire the hall for
nine performances and a benefit and listen you thief what's the
idea of babbling about twenty kopeks to your name are you too
proud to pawn your watch the way I did everybody is willing to
make me the scapegoat everything is on my shoulders everybody
wants the leading part and when it comes to shelling out money,
nobody home. Listen this is my last try if Bessarabia works out,
fine, if not you can all go to the devil I am going to Rumania to
collect a new troupe that will make man and God rejoice, meanwhile get everything ready but don't run up any bills we are coming Friday evening and Saturday night we have a rehearsal and
Sunday we start performing and listen let me tell you that your
censored plays have been on the trash pile for a long time and I
get letters from all over the world with guarantees of engagements
but I have turned them all down because first I will run through
Bessarabia and then we will see.

With kindest regards and best wishes from your friend and
director,

Albert Shchupak

3   THE HOLENESHTI PUBLIC

Drunkards who hadn't tasted the bitter drop in
months, starvelings who had long been denied a bite to eat, couldn't
have thrown themselves on food and wine more avidly than the people
of Holeneshti threw themselves on the Yiddish theater.

Opening night found not only Rapalovich's courtyard but the
whole street in front of his house overflowing with people. The crowd
was so thick, you couldn't have thrown an apple among them. But not
everybody was prepared to go in. In the first place, tickets cost money
and money was a scarce commodity in Holeneshti. In the second place,
theater wasn't everybody's dish. It was well enough for young folks,
for women and children to watch the antics of comedians. But older
men, respectable citizens, some of them greybeards with daughters old
enough to be led under the marriage canopy, would have nothing to
do with such frivolity. Still, even these solid citizens were not exempt
from that plague of mankind, curiosity. Where is it written, they

12

argued, that a man shouldn't take a look from outside through a chink in the wall at what is going on in the theater?

Against such chink-in-the-wall spectators the management hit on a remedy, a water-sprinkler from which gushed a cold stream of water. This method worked more efficiently than a squad of police and it was cheaper.

Its inventor was none other than our acquaintance Sholom Meyer, the *schlimazl*. What his function in the theater was is hard to explain. He was nothing and at the same time everything—bookkeeper, cashier, scene-shifter, ticket seller, and prompter. And when necessary he turned actor. To call him an accomplished artist would be exaggerating. But he was better than that, a hard worker, as faithful to his master as a dog, as Shchupak the director was well aware.

Most important of all, from the viewpoint of the public, Sholom Meyer was in charge of passes, candidates for which were plentiful in Holeneshti.

First and foremost was the Rapalovich clan, some twenty-odd souls. Rapalovich could afford to pay the price of admission many times over, but why should a man pay to enter his own barn? As the doors of the theater were flung open, Rapalovich, followed by his children and grandchildren, the cashier and wet nurse and other hangers-on, marched in and filled the first rows. When Sholom Meyer asked for tickets, Ben Rapalovich looked him up and down and said in a loud voice, "Take those sawed-off stumps of yours out of my sight before I pound you into cornmeal mush."

Sholom Meyer immediately discovered that he was needed elsewhere. And there were others who demanded passes. Take Yechiel the Musician. Who would have thought that a mere fiddler would boast such a large family? And what about the other members of the orchestra? And the wig-maker? And the carpenter, the smith, the tailor, the shoemaker? All had wives and children. And that juicy morsel of a landlady. Was she to blame that she had two younger sisters and a mother as deaf as a post? Enough that she supported them with food and lodging. Was she obliged to buy theater tickets for them, too? And Simon-David the teamster and Chaim-Bear the porter, who had helped cart the scenery from the train. Let Albert the director gnash his teeth and tear his hair, let him fall in an apoplectic fit and drop dead altogether. Whoever had passes coming to him managed to get them. And if someone walked in without even a pass—well, let him come in.

You must never argue with the public.

Not the entire audience came in free. Many paid their last hard-earned ruble for a ticket, borrowed from friends, or pawned their last trinket or heirloom. When your children begged and pleaded and wept to go, you had to have a heart of stone to refuse them.

But what could you do when you had no money at all, no one to borrow from and nothing to pawn?

Into this last category fell Israel the Cantor. The income from both of his occupations didn't provide for luxuries like theater tickets. Reizel pleaded as hard as the other young people in town to be allowed to go, and Leah racked her brains for a way. Let the gossips wag their tongues, let them say she spoiled her only child, raised her on sweets and confections. Reizel must go to the theater.

And Leah found a way. Since Rapalovich's son Leibel was her husband's pupil, and since the entertainment was to take place in Rapalovich's barn, both the pot and the spoon were kosher. The whole thing was made to order. First she broached the subject to Israel, who would have nothing to do with it. His pride wouldn't allow him to speak to young Leibel. But where her child was concerned, Leah the Cantor's wife was willing to swallow her pride. As Leibel was about to leave the *cheder* that day, she drew him aside.

"Leibel, I have a favor to ask of you."

Leibel flushed and stared at his teacher's wife. A favor of him?

When he heard her request, his cheeks grew even redder. He was quite willing, he said, to speak to his mother, who would speak to his father, who would speak to his mother, who would ask his father. . . . Leibel stopped in confusion. But the meaning was plain. He would do it. Here Leibel's grave blue eyes met Reizel's dancing black ones, which seemed to say, "You're wonderful, Leibel. I know you can do it. If you only want me to go to the theater, I know I will go."

That same afternoon Leibel brought back the answer. He had spoken to his mother, who had spoken to his father, who said that if Reizel came to their house that evening she could go to the theater with them.

Reizel's face became radiant. She threw herself at her mother, hugged and kissed her, and, humming a dance tune, began whirling her mother around. Leah pushed her away, laughing.

"Have you gone out of your mind, child? Better hurry and get washed and dressed. Then I will braid your hair for you. After all, you're going out among people tonight. Have you ever seen such a thing?"

14

That evening Leah herself escorted Reizel to the Rapaloviches' and entrusted her daughter to Beilka's care.

"You know she's my one and only child, the apple of my eye."

Beilka looked at the young girl and what she saw seemed to meet with her approval. "Don't worry," she promised, "I'll watch over her as though she were one of my own."

Left alone at the Rapaloviches', Reizel felt uneasy at first. She was surrounded by so many strangers, who all seemed to devour her with their eyes. And the questions they asked her, each one separately and all together. "How old are you?" "What is your name?" "Where do you live?"

And all those eyes. They wouldn't stop boring through her.

Her own eyes were drawn to everything. Reizel had never, in her wildest dreams, beheld such a house. Such a multitude of rooms, so much furniture, so many tables, chairs, beds, mirrors, and knick-knacks, and the supper table set with such a profusion of dishes. Such bowls of fruit, so many different kinds of preserves. And the noise, the clatter, the talk, the laughter. So that's what being rich meant.

Reizel had known that her father's pupil Leibel was the son of the richest man in town. But just what that meant had never been clear to her. That it was good to be rich and bad to be poor she had heard from her mother not once, but a thousand times. "Pawn your empty purse and become rich." "Luck always favors the rich." "The rich are even welcome in the next world." Until now these proverbs had been empty of meaning. Now she sat at a sumptuously laden table surrounded by gay, carefree faces. For the first time in her life she felt a twinge of envy. Then her eyes met a pair of grave blue eyes, the only familiar eyes there. They seemed to be saying, "Are you happy with us? I am so glad you are happy." Her heart stirred and she felt an unaccustomed delicious warmth steal through her limbs.

4 THE CURTAIN RISES

The theater was filled long before starting time. Who wanted to take a chance on being late? Late arrivals had to sit in each other's laps, and the last to come in stood squeezed in the aisles or

15

flattened against the walls. They felt greatly put upon; they had paid good, hard cash for seats, and where were they? Low grumbles were heard, then louder complaints, then a hue and cry. At the peak of the hubbub Sholom Meyer, resourceful as always, gave the musicians a signal to start up a tune. Hearing music, the audience thought the curtain was about to go up, settled down as best it could, and quiet descended.

But the music stopped and the curtain remained drawn. From behind it came shouts and curses, the sound of running feet, furniture being moved, hammers pounding. The audience became restive, children wriggled in their seats, pounded on the floor, and clamored loudly for the show to begin.

Among the young people eagerly waiting for the curtain to rise was a young couple, a boy with fair hair and blue-grey eyes and a vivacious, dark-eyed girl with dimpled cheeks. They sat close together, oblivious of everyone around them, who were equally oblivious of them. Who had eyes for Rapalovich's young son and the Cantor's girl with the curtain before them?

This was the first time Leibel and Reizel found themselves so close to each other. They had seen each other often enough at her father's *cheder*, but there Leibel had to keep his eyes on his books. And Reizel's mother, Leah, was strict. She wouldn't let her go near any of the pupils. "A girl," she would say, "has no business with boys. For a girl is a girl and boys are boys. Did you ever see such a thing?"

Leah wouldn't even allow Reizel to sing when the boys were at their studies. And Reizel loved to sing better than anything in the world. Sometimes she forgot her mother's prohibition and a melody burst from her lips. When that happened the boys stopped their reading and listened with bated breath. And later, at home, more than one of them remembered and sighed and dreamed of the teacher's daughter.

For Leibel it had been more than a passing sigh or a dream. Reizel's face and voice haunted him at all times. More than once, in the *Gemorah* held in front of him he saw not the fine print of the text but Reizel's vivid face.

Many times he had sought excuses to linger behind the others to speak to Reizel only to have that mother of hers come between them. On her part, Reizel, too, had stolen glances at her father's pupils, seeking out Leibel among them. Not because he was the wealthy Rapalovich's son, which had meant little to her, but because of what her father had said about him, that he had a good head on him, and

16

a fine voice. Israel was no mean judge of those two abilities.

Leah, of course, interpreted this in her own way. "Why not? It's a rich man's luck to have gifted children. Have you ever seen such a thing?"

Now Reizel and Leibel sat close to each other on a single bench. Leibel could feel her nearness: he thought he could hear her heart beat. Or was it his own heart pounding? He wanted to say something to make her eyes sparkle and her dimples come out. But his throat felt too tight. Reizel wanted to speak, too, but couldn't think of anything to say. So they looked at each other wordlessly.

All at once they realized how fast time had flown, for now the lights went out one by one. Voices whispered on all sides.

"Oooooh."

"It's as dark as in Egypt during the plagues."

"Ow. My foot."

"Whose fault is that? You have a sore foot, so leave it at home."

"Be quiet. *Shah.* Let it be quiet."

"The devil with you—be quiet yourself."

The audience drew a long breath, shivered, and was still. Leibel didn't know how it had happened, but all at once Reizel's hand, a warm, soft hand, was clasped in his own. He gave it a light squeeze, as though to say, "Happy?" And she replied with a soft pressure which meant, "Very."

The curtain had risen.

For the people of Holeneshti the theater was a bit of luck which had dropped down on them from the clear sky. But for Rapalovich's son and the Cantor's daughter it was more. It was sheer heaven. It was a return to the legendary Garden of Eden. Night after night they went there, occupied the best seats, and beheld the wonders unfolding before them.

A new world had opened up for them in which people disguised their features, dressed in peculiar garb, strutted about, spoke strange words, danced and sang, and acted out scenes which evoked gales of laughter or melted you in tears.

Who were these people? Were they ordinary human beings?

Impossible. They weren't mortals such as you and I, but spirits and demons, or else angels from heaven. Their every gesture and movement, the way they walked forward or stepped back or even stood still was a marvel. They must be bewitched, along with everything around

17

them. From the moment the curtain went up, Reizel and Leibel fell under a magic spell, forsaking the earth for a region of spirits and fairies, demons and angels.

However, when the curtain went down, the magic vanished, the demons and angels gone into thin air. Leibel and Reizel returned to their ordinary selves in the ordinary workaday world. From the topmost pinnacle of heaven they had plunged back to earth. Stunned, they comforted themselves with the thought that the curtain would go up again; again the next night they would soar into heaven.

All the young fellows in Holeneshti envied Leibel because it was in his father's yard that this splendor took place. And all the girls in town were dazzled by Reizel's good fortune in her sudden elevation to the seats of the mighty.

And Reizel's mother, Leah, wasn't above boasting about it. What if she had found favor in the eyes of the rich? Didn't a child like Reizel deserve it?

Still, lest people jump to the wrong conclusions, Leah was careful to explain how it had all come about. "How did my child fall in among the Rapaloviches? Wait, I will tell you. I happened to run into Beilka Rapalovich at the market one day. 'Good morning,' says she. 'A good day to you,' say I. 'And how are you and yours?' she asks. 'God be thanked, and how goes it with you?' 'Don't ask,' she tells me. 'There's bedlam at my house. Some kind of theater has come to town, and they set it up in our barn. You can imagine the excitement among my boys and girls. And how is *your* daughter? I've been hearing fine things about her.' 'Thanks,' I tell her. 'It could be worse.' 'Why,' she says, 'don't you send her over to my house?' 'And what would she do there?' I say. 'She'll get acquainted with my girls, go along to the theater with them. Why not?' 'Thanks,' I tell her, 'I'll ask Reizel. If she's willing to go, I'll certainly send her.'"

A lie, every word of it. But what won't a mother do for her child? Leah found further occasion to drop remarks in front of the neighbors.

"Reizel, what did you have for supper at the Rapaloviches last night?"

"Reizel, what time are you going to the Rapaloviches tonight?"

Or later: "If they ask you for supper again, don't turn them down. No use being bashful. Did you ever see such a thing?"

When the performance was over, the audience made a rush for the doors. Earlier everyone had wanted to be the first to enter; now everyone wanted to be the first to leave. Leibel and Reizel were almost carried out in the press of the crowd.

Outside the night was fragrant and balmy, semi-tropical Bessarabian night, velvety-black, pierced with stars and lit by a red harvest moon. The day had cooled off and the thick dust had settled, making it possible to breathe again. The cool breeze carried odors of ripening grain, melons, apples, and pears.

The Jews of Holeneshti walked home from the theater, not sedately, with polite leave-takings like big-city theater-goers, but yelling and gesticulating. In such a crowd everyone feels duty-bound to impart to the next person what he has seen and heard, in a shrill voice, with inflections and gestures. Everyone is convinced that what *he* saw and heard no one else saw or heard. One repeats a joke several times over for emphasis; another imitates the comedian; a third hums snatches of a song. Children tumble under the grown-ups' feet, laughing and shrieking and crying. Young people gather in clumps or loiter in pairs, reluctant to go home. But there is nowhere to go after the theater, and soon the town is quiet again. At home everyone says his prayers, blows out the lamp, and the town sleeps.

In the small house on God's Street where Israel the Cantor lived a smoky lamp burned late. The Cantor and his wife were waiting for their daughter's return.

Israel, a distinguished-looking man with a silky black beard, sat in his night clothes and skullcap, fanning himself and intoning the bedtime prayer. Leah, enveloped in a voluminous white gown that threw into sharp relief her swarthy face and snapping black eyes, sat on her bed, her figure casting a grotesque shadow on the whitewashed wall.

The moment Reizel entered the door, Leah pounced on her. What sort of "comedy" had the actors put on tonight? Which of their friends was there? What did she eat at the Rapaloviches?

Reizel hardly heard what her mother was saying. Her face was aflame with excitement, her heart was filled to bursting, and there was a rapt, faraway look in her eyes. In her ears still rang the voices of the actors declaiming their lines, the strains of the orchestra and the laughter of the Rapalovich clan. Loudest of all echoed Leibel's whisper: "Will you come again tomorrow?"

"Yes, I will come. How can you ask?" She had not spoken, but answered him as always with a pressure of her hand.

Later, as Reizel snuggled down into her pillow, she shut her eyes, and gave herself up to dreams which carried her far off from God's

19

Street, back to her newly found Garden of Eden, to the world of the theater.

5   EXALTED GUESTS

From their childish paradise, our youthful pair, Reizel and Leibel, unlike their illustrious predecessors, Adam the First and his wife, Mother Eve, were not expelled for any lapse of their own. No. It was rank outsiders who, stumbling on their blessed retreat by accident, brought about their fall.

The first to topple from bliss was the Cantor's daughter, Reizel. Here's how it happened.

Early one morning, when the Cantor was at the synagogue and his wife at market, and before the Cantor's pupils had begun to arrive, Reizel sat at an open window, her hair hanging loose and a small red shawl over her shoulders. She was mending her jacket, and as she worked, she sang a ditty she had heard at the theater the night before.

The little goat went to market—
That's the trade you will keep—
To buy raisins and almonds,
Sleep, my child, sleep.

"Bravo, little kitten, bravo!" A hoarse voice called out under her window. Reizel started in fright and saw a strange man with a huge market basket over his arm leering at her. It was the *schlimazl* Sholom Meyer, whose manifold duties at the theater included housekeeping. Every morning, while the others slept, he went to market to buy something for his "children," as he called the actors, to chew on. The way led through God's Street, where this familiar tune sung with such warmth and purity of tone stopped him, as he put it, "dead in his tracks." Looking up, he beheld a dark-haired young girl, a mere child, with a lovely face. Sholom Meyer was not one to admire in silence. The minute she paused, he cried "Bravo, bravo!"

The small red shawl slipped from her shoulders, exposing for a mo-

20

ment her half-formed breasts. This extra fillip spurred Sholom Meyer on.

"Did I frighten you, little bird? You have a voice, let me tell you, that's honey-sweet. Prima donnas would turn green with envy to hear you. May God grant me fortune and luck! And you're something to look at besides. Wait, am I crazy or have I seen you somewhere before? I could swear I saw you sitting on the same bench in the theater with Rapalovich's young whelp. No? Aha. You're blushing. Your face has turned redder than your shawl. Laugh, girl, laugh. It makes you still prettier. Your dimples get bigger and your teeth flash whiter in that gipsy face of yours. May God grant me fortune and luck!"

Reizel was disturbed less by the man's knowing leer and his coarse compliments, which she barely understood, than by the fear her mother might find her sitting half-naked in the window talking to a strange man. She leaped away and slammed the window shut in his face.

That evening, at the theater, Reizel saw the same man again. He winked at her slyly and her face grew as fiery as the setting sun of Bessarabia. Later, during the first intermission, when Yechiel struck up a Yiddish folk tune to show what he could do, and the audience began cracking nuts, chewing green pears, and exchanging wisecracks recalled from the first act, Reizel saw the man pointing her out to the director, a tall, lanky personage in a top hat, with diamonds on every finger. This individual fixed her with a stare of his small, lashless red eyes. And again her face turned a fiery red.

The very next day, after Israel the Cantor had dismissed his pupils for the midday meal, the door opened and two people walked in. Both were freshly shaven and smelled strongly of soap and eau-de-cologne, but the taller of the two presented the more dashing appearance. His small, closely shaven face with its red, lashless eyes surmounted a long neck, brick-red and wrinkled. This in turn reared itself above a huge, snowy-white collar and wide flowing tie stuck through with a diamond pin. Every one of his long bony fingers twinkled with diamond rings. From his massive gold watch chain hung a large gold medallion embossed with his monogram, the two letters, A and S, intricately entwined and set with diamonds, rubies, sapphires, and emeralds. The jewelry constituted the visible testimonials of his Thespian triumphs, showered on a great actor by an admiring public. Actually, were the truth known, Albert had bought them himself, one by one, on the honest toil of the score of starved, brow-beaten, ex-

21

ploited but irrepressible souls who made up his company. On the assumption that a man shouldn't trust anyone, not even his own wife, Albert carried his wealth on his own person, where it was both safe and seen.

On beholding two such exalted guests, Israel rose from the table, his wife Leah brought out two chairs, and Reizel, poor Reizel, blushed.

"Blessed be your appetites—how do we say it?" began Albert in a luckless attempt to meet the Cantor on his own ground. Sholom Meyer took up the greeting from there (who else but Sholom Meyer could pull him out of such muddles) and went on in flowery language:

"Blessings on your food. Eat it with good appetite. Bite, chew, swallow, and don't mind us. We're plain folk like yourselves. This is my superior, the director of the Yiddish-German theater, and I'm his chief assistant, the first fiddle, the top of the cream, so to speak. His name is Albert Shchupak, and mine Sholom Meyer. Now that we're acquainted, let's drink on it, if you have something to drink in the house. If not, send out for a bottle. After that, we'll take a bite with you. I see you're grating beets—it's a delicacy I haven't tasted in maybe a hundred years. May God grant me fortune and luck!"

After the meal was over and Sholom Meyer had stopped for breath, Albert decided it was time to come to the point. By nature he was a taciturn man, but once he began talking he became so tangled in oratory, there was no stopping him. Knowing his chief's weakness, Sholom Meyer stood by to leap to his aid.

"You must understand, my dear Cantor," began Albert, "that I was once myself a choir boy and studied with a cantor. That is, I carried slop buckets, I mean I sang in the choir. I had a fine voice, a true soprano, and I caught slaps, I mean I sang in the pulpit for years, until I grew up and became something in my own right. I began singing at weddings and circumcisions and celebrations of all kinds. Let me tell you, I sang my own compositions which I had myself composed. I would like to show you the book of songs I made up. It was published in a book, let me tell you. There is a sacred song that goes like this." And Albert began swaying and chanting in synagogue style:

Hallowed be thy name, Cipka my wife,
Here at the pulpit, may the devil grab you
This very night!

Before Albert could get to the second stanza of his original composition, a swift kick under the table from Sholom Meyer gave him the

22

signal to halt. Sholom Meyer himself undertook to explain their mission to the Cantor. Long before coming to Bessarabia, he said, they had heard of Israel's fame as a cantor, and since music was their calling, for weren't theater and music like brother and sister or like husband and wife, wouldn't it be only fitting and proper—in short, would the Cantor favor them with a song?

"Something lively," broke in Albert. "Something juicy in Yiddish."

At first Israel hung back, waiting to be coaxed. "Who? What?" he said. "There's nothing to it. The world likes to exaggerate." But even as he spoke, he was rising from the table, wiping his lips, and clearing his throat. Then he asked, "And what, for instance, would you like me to chant?"

Without waiting for an answer, the Cantor raised his head and lifted his voice in a chant from the Days of Mourning, rendered with rises and falls, trills, quavers and arpeggios. He saw the two guests throwing meaningful glances at each other and smacking their lips as though they were being regaled with delicious food or sweet draughts of wine. Thus spurred on, the Cantor sang song after song until Sholom Meyer caught him by the sleeve.

"Forgive me, dear Cantor, your voice is so magnificent we could stay here and listen till sunset. May God grant me fortune and luck, if I'm not telling the truth. But time, time doesn't stand still. We have a whole theater on our necks, with try-outs and rehearsals and other thorns-in-the-flesh. The point is—we have to work. Tomorrow we are putting on a brand-new comedy, *Kuni Lemel*. And so, would it be too much to ask you that before we leave, you favor us with a little dessert?"

The Cantor stopped, taken aback.

"For instance, what kind of dessert?"

"We'd like to hear your daughter sing. We've heard she has such a sweet voice that thirteen Pattis and seventeen Nelsons could hide their heads in shame."

"How do you know my daughter can sing?" burst out the Cantor's wife Leah, unable to contain herself any longer. At this Reizel caught her breath. If Sholom Meyer said he had heard her singing at her window, she would catch it from her mother! But Sholom Meyer's canny eyes had caught the look on her face, and he twisted himself out like an eel.

"A good tale, though a short one. How is it that everyone knows that your husband has such a wonderful voice, a 'coloratura' that the world marvels at? For fifteen years we've traveled with our theater and never heard of a place called Holeneshti, and yet, you see, Israel of Holeneshti is known to us. The whole world resounds with his name. What do you say to that, my dear madam?"

The "dear madam" had nothing to say to this. She was not surprised that the whole world resounded with her husband's name. But to have her daughter start singing in front of two total strangers was something else again. "Let a girl burst into song, just like that, without rhyme or reason, hocus-pocus, one-two-three? Have you ever heard such a thing?"

Israel, on the other hand, did not take it amiss that his daughter had been asked to sing. True, his wife might be right when she argued that "a girl is a girl and a boy is a boy." Still, if once in a blue moon the child sang along with her father, what harm was there in that? And to tell the truth, he didn't mind singing a little more himself. When a cantor gets started he's like the rain—when it falls, it pours.

And he looked at his wife as though to say, "What can it matter if the child sings a bit?" Leah understood that there was no holding him back. She answered him with a look which meant, "Are you still itching to sing? Then go ahead. Your will is my pleasure. Have you ever seen such a thing?"

Israel's face brightened; he cleared his voice loudly and said to his daughter, "When we're asked to sing we can't be so rude as to refuse. The question is, what shall we sing? I'll tell you what. Let's sing 'Lord of the World.' You sing the lead and I'll help out in a lower key. Start, Reizel. La-la-la-la."

Relieved that yesterday's escapade had passed unnoticed, Reizel was glad to sing anything. Especially since she loved to sing above everything else. She could have sung all day long if her mother hadn't forbidden it: "You must think you're an infant. A young woman like you! Did you ever see such a thing?"

Now Reizel placed herself at her father's side, folded her hands behind her back, raised her eyes to the ceiling, and in a voice as sweet and clear as the tone of a violin, drew out a plaintive Yiddish melody.

Lord of the World!
Lord of the World!
We be-seech you hum-bly our pray-ers to he-ar
How much lon-ger are we this ex-ile to be-ar?
How much lon-ger, dear God, will our suf-fer-ings be-e-e?
Can they l-ast, can they l-ast, till e-ter-ni-ty-y-y?

24

Oppressed and driven, we be-eg of The-e-e
How much longer, how much lon-ger can our ex-ile be-e-e?

The two guests sat spellbound and when the song came to a close they remained with their mouths hanging open. Sholom Meyer recovered first and came out with a loud "Bravo" in his rasping voice. But he stopped in confusion, aware that this was unsuitable. Albert Shchupak, for his part, was completely overcome. The simple words and the plaintive melody, in their very artlessness, expressed the suffering and aspirations of a people. They stirred something that lay dormant in his shriveled soul. Or perhaps it was the singer with her charming dimples and her melting black eyes and the voice like the tone of a violin. Be that as it may, Albert Shchupak, on recovering himself, leaped out of his chair, caught the Cantor's hand in both of his hands and with unmistakable tears in his eyes and a tremor in his voice stammered, "Let my name not be Albret." (Be it noted that he was incapable of pronouncing his own name *Albert*.) This expression, "Let my name not be *Albret!*" was the highest compliment the director of the Yiddish-German theater was capable of bestowing on anyone.

Had he been content to end the interview then and there, all would have been well. But Albert was not the man to let well enough alone. The businessman in him came to the fore.

"What a voice! What a throat! What pitch! What tone! Well, well. Listen to me, my dear Cantor. Here you are, buried in the sticks, hiding in a rat-hole. Splashing around like a frog in a mud puddle. Who sees you? Who hears you? All you know is mush and melons, melons and mush, and synagogue chants. It's a pity, a great pity. A gem like that, a rough diamond. I mean your daughter. What will become of her? I ask you, what will become . . ."

At mention of her daughter the Cantor's wife pricked up her ears. Without as much as a by-your-leave, she cut the director short. "A stranger has no business counting the teeth in another's mouth. Our daughter, I will have you know, still has, God be thanked, someone to look out for her."

Albert did not grasp, or else pretended not to grasp, this figure of speech. He continued to address himself to the Cantor.

"What was I saying, dear Cantor? Oh, yes. You people are blind, stone-blind, and fanatical besides. You're sunk in your own ignorance. You know nothing of the outside world. If you could see the girls in my troupe—dolls, every one of them. The prima donna is a girl of refinement just like your daughter. She hasn't got your daughter's looks, but her voice! High opera, no less. If she came to me, your daughter I mean, in three, four years she'd bring in this much." And Albert extended his arms wide to show how much gold their daughter would bring them as a member of his troupe.

Whether the Cantor's wife understood his meaning is hard to tell. What she saw was a wrinkle-faced clown in a chimneypot of a hat making a bid for her daughter, mouthing nonsense that turned your stomach. "May my enemies not live to see the day," she burst out. "What do you take us for, common trash, cobblers or pants-patchers, to allow our own flesh and blood to join a gang of comedians, acrobats, clowns, vagabonds? Have you ever seen such a thing?"

The director's face turned livid and sweat stood out on his forehead. His lips tightened with suppressed fury and his small, lashless eyes became bloodshot. The unmitigated gall of the woman to speak to him this way, to him, the director of the Yiddish-German theater. He would have leaped on her with both fists, if Sholom Meyer hadn't intervened. He caught the director by the sleeve, gave him a broad wink and turned to the Cantor.

"Your spouse is quite right," he said. "You have a wife in a million, may God grant me fortune and luck! But she has one tiny failing—she's a bit too hot-tempered. She didn't understand my friend the director. He was only talking in general about the different callings there are in this world. You know how it is. Everyone thinks his occupation is the best. Every dog is a master at his own gate and every hog thinks his puddle is the deepest. He meant no offense to you or your wife or daughter. We came here, I assure you, only to hear the Cantor sing. We would stay on and on, but we don't want to intrude. I see the Cantor's pupils are beginning to return, and he is anxious to get to work. How is it said? The *Torah* is the best merchandise. So good-day to you, and a happy journey."

"Break a leg on the way," the Cantor's wife sped their departure. No sooner were they out of earshot than she turned on her daughter. "You can kiss the theater goodbye, my daughter. You won't put foot in it again unless it's over my dead body."

Next she would have turned on her husband but his pupils were already seated around the table. Somewhat crestfallen by the turn of events, Israel pulled himself together. Rubbing his hands nervously, he addressed himself to his pupils. "Do you remember, my children, where we left off? Ye-e-es?"

26

6   ENTER HOTZMACH

Rapalovich's courtyard had become a busy place. Something was doing in the barn day and night. Carpenters mended benches which had collapsed the night before, painters touched up scenery, draymen carried in packing boxes, dragged planks and boards in and out, swung ropes under the rafters. There was a constant din of sawing and hammering, shouts, curses, and laughter, mingled with yells of, "Hotzmach, where are you?" "Hotzmach, get a move on you." "Have you lost your eyes, Hotzmach?" "Move that bench, Hotzmach." "A curse on you, Hotzmach!"

Who could this Hotzmach be, wondered Leibel, who always stopped on his way to *cheder* to take in these exciting sights and sounds.

The Hotzmach around whom all this activity revolved was a tall individual, so thin he seemed to be two-dimensional. Head, nose, elbows and chin were all jutting lines and angles. His ears were pointed and even his eyes, sharp, penetrating, hungry-looking eyes, were three-cornered. His narrow triangular face was pockmarked. As often as not he was doubled over in a fit of coughing. His name was really Holtzman, but the director had long ago dubbed him Hotzmach, and the name had stuck.

Leibel and Hotzmach soon made each other's acquaintance. Seeing the boy looking on, he called out, "Hey, whippersnapper, what are you doing here?"

"Nothing."

"Whom are you looking for?"

"Nobody."

"Then who the devil are you?"

"Rapalovich's son."

"Then why are you skulking at the door like a beggar's brat? Come right inside. Tell me, do you smoke yet?"

"Not yet."

"But your father smokes? Your brothers smoke? Next time bring me a few cigarettes."

The next time, Leibel stole into the barn, looking around him to make sure no one was watching, then produced from his pocket a fistful of cigarettes. Hotzmach gathered the gift up quickly in his nimble fingers and transferred it to his own pocket, without changing expression or saying so much as "thank you." Lighting up a cigarette, he inhaled deeply, let out a thin stream of smoke through his pointed nostrils, and was at once seized by a spasm of coughing.

"These cigarettes are tip-top," he gasped. "Who smokes such elegant cigarettes in your house?"

"My older brother."

"Devil take him, he knows his tobacco, that brother of yours." Then Hotzmach lowered his voice. "Tell me, my fine-feathered friend, what do they eat at your house, for instance, with their morning coffee?"

"What do we eat? Sometimes cheese, sometimes eggs . . . coffee cake, cookies, white rolls. . . ."

"Now you're talking. How about bringing me a roll or two next time? But remember, they must be fresh." And as Leibel was going out of the door, he cupped his hands around his mouth and shouted after him, "Don't forget, *fresh!*"

The next morning Leibel produced from his pocket some warm rolls which immediately disappeared down Hotzmach's throat. Then he lit one of the fresh ration of cigarettes Leibel had brought him and smoked with enjoyment.

For these gifts Leibel won an entrance backstage, that holy of holies he had longed to penetrate from his first night at the theater. He watched the rehearsals; he saw with his own eyes how ordinary people transformed themselves with grease paint, wigs, false beards and mustaches, and motley costumes into devils and demons and angels. Backstage was a new world, a gay, free-and-easy, untrammeled, hail-fellow-well-met kind of world. Here one actor cut a caper, another sang a ditty; one stuffed himself with bread and sausage, another tipped his head back and took swigs from a bottle. Still another, crouched in the wings, behind the director's back, taking a forbidden smoke.

Liveliest of all was Hotzmach, who could imitate anyone to perfection. The vitality of the man, his bounce and resilience were unbelievable. He seemed to be built on springs. Nobody worked so hard, nobody ran so fast, coughed so hard, hungered so much, caught so many blows and kicks, and nobody was so quick to recover and laugh

28

at it all as Hotzmach. Hauled out a moment ago by the scruff of his neck by the director, with a swift kick added, there behind the director's back was Hotzmach, mocking the wrinkled red face, the dour expression, the puckered mouth—Albert Shchupak to the life!

Who could help admiring such a man?

Certainly not Leibel.

"Listen, my lad," said Hotzmach one day, "you go to *cheder* every day. Then you must write a fine hand. Suppose you bring me a pen and ink, a sheet of paper, an envelope, and a seven-kopek stamp."

Hotzmach made this request as he sat on the floor backstage with a brush and a can of polish, and the whole company's boots lined up in front of him.

In a few minutes Leibel had produced the required articles and, seating himself on an upturned crate in front of a three-legged stool, began writing what Hotzmach dictated:

"Write thus, my soul:

" 'To my dear, beloved mother, Sarah-Brocha, long life to you! And to my dear, beloved Uncle Zalman, long life! And to my dear, beloved sister Zlatka, long life! And to all my dear, faithful friends, long life!'

"Done, then drive on.

" 'First of all, I beg to report that I find myself, God be thanked, in perfect health, hoping to hear the same from you from the depths of my heart, forever and ever, at all times, Amen.'

"Did you put down the word *Amen*, kitten? Then I love you. Scribble on.

" 'And secondly, I beg to inform you, dear mother, that we now find ourselves in Bessarabia, a land of melons, cornmeal mush, and hefty women. We put on a play every night, and I am happy to report that I take all the leading parts, and after the holidays we begin to work on shares, that is, each actor will get a share of the profits. At present I work for a salary, that is, I get paid every week, not enough to swell my head, but thank God I am not working for nothing. I'm worth much more and I would be getting more, only we have a certain character here by the name of Sholom Meyer, the Lord Himself must have wished him on us. A dog who gets nothing but leavings himself, but he won't let anyone near the table either. I am sending you three rubles and forgive me, dear mother, that it isn't three hundred. It's all I have at present. Buy whatever you need for the holidays and be sure to get Zlatka some shoes. And tell Uncle Zalman to stop drumming *military*

29

service into my ears. I am safe from military service, tell him, and I have him, Uncle Zalman himself, to thank for it. And I beg you, dear mother, have Eli the *Melammed* write a letter for you and ask him when the anniversary of my father's death falls this year. Last year it fell on the third day of *Succoth*. And let me know if you're still on the same job, and don't under any condition forget to buy shoes for Zlatka. I have no more news. Keep well, dear mother, from your son who wishes you all the happiness and luck in the world from the bottom of my heart, forever and ever, at all times. Amen.'

"Now, youngster, hand me your pen and I'll put down my signature."

And Hotzmach rolled up his right sleeve, grasped the pen firmly in his hand, and produced a series of hen tracks on the paper. Then, shoving the letter toward his young amanuensis, he asked with pride, "How's this for Hirsch Bear Holtzman?"

Leibel pored over the hen tracks, but nowhere could he find a Hirsch or a Bear or any other kind of beast.

"My pigeon, why such a wrinkled brow? I see my penmanship is not to your taste. I learned to write all by myself. Everything I know I learned by myself. People have told me that I'd have had a neat hand if I had been taught. But how? When I was left without a father so young, my mother went into service, and my Uncle Zalman, the tailor, took me in as an apprentice. He isn't much of a tailor, just a pants patcher, but when it comes to beating his help, let me tell you, he's a real craftsman. He gave me something to remember him by for life; a pressing iron right on my chest. I've been coughing ever since. My mother apprenticed me to another hack, but I couldn't stand the work because of my weak chest. Then what does my mother do but hire me out to a *melammed,* a teacher of small children. I had to wipe the brats' noses, teach them their prayers, and carry their lunch to *cheder.* Well, carrying lunches wasn't so bad; I could get in a bite and a lick, here and there. But the trouble was I had to carry the children themselves on my shoulders, through the deep mud, and where does one get the strength for that? Then God Himself came to my aid. The Yiddish theater pulled into town. Everyone ran to see it. How could I stay home? I slipped in by the back door. As luck would have it, the director, Shchupak himself, gets the notion to walk through the aisles checking on tickets, picks me up by the collar, boxes my ears, and throws me out. As if that wasn't enough, he pulled my cap off my head. How could I show up at home without a cap? My mother would tell my uncle, and that assassin would murder me. So I waited outside in the bitter frost until the audience had gone home, and fell on my knees before the director. I wept and kissed his hands, asking him to return my cap. I told him everything, that I was an orphan and my uncle beat me. He looked me over from head to foot, with those small red lashless eyes of his, may they drop out of his head, and says to me, 'So you're an orphan and have no home. How would you like to join my company? I'll make an actor out of you.' "

Hotzmach stopped to cough, to give one of the shoes a brush and to light a fresh cigarette. Then he went on with his tale.

"You think, maybe, my mother was overjoyed when she heard of my new job? Not on your life. And my uncle was pleased even less. 'If he goes off with that gang of actors, he'll forget he's a Jew,' he warned my mother. But who listened to him? My head was in the clouds.

"You can imagine I wasn't given honey to lick right off. Shchupak began teaching me the Scriptures, chapter and verse, first with a few cuffs on the ear for the way I polished shoes. 'Is this the way to polish shoes?' Then he made me his valet. I had to do all the dirty work, run errands for him all over town. I needed the head of a prime minister to remember them all. And if the work wasn't just so, the blows rained down. That's the way he's made, his hands itch all the time, may they shrivel and drop off. A month passed, two months and three. I didn't even see the stage. Was it for this, I asked myself, that I sacrificed my future? To become Shchupak's bootblack and chambermaid? Complain? To whom? I didn't dare say a word to Shchupak. Complain to the actors? With that bastard, Sholom Meyer, snooping around? I just had to put up with it, wait a little longer, a year, two years. Finally my day came. A miracle happened."

Hotzmach was seized by a fit of coughing. Doubled up like a jack-knife, he wheezed and gasped, cursing his cough all the while. "May a cholera catch that cough of mine. May it sink into the earth!" He straightened up, gasped for breath, took a puff of his cigarette, picked up the brush, and went on:

"There was a certain actor in our troupe who played the romantic leads, his name was Uchvatevker, a tall good-looking brute, a regular Samson. He got all the fat parts, made love to the prima donna—a regular gallant, a Lothario. He had everything you want, good looks, a voice, he spoke elegant Yiddish-German, and healthy as an ox. So what does God do? This Uchvatevker, this Samson, this lover, drops dead. Dead as a doornail. Well, he's gone. God must have willed it.

31

But what to do without the star? The placards have been pasted all over town, the playbills printed, the box office is collecting money hand over fist, standing room only. Shchupak was ready to slit his throat. 'Hotzmach,' he says to me in desperation, 'can you play the romantic lead?' 'Sure,' I say, cool as a cucumber. 'And why not?' And I began studying the part. We were playing a serious piece, a drama entitled, *Dora, or the Rich Beggar, by Shakespeare, Revised and Improved by Albert Shchupak, Producer and Director.* That's how it stood on the playbill.

"Opening night came. The curtain goes up and they push me out on the stage dressed up as Rudolph, with painted cheeks, a black curling mustache, and a wig. A Rudolph, I tell you, done up to the hilt, in a new jacket, new pants, brand-new boots that still squeaked. Well, why should I drag out the story? You can never predict what an audience will do. Here I was, Rudolph the romantic lover, mustachios and new boots, and the audience gives one look at me and bursts into a roar. They may still be laughing, for all I know. You can imagine what happened when I went up to Dora, the leading lady, took her dainty hand and said in Yiddish-German, just like Uchvatevker, may his soul rest in peace, 'My beloved child, let us wed, for love grows stronger after the consummation than before the consummation.' They must have laughed for half an hour without stopping. I thought they would tear the place apart. The devil himself must have tickled them in the ribs. I could hardly wait until the curtain fell. As I staggered off the stage, I felt Shchupak's hand fall on my shoulder. I cringed, expecting the blows to come down. But his voice booms out, 'You rascal, why didn't you tell me that you were a comedian?' How do you like that? I didn't even have a notion what a 'comedian' was!

"And that's how it began. From then on I began twirling my baton in earnest, that is, playing the comedian every night. First there was *Shmendrik,* then *Tzingating,* then *Kuni Lemel,* then the drunkard in *David's Fiddle* and who knows how many others. I even got a taste of playing *Bar Kochba* and *The Flowers* by Lateiner. And the audience loved me. When I get up and sing '*Maz'ltov, bride and groom,*' they start rolling in the aisles. And when I paste on earlocks and come out in a torn gabardine doing my chassidic dance and singing,

I am a little Chassid,
A merry creature,
I'm a little Chassid,
For that's my nature.

32

Oh, I'm a Chassid,
A chassidak,
And I sing
Hop-tschik-tschak!

I stop the show. I don't have to brag before a whelp like you, but I can truthfully say that Hotzmach has made a name for himself. The only trouble is I'm not allowed to act every night. And whose doing is it? Shchupak's. That blackguard can't bear to see anyone else get the applause. That's how low he is. Wait, wait, I won't be polishing boots for him much longer. Don't worry, my pigeon, my time will come. After the holidays he'll have to give us shares. If not, we'll leave him high and dry and form our own company. We'd have done it long ago, if it hadn't been for that snake, Sholom Meyer. He's green with envy because our prima donna likes me and hates him like poison. He'd like to get me hitched to his sister Ethel-Dvora. He won't live to see the day. Tfui." And Hotzmach spit on his brush and began polishing with renewed vigor.

To Leibel, Hotzmach's tale became part of the folklore of the theater. His admiration for the comedian increased. He spent his every spare moment in or around the barn where Hotzmach worked, ate, slept, and had his being. "A theater," Hotzmach explained, "can't be left alone. Someone has to watch it all the time. Just look around— stage sets, costumes, wigs, scenery . . ."

For his part Hotzmach grew fond of the boy with the grave eyes and shy smile who brought him snacks and pocketfuls of cigarettes and hung on his words like gems of Holy Scripture. To Leibel he poured out all the bitterness in his heart.

"I tell you, youngster, life is hard and bitter, playing the comedian for a fellow like Shchupak. His kind, may they be sowed thick and come up sparse. He thinks he can dazzle us with his diamonds. . . .

"But when all is said and done, I'm still, thank God, an actor in my own right, if only a Yiddish comedian. Let me tell you, my friend, when the curtain goes up, and I step out on the stage, all my troubles vanish like smoke. On stage I'm a different man. Who cares about Shchupak then? Who worries about Sholom Meyer? They're dust under my feet. When I'm on stage I see nobody, only footlights and heads, baldspots, toupees, braids and buns, hats, kerchiefs, caps. Nothing else. Who's equal to me then? Your father with his pot-belly? Let him, for instance, offer me this whole barn and courtyard and all his

33

possessions in exchange for one night on the stage. Do you think I'd change places with him?

"Or let's suppose, for example, they offered me this barn full of gold and the hand of the king's daughter in marriage, just to give up acting and become a workman or a shop clerk. Do you think I'd do it? I'd spit in their faces. Do you hear me, youngster? But you're still wet behind the ears. You can't understand what fascination the theater has. How it pulls and pulls, like a magnet, devil take it!"

"It's exactly the same with me," Leibel blurted out, and confided to Hotzmach how the theater pulled him, too. Long before he had even heard of it, he had acted plays with his friends in *cheder,* scenes from the Bible such as *The Sale of Joseph, The Exodus from Egypt, Moses on Mount Sinai,* and others. He showed Hotzmach how they had done it.

"I come to Pharaoh and stand before him like this." Leibel drew himself up and folded his arms across his chest. In a low voice at first, then with more and more fervor, he declaimed: "I am Moses, the son of Amram, and I have been sent hither by my King, the God of the Jews, of Abraham, Isaac and Jacob, who is known as Jehovah. I have been instructed to tell you, 'Let my people go out of the land of Egypt.' How much longer can you hold them in bondage? How much longer will you torture their bodies, crush their spirits, slay their children, and bathe in their blood? How much longer, you tyrant, you oppressor, you arch-enemy of my people? Do you know with whom you are dealing?" Here Leibel raised his arm, and his voice pealed out, "I raise my right arm to the heavens to show you what I can do!"

"A powerful delivery!" Hotzmach caught Leibel by the shoulders and shook him. "May I drop dead if you're not an actor, a born actor, as I am a Jew! Do you know what, youngster?" Hotzmach began wheezing and caught hold of a post for support. "Blast this cough of mine. I wish it on Sholom Meyer and that half-wit sister of his. And the pain in my side I'd gladly give to Shchupak for a holiday greeting." The wheezing subsided and he turned back gaily to Leibel. "Do you know what I'll tell you, dicky bird? If I were in your place I'd spit on everything. I'd send that fat-jowled father of mine to *cheder* and let him warm the bench with his fat ass. I'd throw all those thick Bibles out of the window and tell the Cantor to chant his prayers by himself. And I myself would . . ."

But at this moment the actors arrived in a body for rehearsal, and Leibel didn't hear what else Hotzmach would do in his place.

34

7   LEIBEL IS CAUGHT

No one in the Rapalovich household would have no-
ticed that food was disappearing from the larder or that cigarettes
were missing if it hadn't been for the ancient grandmother with the
palsied head. She had a sharp eye for such trifles. And her nose followed her eyes. She had smelled out the thief.

But first she must catch him red-handed. Prowling about the house
at dawn, she saw Leibel tiptoe into the pantry; and when he tiptoed
out again, his pockets bulged. Where was he taking his loot? To
cheder? But the rabbi still slept at this hour. Slipping out to the
porch, the old woman saw Leibel dart into the barn. So that's what
the rascal was doing. Consorting with the comedians. Fine company
for the son of Ben Rapalovich!

Now there was a problem. What to do? Speak to the boy? He would
never listen. Modern children! What did they know of the respect due
to an old grandmother? Warn her daughter-in-law Beilka? She was
nothing but a ninny. A good soul, but a ninny. She let the children
walk all over her. No, she would have to speak to her son. He was the
father. And a father was not a mother. He would know how to deal
with the rascal. A sharp reprimand, a good flogging, and the boy would
learn his lesson, once for all.

Slyly the old woman went about her task. She took her son aside
and whispered into his ear what his youngest was doing and with
whom he was consorting. When she finished, Ben turned a pair of
bulging eyes on her. He dismissed the tale. "A cow flew over the roof
and laid an egg."

In short, he didn't believe her. The charge was preposterous. Leibel
would never do such a thing. Leibel, his youngest, his favorite, the
most brilliant of his children? Did she know what the world said about
Leibel? Ben was no judge of learning, but he listened to what the
world said. And the world said that Leibel would amount to something
when he grew up. Only recently he had met Israel the Cantor, and

Israel had launched into eulogies about the boy, enough to make the father's head swim. He thought to himself then, "The boy will certainly grow up to be a famous rabbi." God willed it that through his son he, Rapalovich, would become renowned. At present his fame was confined to Holeneshti. But some day people would flock to him from all over the world and ask, "Are you the famous Leib Rapalovich's father?" And he would answer, "The famous Leib Rapalovich is my son."

And along comes an old crone, his own mother, and insidiously inserts a worm into his ear. His son, she would have him believe, the future world-renowned rabbi and scholar, is a common thief, a hanger-on of a gang of *schnorrers,* mummers, strolling show-players.

Nevertheless, though he had dismissed her tale as old woman's gibberish, still the worm bored its way into his brain. For the rest of the day Ben Rapalovich went about like an angry bear, snarling at his wife, cursing the farmhands.

Beilka, who knew her husband through and through, asked mildly, "What's happened now?"

The farmhands said to each other, "The boss swallowed a cat."

"Father got up on the wrong side of the bed," said the children, and got out of his way.

That night Ben tossed on his bed, sighed and groaned like a bound ox. With an effort he calmed down. As for the old woman, she had a bad dream. She mistook a pear tree for a wild goat.

At break of day, when God Himself still dozed, Ben Rapalovich was already stirring about. It was his custom to rise early, pull on a robe and heavy felt boots, and go outside to inspect the farmyard. He was a strict overseer. As he put it himself, he didn't like to have anyone blow on his porridge. In other words, everything had to be in shipshape order, the lumber stacked, the yard swept, the trash piled in a corner. And every cow had to be in her own stall.

"Hey, butcher-woman, you're a guest at the *rebetzen's* again! A happy holiday to you both."

Thus he addressed two cows who had crowded into one stall. The one he called butcher-woman was a rough-skinned, skittish animal with heavy red flanks. The other was a smooth, meek little cow with the pious look of a rabbi's wife. Ben proceeded to belabor them both with a stick, giving the skittish animal most of the blows. He explained to her why.

36

"You've got a pan of your own to guzzle from. Don't go sticking your snout into your neighbor's pots."

Next he inspected the horses. "Listen, you wise son of the *Haggadah*, stop annoying your fellows, or I'll interpret the law for you as Rashi does in the Bible."

The horses seemed not to understand their master's learned rebuke. They turned their muzzles up innocently, as though to say, "Were you talking about oats?"

Ben nudged one with his elbow, tickled another's throat, patted the mane of a third, and went on to give the farmhands a piece of his mind in their native Moldavian. Suddenly, out of nowhere, the old grandmother appeared at his elbow. She nudged him and whispered, "There goes your pride and joy with full pockets," and vanished.

Ben's heart gave an unaccustomed leap. Old woman's prattle again. But there was his son running across the yard toward the big barn. Ben called out in a loud voice, "Where are you off to so early?"

Surprised, Leibel stopped in his tracks. "S-so early?" he stammered.

"What do you call this, late? I asked, where are you going?"

"Where should I be going?" the boy parried.

"How should I know? That's what I'm asking you."

Leibel was too stunned to think of an answer. He stared at his father in silence.

"What are you glaring at me for with those big lanterns of yours? Did you say your prayers yet or not? Answer me that."

Leibel gratefully snatched at the word *prayers*. "Yes, no. Not yet. I'm on my way to the synagogue to pray."

Ben Rapalovich breathed more easily. Maybe the boy was telling the truth. But as he came closer to his son, he saw that the boy had averted his eyes and was clutching his pockets with both hands. So the old woman had been right. The boy was carrying off the house piece by piece. "What are you hiding?" he bellowed. "Your pockets look mighty swollen to me."

For this Leibel was totally unprepared. He stood as though he had been nailed to the ground.

"So you won't show me. Then I'll have to ride with my ten fingers right into your sacks." And Ben dug his hands into the boy's pockets and pried out white bread, rolls, tea and sugar. Imbedded in a heap of loose cigarettes lay the gizzard of a roast goose.

To say that Ben Rapalovich was a stern parent would not be correct. He never meddled in the affairs of his children. It was Beilka who ran the household. Ben knew only one thing: "You have to pour out the oats." Which meant, "You have to provide." And he provided generously, without asking how much and for what. As for the rest, the children could do as they pleased. They could even bite off each other's noses for all he cared. But on those rare occasions when a child went out of bounds, he felt called upon to exercise his paternal prerogative. Then the heavens split wide open. And the one who suffered the most was poor Beilka.

And so it happened this time. Ben did not content himself with dealing his son two stinging slaps on both cheeks. He led him inside and called the whole clan together. Then he forced Leibel to confess in public what he had done and for whose sake he had turned thief. But even this did not suffice. He announced that he would put the boy through the "ordeal." This ordeal, rarely invoked, was a relic of tribal days, a form of punishment designed not only to chastise the body but to humble the spirit. In vain Beilka wept and pleaded with her husband, in vain did the brothers and sisters beg their father to let him off, in vain Leibel kissed his father's hands and begged to be spared this humiliation. Ben was as unyielding as an Inquisitor at an auto-da-fé. Coldly and methodically he proceeded about the business. And when it was done, his object had been accomplished, and more. The boy had been punished and humiliated. The welts on the boy's body would heal soon enough, but the wound he had inflicted on his spirit would fester. It would leave a scar that would never heal, a memory the boy would never be able to forgive.

By evening Ben's wrath had cooled off. He ordered the whole family to attend the theater as usual. No one felt inclined to go, least of all Leibel. But Father had issued a decree, and it had to be carried out. The family went.

Supper that night had been strangely quiet. Beilka sat with eyes swollen from weeping. She had been unable to comfort her son with words, but she had wept along with him. Leibel hadn't gone to *cheder* that day. But he was present at the family board, though unable to eat. The others sat with their eyes lowered, feeling the burden of Leibel's disgrace on their own shoulders. Only the old grandmother cast her sharp eye from face to face, as though to say, "Each of you should be run through the gauntlet!" The silence was acute, the only sound was that of Ben snorting and champing over his pastrami.

Ben paused in his chewing long enough to observe that no one else was eating. "Good morning to you," he bellowed. "Are your oxen stuck in the mud? Then grease the axles and keep rolling."

For once his metaphor fell short of its mark. In glum silence the diners pushed aside their plates and slunk away from the table. The family did not assemble again until theater time.

Leibel sat in the packed theater with dazed eyes, smarting in body and spirit. His soul was in a ferment and his mind seethed with thoughts of revenge. The disgrace he had suffered burned in him like a live coal. For that he would have to be revenged. His father would live to regret this day. A resolve was shaping itself in Leibel's mind. Not for nothing had he struck up a friendship with a man like Hotzmach. Only yesterday he had had a talk with him and Hotzmach had finished what had been interrupted the day before.

"You fool, empty your father's pockets," he had told Leibel. "Get together a good sum, and come along with us. We're leaving Saturday night. You'll become an actor. May I drop dead if I'm lying."

At the words, "empty your father's pockets," Leibel had been seized with a chill. That meant plain out and out stealing. Then what about the food and cigarettes he had pilfered? Wasn't that stealing? No, said his conscience. His friend had been hungry; he had wanted to smoke. So he had brought him food and cigarettes. That was no crime. But to take money! He shrank from that. And yet he was ashamed to admit it to Hotzmach. He demurred weakly. "Do you think my father will take it lying down?"

"How will he ever find out, you dumb ox?"

"He'll find out I'm gone and follow. He'll catch me."

"How? By pouring salt on your tail? We're going to Bucharest. Do you know where that is?"

"I know where Bucharest is. It's in Rumania, not far from here."

"Then what are you babbling about, idiot? As soon as we cross the border, your father has no power over you. Neither your father nor your mother nor anyone else. You've got them all—you know where. You walk around Bucharest with your hands in your pockets, thumbing your nose at the whole world. Do you understand me or not?"

Leibel understood well enough. But at the mention of his mother he had felt a pang. How would she take his running away? Would she live through it?

Leibel had been torn in half, one half of him desperate to run off with the troupe, the other half hanging back, uncertain, afraid.

39

But all this had been yesterday, before his father had made a public show of him and branded him a thief. The "ordeal" had changed everything. Now nothing could stand in his way. Not even his mother's tears. Let her weep. Let them all weep. His father, too. At first his father would rage and storm, but later he would come to regret his anger. Ah, how he would regret it! When no one saw him, he would weep and call out in anguish, "Where are you, Leibel, my son? My beloved one!" He would be inconsolable, like Jacob when Joseph's bloody coat was brought to him and he was told that his favorite had been devoured by wild beasts. Or like King David when the news came that his son Absalom had died in the forest.

Had died? Wait. Maybe death was the answer. He would die. That would be the best revenge of all.

And Leibel imagined himself dead, carried on a black pall by a score of men dressed in black; behind him his father, beating his breast, and the whole family weeping and wailing, the alms box ringing with a silvery sound, "Alms, give alms to the poor." The whole town was there, all his father's friends, and the boys from *cheder*, the teacher and his wife, and their daughter, Reizel . . . Reizel? Where was she? She hadn't come to the theater tonight? Leibel rose from his seat, the funeral forgotten. What had happened to Reizel?

When the exalted guests had left the Cantor's house, sped on their way by Leah's good wishes, and that worthy woman had turned on her daughter with the pronouncement, "You can kiss the theater goodbye, my daughter. You won't put foot in it again unless it's over my dead body," Reizel felt as though a black cloud had crossed her sky. The mention of death on her mother's lips was as binding as an oath, and Leah never went back on an oath. But the full import of the tragedy didn't overtake Reizel until that evening, when her father dismissed his pupils, her mother lit the smoky lamp, and darkness descended on God's Street.

This was the hour when Reizel donned her Sabbath dress, draped the red scarf over her shoulders, and unfurling the tiny parasol with the silken tassels her mother had bought her, went forth thus miraculously transformed (except for her down-at-the-heels shoes) to her evening at the theater. She left the drab little house, the narrow, ill-smelling street, the petty everyday worries, for the charmed, carefree, brilliant world of the theater.

But no longer. The evil one himself must have sent the two who had

40

prevailed on her to sing, for while she sang, the gates of her paradise had clanged shut. Overcome by her loss, Reizel threw herself face down on her bed and burst into stormy weeping. Silently she decried the fate which had consigned her to these dismal surroundings, to narrow, bigoted people who shut out the big world without ever having tasted its joys. What did her mother know about the theater? What did she know about life at the Rapaloviches? Or about Leibel? And Reizel burst into fresh tears. Behind the curtain she could hear her parents quarreling in low voices. Her mother's voice, low but intense with conviction. "When I say no, I mean no. I have sworn an oath. Did you ever hear such a thing?" And her father's gentle remonstrance. Then the curtain rustled, and steps neared her bed. It was her father. He bent over her and, stroking her hair, whispered endearments. "Reizel, Reizele, Reizeniu, don't cry." Rash promises tumbled from his lips. "Tomorrow your mother will buy you material for a dress. A wool jacket, too. We'll buy you new shoes. Please, Reizele, don't cry." Reizel only wept harder. Behind the curtain Leah heard every sound and began screaming, "Will you both be quiet? I'll hang myself, drown myself, I'll smother myself. Be quiet, Israel. The neighbors will hear and come running."

Indeed, the neighbors did hear and came running. "God be with you, Leah darling. What's happened? Why are you screaming?"

"Screaming? Who's screaming? We were laughing."

"Some laughter."

"You don't like it? Then go. Who sent for you?"

"We came out of friendship, Leah dear. We thought someone was being murdered."

"May my enemies be murdered," cried Leah in a frenzy and banged on the walls until the windows rattled. "They came out of friendship. Did you ever hear such a thing?"

Reizel wept softly into her pillow. This was her fate. To live in this squalor among people who quarreled and cursed. Every day her mother cursed her neighbors. The next day she made up with them. Then they quarreled and cursed each other again, and made up again. And so every day of her life.

And out there? In that other world, away from God's Street? Ah, there people knew how to live. They knew how to smile and be gracious. They knew how to laugh. They were laughing right now at the theater. What was happening at this moment? The show must be in full swing, or maybe it was about to end. Soon the curtain would fall

41

and a storm of applause would break out, with cries of "Hotzmach! Hotzmach!" heard on all sides. And Hotzmach would reappear, exhausted, the paint running in streaks down his sweating face, and he would dance and sing, again and again, the popular encore:

I'm a little Chassid,
A merry creature,
I'm a little Chassid,
For that's my nature.
Oh, I'm a Chassid,
A chassidak,
And I sing
Hop-tschik-tschak.

And with the gay tune ringing in her ears, Reizel dropped off to sleep.

8   FIRE IN GOD'S STREET

It was long past midnight when the bells of both churches began pealing.

Boom Boom Boom—Boom Boom Boom.

Three peals of the bells meant a fire. The bells went on pealing, three peals and a pause, three peals and a pause, until the whole populace was aroused. Holeneshti's fire department was volunteer. Every man, woman and child became a fire fighter. Everyone rushed to the scene, not only to save goods and lives, but to join in the excitement. Rich and poor jostled elbows, enemies made up quarrels, friends exchanged gossip, the town's wits had a heyday. The whole town was lit up brighter than day. It was worth being in Holeneshti just to witness a fire.

At the Cantor's house Leah heard the bells first. Her daughter's crying had kept her from sleep. Remorse gnawed at her flesh. Why, oh, why had she taken that oath? Stinging thoughts swarmed about her like flies. She tossed and turned as though in a fever. In her mind's eye she saw Reizel leaping out of the window and running toward the

42

river to drown herself. Leah sat up in the dark. Was the child sleeping? Had she heard her stir? Tfui. Tfui. Tfui. She spit softly three times to ward off the evil eye, then lay down again moaning and twisting, trying to find sleep. Suddenly the bells broke the silence. Leah sat up, looked out of the window, and saw the angry red in the sky.

"Israel, wake up. God be with you, Israel. Get up. It's nothing, nothing."

Israel leaped out of bed.

"Don't get scared. It's on our street, but far off." She ran to the window. "I'm afraid it's two doors from Ben Zion the *Schochet's*. What do you say, Israel? Two doors from Ben Zion's, right by the synagogue. Am I right?"

"Two doors?" said Israel. "I'm afraid it's right next door to Ben Zion's."

"May thunder strike me! Israel, get dressed. Hurry. The synagogue is lost. What will we do? Quick, Israel, hurry. Here, take my shawl, wrap it around your throat, you'll catch cold. Hurry, hurry."

But Israel didn't have to be hurried. In a matter of seconds he had pulled on his clothes, poured water on his nails, mumbled a blessing, and turning down the proffer of the shawl (it was a hot midsummer night), was on his way to rescue the synagogue from fire.

At fires Israel was always first on the scene. If he could only get someone to lend him a hand, to reach him a pail of water, to throw him a rope, a ladder, a hatchet, he was ready to jump right into the flames. Ordinarily a mild man, a weakling, a wraith, when it came to fires, Israel became a hero, a Samson, a Goliath. To smash a dozen windowpanes with his bare hands and cut all his fingers was child's play to him. To clamber up a steep roof or enter a burning house was nothing. Aware of this, Leah followed him. God knew to what lengths her hero would go, especially when the synagogue was in danger. But what to do with the child? There she lay, fast asleep, the innocent darling. She had fallen asleep in her clothes. Leah resolved to take only a peek at the fire. Only half a peek. Then she'd run back.

But that was easier said than done. How could you tear yourself away? True, it was still some distance from Ben Zion the *Schochet's* and still farther away from the synagogue. Only Asher the Baker was burning at present. Asher himself was to blame. He had been warned, how many times, to shake down the ashes in his chimney. But does a baker listen to reason? Well, it had happened. His house burned like

43

a candle. And his neighbors' houses? They were all covered with straw and dry shingles and huddled close together. With the smallest breeze, the whole street would go up in flames.

The fire fighters threw themselves at the neighboring houses. They splashed buckets of water, wielded hatchets, threw ropes, dragged ladders aloft, and Israel the Cantor climbed to the top of Moishe Bear the Butcher's roof and shouted orders from above. Any second, he warned, the butcher's house would catch fire, and next in line was the house of Reb Samuel the Rabbi, then that of Noah the Assistant Rabbi, then Ben Zion the *Schochet,* and then the synagogue. Not for nothing had the street been named God's Street. Everyone of God's delegates lived here.

"Woe is me," shouted Leah from a safe distance, waving her arms. "What are you doing, you scoundrel, you idiot? You'll ruin your voice. The High Holidays are coming. How will you sing?"

Israel had been right. The fire leaped from the baker's house right on to Moishe Bear's roof, and the cry went up, "The Cantor! The Cantor!"

The Cantor's daughter lay stretched on a pile of logs in Ben Rapalovich's courtyard. Women, crowds of women, shadowy, faceless, glided about her. They bent over the logs and hissed. "Is it burning? It's burning, it's burning."

What did it mean? Were they going to burn her alive? What did they have against her? With an effort Reizel tried to sit up. But she couldn't move a limb. She was bound hand and foot. She heard the dry wood crackling under her, and a red haze swam in front of her eyes. Summoning all her strength, she strained at the ropes that bound her, and they burst. Reizel awoke.

She was at home, in her own bed, still dressed. She heard the bells, sounds of running feet and cries of "Fire!" "Fire!" She looked out of the window and saw the red glow in the sky and crowds running in the brightly lit street. She called to her parents, but no one answered. In a moment Reizel was out of bed and in front of the house.

There she stood as one bewitched. The whole street had come to life. Dark figures flitted back and forth, their faces lit with an unearthly glow, as if in some wild, satanic dance. Still dazed with sleep Reizel lifted her hand to shield her eyes from the glare. Her black braids came undone and she tossed her hair back. The scarf slipped from her shoulders and her white dress turned pink. Two points of

44

fire danced in her black eyes, her vivid face shining as though with an inward light.

"Good evening, little kitten," said a hoarse voice at her elbow. "So you're all alone. That tigress of a mother of yours has gone to the fire. The whole town is there. As soon as I heard there was a fire in God's Street, I told myself I must go and see what's doing at the Cantor's. May God grant me fortune and luck!"

This time Reizel wasn't frightened by Sholom Meyer. She was glad to see a familiar face. Did he know where the fire was?

Sholom Meyer couldn't tell her where the fire was. "What's the difference who's burning, Berel or Shmerel, Hatzkel or Yokel? I see them running, so I run too. Tell me, little one, why weren't you at the theater tonight? I looked for you near that whelp you always sit with."

At his words, the memory of all that had happened came flooding back. Here was a person who would understand. Without stopping to think, Reizel poured out her story into his willing ears. Because she had sung for them, her mother had forbidden her to go to the theater. . . .

"Is that all?" laughed Sholom Meyer. "I might have known it. What a pity, what a great pity that such a rare diamond should lie buried in the mud of Holeneshti among dumb brutes who don't understand its value, fanatical parents who don't know where their child's fortune lies."

Reizel looked at him questioningly. What did he mean?

Sholom Meyer enlightened her.

"The first time I heard you sing—you remember, that morning at your window—I said to myself, 'Here is a prima donna above all prima donnas. May God grant me fortune and luck!'"

Reizel's eyes widened. She a prima donna!

"And when I heard you sing 'Lord of the World,' I said, 'This girl has been created by God to become part of our theater.' That's just what I told our director. 'We can't let that golden voice go,' I said. 'We have to drag her away from here if we have to do it by force.'"

Reizel shrank back. By force?

Sholom Meyer understood her gesture. "How else? We can't permit such a pure diamond to get lost in the mud. Just imagine it to yourself, your first performance. You play the leading part in *Flowers* or *Salome* or *The Sabbath Kiddush*. You come out on the stage in a short dress and little gold slippers. You dance and sing one melody after another. When it's over you bow and the audience falls at your

45

feet. It kisses your hands. Or else you come out dressed as a boy with curly black hair, you look up and give them 'Hot Cakes.' "

Glancing sideways at her to see what impression he was making, he sang in his hoarse, tuneless voice:

I see a boy in the streets,
He's as free as the air.
He strolls around hands in pockets,
Without a care.
Why can't he toil as I do,
In my miserable lot,
Crying aloud, 'Buy hot cakes,
Good people, buy hot cakes, buy hot.'

"With a voice like yours and with your looks you'll lay them out in the aisles."

Since Reizel didn't answer, Sholom Meyer decided to make it stronger. Sidling up to her and stroking her hand, he whispered, "You can thank God, my dove, that you met me. Our prima donna is a well-born girl too, but of poor parents, just like you. She comes from a small town in Poland and she has me to thank for being an actress. I helped her run off from home. It's a good story. Wait till I tell you. Her father was nothing but a . . . ."

Just then Sholom Meyer saw out of the corner of his eyes a figure silhouetted against the bright sky, cutting across the way to the Cantor's house. He mustn't be caught talking to the Cantor's daughter, or the plan that was just taking shape in his head would go to pot. He took quick leave of Reizel with an extemporaneous riddle in rhyme which he threw at her over his shoulder as he ran:

A maiden who's wise
Gets a new dress for a prize.

9   A FIFTEEN-MINUTE INTERMISSION

At the theater a fifteen-minute intermission was about to begin. So the playbill read, but the audience knew better. Thirty

46

minutes was more like it. They left their seats and shoved their way to the doors to catch a breath of fresh air or to find a waiting relative or friend whom they intended to smuggle into the theater, or perhaps to pay a visit backstage. It stands to reason those who went backstage were not respectable householders, but stray souls, musicians, workmen's apprentices, people with nothing better to do. Leibel Rapalovich among them.

At other times, whenever Leibel crossed the proscenium and felt the boards of the stage creak under his feet, he was transported to a new world, where he seemed to be floating in the air. He became one with the actors, assumed their speech, their walk, their mannerisms.

But this evening Leibel had something other than stage marvels on his mind. Without so much as a glance, he passed the prima donna, with her big blue eyes magnified by mascara. He didn't stop to greet the actors who were lounging about, chewing hard apples and spitting the skins out. His goal was Hotzmach.

It was hard to recognize Hotzmach tonight in the garb of Pauperson (for that rip-roaring comedy, *Pauperson and Hungerman*). His costume consisted of a tattered frock-coat, a much-creased but imposing top hat, shoes through which his ten toes stuck out, and tattered pants whose patches included a big ace of diamonds.

This ace of diamonds had made a hit. To patch an old pair of pants with a playing card was a trick which wouldn't have occurred to anyone in Holeneshti in a thousand years. Naively the audience supposed it was Hotzmach's invention and gave him such an ovation that the director, Albert Shchupak, in the part of Hungerman, almost burst with envy.

Hotzmach, of course, considered the laurels justly his. He felt that tonight he had played like a god.

Seeing Leibel wandering about aimlessly, he took it for granted the boy had come to thank him for his performance and perhaps to bring him a tidbit. He called out gaily, "Hey, youngster, what are you looking for? Last winter's snow? Where were you all day, dear heart?"

Leibel asked Hotzmach to bend down. He had something urgent to tell him.

"A secret for the whole town?" And Hotzmach bent over double, almost breaking his thin frame in half.

When he heard the secret, Hotzmach straightened himself to his full height and his sharp eyes glinted like quartz pebbles. He gave Leibel a hearty slap on the back. "Now you're talking, my love. You're one of us now. What did I tell you? Your place is right here with us. If not, may I drop dead."

Scenting a plot, Albert Shchupak sprang to his side. "What place? Which place? Whom are you placing, Hotzmach?"

Hotzmach blanched, but quickly recovering himself, he pointed to Leibel. "He just told me someone grabbed a place in the theater without a ticket."

The words had their intended effect. It was like telling a farmer, "There's a rabbit in your carrot patch."

"Sholom Meyer," yelled Shchupak. "Where's that Sholom Meyer? A plague take him." Then he turned swiftly to Leibel.

But Leibel had already jumped off the stage and was lost in the audience.

That night our hero went to sleep with a full-fledged plan for revenge. He would settle his score with his father, pay him back for the beating and disgrace, for everything, everything!

He didn't have to ponder long. What was there to ponder about? Everything fell into place naturally, as though it had been preordained.

In the middle of the night, when everyone was asleep, he would get up and tiptoe to the cashier's bed. As luck would have it, the cashier slept in the same room with Leibel. He was named Simcha, which means Joy, but Leibel had nicknamed him *Susan v'Simcha,* meaning Gladness-and-Joy. Gladness-and-Joy boasted of being such a light sleeper he could hear a fly buzzing, but everyone knew he slept so soundly you could carry him out with his bed and he wouldn't waken unless you poured a bucket of cold water over him.

In spite of this, Simcha could be trusted implicitly. First of all, he was one of the family, a nephew or cousin of Ben Rapalovich's. Secondly, he was a sober and honest young man, as loyal as a watchdog. He carried the keys of the cash-drawer in his pants pocket at all times. Before retiring, he inspected all the doors and windows and shutters and took a look under the beds. When he undressed he folded his pants and put them under his pillow.

To Leibel, the coincidence of Simcha's sleeping in the same room was heaven-sent. He imagined getting up in the dead of night, putting his hand under Simcha's pillow, pulling out first one pants leg, then the other, extracting the keys from the pocket, and tiptoeing to the table. The only one he feared was the old grandmother in the next room. She slept with one eye open, and that eye so sharp it could see

48

through a wall better than most people could see through strong lenses. Leibel saw himself unlocking the cash-drawer and his fingers closing over bank notes. Hotzmach had instructed him to take paper money. Leibel saw himself stuffing the roll of bills in his pocket, locking the drawer, deftly replacing the cashier's pants under his pillow, then swiftly and noiselessly sliding outdoors, where Hotzmach waited in a wagon that would take them to the railway station.

Leibel had planned one more detail. He would change into a disguise and plant his own clothes at the river bank. Let them think he had drowned himself. They would drag the river and never find his body. They would sit in mourning for the prescribed seven days, and then they would forget him. Time would go by, say ten, twenty years. Leibel, now a famous actor, the director of his own company, would arrive in Holeneshti, engage his father's barn through an intermediary, and set up *his* theater. The whole town would be invited free of charge for the first performance. Let them see what real theater was! When the curtain went up, the whole company would step out on the stage, and in the center would stand Leibel himself, crusted with diamonds from head to foot, just like Shchupak. They would recognize him at once. His mother would fall in a faint. His father would thunder, "Leibel!" and on all sides people would shout, "Leibel!" "Leibel!"

Hearing his name for the third time, Leibel opened his eyes and saw Gladness-and-Joy standing at the head of his bed.

"Simcha, what's happened?"

"What's happened? I've never seen anyone sleep so hard. I kept yelling and yelling. Get up. There's a fire in God's Street. The bells are ringing for the last hour. They could wake the dead."

Thus Gladness-and-Joy, who had just a moment before been awakened and warned not to leave the house.

But how could he stay in and miss the excitement? He resolved to run out with Leibel, "just for a peek." Leibel had his clothes on and was running toward God's Street as though the devil were behind him. He was running away from the fire, toward the Cantor's house, while Simcha ran straight toward the fire.

If our hero lived to a hundred he would never forget that night. In the happiest as well as the most wretched period of his life, when he found himself alone, he would only have to shut his eyes to relive the terror and wonder of that night of enchantment.

In front of her door, floating in an aureole of red, he saw the figure

49

of Reizel. From a distance she looked unsubstantial, like a phantom of fire that would be sucked upward at any moment along with the stars. But as he came close, he saw she was real, and more beautiful than ever. Never had her hair been so black, never had her cheeks been so red, nor her eyes so lustrous. She was a princess, an enchanted princess of darkness and fire.

Reizel saw him and ran up to him, looking back to make sure no one was watching. Breathlessly she told him how she had awakened, all alone in the house. Her parents must have gone to the fire. Did he know whose house was burning?

"I don't know," Leibel said. "I was told there was a fire in God's Street, and I came straight here."

Reizel looked at him shyly. "You came straight here?"

"Even if the fire weren't on God's Street, I would have come straight here." He stopped in confusion. Reizel's eyes clung to his face. She had never been so stirred before. The radiance in his face was more than a reflection from the fire. And the look in his eyes, how intense and warm, and how gentle and steadfast at the same time.

Leibel tried to explain why he had come to her. "On such a night! How could I stay away? I don't care who's burning. Let them all burn. Let the town go up in flames. Holeneshti means nothing to me now . . . in a day or two . . ." He caught her hand impulsively. "If I tell you something, will you promise it will remain a secret between us two?" The pressure of his hand was warm, it made her feel close to him; yet his voice had an overtone of sadness as though he were speaking from a great distance.

"I am going away," he said.

She looked at him with wide, startled eyes. "Going away? Where?"

"Where? I don't know yet."

But he was leaving, he told her, as certainly as this was night and not day. As surely as there was a heaven above them. Involuntarily both of them raised their eyes to the heavens and Reizel felt a sudden chill go through her. She had never seen him so solemn. He seemed suddenly to have grown up, to have become a man. And she was still a child.

In a tremulous voice she asked, "Will you be gone long?"

"Yes, I am going away for good."

"Then we shall never see each other again?"

"Never."

As Leibel explained why he was leaving and with whom he was go-

50

ing, he saw the brightness slowly drain from her face. When he took her hand again, her fingers were icy cold. He felt a pang of regret.

"Then you don't want me to go? You will miss me?"

Reizel shrank back, the color flooding her face again. "No, oh, no. It isn't that." It was only envy she felt. How simple for him. How easy. He had quarreled with his father, and had decided to leave home. So he got up and left. But she? How could she do it so simply? And she had reasons for leaving home, too. He wasn't the only one who suffered humiliation. Her mother . . .

And she told him all that had happened to her the day before. She also told him of the talk she had just had with Sholom Meyer, and of what he and the director said about her voice. She didn't hold back anything.

Leibel wasn't sure how it came about, but they found themselves sitting on the stoop of the Cantor's house, their hands clasped together. And Leibel was lifting her hand to his hot lips and kissing the tips of her fingers one by one. She didn't take her hand away, but kept looking at him with wide, anxious eyes. And looking into her dark eyes, he saw reflected in them all the grandeur and terror, the beauty and wonder of that enchanted night.

What Reizel told him that night in a low, breathless voice, while the noise of the fire-fighting raged about them, was the best news Leibel had ever heard, a lucky omen for both of them. He was convinced the same fate was working for him and Reizel. The fate which had condemned them both to the brutishness and vulgarity of life in Holeneshti had also miraculously thrown them together and awakened the same longings in both of them. Now it was working for their deliverance. Together they would burst their bonds; together they would set out into the wide world to begin a new life, a happy, free, joyous life. They would tread the same path, share the same studies, follow the same muse . . . and some day become famous together, he as an actor, she as a singer.

And Leibel called on the night and the flaming heavens to bear witness that they would never part from each other. Solemnly they joined hands and plighted their troth. They would cling to each other no matter what happened, no matter how far they wandered. As they grew up and became man and woman, they would work in the same theater, travel together over the whole world. Together, one day, they would return to Holeneshti to visit their parents. How people would

51

envy them and marvel at them. They would point. "Look at the happy pair." For they would be betrothed then. Betrothed? No, they would surely be husband and wife. For weren't they betrothed now?

Leibel said, "Remember that first night in the theater?"

Did she remember? That was a night she would never forget. She could have sat there forever.

And they talked on and on, recalling incident after incident, scene after scene, off-stage and on-stage. Everything that had happened to them was entwined with the theater. And so it would be always. God Himself had willed it that way. He had sent each of them a messenger, Sholom Meyer to her and Hotzmach to him.

They looked up at the sky again. It was no longer a hectic red. The fire was dead. Stars appeared once more in the deep darkness of the summer night. First one star, then another, then another. The whole sky was sprinkled with stars. But they didn't stay in one spot. A star blazed, then flickered, and was gone. In its place appeared another, then it, too, flickered and disappeared.

"Look." Reizel pointed, her voice trembling with fear. "The stars are falling." Leibel laughed with gentle condescension. "Don't be frightened, Reizel," he said. "It's natural for them to fall. Stars always seem to be falling. But they don't really fall; they wander."

And like an older and wiser brother, he explained to her the mystery of the stars. Each was the soul of a human being. Wherever a man's star wandered, he had to follow. That was why the stars always seemed to be falling.

"Stars do not fall; stars wander," Leibel repeated in a low voice, looking at the sky from which the crimson faded rapidly. Only one corner still glowed red, and that, too, was paling. The noises were dying down. The dark mass at the end of the street was breaking up into smaller clumps and then into single figures which separated and scattered in all directions. Voices and footsteps were coming closer. Soon Reizel's parents would return and find them together on the stoop. They must part, though they could have stayed forever.

Reluctantly Leibel arose and took his leave.

10 A HAPPY WEEK

It was Saturday night.

All trace of the Sabbath, the gracious and holy Sabbath, was gone from Holeneshti.

Gone were the jaunty youths and coquettish maidens dressed in Sabbath finery who had promenaded up and down "patrician street" chattering Russian, a limping, corrupted Russian, but still Russian.

Gone from God's Street were the men in their Sabbath gabardines and the women with diamonds twinkling in their ears, pieces of glass, but still "diamonds."

Gone were the children who had been playing the new street game, "theater." The broiling Bessarabian sun had set long ago; the dusk of the mild Bessarabian evening had taken its place. Here and there in the sky shone a faint star.

Devout women had long ago finished intoning "The God of Abraham, Isaac, and Jacob" in the dark, and were now busily lighting lamps and rekindling their cooking fires.

The "holy Sabbath departing hence" left a sadness in the air. Pious men had long ago finished chanting the blessing over the *Havdalah* candle which marked the Sabbath end. Some were already singing hymns, or briskly ushering in the new week with prayer. Even into their merry voices crept a note of melancholy, regret for the day which had just passed. How hard to relinquish the "expanded soul" granted the Jew on the Sabbath, how painful to part with the lovely and gracious Sabbath Queen!

"A happy week! A happy week!" announced Israel the Cantor and put out the *Havdalah* candle with a deep sigh. Mechanically he began rattling off the next prayer, accompanying himself with a brisk snapping of the fingers. He looked over at Leah and thought, "Now she'll start nagging about money and shoes and other everyday things."

"A happy week! A lucky week!" answered Leah, also with a deep sigh. But she wasn't thinking of her husband. She was worried about

Reizel, who sat pensively in a corner. What was the child thinking of? It was unlike Reizel to be so silent. Leah had long since repented her harshness. It was a sin to treat a one-and-only darling in this way. But what's done is done, thought Leah. Especially now that the theater was packing to leave, this very night, and good riddance. Less commotion and bedlam in town. Holeneshti had got along without a theater until now, it would manage again. And the child would forget in time. A child was only a child. She would buy her a pair of new shoes, and bring her candy and sweets from the market, and the wounds would heal. . . .

The market! Tomorrow was market-day, and here she was without a kopek to her name. A whole week coming . . . did you ever see such a thing? Absorbed in her housewifely concerns, Leah forgot about Reizel's grievance.

And Reizel herself? Reizel was far, far away from such matters as shoes and markets. Far, far away from Holeneshti. Where would she be tomorrow this time? Nobody knew except Leibel and herself and two others, the director of the theater and Sholom Meyer. Only this morning she had talked with Sholom Meyer while everyone was at the synagogue, and they had agreed that tonight, at the stroke of twelve, she would . . . She knew what she would do. And Leibel knew, too. And no one else, no one.

She savored the sweetness of knowing something her mother had no inkling of. Sholom Meyer had been right when he said, "She has no business locking you up in the house like a bird in a cage. Never letting you out of the house, trailing after you every step, not allowing you to raise your head. 'Don't sing for strangers.' 'Don't go to the theater.' 'Stand here.' 'Sit there.' 'Do this.' 'Don't do that.' Are you her slave?" Well, it would serve her mother right. Tomorrow morning when she got up and found that "the bird had flown from the cage," then she would be sorry. But it would be too late. Reizel would be gone. Then her mother could have herself a happy week. A happy and lucky week.

Reizel's heart ached only for her father. He deserved no blame for this. He had loved her. How close they had been to each other. Who would play *dreidl* on *Hanukah* with him after she was gone? Who would steal the *afikomen* on Passover? Who would go with him to the synagogue on *Simchas Torah*? And who would sing hymns with him on Saturday night?

She recalled his favorite song, "The Messiah," in two parts, his in

54

Yiddish and her responses in the peasant dialect. It went like this:

He—And what will come to pass?
She—The end of our exile.
He—Where will Jews go then?
She—To the land of Israel.
He—What will come to pass there?
She—We will meet our savior.
He—Who will be our savior?
She—The blessed Messiah.
He—When will this take place?
She—Soon, in our own time.
Both (very fast)—Day of gladness, day of joy,
   Day of friendship and deliverance.
   Day of gladness, day of joy, etc., etc.

"Have you had enough of 'day of this and day of that'?" her mother would interrupt, bringing the samovar. "Drink your tea now. Did you ever see such a thing?"

How merry and gay, how carefree and foolish she had been then. Such a short time had passed, and yet how long ago it seemed. A wave of sadness engulfed Reizel. Her throat felt tight and her eyes stung. Any minute she would burst into tears. Her father, noticing her mood, bent down, still reciting the prayer, to stroke her glossy black braids. In a low, tender tone he asked, "Daughter, what is it?"

"Nothing," she answered in a choked voice. "Nothing. A happy week!"

And hiding her flushed face against her father's breast, she hugged him close.

At the Rapaloviches', Ben had also finished the *Havdalah*. He performed the rite with pomp and circumstance, the whole family gathered around him. When he was done, they all intoned in one voice, "Blessed be the Lord, A-amen."

Ben's *Havdalah* was something to listen to. He began in a loud resonant voice, each word clear as a bell, faltered in the middle and fell into mumbling under his breath, then recovered, the words ringing out again, and finished in style with a long drawn-out A-amen. Blowing out the candle, he promptly got back to business. He stuffed his pockets with bills (like all pious Jews, he had emptied them for the Sabbath), roared out, "A happy week, a good year," and signalled to the cashier to count up the week's receipts.

And Simcha rolled up his sleeves, opened the cash-drawer, and settled down to his money-counting.

Joy-and-Gladness, the expert, spit on his thumb, the crisp notes crackling and flying under his fingers. First came the ample hundred-ruble bank notes which Ben called "sheets," then the dainty white twenty-five-ruble notes, the fiery-red tens, the sky-blue fives, and last of all the "small stuff," the faded green three-ruble bills and rumpled yellow singles.

As the cashier counted the money, Leibel sat immersed in his small prayer book and counted along with him. When Simcha tackled the "small stuff," Leibel lost count, but he kept on watching surreptitiously as he prayed. The stacks of money rose like a wall between him and the prayer book. "Where will it be by midnight?" he thought. And answered with grim satisfaction, "In *my* pocket."

Suddenly he was seized by a panic, and to cover his trembling, chanted and swayed with renewed vigor.

Ben and the cashier were too absorbed to notice, but his mother who sat nearby, observing the fervor with which he was praying, swelled with pride. How wrong to have put him through the ordeal. For what? For giving a poor, starving actor part of his lunch? Was that such a crime? If only Ben could see him through her eyes, if only he would take one look at that bright, innocent face bent over the prayer book!

But Ben was far too engrossed in his money to look at his son. The paper packets disposed of, he and the cashier now turned to the silver. At counting silver Simcha was even more of a whiz. The coins fairly flew through his agile fingers as he piled them in heaps. Next he attacked the copper, at whose dull clink Leibel thought scornfully, "These I don't need." The fat paper packets would be enough.

Leibel watched Joy-and-Gladness put the money back. In that drawer now lay all his hopes and his dreams. Money was a temptation, the Evil Spirit Incarnate, he had often heard from his teacher and from other wise men. They warned, too, that the Evil One was hard to resist. Now he knew what they meant. Satan held him fast in his two hairy paws. Useless to struggle. Leibel didn't try. On the contrary, he prayed for Satan's success. For if he failed, if, God forbid, he were caught . . . May that hour never strike, prayed his heart. For then he would surely be lost. Lost to both worlds. And Reizel? What would become of her? If he failed, that would be the end of all their hopes and ambitions and dreams.

56

"*Maz'l-tov*, the wedding guests have arrived to sweep the barn of the Jewish filth!" roared Ben, rising from the table—which meant that the teamsters had arrived to clear the barn of the Yiddish theater.

Ben Rapalovich could have whipped himself a dozen times over for having rented his clean, spotless barn to the actors. A herd of swine, he said, couldn't have polluted the barn and courtyard the way these vagabonds had done. He despised these tattered *schnorrers*, as he called them, as a good Jew despises pork. Most of all he despised that dressed-up clown, Albert Shchupak, who reciprocated with equal disdain. To Albert, Ben was "that Bessarabian potbelly."

Out in the yard worked Simon-David the Teamster with his vans, four vehicles in all, the last a tall wagon called the *Harba*. Ben greeted him. "Look who's here. A guest, Simon-David, a guest. Tell me, dear heart, how much do you get, for instance, from these tramps for carting away their corpse?"

"Nothing with nothing. *Ashri-haish*. Woe to the poor driver," answered Simon-David with a quotation from the Psalms, and at once started complaining how poor business was. He spread out his fingers and counted off his liabilities: "First, a horse has to eat; second, I have to pay drivers; third, oats are dear; fourth, a wagon needs greasing. Then I need a peasant to help, and a peasant is a thief. . . ."

When he ran out of fingers, Simon-David dismissed the whole thing with a wave of his hand and another quotation, freely interpreted, "With the head sunk in the earth."

Simon-David the Teamster, more businessman than teamster, owned a house of his own as well as three pairs of horses, sent his children to *cheder*, and, himself laid claim to scholarship, knowing by heart the Psalms, from which he was always spouting quotations.

Simon-David had made a deal with Shchupak to transport the theater, actors, props, and luggage, to the station in Ploesti and not a step further. He would come Saturday night without fail, even if the heavens should rain stones. He would take them to Ploesti, but from there they had to go on alone, even if they had to "ride by sleigh to the Promised Land."

Now Simon-David had arrived, and the theater had not yet packed its bags. Shchupak ran about like a hen with its head cut off. He had never been so jumpy. He conferred in whispers with Sholom Meyer, quarreled with the actors, cursed Hotzmach, and swore at the crowd assembled to watch.

The whole Rapalovich tribe streamed outside after Ben—sons and daughters, sons-in-law and daughters-in-law, the nurse, the cashier, the cook. Even the grandmother was there casting her sharp eye about. Who knows—in the blink of an eye, between a yes and a no, something might disappear into the wagons that didn't belong to the theater. Only Leibel was missing. Hotzmach was nearly out of his mind. He couldn't find the boy anywhere. Suppose the youngster had regretted the whole scheme. A fine spot that would leave Hotzmach in. He'd be a King of Fools in his own eyes. Remain Shchupak's handyman for the rest of his life, get hitched to that hag, Ethel Dvora, let a pestilence overtake her and the rest of them. Let them not live to depart from this place; and if they did, let them burn alive before they reached their destination.

"Hotzmach, what the devil are you mumbling there?" yelled Shchupak.

"I'm not mumbling, I'm studying my part."

"Fine time to study your part. May you roast alive. Come here, you idiot."

"Amen, the same to you. I'm coming, I'm coming." Hotzmach ran, coughing and looking around for Leibel.

Why wasn't Leibel in the crowd watching the theater depart? Such goings-on in his father's courtyard and Leibel not there? Hard to believe.

Leibel was doing penance. He was praying to God, asking forgiveness for the sins he was about to commit. He repeated the Psalm of David which his teacher had told him could remedy every trouble. And Leibel was sorely troubled. Not only would he soon become a full-fledged thief, he would wound his mother; not only was he running away from home, he was also abetting the Cantor's runaway daughter. Fervently he recited while hot salty tears poured from his eyes.

Incline Thine ear, O Lord, and answer me;
For I am poor and needy.
Keep my soul, for I am godly;
O Thou my God, save Thy servant that trusteth in Thee.
Be gracious unto me, O Lord;
For unto Thee do I cry all the day.
Rejoice the soul of Thy servant;
For unto Thee, O Lord, do I lift up my soul.
For Thou, Lord, art good, and ready to pardon,

58

And plenteous in mercy unto all them that call upon Thee.
Give ear, O Lord, unto my prayer;
And attend unto the voice of my supplications.
In the day of my trouble I call upon Thee;
For Thou wilt answer me.

"What's Leibel praying about so hard?" his brothers and sisters asked, as they ran past him into the courtyard.

But Leibel paid no heed to them and read on:

But Thou, O Lord, art a God full of compassion and gracious,
Slow to anger, and plenteous in mercy and truth.
O turn unto me, and be gracious unto me;
Give Thy strength unto Thy servant,
And save the son of Thy handmaid.
Work in my behalf a sign for good;
That they that hate me may see it, and be put to shame,
Because Thou, O Lord, hast helped me, and comforted me.

"God be with you, Leibel. Don't you want to see what's going on outside?" asked Joy-and-Gladness, who had rushed in all agog with excitement.

Leibel looked up with a start, kissed the Psalter devoutly, and ran outside.

Leibel went out with spirits refreshed and uplifted. The dark summer night bent over him with its million watchful eyes. The stars had never seemed so close. His senses sharpened, he felt he could see, hear, and smell more acutely than ever. God had heard his prayer and would grant forgiveness. . . . Suddenly Leibel felt something warm and furry rub against his legs. It was his old friend Terkish who, having caught Leibel's attention, leaped up with short, joyous yelps, as if to tell him of the going-on in the courtyard.

Between Leibel and Terkish was an old and tried, though forbidden, friendship. What business had a young man past *Bar-Mitzvah* to be playing with a dog? Especially a cur like Terkish whom everyone kicked around? But just because of this, because Terkish was such a red-eyed, one-eared *schlimazl* of a dog, Leibel loved him. When no one looked, he would bring him crusts of bread, or if he could find no bread, cake and cookies and even candy. Terkish would eat anything. Terkish had plenty of dog-wisdom. With no one in sight, he leaped right into Leibel's face. But let someone appear, and Terkish turned away and pretended to lick himself.

59

"Who'll bring you scraps from the table?" Leibel asked, stroking the dog. "Who'll look out for you when I'm gone?" But Terkish didn't know his friend was saying goodbye. He had more pressing things to worry about. Hungrily he shoved his damp nose into Leibel's pocket.

Looking at Terkish, Leibel thought of the other friend he would leave behind, the white colt his father had given him for a *Bar-Mitzvah* gift. Pious men had been shocked at what they considered a blasphemous gift. Who but an ignoramus like Ben would do such a thing? In derision the colt had been named "The *Bar-Mitzvah* colt."

But though Leibel was a brilliant Talmud student he also had a passion for horses, inherited, no doubt, from his father, of whom people said that he had "a horse's soul." All winter Leibel had fed the colt, groomed him, played with him in every free moment. This spring, when the colt was a year old, he had begun training him to the saddle. The colt shied away from the grooms. He let no one but Leibel come near him. True, when Leibel tried to mount him, the colt pawed the ground, reared up on his hind legs and threw Leibel head over heels into the mud. But Leibel was not discouraged. Such was the nature of horses. Before they were broken to the saddle, they threw their masters more than once. After his fall Leibel limped for a few days. As soon as he recovered, he tried again. Again the colt threw him, but this time with less violence. Leibel didn't lose hope. Any day now, the grooms predicted, his colt would be ready for the saddle.

And now Leibel was leaving. Who would take care of his colt? Who would feed him and water him and tickle his throat? Who would break him in? With dragging steps Leibel entered the stable. Hearing steps, the colt turned his spotted face around, his nostrils flaring and his eyes shining in the dark, and neighed softly.

"Goodbye, little horse," said Leibel, stroking his warm smooth hide. "Do you know that I'm leaving, or don't you?"

No, the *Bar-Mitzvah* colt didn't know that Leibel was leaving him. He shook his mane slightly, his hide shivering under the boy's touch, and pricked up his ears to hear what his friend had to say next.

A horse remains a horse.

11 SHOLOM MEYER MAKES A SPEECH

In vain did all of Holeneshti flock that Saturday night to Ben Rapalovich's yard to speed the Yiddish theater on its way. Sholom Meyer told them in no uncertain terms, punctuating his words with curses, that it was no use waiting. It would be hours before the theater would be packed and ready to leave. But the Holeneshti theater lovers turned a deaf ear. Everything in the world must come to an end, and eventually the theater would be ready to leave. And how could Holeneshti allow a Yiddish theater to depart without half the town escorting it at least part of the way?

This didn't sit well with the director and his lieutenant. To carry out their bit of business on God's Street they must get rid of all witnesses. What to do? Sholom Meyer climbed up on the tallest wagon, faced the crowd and launched into a speech.

"Honored public, ladies and gentlemen. In the name of the director of the Yiddish-German theater and in the name of the whole troupe, I have the honor of conveying to you our heartfelt thanks for the patronage given our theater. During our entire stay with you, and I say this with deep pride, our theater was never empty. And not only inside. The outside was besieged at all times as well. This shows how much you value Art, and in what esteem you hold Yiddish theater. I want to beg your pardon a thousand times for any harsh treatment I may have accorded to you. In plain language, forgive me for the times I cursed any of you or threw you out of the barn or turned the hose on you. Man is less than an angel. I don't know about you, but I assure you our troupe will never forget Holeneshti. Honored public, our theater is about to leave, perhaps for a long time. We would be delighted to have you escort us out of town. But it pains me to inform you that we will not be ready to stir from here until morning. If you wish to make us happy, please go home to sleep, and, God willing, in the morning you will come back. At that time you will be most welcome."

The speech had a tremendous effect, especially the word "welcome" which he pronounced in high German. The honored public gave him an ovation. They shouted *Bravo* over and over. Then they yelled *Hurrah*. And even that wasn't enough. They began calling, "Hotzmach, Hotzmach, give us a *Chassid'l*."

Sholom Meyer climbed on his perch again, begged their pardon, and told them their yelling and hurrahing was in vain. Hotzmach would not appear. The theater was closed.

But the noise did not subside. On the contrary, the shouts of *Hotzmach* and *Chassid'l* grew louder. Sholom Meyer saw that he could accomplish nothing with kindness. And so he unpacked the water-sprinkler and set it up. This method worked like a charm. In a few minutes the courtyard was empty.

Having waited an hour or two for the town to go to sleep, Shchupak collected the whole troupe, as well as Yechiel and his musicians, and led them all to a cellar to drink wine and make merry as God had ordained.

The actors were dumbfounded by Shchupak's generosity. He set up one round after another. "Drink, children, drink. What did I say? Pour the wine and drink."

At the height of the carousing, Sholom Meyer sidled out the door of the cellar and glided away like a shadow toward God's Street.

Isaac of old led to the altar by Father Abraham couldn't have felt greater terror than our young hero on the way to Ploesti that night. Sitting next to Hotzmach on top of the wagon, Leibel listened to the beat of the horses' hooves and the rolling of the wheels, and his limbs trembled and his teeth chattered with fear. Only with fear? A ride such as this could have shaken the innards out of a calmer man. It had been Sholom Meyer's idea to put Hotzmach in charge of the baggage on top of the *Harba,* which rattled and lurched and swayed as though it would fall apart any minute. But for once Hotzmach didn't give a hoot in hell for Sholom Meyer or the director. He could snap his fingers at them both. In his bosom lay a packet that warmed his skin like a poultice, and filled his heart with ineffable joy.

Leibel had handed him the packet with trembling fingers cold as ice.

"How much is in it?" asked Hotzmach in a whisper the driver wouldn't overhear.

"I don't know myself," Leibel whispered back, and Hotzmach could hear the boy's teeth rattle.

62

"Why are you shivering, kitten? Are you cold?" asked Hotzmach, with the tender solicitude of an older brother.

"No-no. I am w-w-warm," Leibel answered.

"S-so, you are w-w-warm," mimicked Hotzmach. "May no worse fever shake you. Here, let me wrap my stole around you. It will comfort you like a mother." And Hotzmach quickly undid a bundle of clothes and pulled out of it a ragged misshapen garment.

Why call this rag by such an exalted name? It is possible that at one time, when it had belonged to Shchupak, it had been worthy of the name *stole*. But that had been long ago when Shchupak was still a plain actor, or maybe even before that when he made the rounds of weddings and circumcisions singing his "sacred songs." At any rate, when Albert decided to bestow his mantle on the comedian, he had made a histrionic ceremony of the occasion. He had assembled the whole company, announced in a pompous speech that he was presenting Hotzmach with a gift, then draped the rag over Hotzmach's scarecrow figure and twirled the poor comedian around to show off its splendor.

"Look," said Shchupak. "Isn't this mantle a beauty? Doesn't it sit well on him? Like the stole of a priest? It once had a rich velvet collar and a cape on top. I bought it ready-made, a real bargain. Heh heh. Let my name not be Albret." And overcome by his generosity, he wiped a tear from his red-rimmed eyes.

Hotzmach, parading behind Shchupak's back in the ragged coat, struck up an attitude so much like the director's that the audience could hardly tell who was the donor and who the recipient.

Yet this "stole" had served Hotzmach through the years as tenderly as a mother, in turn an overcoat and raincoat, featherbed and pillow, blanket and robe. And now it came in handy to cloak the youngster, who was shaking like a lamb led to slaughter. Hotzmach bent down toward his protégé and comforted him like a small child.

"What are you afraid of, silly? Before you know it, we'll be in Ploesti and from there it's a hop and jump over the border. By the time your folks wake up you'll be out of their reach."

This thought tickled Hotzmach so that he laughed softly to himself until his laugh turned to a cough and he began cursing under his breath.

Leibel paid no attention to him. He could swear he heard someone running behind them, panting. He stuck his head out of the stole and, twisting around, saw the dog Terkish running behind the wagon, panting loudly. How did the dog get there? Someone must be following in a wagon and the dog was running ahead. A cold sweat broke out over his body. Then he heard the wheels of a wagon.

"I'm lost," Leibel thought, and prepared for the worst.

But it was only Simon-David, who had caught up with them. He shouted to the driver, "Still crawling along? I thought you were halfway to Ploesti by now. Crack your whip over the nag's back or give it to her in the legs, you dumb ox."

And without waiting for the driver to lift his whip, Simon-David cracked his own whip over the horses' flanks. Then he yelled, "When you get to Ploesti, tell the other drivers to change harness and go straight back. Not to wait for me. Do you hear me, or are you asleep? Giddap, children, giddap."

As Simon-David turned his own horses around, Leibel wiped the sweat off his face and thanked God for his narrow escape. He stuck his head out again, and there, from the back of Simon-David's wagon, suddenly shone at him a pair of familiar glowing dark eyes. He half rose from his place and screamed, "Reizel!" But before his cry reached the other wagon, Simon-David swung completely around and with a whistle and shout and crack of the whip drove off in the same direction from which he had come. In the twinkling of an eye the wagon had disappeared in a thick cloud of dust, leaving behind the odor of horses and the strong smell of tar.

Leibel's head whirled. How could he have seen Reizel in Simon-David's wagon? And if it was Reizel, why had Simon-David turned back? Weren't they both going in the same direction?

Leibel tried to pierce the gloom of the road behind them, but he saw only old Terkish still running behind. Poor Terkish. He felt a pang for the dog and for his other friend, the colt, left behind.

"A cholera seize them both!" exclaimed Hotzmach.

"Seize whom?" asked Leibel.

"Shchupak and that bastard Sholom Meyer. Did you see how they spread themselves out in Simon-David's wagon as though they were in their father's vineyard?"

Leibel looked at Hotzmach with amazement. He hadn't seen anyone but Reizel. What was going on here?"

Hotzmach went on muttering to himself, "One thing I can't get through my head, even if you chop it off with an axe. Why the devil did they turn back? I'll have to ask that crawling donkey of a driver.

Hey, uncle!" He raised his voice. "I'm sorry to wake you out of your nap. It's time to get up for prayers. Can you tell me where that other road leads, the one Simon-David took?"

"Eh? The other road?" The driver turned a sleepy face to Hotzmach. "That's the road you take when you want to go to Novoseletz, that is."

"To Novoseletz?"

"Eh. To Novoseletz."

"Where do you get Novoseletz? We're going to Ungeni, not to Novoseletz."

"Eh? We're going to Ploesti, that's where we're going."

"I know we're going to Ploesti," said Hotzmach impatiently. "At Ploesti we take the train to Ungeni. That's on the Rumanian border. Novoseletz is another border."

"Eh. Another border. If you want to go to Novoseletz, that's the road you take."

"What do you mean Novoseletz. Who's going to Novoseletz? We're going to Ungeni," shouted Hotzmach at the top of his voice.

"We're going to Ploesti," said the driver calmly.

"May a stone fall on your head. I tell him Ungeni and he tells me Ploesti. Go reason with a teamster."

Hotzmach spat at the driver's back and whispered to Leibel, "A country bumpkin."

But Leibel was too absorbed in his own thoughts to hear him. What was happening to Reizel? Where were they taking her?

"Do you know what, my little songbird?" said Hotzmach. "I think Shchupak and that bastard Sholom Meyer forgot about meeting us at the station and turned back to Holeneshti. But the question is," he pulled his derby over one eye and mused aloud, "the question is, why did Simon-David tell the others not to wait for him? It doesn't make sense." He stroked his beardless chin. "I believe the bumpkin is right. They went off to Novoseletz."

His mumble turned to a low chant. "Now the question is, why did they send the whole company and the decorations to the Rumanian border, and go the other way themselves?" He remained silent for a moment, then answered himself in the same manner, as though he were chanting the Talmud. "Tha-at's the question."

Part II

12 URIEL ACOSTA

Holtzman, Shwalb & Co., a traveling Yiddish theater, roamed for several years from town to town over Rumania, Galicia, Bukovina, and even strayed into such big cities as Vienna, Berlin, and Paris. Wherever it went it created a sensation. If we accepted the word of the newspaper blurbs, we would have to assume that nothing like it had ever been seen or heard in the world before.

Yet Holtzman, Shwalb & Co. was no ordinary theater troupe, but a theater without a "prima donna as pretty as a picture" who "drew packed houses"; without a "comic" at whose antics the audience "would slit its own throat"; without the songs and dances and vaudeville capers which the Yiddish public then loved so well and which it doesn't despise even today. The success of the troupe hinged on one personality, a young actor by the name of Rapalesco.

According to report, this Rapalesco could work wonders, "turn snow into lumps of cheese." Critics compared him to Zonenthal, Barnai, Passport, Irving, and other great Thespians of the day. Wherever he appeared, crowds flocked to see him and to marvel at the magnitude of this star rising on the horizon of the Yiddish stage.

With what tricks and wiles did this young actor dazzle his audience? Did he startle them with wild outcries and grimaces? Did he amaze them with extravagant gestures and melodramatic effects? Charm them with the simpering airs and mincing manners so often affected by Yiddish artists? Not at all. According to the critics, he won his audience with his very lack of artifice, with his candor and simplicity, by acting at all times and in all roles true to life, as natural and straightforward as nature itself.

"Without Rapalesco," wrote one reviewer, "this troupe is nothing but a circus, a bunch of spiritless amateurs as dark as the grave, and as lifeless as a cemetery. But the moment young Rapalesco steps out on the stage, all the corners light up, the play springs into life."

This Rapalesco had distinguished himself particularly in the title role of the play *Uriel Acosta*. "Last night," wrote a critic, "I went to see the troupe Holtzman, Shwalb & Co. perform *Uriel Acosta*. I saw the rising young star, Rapalesco. Words cannot describe the impression he made on me." This same critic then went on to describe the indescribable in three and a half columns of rhapsody, ending, "If only Karl Gutzkow, the author of the play, could rise from the dead and see the Acosta that Rapalesco has created!"

Thus the critics. And the public? The Yiddish theater-going public, never granted a surfeit of distinguished actors, fought for tickets and shouted itself hoarse at every performance, the majority drawn not by interest in the drama but by sheer curiosity. Say what you will, "the whole world can't be crazy." Once in the theater, they responded in spite of themselves to the vitality of Rapalesco's performance. Here was an actor who with simple words and gestures touched their very heartstrings, aroused half-buried thoughts, awakened slumbering emotions.

And they asked each other: Who is this young unknown; this rising young genius? Where does he come from? What is his real name? They could learn only that his name was Leo Rapalesco, that he came from Rumania, from Bucharest, and that he was still very young, a mere stripling of eighteen or so. That was all.

However, the reader, of course, must have guessed that Leo Rapalesco was none other than Leibel Rapalovich of Holeneshti.

The senior director of Holtzman, Shwalb & Co. was Bernard Holtzman, a tall personage, thin and slightly stooped, with an imposing top hat, a white vest with gold buttons, and a clean-shaven but sickly-looking face with black sideburns. His sallow complexion and sunken eyes attested to his ill health. He suffered from shortness of breath and a wheezing cough. The many doctors he had consulted told him the same thing. He might go on living for years with this cough, or he might give up the ghost any morning. They advised a

70

trip to summer climate and, above all, rest. Holtzman laughed. It's easy to say, Go away and rest. And what would become of his *cheder,* meaning the theater? There were wolves aplenty sharpening their teeth against his troupe and eager to lay their paws on young Rapalesco. The cholera take them before he would let "the kid," as he called him, out of his grasp. He had sweated enough to make an actor of him. What would have become of "the kid" but for Holtzman? Nothing with nothing.

By now the reader must have guessed that Bernhard Holtzman was none other than our old acquaintance Hotzmach.

No comedian any more, dancing and singing "I'm a little *Chassid.*" That's over and done with. Hotzmach has turned businessman. The whole theater rests on his shoulders. He makes good money these days and is saving up so that he can retire some day and rest. He has also become the head of a household. Not a wife, God forbid. Hotzmach has taken an oath never to marry as long as he lives, for which he holds Shchupak's old side-kick Sholom Meyer responsible. "That bastard, how anxious he was to get me hitched to that half-wit sister of his, may a cholera take them both."

Holtzman, though Hotzmach no longer, still smolders with anger recalling the days when he shined shoes for Shchupak and Sholom Meyer tried to marry him off to his sister Ethel Dvora. What actually happened between him and Ethel Dvora and why he still holds a grudge against her no one will ever know. But Holtzman has sworn by the name of his father, may he rest in peace, never to marry, not even if "they" were to offer him a stack of gold this high. True, once or twice he stood on the verge of breaking this oath. But he was given to understand, and not in the most refined language, that such a cadaver, with one foot in the grave, had better espouse the Angel of Death. Holtzman had answered with curses. Let *them* espouse the Angel of Death. He would outlive them all.

To cover his disappointment, he had sent for his mother and his sister Zlatka. Now he was the head of a family. His mother kept house for him, and his sister Zlatka he had turned into an actress. Not a bad-looking girl, Zlatka, though a bit countrified still, with work-roughened hands and a pointed reddish nose, young and bashful, but never mind. There are plenty of men after her, both actors and non-actors. Even Holtzman's partner, Isaac Shwalb, has made it clear he wouldn't be averse to the match. But Holtzman has another prospect in view.

71

Right in the center of the old, old town of Chernovitz, ancient capital of Bukovina, stood a large hotel named "Under the Black Rooster." Its windows overlooked the shops and stalls as if rejoicing in its eminence. It waited for guests, and well it might. On the patronage of such as the Yiddish theater troupe, Holtzman, Shwalb & Co., the Black Rooster would never grow rich. The whole company occupied a mere few rooms and its members ate their meals in the Yiddish restaurant—those who had the price of a meal. For this was the lean period toward the end of the month, when the actors lived on studying their lines, rehearsing their parts, and playing "tertel-mertel," a card game with all the virtues. It doesn't tax anyone's brains; it doesn't call for a set number of players; it can be played sitting or standing. For this reason it is popular with actors, musicians, shipping clerks, and others who have no time to spare and want to get in on a quick game, standing, so to speak, on one foot.

The room in which the company played "tertel-mertel" was so clouded with smoke you could barely see your hand in front of your face even in broad daylight. At the head of a long table sat the banker with a large plate, his "bank," in front of him. At this moment he happens to be Isaac Shwalb, Holtzman's partner, a man with a large beardless face as red as raw beef. His face is even redder than usual as he lays out the cards. Luck has been against him all day. For every card he turns up he has to pay out from the bank. As if that weren't enough, the winners gloat over him. Grasping hands stretch out to him from all sides and taunts fly about his head.

"Shwelbele, two crowns for me and two boils on your red face."

"Here, Shwelbel, I've got the top card. Pay out four times."

"Shwalb, I'll strip you naked as the day you were born."

"I'll have three pints of your blood, Shwalb."

"Death you will get from me, death."

"Aha, bastard, you lost. Pour out the sugar."

The more they curse him, the more rattled he gets; and the more rattled he gets, the more he loses. The embers fanned, he burns like a straw roof.

"Imbecile! Throw up the game. Let someone else take over the bank. Can't you see, hound, the odds are against you?" This Holtzman counsels him like a faithful comrade and partner, but Isaac retorts, "Get out, you asthmatic dog, you dried-up old bachelor. Who asked your advice?"

And Isaac Shwalb feverishly shuffles the cards and looks with blood-

72

shot eyes into the emptying plate. With a sigh he reaches into his inside pocket and produces a bulging wallet. The crowd gets a new lease on life.

"You're driving to Kishinev, Itzikel? Drive, drive, thief, and get buried nine ells deep," shouts a dried-up old actor with a huge Adam's apple; and Zlatka Holtzman, the director's sister, sputters with laughter. All eyes turn on her suddenly, and she blushes to the tip of her pink nose. Just in time Rapalesco comes to her aid. He speaks up from across the table and offers to buy a card in partnership with her. "The ace of clubs," he says. "Clubs are lucky today." She looks at him gratefully, her heart in her eyes. If he would only come closer to her. As though guessing her thought, Rapalesco pushes through the crowd and walks up to Zlatka who almost faints with joy. God in Heaven! How handsome he is! He turns and smiles down at her as though the heavens themselves had opened up and the sun shone in its glory. What matter if he smiles at the next one in the same way? As long as the heavens are blue and the sun shines on her.

Having sold more than half of his deck, the banker gathers up the coins thrown on the table and piles them into the plate. Slowly, cautiously, he begins laying out cards from the other deck. The crowd follows every motion with greedy eyes; the noise and tumult and laughter grow louder. Again Shwalb is the loser. He is burning and paying. Then a shout goes up. "The ace of clubs. Who has the ace? Rapalesco. Who else? Speak up, Rapalesco. Ask for your money."

"We won," says Rapalesco to Zlatka. Her face glows, not because they won, but because he is speaking to her. He shows the banker his card, and the crowd envies him openly. "A lucky fellow." "Wins every time." "Someone crossed his path with full buckets." Then they turn on the banker, venting their spleen on him.

"Shwalb, the ace. Four to one. The odds were against you. Pay up, Shwelbel, pay up."

"I'm paying, I'm paying," says Isaac, counting out the money and handing it to Rapalesco with good grace. Rapalesco is not like the others. He doesn't gloat when he wins nor curse when he loses. He is a different sort altogether. Everyone in the company loves Rapalesco, and the one who loves him most—why should we deny it—is poor Zlatka.

Poor Zlatka. She scarcely knows how it happens, but every time she sees Rapalesco she goes to pieces. When she has to act opposite him

73

on the stage she goes numb all over, often forgetting her lines and missing her cues. Then she catches it from her brother, the director, who is stricter with her than with anyone else.

"Well, well. You acted like a regular cow today. When Uriel Acosta said, 'You can shut your eyes, all of you. You, blind mother, shut your eyes, too. Enough. Let me go . . . I am leaving . . .' then you, Judith, must run to the window and come out with this speech, 'Ah, he's running . . . all out of breath . . . and straight for the synagogue. It is I, I who am responsible for this.' But what do you do? You stand there like a lump of clay! And when the prompter tells you, 'To the window, to the window,' you hear him like a gnat. He motions with his hand and you look at the door. Your hands and feet, little sister, should be chopped off for such acting."

Zlatka knew better than anyone that her hands and feet should be chopped off for such acting. But was she to blame? The moment she walked on-stage and saw the mother of Uriel Acosta, dressed in black, her heart failed her. And when she heard the words, "Free, Judith? You shall never be free," then everything turned dark before her eyes. It seemed to her that the blind woman was not Esther, Uriel's mother, but a huge black crow, croaking doom.

Poor Zlatka. Was she to blame for losing her heart to this youth? She had never met anyone like him in her small home town. Why had she ever strayed from it? Why couldn't she have been left there? She did well enough, learning to sew shirts, and beginning to earn a little money. Then her brother had to start sending letters and telegrams. He wouldn't leave them alone. So they had come, she and her mother. At once he went to work making an actress out of her. First they tried her as a *soubrette;* put a short dress on her and shoes so tight they pinched her toes and almost made her eyes pop out of her head. When she complained, her mother said, "Just imagine to yourself that you're working for strangers, and they tell you to climb on the roof. Would you be any better off then?" Next her brother tried to make a prima donna of her. But she had no voice. "You squeal, little sister, just like a cat when its tail is stepped on."

Zlatka breathed easier when she was given the part of Judith in *Uriel Acosta*. Not because she particularly liked the part, but because now she could be closer to the handsome blond youth with the melting blue eyes. For his sake she was willing to go through the torture of learning strange words whose meaning she didn't understand. For his sake she went on the stage, though she despised it, footlights, the

74

costumes, actors, the whole of it. And most of all she despised and feared her brother's partner, Isaac Shwalb, with his huge red face and his revolting attentions. He followed her around, chucked her under the chin, pinched her cheeks, and asked, "Do you love me?" until she was ready to scream. He would bring that ugly red face close to hers and whisper endearments. "Little apple, do you love me, little apple?"

Zlatka would have run away if she wasn't afraid of her brother, and if she could have seen Rapalesco any other way. Rapalesco. The name itself was a song. She repeated it over and over to herself like a refrain. More than once, lying in bed, she pulled the cold pillow from under her head and, pressing it to her breasts, whispered the words of Judith. "If I could only clasp him to my breast."

In the morning, on waking, her first thought was of him. Soon she would stand beside him, drinking in his words, "Judith, Judith. On every page it is written in letters with garlands entwined, what we have come to mean to each other."

And when she saw him, she went to pieces completely. Holtzman alone saw her confusion and understood what it meant. He thought to himself, "One party, the bride, is ready to march under the canopy. If I were only so sure of the groom."

No one knew as well as Holtzman what a treasure he had in young Rapalesco. And no one could have guarded him more carefully, like something of rare value entrusted to his care for which he would some day have to give an accounting. He kept a jealous eye on the boy's every move. If someone said a superfluous word to him, Holtzman heard it. If anyone threw an unwonted look in his direction, Holtzman intercepted it in mid-air.

But all this wasn't enough. Rapalesco, still young, needed a mother's care. And when Holtzman sent for his mother, it was not so much for his own sake as for that of "the kid." And his instinct proved right. In Sarah-Brocha, Rapalesco found a new mother.

In appearance Sarah-Brocha, tall and angular, with large work-roughened hands, put one in mind of a worked-out cavalry horse. But the more Rapalesco came to know her, the more he appreciated her sincerity and innate good nature. She was a woman without pretense or humbug. "What was on her lung came out on her tongue." For instance, she couldn't stand to see Rapalesco sleep so late in the morning. She woke him at crack of dawn. Holtzman objected. "Do you know who he is? His father is stuffed with money." "Fiddlesticks,"

Sarah-Brocha answered. "So what if his father is stuffed with money? Does the son have to loll in bed past noon?" She also laid down the law about eating and drinking. Before Rapalesco left for the theater, she caught hold of him, "Drink your milk, then you can go play-acting."

Rapalesco first felt the touch of her coarse work-roughened hands on his body when he lay sick with influenza, after a strenuous week's engagement, in a small town in Galicia. Alarmed, Holtzman sent for the doctor, who recommended sweating. "Sweat, did you say?" Sarah-Brocha rolled up her sleeves and went to work. She rubbed Rapalesco with spirits and vinegar, spooned hot raspberry cordial into him, piled blankets and featherbeds on top of him. For good measure she added Holtzman's famous "stole." Rapalesco swam in rivers of sweat. Sarah-Brocha nursed him day and night, mopped his wet brow, forced medicine down his throat, and loudly cursed the mother who had allowed such a nestling, such a tender young bird, out into the world among these actor-tramps.

Later she told Rapalesco that, as he tossed and groaned in his fever, he had called on his mother. "You named someone else, too. Some Reizel. Is she a sister, this Reizel?"

Rapalesco said nothing. Let it be a sister.

He had never uttered Reizel's name to anyone, not even to Holtzman. But her memory remained in his heart. The mystery of her disappearance still plagued him. He recalled that night when he and Holtzman had fled to Jassy, and from there on the train to Bucharest, where they learned that the troupe had been left high and dry at the border, without a groschen. Later they heard that Sholom Meyer had arrived at the border town alone, had picked up the theater baggage and properties and gone off, no one knew where. The other actors had scattered, some going home on foot, others remaining to starve in Rumania.

Of Reizel he heard not a word.

13 HOLENESHTI DOESN'T SLEEP

Of all the people in Holeneshti who had been affected by the disappearance of the young couple Ben Rapalovich alone neither wept nor wailed nor wrung his hands, but calmly and without fuss went about doing what had to be done.

First he ordered everyone to silence. And they quieted down. Then he issued a command, "Let the horses be harnessed and the 'brass button' be summoned." In Ben's language this meant the police lieutenant, with whom he was on "thou" terms.

"Take all you want," he said to the police lieutenant. "Strip me to my bare skin, but bring back my child."

Hard to believe a person could change so much in one day. Ben's usually plump, ruddy cheeks looked bluish and sunken. Even his belly, usually as tight as a brass drum, had slackened and hung down to his knees. His manner changed. He didn't shout or bang with his fists or break chairs. Somber as a ghost, he drifted through the house, refusing to attend to the farm or even to face the light of day. And here lay his wife, mortally ill. A heart ailment, the doctor said, and she needed to be soothed and comforted. How could he comfort her when his own head had just been split open by an axe, with his best and dearest, most treasured possession snatched from him?

"Take as much as you want," he told the police lieutenant again. "Strip me to my bare skin, but bring back my child."

The police lieutenant looked at Ben with amazement and pity. He had never seen him so distraught. He put his hand on Ben's shoulder and said in a voice meant to be reassuring, *"Budyet charosho.* All will be well. Pour us a drink."

And the "brass" went to work to solve the mystery of the young couple's disappearance. With their usual single-mindedness they dispensed with formalities and went straight to the heart of the matter. The finger of authority pointed at the Cantor. He, said the police, and he alone, knew where the young couple had gone. He refused to talk?

Well, let him sit for a few hours in the "stone cell" and get acquainted with the mice and the roaches, and his tongue would be loosened. And they would have clapped Israel into jail but for the quick wit of his wife, Leah.

Leah, as soon as the first wave had passed, felt her strength return and her brain clear. Without doubt, this calamity smacked of the Yiddish theater. She had a hundred and one signs to prove it. How? Never mind. A mother's heart knows. She had felt it in her bones the moment those two *schlimazls* had crossed her doorstep that they were out for her blood. But where had her eyes been? She had been blind, stone-blind. And God had punished her for her negligence. But now her eyes were wide open. Everything was clear, as clear as day. Not one person but many had a share in this calamity. First of all, there was that strumpet Necha, the landlady of the inn, with those two brazen-faced sisters of hers who were ha-ha-ha and he-he-he with everyone, separately, all day long. The actors had lodged at the inn, and the three women had been *kitzeniu-mitzeniu,* hand-in-glove with them. They must know everything. And what about Yechiel the Musician? Why had he spent all Saturday night carousing with the actors in Henich the Vintner's cellar? And Henich himself? Also a saint in a bearskin coat! Hadn't his oldest girl run off three years ago with a government clerk? Let the police go after them instead of meddling with her innocent husband. Did you ever see such a thing?"

Thus none other than Leah opened the eyes of officialdom. She, so to speak, put weapons into their hands and gave them a lantern to seek out the truth. Not only did the police set her husband free at once, but they seized the above-mentioned suspects and put them through the third degree. At first they denied everything, but when they realized that all the police wanted of them was information about the Yiddish theater and the runaway couple, they unsealed their lips and poured their stories forth.

The first one summoned was Henich the Vintner, a man well along in years, with hair as white as a dove but cheeks as plump and rosy as a young man's, and a comfortable, Bessarabian potbelly. Though none too quick, he had one virtue—he was a truthful man. And he told his story straight from the heart, as though he stood before the Throne of the Almighty Himself. Here is what happened, he said:

Every Saturday night for years, ever since his start in the wine-making trade, it had been his custom to light a candle and descend into the cellar to examine his wines and see which must ferment and which must be filtered, which diluted and which made stronger. Now there is one kind of wine you pour into bottles and cork so that it won't mold, and another kind which you leave alone to age by itself. For when all is said and done, what is the secret of wine-making?

Here the police rudely interrupted, informing him they were not after the secrets of wine-making. People had reported having seen the actors tippling in his cellar all Saturday night.

At the word "tippling" Henich cackled with laughter. Everything is called tippling. Here is what happened. He was standing in the cellar Saturday night, tending to his wines, when a message was brought to him that the actors had come to drink wine. He dropped everything and went to meet them, thinking, they will drink and drink, the wine will start flowing. In the end it turned out that from all their "tippling" they drank three bottles of red wine and one of white. All they did was talk about wine. And Henich had a maxim that those who talk about wine don't drink it, and those who drink wine don't talk about it.

"True, very true," the police cut him short, "but what do you know about the runaway pair?"

It turned out that about the runaway pair Henich knew as much as they. Here is what happened: When he got up Sunday, first thing in the morning, as was his custom, he went down to the cellar to look at his wine. . . .

"Enough wine!" said the police, and went to work on Yechiel the Musician.

Yechiel was a man with a thick mane of hair, a gold signet ring on his finger, a tall hat, and an imposing stole like a priest's. But his health wasn't too good. He always wore a muffler wound about his throat and he spoke in a hoarse whisper. Yechiel would have it understood that this came from playing the fiddle. But his colleagues the musicians insisted it was something else. Yechiel, a gay dog, carried on "affairs" with half the married women in town. His wife Hannah Pearl made no scandals. She wasn't that kind. A patient woman, Hannah Pearl, but only up to a point. Everything can be endured, up to a point. And so Hannah Pearl gave it to him now and then, but only when no one could hear. She wasn't that kind. She hated a scandal.

Usually quite voluble, Yechiel had trouble telling his story, perhaps because Hannah Pearl stood at his elbow. He ran his fingers through his hair, and cleared his throat several times, but when he tried to speak, his tongue became twisted. Tryouts and rehearsals, rehearsals and tryouts, orchestras, musical scores . . . aside from these he knew nothing; and if his colleagues insinuated that he had been carrying on with the prima donna, they lied in their teeth.

"*Charosho*," said the police. "Very good." About his carryings-on with the prima donna they would talk later. And now would he be so kind as to tell them what he knew of the pair who, it was said, had run off with the theater troupe last night? About this Yechiel swore up and down that he knew nothing.

Yechiel thought they had done with him. But instead they locked him in another room, and told him to wait until they called him again. In the meanwhile they turned to Necha and her two sisters. And here they found themselves with a bull by the tail.

They could not understand why Necha flew into such a rage when they called her up for questioning. Was it because she was such an innocent soul on whom no shadow of suspicion could fall? Or something else? But she erupted like a volcano of profanity and refused to quiet down. She poured fire and brimstone on the heads of her enemies who begrudged her a livelihood; she turned to cinders and ashes all who spoke ill of her. Let their mouths twist to one side. Let their tongues be cut out. Let their eyes fall out of their sockets. Let them lose arms and legs, and hobble around on crutches. Let them bury father and mother in unhallowed ground and never bring them to a consecrated grave. Let them go begging from door to door, they and their children and children's children to the last generation, dear Lord in Heaven, dear, kind, merciful Father. Amen.

But the curses didn't help Necha. The police warned her if she told what she knew, well and good. If not, she'd join Yechiel the Musician in the lockup. At that she stopped cursing and began talking.

She herself, said Necha, was a widow and kept an inn. "That's to say, an inn. It's nothing but a barn, a kennel, a stable. I'd have closed it up long ago, but what can I do when my husband, may he rest in peace, left me a bomb?"

The officials jumped. "A bomb? What kind of bomb?"

She meant the house. "A broken wreck, a ruin nobody will take, unless I give it away. Everybody who comes to see the place tells me it isn't a bad house, if it only stood in the market place. So I ask you, should I take it on my shouldres and carry it over to the market place?"

80

"No, no. Leave the house where it is. Better tell us what you know about the Yiddish actors who lodged with you."

Necha's feelings weren't hurt at this snub. "The actors, you say?" Very well, she'd tell about the actors. It was Saturday night and she had just finished saying "God of Abraham" and was putting on the samovar for tea. "All of a sudden, one of the actors walks in, the one they call Sholom Meyer, the *farshlepte krenk,* and he says to me, 'What will you take for your bearskin coat and your winter shawl?' I looked at him as though he had gone out of his mind. '*Schlimazl,*' I say, 'what do you want with a wool shawl and a fur coat in summer?' And he says to me, 'It's none of your grandmother's business. If I need it, I need it.' He fastens himself to me like a leech, won't let me off till I bring him the coat and shawl. Then he asks, 'What will you take for these old rags?' 'God in heaven,' I tell him, 'if they're old rags to you, why do you want them?' And he again, 'It's none of your grandmother's business.' So I name a price and he almost jumps out of his skin. 'Are you crazy or just out of your head?' So we bargain for a while, back and forth. He to me, 'Old rags,' and I to him, 'Then don't buy.' Until we strike a deal and he hands over the money. I think to myself, 'God in heaven, what does a man want with a woman's coat and winter shawl? And all of a sudden, just before leaving town?' And I decide to keep an eye on him and see what he'll do. In the meantime the rest of the *schlimazls* arrive from the theater, drink their tea, and begin to settle their accounts. May each of them get a boil this big for every half-ruble they rooked me for. Then off they go to Henich's cellar to drink wine. Why, all of a sudden, before leaving, wine? May I know as much of harm. Well, let them drink and grow strong. It isn't my money they're tippling away. And I had something else to rack my brains with. Why did Sholom Meyer buy a fur coat in summer, and a woman's coat at that? Better yet, if he had packed it away with the rest of his things, I might have thought, he wants to bring someone a gift from Holeneshti. If so, I let it go too cheap. But in the end, what does he do? He takes the coat and the shawl and says to me, 'Let them hang on the wall here till the last minute.' How do you like that? Sometime around midnight, he shows up and takes the coat and shawl and sets off. I ask him, 'Where to?' And he says, 'It's none of your grandmother's business.' 'With your head sunk in the ground,' I tell him. I was ready to go to bed, but how can I when the actors are off somewhere in Henich's cellar and they still have to come back and tell me goodbye? After all, they were guests such a long time, they can't leave without a godspeed.

81

Well, it's long after midnight. I look outside. Aha. A wagon. A second. A third. The whole company is here. 'Goodbye.' 'Happy journey.' I look at the last wagon, Simon David's, and there sits their director and right next to him a woman wrapped up to her eyes in my bearskin coat and winter shawl. Her face is covered; all I can see is her eyes. But they look familiar. God in heaven. Who can she be? I know all their women, scarecrows every one of them, each homelier than the next. And this one looks like a bonny thing, with shining black eyes like a gipsy's. I could swear I knew her. If only they stopped long enough for me to get a good look. But they've just driven up and the next second it's 'godspeed' and they're off. All night long I didn't sleep a wink. Lord, Lord, who was the girl with the gipsy eyes? Then in the morning when I heard the story going around town, I grabbed my head with both hands and called to my sisters, 'Give me straw to chew and call me a heifer.' "

In short, heaven and earth had sworn that a secret must out, that truth will rise like oil upon the waters. May God grant her fortune if she hadn't known this would happen. But why couldn't it have happened to her sisters instead? Didn't they go to the theater every night? Why hadn't her sisters made eyes at the *schlimazls* like the Cantor's daughter?

At this a wild cry arose. "Hold your tongue, hussy!" And like an enraged lioness, Leah, the Cantor's wife, leaped at the woman's throat, ready to choke her. Luckily the police pulled the two women apart in time.

14 THE EXPEDITION AFTER THE RUNAWAYS

The upshot of all this questioning was this: the police officially proclaimed that "the son of Ben Rapalovich, Leib, aged fourteen, and the daughter of the Cantor, Reizel Spivak, aged fifteen, ran away Saturday night with the Yiddish theater to the Rumanian border, and the aforementioned son of Ben Rapalovich, Leib, stole from the aforementioned father, Ben Rapalovich, a sum of money in such and such an amount."

Their duty done, the police retired. All that remained was to follow the criminals, apprehend them, and recover the money. Ben Rapalovich did not delay. He at once fitted out an expedition at the head of which he placed his older son, Anshel.

Anshel, a dapper young man of about twenty-two, pasty-faced and red-lipped, had a handsome, closely trimmed black beard and thick curly black hair. Though far from a numbskull, Anshel had never loved school. As a boy he had refused to go to *cheder,* though you beat him black and blue. Realizing that he couldn't make a scholar of this son, Ben declared, "You won't learn your lessons; you can graze cattle."

In other words, he would make a farmer of him. And this suited Anshel to a T. He rode horseback like a Cossack, spoke the Moldavian dialect like a native, understood the nature of melons, and could tell at a glance which tree would bear fruit and which was fit only for firewood.

Only recently Ben had found him a suitable match, a girl without beauty or talent and sickly besides, but of a well-connected family in Beltz. When the groom saw the prospective bride, his heart was riddled with holes, but he knew it was useless to protest. Ben was eager to buy himself "honors" and when Ben wanted something badly enough, nothing would stand in his way.

Returning to Holeneshti, Anshel soon found solace at home in the person of the nursemaid, a comely young wench as vigorous as a young mare. True, the nursemaid objected at first and threatened a scandal. But what did a wealthy man's son care about scandals? Especially Anshel who had been slapped in the face by every girl in town? It goes without saying Ben knew nothing of his son's amorous adventures. Only Beilka, the mother, knew what went on, and she kept her peace, secretly praying that when her son married he would settle down.

This was the ambassador whom Ben Rapalovich selected to bring back the runaway Leibel. Along with him he sent the cashier Simcha with a substantial sum of money and instructions to spare no expense but bring the rascal home at any cost.

The expedition also carried official "documents" empowering them to bring Leibel back in chains, if need be. And his parting word was, "Remember, with kindness."

By the time Anshel and Simcha reached Jassy, they found all the actors gone. They were told that some young fellows with broken shoes and clean-shaven faces had been seen straggling about town recently; but where they had disappeared to nobody knew. The two envoys pushed on to Bucharest.

This was Anshel's first visit to the big city. He had long dreamed of this opportunity. As soon as he was married and became his own master, he had promised himself he would run down to Bucharest, and have his fling. And here he was, not married yet, and with plenty of money to spend. It was, as they say, "a kosher pot and a kosher spoon"; so he could gorge himself.

The only fly in the ointment was the presence of the cashier. But, in the first place, who listened to him? And, in the second place, Simcha was also human and a bachelor besides. To top it off, the cashier was not the boss, but an underling. Where the employer's son led, he had to follow.

Simcha agreed that they must stop at the best hotel in town, the *Hotel Datchio* in *Strada Podemagoshoi*. "God knows," he said, "it's costing this much, let it cost a little more. Especially since your father said not to spare any expense, and if we ran out of money to write, and he would send more."

But when he learned how much the *Hotel Datchio* charged, the poor cashier grabbed his head with both hands. Anshel calmed him down. "Don't be a fool, Simcha. When you're on such delicate business you can't live like a hog."

The *Hotel Datchio* got its renown from the fact that during the Russo-Turkish war the great Osman Pasha had lived there. It was also noted for its café-chantant, "Paradise," where the beauteous and celebrated Rumanian Chanteuse, Marinesco-Malinesco, sang her celebrated Russian songs, "Stormy winds are blowing" and "I want to tell you, tell you." Stopping in such a hotel was indeed paradise. But living in paradise costs money. On getting the first week's bill, Simcha almost had a stroke. But Anshel reassured him again. "Idiot, who cares about money? When a human life is at stake? We've got to find the boy."

Simcha shrugged but gave in. If the boss was eager, then he was willing. They began to live like God in Odessa. They hired a carriage by the hour and drove all over the city, visiting all the parks, museums, galleries, and stopping in all the theaters, circuses, cafés and cabarets, where, as Anshel cleverly pointed out, they were most likely to encounter the runaways.

The "Paradise" was Anshel's favorite. "Mark my words," he told

84

Simcha, "we'll nab them right in this spot. Let's sit at the table in the corner. From there we can see everything."

Reluctantly Simcha agreed. From their table they could see everything, including the entrance. Anshel ordered like a lord. The chorus girls, flitting around in short red skirts with gold trimming and tiny rakishly worn red chapeaus edged with gold, delighted him. Most of all he was taken with the harpists. As their thin, nimble fingers strummed the strings, they nodded their little heads and fluttered their lashes and smiled, smiled straight at him, Anshel.

One night, the two envoys were sitting at their usual table drinking *Dulshatza,* a sweetened fruit punch. Anshel was in excellent spirits, but Simcha was dejected. His heart bled for the money they were frittering away. "Here we sit in Bucharest, looking for nothing, and money blows away like trash in the wind. Woe, woe, what will the end be?"

Simcha, in spite of his name, "Joy-and-Gladness," was a gloomy soul. Thin and sallow, with round bulging eyes, a perpetually plugged nose, and a thick upper lip, covered by a ragged, drooping mustache, he looked as though the whole world had fallen on top of him. He could see nothing in the Café Paradiso to revel over. Here's the orchestra dinning away, like any other, he thought. Here's the crowd making merry like Holeneshti on bath day. They're throwing rubles around. Money is honey! What do they lack? Headaches? The harpists, dancers, soubrettes, and other pests cavorting around, women dressed in outlandish costumes, others only half-dressed, and still others hardly dressed at all—he had no interest in them. Not even in Marinesco-Malinesco, herself, who appears, like a dessert, after dinner. Let her roll her eyes, flash her diamonds, and sing "Stormy winds are blowing," then "I want to tell you, tell you." Simcha doesn't care, though everybody else sings along with her, "A-strolling we will go, will go," Anshel louder than anyone.

She sees Anshel and winks an eye. Overcome with rapture, he winks back. Her number finished, she sweeps down from the stage and approaches their table. Anshel leaps up to make a place for her between him and the cashier. A gust of perfume assails their nostrils. Simcha's nose, unaccustomed to such fragrance, begins to twitch, and he explodes into sneezes. Anshel calls out, "Good health to you," and Simcha wishes he could hide under the table.

"Domniulu," says Marinesco, tapping Anshel playfully over the arm with her fan. "A handsome young blade like you drinking *Dulshatza!"* Or as we would say it, "A buck like you drinking chocolate sodas!"

85

Anshel melts at the compliment. He summons the waiter with a lordly air and inclines his head toward the singer as though to say, "What's your desire, lovely lady?" The lovely lady desires champagne. He orders champagne and inclines his head again. "What more do you wish, Princess?" The Princess wishes roast pheasant. Then she calls for a liqueur. *Chartreuse,* she calls it. *"Chartreuse,"* repeats Anshel, as though the word hadn't just been born on his lips. Next the lady wants pineapple. The waiter regrets, they are out of pineapple. Anshel waxes indignant. What sort of answer is that? When a lady wants pineapple, let there be pineapple. Simcha pulls at his sleeve and whispers, "It will cost you a fortune." "Donkey," Anshel whispers back, "do you see the diamonds she's wearing? Do you know what they're worth?" No, Simcha doesn't know, and he doesn't care. He only knows their wallet is flattening out. He told Anshel this morning, and Anshel yelled, "Donkey, then why don't you write home for more money?"

"What should I write?" asked Simcha.

"Write that we're hot on their trail. Write that we're working night and day looking for them. We've been driving all over the city hunting for them and others are helping us hunt. But it costs money, plenty of money. Nobody will do it for nothing. Tell my father to rush more money."

The champagne arrived in an ice bucket and Anshel popped corks and filled three glasses with the sparkling liquid and drank to the singer's good health and saw to it that Simcha drank, too. Why should he sit there like a corpse at a feast? It didn't look right. Having drained one glass and another and still another, Simcha became more cheerful. His forehead began to shine, the ends of his mustache twitched, and the semblance of a smile appeared on his thick lips.

One might say this was the first time in his life that "Joy-and-Gladness" had been joyful and glad. All at once everything around him became hilariously funny. Especially Anshel, who was trying to embrace Marinesco. Simcha waved his empty glass in the air, and rolled from side to side with laughter. But all of a sudden he stopped; his drooping lids flew open, and he stared with bulging eyes at the door.

He had seen two persons enter the café-chantant, one tall and thin, the other shorter and stockier. It seemed to him the arrivals had thrown one look at him and Anshel and had darted back. Before Simcha had time to turn to Anshel and scream, "Here he is, here he is, as I am a Jew!" they had vanished.

86

In vain Simcha ran after them like a crazed man. In vain he swore that he had just seen Leibel at the door with his own eyes. Anshel wouldn't believe him. He had imagined the whole thing, he said. The wine had gone to his head.

The cashier Simcha, though tipsy, had made no mistake.

As soon as Hotzmach and Rapalesco arrived in the beautiful city of Bucharest they set out to see the sights. "We have to study the stage, my songbird," Hotzmach told Leibel. "Canvass all the theaters and cabarets, look over the business possibilities. We can't remain idle forever. The world won't hand us a living. We'll have to scratch for it ourselves."

To Leibel these words sounded prosaic in the extreme. His soul yearned toward the stage, but not as a trade. He aspired to something loftier which he himself didn't fully understand as yet. He begrudged every day, every minute passed in idleness. He would have liked to throw himself into acting at once. But if Hotzmach said they must study the stage first, he must know what he was talking about. And so he went along with Hotzmach to "study music, theater, and art."

From tent-shows and coffee houses in the slums they worked up to the music-halls and cabarets, the legitimate theaters, the fashionable café-chantants and night clubs, omitting no type of entertainment hall. In each, Hotzmach learned a new angle or trick, sampled a tidbit to use later for his own purposes.

"Take a look, my songbird, how they put on a show," Hotzmach would say. "Do you see stage sets? Do you see dresses? Shoes? Stockings? The devil take money. Not in vain is it written, 'Silver and gold on pigs are seen.' "

". . . can wash a pig clean," Leibel corrected him.

"Have it your way," Hotzmach said, tapping his inside pocket with a significant gesture. "As long as we've got it. Lucky we stopped in this town. What we pick up will come in handy. Wait till you see the theater I'm going to set up. It'll make man and God rejoice. A plague on Shchupak."

Leibel saw the stage in quite a different light. To him the acting was everything. He imagined himself on the boards, speaking immortal lines. The vision made his face flame with excitement and his breath come in short gasps, leading Hotzmach to believe the boy was bowled over by the costumes and the decor.

"See, my treasure, that's how they trick out a show. With sparkle

87

and glitter and color. Knocks your eyes out. That's the kind of show I'm going to put on. A plague on Shchupak."

Hotzmach yearned to become another Shchupak, a director and manager of his own theater. Why not? God had wrought greater miracles. The best example was Shchupak himself, once a servant, then a choir boy, then a street singer who sought out weddings and circumcisions, and look at him now—a director hung with diamonds, the devil take him! As long as Hotzmach had nothing to eat, he had to slave for that bloodsucker. But now that he had the wherewithal—here he tapped his side-pocket, and involuntarily his shoulders straightened and his head rose—now he could laugh at Shchupak. Wait, wait, Hotzmach would show him up yet. He would collect a company of the best actors and actresses; he would bring them to the town where Shchupak was performing with his clods and sticks; he would rent the same theater from right under his nose, and make him sorry he had ever been born, him and his lieutenant Sholom Meyer, may they both get the sunstroke and burn alive on a hot summer day!

Leibel, too, wished himself in the same town as Shchupak, but for other reasons. Wherever Shchupak was, there Reizel must also be, if she hadn't been caught before this. The thought of Reizel seized by her pursuers sent a cold chill through him. Hotzmach, noticing his sudden silence, asked, "What's wrong, dear boy? Afraid you'll be found? May I drop dead if anyone would recognize you now, in your new duds. You can forget Leibel Rapalovich of Holeneshti."

Hotzmach was right. Who would know either of them now? The birds had shed their dusty old feathers and donned brilliant new plumage. The day they arrived in Bucharest Hotzmach had his face shaved clean except for two narrow sideburns which his mirror told him gave his countenance distinction and charm. In a large clothing store he had himself outfitted in a new suit of the latest cut. To this he added a shiny top hat, a cane with an ivory handle, patent-leather shoes, and bright yellow gloves.

"What do you say, my songbird? Would anyone say this was Hotzmach?"

"Nobody in the world," agreed Leibel happily.

No less did Hotzmach rejoice at the change wrought in his young friend. Gone were the Talmud student's black coat and countrified cap. Leibel was now attired in a short, modish coat and striped trousers. On his head sat a jaunty derby, and he, too, carried a cane and yellow gloves.

88

Decked out in their new plumage, they enjoyed what Bucharest had to offer. At shop windows they stopped to admire but not to buy, Hotzmach guarding their money jealously against the time they would set up a theater. But they ate well. Hotzmach never seemed to get his fill of good food. He who had hungered so much in his life ate as though each meal were his last. After eating, they rested. He who had labored so much in his life couldn't get enough rest. And then, when darkness came, they set out again on their studies.

For those who pursue the study of "music, theater and art," life starts at night. And for fugitives it is certainly healthier to wander about the streets as little as possible in broad daylight. Only yesterday Leibel had told Hotzmach he had seen his brother Anshel and his father's cashier flying past in a carriage.

"You've been dreaming," laughed Hotzmach. "Brothers and cashiers! Nonsense! Even if they saw you, they'd never recognize you. Do you know, my boy, what we need now?"

"What?"

"New names."

"Why?"

"Why? I lie awake nights worrying about it. Suppose we set up our own theater and we arrive in some Yiddish town. The billboards go up with our names. I put up my real name, Holtzman, Bernhard Holtzman. Who will ever know Holtzman is Hotzmach?"

"You're right. Holtzman sounds better."

"You see? But what about you? Rapalovich is no good. Someone who knows your father might catch sight of it. I lie awake nights and that's what I think of. We'll change your name to a Rumanian one, ending in *esco*. Margolis-Margolesco, Rapalovich-Rapalesco. Get it? The First Yiddish Rumanian theater. Bernhard Holtzman, Director. And under it, Rapalesco of Bucharest, Leading Artist. How do you like it? Hotzmach has good ideas, no?"

And without waiting for an answer, Hotzmach caught his friend by both hands and danced him around the hotel room, singing to the tune of a popular song of the day:

Holtzman-Rapalesco
Rapalesco-Holtzman.

Since meeting Hotzmach, Leibel had never seen him sad or dispirited. Even under the thumb of Shchupak he had remained a gay, irrepressible soul. But never had Leibel seen him so light-hearted as

89

now. Life fairly spurted from him. He seldom coughed any more and he had almost stopped swearing. Only once in a while, in speaking of Shchupak or Sholom Meyer, did an oath escape him.

A few days later their tour of "art, theater and music" took them down to the "Paradise" where we left Anshel and Simcha.

We say "down" because, as with other paradises, they first had to descend into the underworld. They had to secure admission cards, make turn after turn and go down before they could go up.

In their pursuit of "art, music and theater" the two friends had become somewhat accustomed to the gay café-chantant atmosphere, but not to the extent that they could walk up directly to a table, seat themselves, ring the bell, and nonchalantly call out, "Wai-ter." Therefore, when "Paradise" proper opened up before them, they hesitated at the door, staring.

"The devil take money!" Holtzman ejaculated under his breath, when, about to take a tentative step toward the nearest table, Leibel caught him by the arm. "There they are," Leibel said, in an urgent whisper.

"Who?"

"My brother Anshel and our—"

"Go on, you—" Holtzman began in disbelief, but following Rapalesco's pointing finger, his expression changed to dismay.

The two turned and fled. Not until they were three blocks away from the café and deep in the stream of pedestrians did Holtzman slow down long enough to say, "That brother of yours looks like some customer! Who was the fellow with the chewed-off mustache?"

"Didn't you recognize him? That's our cashier, 'Joy-and-Gladness,' " said Leibel, through chattering teeth.

Holtzman instinctively felt his pocket and hastened his pace.

"Thunder strike them! Do you know what, my songbird? I wouldn't care to meet up with them. And neither would you, I imagine. Let's leave them to their paradise and get a move on."

"Where?"

"Wherever our eyes lead us. We'll leave Bucharest. As it is written, 'He who changes his abode changes his place.' "

"It is written, 'He who changes his abode changes his luck,' " Leibel corrected him.

"Have it your way. The main thing is, we've got to leave town, and the quicker the better. Listen, let's walk a little faster. Better yet, there's a droshky, let's get in, and tell the driver to whip his horse on. The devil take money."

A few hours later the two friends were seated in a compartment of the Bucharest-Budapest Express. And since it was a cool night and they were lightly dressed, Holtzman produced from his valise the faithful old "stole" and wrapped it snugly about Leibel.

"Cuddle down, my bird, like this, or you'll catch a chill. How do you say it is written? 'He who changes his place . . .' "

" 'He who changes his abode changes his luck.' "

"A clever saying, as I am a Jew." Holtzman caught at his side-pocket, was seized by a fit of coughing and, as he coughed, he cursed Shchupak and Sholom Meyer with deadly curses.

15 GETZEL BEN GETZEL AND A FLOOD OF PLAYS

In later years Leibel never retained a clear memory of his early travels with Holtzman. The tours from Rumania to Hungary, then back to Rumania, then to Galicia and Bukovina ran together like a confused dream. He could scarcely recall more than the names of towns and cities, Mukvatsch, Marmorosh, Bereksoz, Ungvar, Grosvardein, Brailo, Piatro, Galatz, Bamashan; Tarnov, Tarnopol, Przemysl, Yaroslav, Stanislav, Brody, Zlotchev, Sinyatin, Hisyatin, Krakov, Lemberg. . . .

Of them all only Lemberg stuck in his memory, for in its Yiddish theater events occurred that caused an upheaval in his life and spurred his growth both as a man and as an artist.

The Lemberg Yiddish Theater of that day was a monopoly, the monopolist an individual named Getzel ben Getzel, who boasted that he had come into the theater by inheritance from his father, who in turn had received it as a grant from Emperor Franz Josef when the latter had passed through Lemberg. His boasts might be open to question, but this much was clear. In Lemberg there existed only one Yiddish theater and one director, Getzel ben Getzel, and God help the upstart who tried to trespass on his territory. Those managers of road

91

companies who had attempted it warned their children and children's children to stay away from that accursed place.

And "monopoly" was to Getzel ben Getzel an all-inclusive term. He deferred to no one, least of all to his public. What did the Yiddish public know anyway? "The masses are asses," Getzel maintained, and on that premise he gave them straw to chew: "Shminder Legetz at the Auto-da-fé," "The Bloody Inquisition of Sobieski's Reign," "Isabelle, Tear My Skirt," and other pearls of drama and tragedy such as were fished up from the deep brain of a Shchupak or Sholom Meyer between sunrise and sundown.

Such modern dramas as "The Golden Land: A Bloody Tragedy," "The Destruction of the Temple: A Dramatic Operetta," "By the Waters of Babylon: A Comedy with Songs and Dances" were too heavy for Getzel's taste. Recently he had introduced a lighter repertory in literary vein: "Hinke Pinke," "Shloima Gorgel," "Jump into Bed," and "Velvele Eats Compôte." He didn't believe in indulging his public. Whatever he chose to give them, they would lick their fingers and come back for more.

But Getzel had underestimated his public. Lemberg, not entirely abandoned to the Philistines, had its men of refinement and taste, though he turned a deaf ear to their plaints that he change his repertory. Finally the malcontents took their cause to the press, which carried vitriolic attacks on the theater of Getzel ben Getzel. That he considered the last straw. You could, if you liked, attack him in public with curses or blows; he was a match for anyone with tongue and two fists. But to write him up in the papers! That he would not brook. For such effrontery you crushed people's bones. And Getzel did not stand alone. He had loyal partisans who would go through fire and water for him.

And yet in the end Getzel ben Getzel resorted to the press himself. A letter appeared challenging the critics: If they wanted new plays, let them write them. If the director found their offerings worthy of production, he would not only receive them with thanks, but would pay for their labors as well. He was not one to accept something for nothing.

For the press this represented no small triumph. Here appeared clear proof that the pen was mightier than the sword. The printed word had cracked the armor of Getzel ben Getzel. Exhortation appeared urging all writers to begin creating new vehicles for the Yiddish stage: "In the expression of the people's spirit hangs the pride of the

92

nation, and in true folk drama lie all the national cultural values, etc., etc.," and ending with Napoleon Bonaparte's apostrophe to the Pyramids.

The writers needed no urging. Unfortunately neither did anybody else, least of all those bright young men without occupation who lived off their fathers-in-law and nursed a secret ambition to become *literati*. People from all walks of life, tailors, carpenters, cobblers, and blacksmiths, laid aside their accustomed tools and took up pen and ink. The town of Lemberg, they said, went shoeless and coatless; fences fell into disrepair; and horses limped on sore feet. But literature burgeoned and flowered. Getzel ben Getzel was besieged. A veritable flood of tragedies, comedies, operas, and melodramas rained down on his head.

Getzel received each aspirant in a cordial manner and arranged for an audition before the whole company, according to world-wide custom. True, the actors of the Lemberg Theater were not the most discriminating judges of the art of playwriting, never having come to close terms with literature. But on the other hand they were a fun-loving crew, always on the lookout for some innocent sport.

When a playwright appeared for an audition, Getzel introduced him to the company and led him ceremoniously onto the stage. Then the spotlights played on him and actors and director gathered in a box in the darkened theater. The reading began. "Louder," shouted the actors, "louder." Naturally the author raised his voice. "Louder," they yelled. "We can't hear you." The poor author shouted louder and louder until his voice became a croak. When he was through reading, he looked around to note the effect, and found that he had been reading to empty seats. The director and actors sat elsewhere deep in a game of "tertel-mertel."

It was to this director, Getzel ben Getzel, that Holtzman came with his small troupe, composed of some young fellows, among them Leibel Rapalovich, by now playing leading roles under his new name of Rapalesco.

After his first audience with the Czar of the Lemberg Theater, Holtzman declared that Shchupak was a babe in arms compared to this local Yokel ben Fleckel, as he promptly dubbed the director. It would be easier to transplant the whole city of Lemberg than to sway Getzel ben Getzel an inch.

But Holtzman had flint in his soul, too. With him it was not so much a matter of money, at this point, as of pride. He had made up his mind once and for all that Lemberg must see his troupe perform, if only one time. And so he let the oak have his way. He gave in to terms which he wouldn't have accepted from anyone else.

When the contract for the first three performances had been signed by both parties, the two directors repaired to a nearby restaurant for a snack. They sealed their pact over a bottle of *schlivovitz*. Then Holtzman asked Getzel ben Getzel in all seriousness, "Tell me, my dear Yokel ben Fleckel, does it ever happen that the cholera should stray into your town?"

"God has spared us until now. Why do you ask?"

"A pity. There'd be some hope of getting rid of you then."

In such pleasantries the meal passed. When they had finished the wine and had their fill of goose livers and other such dainties, they smoked cheap cigars and sat back satisfied with the world and with each other. But when the time came to settle the bill, Getzel ben Getzel suddenly remembered he didn't have a thaler on him, and was about to make a hasty departure when Holtzman caught his sleeve. "Hold on, Herr Yokel, it isn't becoming for the director of the Lemberg Theater to sneak out the back door."

However, Holtzman figured he didn't have to rely on such jibes for revenge. He calculated on dealing Getzel ben Getzel a death blow from which that tyrant would never recover.

As it had happened elsewhere, so it happened in Lemberg. Rapalesco, after the first performance, had the audience eating out of his hand. How did he do it? He moved and spoke simply and naturally, even as you and I, and yet, marvel of marvels, you couldn't keep your eyes off his face. You held your breath to hear every word. The other actors appeared like painted dummies beside him.

People turned to each other and asked, "Who is he, this creature?"

"The devil knows—some Rapalesco of Budapest."

The second night the theater was packed to the doors, and the third night people had to be turned away. Getzel ben Getzel dogged Holtzman's footsteps, begging him to remain for at least three more performances. It is certain the two directors were eager to be rid of each other, and yet they renewed the contract. True diplomats, each had a trick up his sleeve.

Getzel ben Getzel watched the public fighting for seats and his head whirled. What were the idiots drooling about? Every gulden the box office took in added to his frenzy, though three-fourths of the receipts went into his own pocket.

During the last act, with the theater as crowded as a hencoop and

94

the applause at its loudest, Getzel ben Getzel decided to see for himself. He hid in the wings and watched, his eyes not so much on young Rapalesco as on the enraptured audience. What was it all about? A young bird like that. He didn't even seem to be acting, And yet the audience was eating him up. Well, if that was what they wanted, he'd give it to them. He'd entice the fledgling into his own coop. Catch the goose that was laying these golden eggs. But how? Go right up to him and lay a proposition before him that would turn his head? The young fool would run and tell his director. And Holtzman was no one to trifle with. No, he must strike through another. He had it. He would use his new prima donna, Henrietta Shwalb.

Who this new prima donna was and how he had found her can be told in a few words. One evening Getzel had seen, entering his theater, a plainly dressed young girl who struck him at once with her "neat waist and majestic figure." He tried to size her up. Was she a seamstress? A parlor maid? "If I could get this girl into my theater, I could make a prima donna of her," he said to one of his henchmen. "Find out where she works."

"I know her brother," replied the other. "Shwalb is his name, Chaim-Itzik Shwalb, a tobacconist who peddles cigars and cigarettes."

"The one with the big red face? I just slapped it for him the other day and threw him out of the theater for butting in on a rehearsal."

"What's the difference? I'll talk to him, if you like."

"Good enough, but don't let him get any big ideas, you understand."

And so it came about that Henrietta, still called Yentel, came to the house of Getzel ben Getzel. Her brother, who had escorted her, remained outside, mindful of the slaps.

The director, Getzel ben Getzel, had just got up and padded around in his bare feet as he offered Henrietta a chair. She thanked him but said she would rather stand. He asked her, "Where do you work?" She replied she had a good job. "How much do you make?" Fifteen gulden a month besides clothing. Her clothing allowance came to ten gulden more, and she picked up another six or seven on the side.

"How much is that altogether?"

"Count it up."

The director began hunting for pencil and paper, but gave up and asked how she would like to make fifty gulden a month. She said fifty gulden was good pay, but it depended on the kind of work.

95

"No work at all," said the director. "Only acting in the theater. What's your name?"

"I'm named Yentel, and my family name is Shwalb. There's my brother and me."

"Yentel. Pheh! What kind of name is that? Henrietta, Henrietta Shwalb." He rolled the name on his tongue and found it good. "Where's your brother?"

"Waiting outside."

"Well, send him in. I'll settle with him."

The director was mistaken in thinking he could settle the matter quickly with Yentel's brother. Chaim-Itzik presented a special complication. The humble tobacconist had stage aspirations himself. How could anyone have guessed that in this big-bellied, bowlegged creature there lay buried the soul of an artist? Not for nothing did he haunt the theater and shove his way backstage in spite of kicks and insults.

And so, when Chaim-Itzik Shwalb heard the director's proposition, he said to himself, "My day has come." Taking his courage in both hands he spoke up. "I will let you have my sister for an actress only if you take me in as an actor."

"What kind of actor will you make with that face?"

Chaim-Itzik swallowed hard. He had been told more than once that he had the face of a villain and the eyes of a thug. Now he lowered his eyes and said quietly, "What kind of face do I have then?"

"The face of—I don't know what."

Chaim-Itzik sighed deeply.

"Do I have to come out on the stage as I am? I can put on make-up, disguise myself. Do you think I don't know about these things? I, too, have been an actor."

"Where did you act?"

"With the Purim Players. I still play every Purim. I dare anybody to show me a better Haman."

"That may be. That may very well be. But what will you do with that balloon?"

Chaim-Itzik glanced down at his belly. "I can lace myself up. Do you think I know nothing? I've watched your actors backstage, and they're no different from the Purim Players."

Getzel took umbrage at this comparison. He barked, "And what will you do with your voice?"

"I have a voice like everybody else."

"That's what you think. Your voice is a squeak."

"Who squeaks? Do I squeak?"

"Who then? Do I squeak?"

"You're just baiting me," said Chaim-Itzik, rising with dignity. "Good day to you. If I'm not good enough to be an actor, then my sister can't be an actress."

Getzel saw he had no way out, though he shouted "Hear O Israel" from morning till night. If he wanted the sister, he had to accept the brother.

Once the bargain was made, Getzel's headaches began. Henrietta had no talent and no voice, but she had a "trim waist and majestic figure." But what to do with that clod, her brother? Were he content with bit parts, Getzel could figure that Henrietta cost him ten gulden extra a week, and let it go at that. But the cigarette peddler hankered after the heavy roles. Getzel was in no position to quibble, with business so poor lately. He needed an actress like Henrietta, with looks and a figure. If that didn't do the trick there was no justice in heaven.

And so Getzel ben Getzel had announcements printed acquainting the public with the news that a well-known singer and actress, famous for her "neat waist and majestic figure" was arriving shortly from Buenos Aires to join the Lemberg Theatre.

Meanwhile he went to work training Henrietta. He taught her the routines, drummed a few simple tunes into her, and above all showed her how to wear clothes so as to look dressed yet not dressed, revealing just enough of her charms and not too much. The debut of this renowned star from Buenos Aires caused such a furor that the director's heart swelled with pride. The gallery's endearments, "Shwelbele," "Kitten," "Canary," marked her an instant success.

But the tobacconist was another matter. "How can you send this baboon on the stage?" Getzel asked in despair. Chaim-Itzik's perfectly memorized lines came out like the bleating of a calf. Lace him however tightly, he still waddled. Was that his fault? Could he help it if he had been born with a thin voice and bowlegs? In the part of a villain he thought himself superb. No one could roll his eyes so fiercely or work his face into such contortions. Not for nothing had he made a name for himself among the Purim players for his performance of Haman.

16 THE PRIMA DONNA AND HER ADMIRERS

There's a saying that "if you want a thief badly enough, you will cut him down from the gallows." And in the end Getzel ben Getzel had to take the despised Chaim-Itzik, or Isaac Shwalb, as he now called himself. He even had to take him into his confidence in the matter of winning over "that Bucharest bird for whom the public went crazy."

Isaac Shwalb knew where he stood with the director. He knew his colleagues despised him, that they would as soon drown him in a spoonful of water, that they ridiculed his acting and called him "Oaf," "Lout" and "Stick."

It was all a matter of luck, Chaim-Itzik felt. If the truth were known, he was not the worst actor in the world. There were plenty of Yiddish actors in other cities inferior to him, comedians who fancied them-selves tragedians, and vice versa. And yet they got by. They were ac-cepted, even praised. "Without luck," Chaim-Itzik sighed, "you might as well never be born."

Yes, Isaac knew. He realized that his sister was his salvation and for that reason he kept a sharp eye on her. For the public anything went; she could appear on the stage naked. But off-stage—beware! Then his prerogative as an older brother came into play. And he was a vigilant brother, as Henrietta's numerous admirers learned to their sorrow. "That brother of hers has the fist of a bone-crusher. May it wither and fall off altogether." This didn't prevent any of them, from the meanest bit-player to the director himself, from trying.

Yes, Henrietta was now prima donna of the Lemberg Theater. What could the former prima donna, poor thing, do? Her superior acting and voice availed her nothing against Henrietta's youth and her pretty face and figure. That, alas, is the way of the world. Even in Paris, they say, a pretty face plays the leading role.

In Henrietta, no one could have recognized the former Yentel. First of all, there was her new hat, a genuine panama with ostrich plumes.

98

Her carriage and gait were those of a duchess born to the manor. Her admirers no longer contented themselves with sending her oranges. Now she received gifts worth all of twenty gulden, or maybe twenty-five or even thirty. And as testimony to her elevated station, Henrietta now kept a servant girl who carried her wardrobe to the theater.

To tell the truth, Henrietta was not above lending her maid a hand at the washtub or ironing board, when no one looked on. And many a wrangle took place between them. Once Henrietta missed a collar and chemise and accused the maid. She went on to upbraid the girl for being too chummy with her brother Isaac, and the girl taunted Henrietta with her own free-and-easy manners. It would have come to blows if Isaac hadn't arrived just in time and found the missing articles among his play scripts. How they had got there the devil alone knew.

The maid burst into tears, and Isaac wanted to know why she was bawling. She told him of his sister's slurs on her character, Isaac grew incensed and . . . but enough. We are not concerned with the private life of actors. Suffice to say Henrietta, now a prima donna who carried herself with the air of a princess, wore genuine panama hats with ostrich plumes, received valuable gifts from her admirers, kept a personal maid, and everybody in the Lemberg theaterworld, married or single, paid court to her.

And private individuals as well, in no way connected with the theater. And each believed himself the only one at the fair. For Henrietta, though no genius, was clever enough to know how to keep men dangling. But that was as far as it went. Her brother saw to that. For this reason Getzel ben Getzel summoned Isaac Shwalb to a conference behind locked doors. From it Isaac went straight to his sister and began extolling the young artist from Bucharest.

"Do you understand, Henrietta? I want you to make up to him, so he won't want to leave Lemberg. Don't ask me why. You'll see later. The rest you'll understand for yourself, if you have a brain in your head."

Isaac's injunctions were superfluous. The prima donna had already marked the young man with the grave eyes and fair hair as her legitimate prey. Not because of his looks or his talent, but simply out of pique. Used to having men fall like flies at her feet, Henrietta was nettled that young Rapalesco took no notice of her. She never sat still in his presence; she danced and twirled and disposed herself in alluring attitudes, she pouted and smiled, acted forward and coy by turns; whatever the occasion, she laughed to display her white teeth. But to

99

no avail; it was like the old, old story of young Joseph and Potiphar's wife.

Everyone except Rapalesco himself was aware of what went on, and eager for the romance to develop. Each had his own axe to grind. Getzel ben Getzel wanted Henrietta to seduce Rapalesco to keep the actor in Lemberg. Henrietta played the game for the sheer love of the sport. Isaac Shwalb had his own reasons. He was tired of playing watchdog. High time she made a suitable match. No telling into whose hands a rattlebrain like Henrietta might fall. To further his design, he attached himself to the young actor's director, Holtzman, and they became cronies. And Holtzman, as clever as they, and maybe a bit cleverer, laughed up his sleeve. He saw it as a means of getting the whole mess of fish into his own net, Henrietta and her brother along with some of Getzel's young actors. Why not? Let that Yokel ben Fleckel be left high and dry with his inheritance and his henchmen. Furthermore, he had an eye on Henrietta himself. Who knows, she might get used to him in time. He couldn't remain a bachelor forever. What if she appeared cool to him now? There were ways. A sweet word, a gift here and there, after all, money talks!

One thing only puzzled and disturbed Holtzman. Why did the foolish boy run from her advances? Why had he become so moody all at once? What had happened in Lemberg to upset him? Perhaps we have the answer.

The very first evening Holtzman brought his troupe to Getzel ben Getzel's theater, he noticed a familiar figure in the wings, that of a plump little woman built like a top. But since the wings of the Lemberg Theater were illumined by the glow of a single smoke-blackened lamp, he could not make out her features clearly. One minute he thought he knew her; the next minute he wasn't sure. However, when the little woman came up to him and opened her big laughing mouth, he knew. She, too, had recognized him. Holtzman stared for a moment, then sprang back with a cry.

"Braindele Kozak!"

"Hotzmach!"

"Shh, don't let on we know each other. Woe is me! What's happened to you? You've become wider than you are long. You're working here for this Yokel ben Fleckel? How long? And where's our friend Shchupak? And that bastard Sholom Meyer? And his half-wit sister? May a cholera strike them all in one day."

"Amen," answered Braindele Kozak with a laugh. And because the bell had sounded, and the stage manager was driving the actors before him, shouting that the curtain was going up and the public was tearing the theater to pieces, they had to part until the end of the first act. But not before they had agreed not to let a soul know that they were acquainted.

Holtzman went straight to Rapalesco's dressing room and imparted the news to him. He had just run into one of Shchupak's actresses, Madame Cherniak, or Braindele Kozak. He must remember her from Holeneshti, a short, plump woman. And he warned Rapalesco to pretend, when he met her, he had never seen her before.

Rapalesco's dressing room was no more brilliantly lighted than the wings. Besides, he stood at a grimy, cracked mirror, applying his make-up. No wonder Holtzman's usually quick eye didn't note the change that had come over his friend's face.

"What did you say her name was?"

"Braindele Kozak."

"Braindele Kozak? I don't remember anyone by that name. You'll introduce her to me. How do you like my make-up?"

"Excellent. After the first act you'll meet her with the rest of the troupe. Pretend you're seeing her for the first time. Why should anyone know who, what, where? Understand?"

"Certainly. What time is it? Who goes on next? Is that my cue? Well, one, two, three."

"With the right foot," Holtzman wished him, and adjusted his wig.

Rapalesco did not play his best that night, though not badly enough to disappoint the audience. The tumultuous ovation he received at the end of the first act bore witness to that. But Rapalesco felt that he had acquitted himself like a cobbler. For such acting he deserved to have hands and feet chopped off and to be recruited into the army. He had muffed cues, skipped lines, added others, garbled whole speeches.

After his curtain calls he rushed into the dim dressing room, his eyes smoldering as though in a fever; but it provided no refuge. The cubicle overflowed. The whole Lemberg Theater company had crowded in. The actors pressed to congratulate him, some with sincere admiration, others with ill-concealed envy. During the introductions it seemed to him, in his fevered state, that he was reviewing a procession of birds and beasts. One struck him remarkably like a goat, another like a rooster, a third, who had green eyes and kept licking his lips,

101

like a cat. The director himself, Getzel ben Getzel, was performing the introductions: Bendek, Slayen, Shwalb, Frau Tzimring, Madame Katz, Kurtzling, Prima Donna Shwalb, Fraulein Shtender, Stotichik, Madame Cherniak. . . .

Rapalesco knew her at once. And Braindele Kozak recognized him too, though he had grown considerably, and wore a costume and make-up. She had seen Leibel often enough in Rapalovich's barn in Hole-neshti, hobnobbing with Hotzmach. In the hubbub she nudged Holtz-man and asked, "So this is your Rapalesco of Bucharest? The land-lord's boy from Holeneshti. Ha ha!"

"Shhh," Holtzman warned her, and stepped on her foot. "Not another word. Let's talk about something else."

"About what, for instance?" And looking into his shrewd grey eyes, she thought, "How a person can change. Who'd ever guess this is the same Hotzmach who used to shine shoes for Shchupak and catch kicks all around like a stray dog?"

"Where in the devil's name is Shchupak now?" asked Holtzman. "And Sholom Meyer? And the others?"

No sooner had she answered one question than thirteen others sprang from his lips. All he could think of was Shchupak, and here she was dying to hear about Rapalesco, this famous young actor from Bucharest, whom everybody was crazy to meet.

As for the young actor himself, he appeared restless and taciturn, unaware of what was going on. He looked over people's heads, seeking someone with his eyes. At last he found her, the chubby little woman, round as a top, in a corner with Holtzman. He wanted to run toward her, to shout, "Have you seen or heard of a girl named Reizel? You must know whom I mean? The Cantor's daughter from Holeneshti." The words fairly tore at his throat to come out. But beasts and birds bobbed in front of his eyes, and the bleating and crowing and cackling assailed his ears.

Then a newcomer appeared in the wings, a short, well-dressed man with a bald skull, flashing gold-rimmed glasses and huge buck teeth gleaming from his wide grinning mouth. A path was made for him as cries rose, "Children, here comes Dr. Leviathan."

"He knocks a teakettle" is an expression which didn't spring from our own soil. We borrowed it from America. "To knock a teakettle" doesn't mean, God forbid, to slander anyone. He who "knocks a tea-kettle" merely babbles or rants; his ears do not hear what his tongue is saying. Where does this expression come from? Why a kettle and not a samovar? And how does one knock this teakettle? We leave these profound questions to the savants of philology and anthropology. They might find their source in such phrases as "sounding brass and tinkling cymbal," or "a tale told by an idiot full of sound and fury," or in the primitive beating of tom-toms. . . . Let the scholars worry their heads. We will not presume to dabble in another's craft, take a livelihood away from its rightful practitioners. We'll stick to the teakettle.

Holtzman, who never let his eye stray far from Rapalesco, saw the stranger shove his way to the boy's side. Quitting Braindele Kozak, he wedged himself in between the two. He measured the stranger with his sharp eyes and asked, "What is it? Whom do you want?"

The stranger, perceiving the elegant figure of the director with the top hat and the sideburns towering over him, took from his pocket a visiting card, which read, "Dr. Julius Levias."

Holtzman looked at the card, then at the doctor, and thought, "What sort of creature is this?" But one of the actors drew him aside and whispered that this Dr. Levias, or Leviathan, as the actors had nicknamed him, was a well-known physician, a scholar of note, a great lover of Yiddish theater, and a Maecenas who was worth half a million.

Neither the title of doctor nor the nickname "Leviathan," nor yet his reputation as a scholar and patron of the arts impressed Holtzman so much as the "half a million." On hearing that, he returned to the little doctor with outstretched hands and gave him such a hearty welcome that it startled everybody.

Recovering from this enthusiastic reception, Dr. Levias asked Holtzman in German, was he indeed the impresario of this talented young artist?

Very likely this was the first time in his life Holtzman heard the word "impresario." It was too much for him to digest at once. He replied, in what he fondly believed to be German, but what was no more than Yiddish stretched out with broad *a*'s. Indeed he was the boy's impresario. He himself was a Russian by birth, but the boy hailed from Bucharest, that is, not Bucharest itself, but an hour and half's journey from there.

Perceiving that the "impresario's" German was a bit Hebraic, Dr. Levias shifted to plain Yiddish. Hearing Dr. Levias speak Yiddish "like everybody else" Holtzman's own tongue was delivered from

103

bondage, and he launched into a long and involved tale of how he had made an actor of the youngster. It began, he said, in Bucharest, where he was acting at the time. A poor workingman came to see him about his son, who showed talent. He took to the boy at once and told the father, "I must make an artist of your son." Said the poor workingman, "What do you mean, *artist?* What kind of trade is that?" And Holtzman laughed with delight at his own joke. And the doctor's eyes sparkled with interest behind his gold-rimmed glasses.

And Holtzman kept hammering away, knocking the teakettle for all it was worth. Tall tales concerning himself and Rapalesco poured from his lips, each more extravagant than the one before. Only a German Jew like Dr. Leviathan could swallow them whole. Rapalesco fidgeted in growing embarrassment. Holtzman himself began to suspect he had gone a bit too far. But he didn't know how to stop. He was not a liar by nature, but rather by circumstance. His flight from Holeneshti had forced him to manufacture stories whenever he met a new person. A fugitive can be forgiven his lies. Whom does he harm except himself? A woman turned witch, they say, is worse than a born witch. And a made liar is even worse. A born liar is no more than a person with a talent. Each lie falls from his lips rounded and perfect, a real work of art. But the inventions of a made liar take on an unwieldy shape and bristle with contradictions.

Holtzman had now launched on a tale about King Carol of Rumania. How he would get rid of King Carol God alone knew. Luckily at this moment the stage manager appeared.

"What's going on here? Out there they're bringing the theater down, and here they stand around chattering and smacking their lips like guests at a Sabbath dinner."

The first guest performance at the Lemberg Theater was over, but the public refused to budge. The curtain had been raised and lowered many times, but the cries of "Rapalesco, Rapalesco" still rang through the hall.

"Let them howl with the toothache," drawled an actor with a pockmarked face, as he struggled with his coat. The torn lining of the sleeve had become twisted and he could neither get his arm in nor pull it out.

"Shall I?" asked the stage manager, as he held the block that raised the curtain.

"Enough. They've had enough for their money," said Holtzman.

104

But there was no help for it. The guest from Bucharest had to show himself on the stage once more. Still the public went on applauding and stamping their feet and shouting itself hoarse. "Rapalesco! Rapalesco!"

"That's the end. I won't come out any more," said Rapalesco petulantly. He threw off his wig, unglued his mustache and began wiping off his make-up. All eyes were riveted on his face. The actors' grudging glances took in his fair tumbled hair, his unblemished young skin, his clean-cut features. How had this fresh-faced youngster achieved such a triumph? Before he stepped out on the stage, they had expected God knows what, a voice to make walls vibrate, a step to make the floor quake, acting that would shake the roof. They had expected something out of this world. And in the end—What? Where? Who? He had walked across the stage without causing a board to creak. He had spoken in an ordinary voice. He had made hardly any gestures. Was this acting? Not as they knew it. Then why did the audience go wild? Fools, asses, kine—every one of them. This was no actor. He simply had luck. That was it. You had to have luck.

That's how the envious actors consoled themselves as the roar of applause swept over their heads without sign of letting up.

But everything in the world must come to an end. Even the curtain calls of an actor on the Yiddish stage must come to an end. At last the audience started to leave. The lamps were turned out one by one, and in a few more minutes the theater was empty.

Only one person remained behind, Dr. Levias, or Dr. Leviathan, who had extended an invitation to the actors of both troupes to accompany him to a café as his guests.

The Lemberg actors knew their Dr. Leviathan well. They knew how far his open-handedness went. He wasn't one to squander money on Yiddish actors. Compliments and fine words he gave without stint. But with his pocketbook he was chary. Still, even a kind word is better than nothing. Praise can gladden the heart and make the soul rejoice. An artist, no matter how secure in his greatness, will never scorn flattery. . . .

If Dr. Levias was lavish in his praise toward others, he literally smothered our young hero with *kudos*. After every act, he ran backstage to Rapalesco's dressing room, and thanked actor and impresario almost with tears in his eyes. After the last act he went into such ecstasy that he embraced Rapalesco and kissed him soundly on both cheeks. Then he took Holtzman aside and expressed his appreciation

105

again in fervent language, pressing both hands to his heart as though to say, "I am indebted to you from the bottom of my soul."

The actors who witnessed this scene envied Rapalesco anew. They thought to themselves, "This Leviathan doesn't throw his money around. Still, he's a German and an eccentric besides. He might take it into his head to give the young fellow his gold watch or diamond ring. Or maybe he will go completely out of his mind and transfer some of his property to his name."

Holtzman, who didn't know this Maecenas so well, placed even higher hopes on his generosity. "He's gone wild about the kid," he thought. "Maybe he'll give him a few thousand thaler; or he might come up to me and say, 'God has seen fit to bless you with a treasure like Rapalesco. He has blessed me with money. Let's combine our fortunes and set up a theater in partnership.' Why not? The Lord alone knew what a Maecenas might do, a lover of the Yiddish theater and a millionaire into the bargain."

So when the doctor extended to Holtzman a personal invitation to accompany him to a café after the performance, he joyfully went to impart the news to Rapalesco.

"Do you know what, my dear songbird? This doctor, this Leviathan, has invited us all to a café."

"All of us?" And Rapalesco looked around eagerly for the short, plump woman named Braindele Kozak.

The applause of the audience and the fine compliments of Dr. Leviathan hadn't driven her out of his head She was the one person in the world who might bring him news of Reizel's whereabouts.

Reizel's image stood fixed in his mind just as he had seen her the night of the fire in God's Street, a princess of fire and darkness. She had become his betrothed that night and this she would always remain. Tonight her image shone more vividly than before. He could almost see her and touch her now that Braindele Kozak had turned up to tell him about her.

For that reason he looked at Braindele Kozak with favor, though this little woman was as round as a barrel, with legs and arms like fat sausages. Above the voluminous red cape that almost engulfed her, her face, as white and round as a full moon, held eyes with an Oriental slant, though her eyebrows were extraordinarily thick. She smiled almost constantly and moved about lightly with a dancing step. Looking at her, no matter how heavy-hearted you might be, you couldn't help smiling. That was Braindele Kozak.

106

Leibel wished all the actors of both troupes would sink into the earth or vanish so that he could be alone with her. But they stood close around him as though they had been expressly hired for that purpose.

"Why are you taking so long?" Holtzman asked, and helped Rapalesco get dressed, putting a scarf around his neck to ward off the chill night air. Then he took him by the arm and they started out. After them the whole crowd burst out of the theater like noisy boys let out of school.

Outside the doors of the theater stood a carriage and horses, a rare sight for the Lemberg Theater. The actors looked and marveled. Dr. Leviathan had ordered his own carriage and horses to take him and the two guests of honor to the café. The three of them boarded the carriage and Holtzman could not restrain himself from exclaiming, "The devil with money!" Then Dr. Levias turned to the actors below him. "And so, gentlemen, to the Café Monopol."

Again the actors looked at Rapalesco with envy. Someone muttered, "As Rashi says, 'He who rides on horseback, and he who walks on foot.'" And another added under his breath, "You have to have luck. The boy was born with a caul."

"Wrap this around you," said Holtzman to Rapalesco, drawing the carriage robe around his shoulders and covering his legs with another. The doctor gave orders to the coachman in German and the coachman shouted to the horses in horse-language. Overhead the stars shone, the night breeze caressing their faces. Rapalesco turned to look back at the actors pointing to him. They envied him, the fools. He would a thousand times rather be walking with them under the stars and talking to the little actress Braindele Kozak.

17   THE CAFE MONOPOL

In the carriage beside the brilliant young actor and his distinguished impresario, Dr. Levias was enjoying to the full his role of Maecenas, connoisseur of the drama.

Every normal person has some one peculiarity. With Dr. Leviathan it was theater. When he took off on that subject, no one could stop him. When the clock is out of order a certain wheel will begin to turn at a touch and continue to turn without stopping. Clockmakers can slow down the motion of the wheel until it can hardly be seen. But in the case of our Maecenas, the wheel called "theater" remained permanently out of order. The actors of the Lemberg Theater, aware of this, took care to touch the wheel.

But Holtzman and Rapalesco, ignorant of the doctor's weakness, listened with wide-open ears and bated breath. If Dr. Levias had not possessed fame as an art patron and a small fortune besides, Holtzman would never have tolerated such talk in front of the "kid." He would never have permitted him to inject this deadly poison or "antimony," as he called it, into the boy's veins. Imagine telling him he had no right to appear in such common roles with such small-time actors. A God-given talent like his should find an outlet in classical roles, and in Vienna, Berlin, Paris. The boy, insisted Levias, should go out into the world and see how real drama was performed. He should meet the great artists, the stars who lent luster to the wide theatrical heavens. And so on and so on, Holtzman marveling at the quantity and variety of his high-flown words.

To Rapalesco the doctor's talk had a different significance. In these words he found a truth that echoed something in his own heart. He understood that he had a long and arduous road to travel before he could say to himself in all honesty, "I am an artist." His instinct told him that though the Lemberg audience had smacked its lips over his performance, it left a great deal to be desired. He must see more, study hard, work unceasingly before he could develop the talent that he knew lay in him. And for that he needed contact with the theaters of the big cities.

When he had broached this before, Holtzman had scoffed: "Fool, who ever told you actors are made in a factory? Look at me. Where did I learn the art of comedy? Not in Shchupak's kitchen, may his name and memory be blotted out. Yet let anyone tell you I'm not a comedian and you'd be the first to spit in his face. Isn't it so?" Rapalesco assured him that if anyone tried to belittle his friend's acting he'd gladly spit in his face. "Then what are you babbling about? Do you think I'm not faithful enough to you? That I don't have your good at heart? Or are you getting tired of me? Tell me, little songbird, don't be ashamed."

Rapalesco assured him he knew Holtzman was faithful to him, and that he didn't even begin to get tired of him.

108

"If so, spit on those foolish notions of yours, and let's get to work. We'll travel about a bit longer until we save up enough to open our own little theater somewhere with a sweet little prima donna, and all the other trimmings. And the devil with money."

Thus ended their talks. But the young artist was not satisfied. He continued to dream of the great world; he yearned to sit at the feet of the masters, to emulate them and learn from them. Rapalesco was young and naive enough to feel that the theater was a temple and the artists its high priests. Whenever he walked upon the stage, he did it with the high seriousness and the sense of dedication of an acolyte approaching a shrine, each step calculated with precision, each look measured and weighed. He didn't expend a single extraneous motion or utter a superfluous syllable.

In Dr. Leviathan's words, therefore, Rapalesco heard echoes of his own innermost desires. If to Holtzman the doctor's talk was so much moonshine and poppycock, to put up with only because of the doctor's wealth, to Rapalesco his words were as holy as the Law given unto Moses on Mt. Sinai.

"Listen to my advice," he said. "You must take the boy to Vienna, our Vienna. Take him to the State Theater, our State Theater, and show him how real acting is done on a real stage. Let him have a look at Zonenthal, our Zonenthal . . .

"Who's Zonenthal?" both asked in one breath.

Dr. Levias threw them a pitying look. So might he have looked at two barbarians who didn't know what to do with a knife and fork.

"You've never heard of Zonenthal? He's the mentor of all actors. He is also a Jew, and came to Vienna as a young boy, a tailor's apprentice. When he saw the famous Davison perform, he threw up his tailoring and in a few years became the world-famous and beloved artist, Zonenthal, our Zonenthal, who . . ."

"Does he have this other stuff?" Holtzman broke in, in an attempt to turn the wheel the other way.

Dr. Levias looked at Holtzman inquiringly. "What other stuff?"

"That which I like and you don't despise either." And Holtzman rubbed two fingers against his thumb in a meaningful gesture.

Dr. Levias understood and burst out laughing.

"Oh, so that's what you mean. Zonenthal is a millionaire." He drew out the word "mil-lion-aire."

Whereupon Holtzman's eyes flashed in the dark and the unknown Zonenthal grew three heads taller in his estimation and the city of Vienna assumed unparalleled charm.

"The devil take money. If the trip didn't cost so much, and if we could get to this here Zonenthal, I'd take Rapalesco along and we'd run down to Vienna."

"Ab-so-lutely," said Dr. Levias. "I can give you a letter of introduction to him, if you wish."

Holtzman almost leaped out of the carriage.

"You are acquainted with him personally?"

"I am acquainted with all the great artists in the world."

With this modest statement Dr. Levias attained the stature of a giant, to Holtzman because he was on speaking terms with a millionaire and to Rapalesco because he knew a great artist. Though Rapalesco had heard the great man's name for the first time, something told him that this was the deity he had worshiped since childhood.

Holtzman imagined himself and Rapalesco arriving in Vienna. He saw the great Zonenthal receiving them with open arms. After auditioning the "kid," he turned to the "impresario." "What is your wish, my friend?" Holtzman answered with due modesty, "What should my wish be, Herr Zonenthal? You're a man who understands such things. My wish is to have a little theater of my own, with a sweet little prima donna and all other trimmings, and to the devil with money!"

In Rapalesco's dream, woven of different threads, he saw Zonenthal as a supernatural being, his guardian angel, teacher and mentor, who would show him the path he must take to realize his dreams.

"Gentlemen," said Dr. Levias, as the carriage stopped in front of a brightly lighted entrance. "Gentlemen, we are at the Café Monopol."

In every town of consequence there is a coffee-house where actors like to congregate. In Lemberg it was the Café Monopol. There if you liked, you could play chess or dominoes or dice; if you felt so inclined, you could join in a game of billiards; and if you wanted to badly enough, you could risk a game of cards.

Naturally you didn't jump into a card game the moment you entered. A game of cards likes a closed door and drawn blinds. For this purpose the Café Monopol had set aside a small room, well in the back, away from prying eyes. And since the actor hasn't been born who doesn't relish a game of cards, this room always swarmed with Yiddish actors and was so filled with smoke as to obliterate the light of day. In Lemberg, if you wanted to see a Yiddish actor, you walked straight through the Café Monopol to this back room.

On this evening the actors swaggered into the café and spread them-

110

selves out at the tables as though ready to eat and drink everything the place had to offer. But when the waiters asked, "What is it the ladies and gentlemen require?" it turned out that the ladies and gentlemen required nothing as yet. They were waiting for "some people," at whose expense they proceeded to amuse themselves. The chief butt was "Dr. Leviathan." One actor caricatured his way of holding his hands in his pockets, peering over the rims of his glasses, and sputtering through his front teeth; another mimicked his way of applauding Rapalesco with his hands and his feet and his whole body; a third pantomimed the appreciative kiss on both cheeks, and Rapalesco's shrinking back in fright.

Yiddish actors are a fun-loving lot, on the whole. Not without reason are they called *farshlepte krenk* which means literally a dragged out or a lingering illness. When a *farshlepte krenk* attaches himself to his victim, he is like a persistent rash, seldom fatal, but annoying and irritating. A *farshlepte krenk* is seldom gloomy. With or without cause for merriment, he is always willing to laugh. If a remark is witty he laughs. And if it is foolishness, then he certainly has reason to laugh. . . .

They well knew what was going on in Dr. Leviathan's carriage. They knew he had instructed his coachman to take a circuitous route "for fresh air," that is, to give him a chance to spout. The actors could wait. A Maecenas with money doesn't have to cater to *them*.

When Dr. Levias made his entrance, the whole company rose to its feet as one man, and respectfully gave him the seat of honor, which he took with the air of a man who knows his place. Then with a nice regard for protocol he placed Rapalesco on his right hand and the impresario on his left. At once the tone of the gathering rose to a higher plane. Dr. Levias jingled the bell, and the waiters, bowing low, gazed into the doctor's eyes with breathless suspense as though the words about to issue from his lips contained something of supreme import. But Dr. Levias, not ready to speak, first rubbed his bald pate carefully with his diamond-ringed hand, then wrinkled his brow, and with half-closed eyes looked over the rims of his glasses at some vague point in the distance like a person about to solve a great problem. At last the words came. The doctor desired the waiters to be so good as to bring beer, a stein for each person, and some kosher wurst for a snack.

The beer served, a plate of kosher wurst placed with a flourish in the center of the board, Dr. Levias rose to his feet, like the chairman of a board of directors at its annual meeting. By way of a toast he

111

launched into a long and brilliant discourse, in high German, sketching in a "brief summary" of the history of the theater in general, from the time of the great Shakespeare to our own day. The names of books, plays and authors poured down like hail on the heads of the starved actors, who couldn't refrain from casting longing glances at the beer and at the kosher wurst, which gave forth an enticing aroma of spices and garlic. Here and there a listener surreptitiously sampled the beer, knowing that before Dr. Levias finished with Shakespeare, they could all dispatch their beer and wurst three times over.

At last Dr. Levias, himself aware that he had dwelt long enough on the background, skillfully jumped from Shakespeare to the "father of the Yiddish stage," Goldfadden, and his successors, hurrying on to the artists of the Lemberg Theater and of all the traveling theaters which wandered from town to town bearing aloft the standard of Yiddish Art. Of these the most significant was their young guest from Bucharest, the already well-known maestro, the talented Rapalesco, whom they had the honor of welcoming into their select circle tonight.

"This young artist, ladies and gentlemen," Dr. Levias informed his listeners, pointing to Rapalesco, "this young artist has flared up before our eyes suddenly and unexpectedly, as a scintillating celestial body, unknown to astronomy, sometimes flares up suddenly and unexpectedly in the vacant heavens. Thus has this wandering planet, this unknown star, Rapalesco, drifted our way and lit up with his brilliance the whole sky of the Yiddish stage. But not for long, ladies and gentlemen. He will only remain with us a short time, like all the great wandering stars which flare up one moment and are gone the next. I will now propose a toast, ladies and gentlemen," the doctor concluded his speech, "I drink to the wandering Yiddish stars, Hoch!"

The actors responded with a triple *Hoch!* and addressed themselves promptly to what remained of their beer and the wurst.

Sometimes an incidental word is enough to stir up a whole pack of forgotten thoughts and memories. The two words, "wandering stars," carried Leibel back to Holeneshti. He and Reizel had spoken of wandering stars the night of the fire in God's Street. Reizel had seen falling stars and had moved closer to him, afraid. "Look, the stars are falling from the sky!" And he had calmed her. "Stars do not fall, silly; stars only wander." And he was drawn back to that night of terror and grandeur, of beauty and enchantment.

"To our wandering stars!" said Dr. Levias once more, raising his glass. Then he rang for the waiters, settled the account, and bade the actors good night until the next evening's performance.

112

"Auf wiedersehen."

"Blessed be your going!" one of the actors flung after him when the doctor was already out of the door.

"Everything comes to an end," said another with a deep sigh.

"There is nothing eternal under the sun, as Don Pedro once said."

"Idiot. There is nothing new under the sun. And it was Moses who said it."

"Perhaps you mean—King Solomon?"

"Let it be King Solomon. Children, to work. The night doesn't wait."

And the crowd rose from the tables and made for the little back room.

Inevitably, when Yiddish actors sit down to a game of cards, they single one out as the scapegoat, the butt of jokes, wisecracks, and mainly curses. Among the actors of the Lemberg Theater, Isaac Shwalb most often filled that role. Then they never called him by his right name, but Chaim-Itzik, or Itzikel, or the diminutive Shwelbele; and *nom-de-plumes,* such as "Bassdrum," "Potbelly," "Redface," "Haman," "Mondrish"—whatever came into their heads. But if you think Isaac Shwalb was offended, you don't know your man. When he played cards, he was oblivious. Neither insults nor blandishments could touch him. He played cards, as he did everything else, be it acting or eating, with singleness of mind.

After Isaac had dealt out the cards and counted the money, he began laying out "the little people," as he called the cards. He went about it with deliberation, naming each card in turn according to the consecutive letters of the alphabet. *Aleph*—Appletree, *Beis*—Bathhouse, *Gimmel*—Goat, *Daled*—Devil, *Hey*—Hare, *Vov*—Vineyard, *Zayin*—Zebra, and so on.

Say what you like, the tragedian Isaac Shwalb played a villain only on the stage. Elsewhere he was meek as a lamb. "A rare jewel," his colleagues called him. "Only he should have had his throat slit before he was born."

A black cat must have crossed his path, this evening. Luck was against him. He and his sister Henrietta kept losing, and they blamed each other. Shwalb reproached her with "burning money." She retorted it was her own money she was burning. He told her, "Scrub floors." She told him, "Roll cigarettes." He told her. She told him. The crowd grew merrier still.

Little by little the two directors, Getzel ben Getzel and Bernhard

113

Holtzman, were drawn into the game. They had sat apart at first, watching the common herd amusing itself. Then each threw a coin into the pot, not, God forbid, because he wanted to win, but just for the sport, to see who would come out on top. As blind luck would have it, they both lost. This forced them to try once more, to recoup their fortunes. Again they lost. Now the fever took hold of them, and they entered the game in earnest. Playing, they lost sight of everything but the three goals in front of them—the banker, the cards and the pot.

Cards flew faster from hand to hand. Faces flamed and eyes burned. Coins clinked. The hysteria mounted. The players pounced on the money. They scrabbled for cards. Some laughed; others sat glum. Some looked pleased, others disgruntled. But pleased or not, silent or noisy, everyone reached fever pitch, ready to leap at each other's throats, to devour each other alive.

Only two people stayed out of the game, Rapalesco and Braindele Kozak. Not because they were above such things. On the contrary. It was said of Braindele Kozak she could outgamble any three men. To win a groschen from her was like extracting wine from a stone wall. When she won, she hid the money deep in her pocket. When she saw the cards going against her, she stopped playing.

As for young Rapalesco, he didn't despise cards either. But he played in a different way, less concerned with winning or losing than with the game itself. The fortuitous twists of the game held a fascination for him.

The others were so absorbed they didn't notice that Rapalesco and Braindele were not playing. If he hadn't been mistaken, Rapalesco began, he had seen Madame Cherniak in Holeneshti. No, he had not been mistaken, Madame Cherniak assured him. Their talk drifted aimlessly from Holeneshti to Shchupak's theater and to theaters in general, until Rapalesco asked carelessly, "And what has become of Shchupak? Where is he now?"

"Where's Shchupak?" She laughed her wide-mouthed laugh. "May he rest in peace." And she made a motion as though dismissing him from this world.

Rapalesco started, "Is Shchupak dead?"

Madame Cherniak laughed again, displaying her white teeth.

"Shchupak dead? A fellow like him wouldn't do anything so rash as to die. He's strong and healthy in body and limb, but his mind has been touched, poor fellow. Aside from carrying on with three

114

wives at once—a scoundrel like that can afford three wives—he tied another millstone around his neck, and it's dragged him so low, let us hope he'll never get up again."

Yes, he was really down on his luck now, said Madame Cherniak. He had hit rock bottom, had spent every groschen he saved, pawned all his diamonds. And whoever knew Shchupak and his diamonds knew what that meant. And all for what? For a girl he had deluded himself into thinking would become his salvation, his support and mainstay, his diamonds and all. He planned to make a prima donna of her. But there's still a God in Heaven. And what does God in His infinite power do? This girl, this prima donna, meets a great singer, Marcella Zembrich, at a concert. Marcella Zembrich takes a fancy to her, gets her away from Shchupak and places her in a conservatory in Vienna. Well, isn't that enough to drive him insane? Losing a little prima donna like that on whom he'd staked his whole future? And what a prima donna! When you hear her sing, you feel the world might as well come to an end. And a beauty in the bargain, young and fresh as a rose. Her name was Rosa, Rosa Spivak.

"Reizel?"

The name had escaped Leibel's lips before he could stop it. His fair face blushed a furious red, and though he tried to hide his confusion it was too late. Madame Cherniak had noticed. The stage had apparently not taught Rapalesco to dissemble in real life. With one word he had given himself away.

18 SOME ARE HANDSOME— SHE IS CLEVER

When Braindele Kozak heard Rapalesco call out Reizel's name, she could restrain herself no longer. She clapped her hands and exclaimed, "Oh. Oh. Some are handsome—I am clever."

Yes, some women had beauty, but she had brains. And a quick eye. The moment she had clapped her eyes on this "Leo Rapalesco of Bucharest" she had guessed it was "he," the boy she had seen with Rosa Spivak in Holeneshti. Now she knew why Rosa had put up such a struggle, why she had cried and carried on so. A young man like this was worth pining for.

She had spoken out loud and Rapalesco heard. "She pined for me?"

Madame Cherniak slapped him playfully over the arm. "Listen to the young innocent, he pretends he doesn't know what I mean. Poor fellow, so young and he already knows how to strike poses. Did she pine, for him, he asks. The poor girl was beside herself. She wouldn't be consoled. It happened one time in—wait now, what was the name of the town?" She couldn't recall. They had stopped in so many towns. They had roamed the country like gipsies with Shchupak. Spent the day in one place, the night in another. . . . Shchupak didn't dare spend much time in one place. His wives were always chasing after him. One after another descended on him like Pharaoh's plagues. May a plague descend on him in earnest. And what a trouple he had. One clod worse than the next. If it hadn't been for her acting and Rosa's singing he could have gone from house to house begging or given up the ghost altogether. The whole theater owed its success to the two of them, especially to Rosa's *lieder*. What *lieder!* What singing! Madame Cherniak had been the first to predict the girl would become famous for her singing. Time and again she had told Rosa her place wasn't here with these tramps. . . . Shchupak gave out that she was a niece he had brought down from Warsaw. What a laugh. But if Shchupak said a niece, let it be a niece. What she didn't guess herself Braindele wormed out of Shchupak's henchman, Sholom Meyer. Rapalesco might remember him from Holeneshti.

Of course Rapalesco remembered. A short, lively character with a derby. A regular clown.

"A clown!" Braindele snorted. "A bandit, a rascal, not a clown. A regular scoundrel, a thousand times worse than his employer. Faithful to Shchupak as an old dog, the devil alone knew what kept them so close to each other. Wherever you didn't sow them, there they sprang up, like thistles. And always together."

And she went on to revile Shchupak and Sholom Meyer, while Rapalesco waited impatiently for her to get back to the subject of Reizel. She saw his impatience and said, "Yes, where was I? I was talking about Rosa Spivak. She came to me one day—I can't remember what town we were playing then—and asked me if I knew how to tell fortunes from cards. Why cards, all of a sudden? I told her there was a fortune-teller in town who was better than I at it. Rosa fell on my neck, 'Darling, precious, sweet Braindele, take me to her.' 'What's the hurry,

116

my little bird?' She wouldn't tell me, but insisted I take her right away. An impulsive, spirited girl that Rosa, temperamental as you find them. No predicting what she'd do next. Sometimes, out of a clear sky, she'd start weeping, hide her head in her pillow and weep, wouldn't eat, drink, talk, or do anything. Just as suddenly she'd catch you by the hands and start dancing. Temperamental! Or when the notion took her, she'd start singing, and sing and sing like a nightingale.

"Well, where was I? Oh, yes, about the fortuneteller. So we go to the fortuneteller. Good enough. We come in. The fortuneteller, an old witch, cunning as they come, looks her over, and begins laying out the cards. She turns up a heart. That means love. Then a diamond. That's a blond young man. Then a six, which means a journey. And another six and another. All this time the witch didn't take her eyes off Rosa's face. She tells Rosa a blond young man was in love with her, that he thought of her day and night. He longed for her, body and soul. I tell you, she laid it on thick. This blond young man, she said, is dying to find you, but he doesn't know how. For you are both on a journey, both traveling, always moving, never in one place, he there and you here, you there and he here. You love each other, she said, dearly, but your paths can't cross. You both wander, you keep on wandering like the stars, like the stars in heaven. . . .

"The old witch told her more things. I don't remember them all. But I remember that when we left the fortuneteller, Rosa threw herself on my neck, and began kissing me, and crying and laughing at the same time. . . . So now I understand everything," Braindele finished, her round moonlike face lighting up with a knowing smile. "Now I know who the blond young man was."

It was long after midnight when the players wound up their game and went their separate ways, some chastened, others elated, some burning with regret and others with anger at themselves, at each other, and at the whole world.

As though for spite there wasn't a single droshky to be found in the streets of Lemberg, and Holtzman and Rapalesco were forced to walk all the way from the Café Monopol to their lodgings at the other end of town.

It was an autumn night, one of those end-of-the-season nights which is neither summer nor winter, neither warm nor cold, a plain run-of-the-mill night. Then why was Rapalesco so elated? Why was he suddenly moved to embrace his friend Holtzman, his dear, beloved Holtzman, in the middle of the street?

Holtzman turned on him as though he had suddenly gone out of his mind. "What's come over you tonight, my dear songbird?"

Holtzman, in no mood for embraces, was furious for having permitted himself to be drawn into the game. The devil himself must have pushed him. The first few rounds he had won. Then why hadn't he grabbed his capful of nuts and gone home? But no. His palm started to itch. He had to go on playing. Man's eyes are always bigger than his belly. And besides it would have been bad policy to turn down the director, Getzel ben Getzel.

"May a cholera snatch him and my cough together."

A bad sign. When Holtzman began coughing, and cursing his cough, it was a sure sign of a bad mood. But Rapalesco was in a jubilant mood. Even that wouldn't describe it. His heart sang. Blessed be this night, it sang. Blessed be the world. The beautiful, lovely world. All the way from the Café Monopol to their lodging he couldn't stop talking and laughing and singing. Holtzman peered into his face. "What's happened to you, kid?" The boy's face spread in one smile from ear to ear. Dr. Leviathan's compliments must have gone to his head, Holtzman thought sourly.

They arrived at their lodgings almost at dawn, and had to stand outside ringing and ringing until they were admitted. They had undressed and prepared for bed, but Rapalesco was still in his jubilant mood. He couldn't stop talking and laughing. And his talk sounded peculiar to Holtzman—disjointed, crazy. "Yes," he was saying, "I certainly like Lemberg. A wonderful little town, Lemberg. A jewel of a town. I like the name, too—Lem-berg. And the people. Wonderful people. And they have a fine theater here. And the artists —wonderful fellows all of them."

"And the director, Getzel ben Getzel, is he wonderful too?" Holtzman put in.

"Why not? A splendid fellow, this Getzel."

"A black year on him," said Holtzman, and got ready to blow out the lamp, but Rapalesco held him back. He wanted to talk longer.

"Are you crazy? It's almost day."

"Just a little longer," begged Rapalesco, and laughed at himself.

"What do you want to talk about?"

"Let's talk about Dr. Levias."

"What's there to say about him? A German Maecenas with a tongue that wags at both ends."

118

"Tell me what you think about going to Vienna. Ahhh, Vienna!"

"What should I think about Vienna? How can we drop everything and tear off to Vienna? Have we got thieves' gold to squander, or what? Now if your doctor would pay our expenses. . . . He can stand it. He's got money to burn."

Rapalesco became thoughtful. "Of course he'll pay our expenses. Why not? A wonderful man, this doctor. A rare jewel."

"Everyone's a jewel to you. Everyone's wonderful. Now let's go to sleep. Sleep. Sle-ep."

Holtzman stretched his long stringy neck from under the covers, puckered his lips, and blew out the lamp. He shut his eyes and tried to settle himself to sleep. But Rapalesco persisted.

"That plump little woman, Braindele Kozak, isn't she charming?"

Holtzman's eyes flew open. He leaned forward on his sharp-pointed elbow and stared into the darkness that was slowly becoming diffused by the wan light of day. Until this moment he had completely forgotten Braindele Kozak. Now he remembered how she and the "kid" had sat with their heads close together all evening. What could they have talked about? He couldn't forgive himself for becoming so engrossed in the game as to forget to keep an eye on the kid.

Holtzman sleepily asked Rapalesco what they had talked about.

Carelessly Rapalesco answered. What should they talk about? Nothing important. Nothing at all. And he began spinning a yarn, marveling, as he talked, how easily the lies tripped off his tongue. He laughed at himself. Could he, too, be learning how to "knock a tea-kettle"? But when he stopped to ask Holtzman a question, he got no answer. Apparently Holtzman was asleep.

Holtzman slept restlessly. Something stirred in his breast, tried to tear itself out of his throat. A hoarse rattle came out, and he turned over, awoke, and began coughing and cursing his cough. Then he dropped off to sleep again; again the rattle in his chest woke him. Again he turned over, and began coughing and cursing, then slept again and woke again.

How could anyone sleep on such a night, Rapalesco wondered. A strange night. Half-wintry, yet delicious. A night to sing about. Blessed be this night, his heart sang. He jumped out of the bed, opened the window wide, and leaned out. He inhaled the cool, damp air. His eyes roved the sky. The stars had faded, but high in the heavens hung a pale crescent moon. Soon it, too, would dissolve. The pale blue of the sky was turning grey. Dawn was coming. Soon the new day would be here. For him it was the same—night or day. God had created

119

both. He had created the world, the wonderful, glorious world, in which the very cobblestones made music. How could he sleep when he was so full of this music? How could he sleep when he wanted to sing?

19 THE CHESS PLAYERS

The directors of the two rival theaters, Getzel ben Getzel and Bernhard Holtzman, were not, heaven forbid, mortal enemies engaged in a death struggle, but only intent on outwitting each other. Each planned his campaign carefully, covertly watched his opponent, set a trap here, an ambush there, and pounced when he thought the other wasn't looking. Which is called "playing a good game of chess." And the player is no thief, swindler, or liar, just a clever chess player.

Holtzman was gifted with a keen sense of smell. His sharp nose had sniffed out in advance which way the wind blew. Everyone danced about Rapalesco, looking at him the way a cat looks at a bowl of cream. But Holtzman pretended to see nothing. Dance, children, dance. You're dancing at your own funeral. Cunningly he set up his countermoves.

First of all against Isaac Shwalb, whom he had noticed fawning on Rapalesco. That master-player Holtzman could have taken a pawn like "the potbelly" right off, but he chose a subtler play. He invited the tragedian to a restaurant and over a glass of beer and a cut of sausage, he assured Shwalb he thought him a superlative actor, much too fine a tragedian to waste himself on this Yokel ben Fleckel. With these words he bought Shwalb at once. Shwalb confessed to Holtzman, in strict confidence, of course, that he would have left that exploiter long ago if it hadn't been for two things. First, he was bound by a contract which still had three full years to run. Second, he was short of "thread." If he only had the means he would have shaken the dust of Lemberg from his feet long ago. With a prima donna like his sister he could land on his feet anywhere. London, they said, was a slightly bigger town than Lemberg, no?

120

"Slightly bigger," Holtzman conceded, and took a sip of his beer.

"And the theater there is a bit finer, no?"

"I believe so," Holtzman said, taking another sip.

"Much finer," said Shwalb. He had a brother in London, he said. Also a tobacconist. That is, he had once sold cigarettes. Now he was a "businessman." He had sent his photograph recently. A fellow with a stomach like this, and a gold chain and a diamond ring. "I'd never have recognized him. He keeps writing me to come to London, and bring our sister. Then we'd find out what life was."

Holtzman heard him out. "Your brother talks sense, believe me." Hadn't Holtzman himself wanted to go to London? A fine little town, London, they said. One could really get ahead there. The thing to do was to get together a *cheder,* that is a company that would knock their eyes out. He knew just what his own company needed—the right kind of tragedian to play "heavy" roles, and a good-looking prima donna. If he only had those two, he'd be all set, and the devil with money!

A half-hour later when Holtzman and Shwalb left the restaurant, each with a thick, strong-smelling cigar between his teeth, they shook hands with great warmth and smiled knowingly at each other.

When the Lemberg actors saw how that burr, Holtzman, had attached himself to "Potbelly" Shwalb, they at once began carrying tales to director Getzel ben Getzel. "Our Itzikel," they whispered into his ear, "is buttering up that braggart from Bucharest. They're as thick as thieves." Whereupon Getzel summoned the tobacconist to him at once.

When Isaac Shwalb appeared, Getzel invited him into his office for private conference, first taking the precaution to lock all the doors and windows and make sure that no one was listening at the keyhole. When Shwalb came out, his face flamed like a bonfire and he sweated from every pore. He must have got it in the neck, his colleagues exulted. But Isaac kept his own counsel. Possibly he was playing a game of his own, dancing, as they say, at two weddings at once, playing the two directors off against each other. At any rate, that was the conclusion Holtzman arrived at, and made a new move, at Braindele Kozak.

Now the Lemberg actors had a fresh piece of business to chew on. Why was the Bucharest director so friendly with Braindele Kozak?

"Watch the two turtle doves billing and cooing."

"Maybe we'll dance at a wedding yet."

121

"*Maz'ltov,* in a lucky hour."

"Two clowns romancing."

Who would have guessed Holtzman was using Braindele to approach Henrietta. He began by engaging Braindele in an intimate conversation, and inviting her for a walk. Why not? They had known each other of old. Why not renew their friendship? They wound up in Braindele's room in a cosy *tête-à-tête.* Holtzman told her how happy he was at this reunion with an old friend. Only one thing was lacking. If Shchupak were only here!

Braindele raised her eyebrows, trying to guess at his meaning.

"He'd have fallen down in a fit."

"Amen. From your mouth into God's ears."

She almost said "thy" but caught herself in time. Lord, Lord, how a man could change. If Shchupak were here and took one look at his Hotzmach, he would surely have thrown a fit.

Even his language was different. Hotzmach the comedian talking about "business," "investments," "capital." Hotzmach and capital! What a laugh. He boasted he had a nice little sum of money saved up. He couldn't call himself a capitalist yet, but he'd gladly match his bit against Shchupak's. The other had diamonds and he had cash. Cash was better than diamonds, any day. The devil with money!

"Leave Shchupak alone," said Braindele. "He has more headaches than diamonds now."

"I won't believe it until I see it with my own eyes. And I won't rest until Shchupak takes a turn at polishing my shoes, may the cholera snatch him and my cough together."

As always, at the mention of Shchupak, Holtzman became agitated and began coughing and cursing his cough. Calming down, he hooked his thumbs into his vest, and began striding up and down Madame Cherniak's room, examining the tips of his shoes, and boasting of his wealth. Suddenly he caught himself, stopped pacing, and insisted that he had earned every ruble of his money, so help him God, himself.

"Amen, and why not?" Madame Cherniak bridled at this. He had no call to apologize. She was not one of those who thought it a disgrace to have a little money. The disgrace was, rather, to be a pauper, a have-not, like those loafers and vagabonds, who went about—if he'd excuse the expression—without an undershirt on their backs, and knew only how to play cards, to fritter away their last coin, to swindle and beg, to make loans and forget to pay. She had nothing but scorn for those wastrels. Couldn't one be a good artist and still look after his money? For what is a person without money?

122

"A body without a soul." Holtzman caught her up, in the same tone. He recalled that even in the old days she had kept her money in a "knot." The actors used to say, "She's as stuffed with money as with years." If she'd only kick the bucket and let them inherit.

They went on in this manner until by degrees Holtzman led the conversation around to more serious business. How much longer, he asked, could she remain a serf to this Yokel ben Fleckel? Wouldn't it be a thousand times better for her to throw in her lot with him? To go on, together, hand in hand? Together they couldn't be beat. They had each been through the mill, they knew how to make money and how to salt it away. To earn a groschen wasn't so hard. The trick was knowing how to hold on to it.

"That's the trick," Braindele agreed, nodding vigorously.

"Too many slobbering mouths waiting to get at it," said Holtzman.

"Too many slobbering mouths . . ." Braindele repeated with emphasis.

And so it went, until Holtzman reached the heart of the matter.

"We must snatch that pretty little heifer away from this Yokel ben Fleckel."

"A pretty little heifer," echoed Braindele Kozak. She was delighted with the trend of the whole conversation and pleased with herself for guessing whom he meant. "A pretty little heifer." That suited Henrietta down to the ground.

Encouraged, Holtzman went on, giving her to understand, half in earnest and half in jest, why they must snatch the little heifer away from Getzel ben Getzel.

"A good-looking prima donna, though she be as stupid as a calf, is a business asset."

"A business asset. Ha ha." And Braindele laughed. What next?

"She'll bowl them over like a wonder-working rabbi with his tricks," added Holtzman, still half in earnest and half in jest.

"A wonder-working rabbi. That's good. That's very good." And Braindele slapped him coquettishly on the arm and laughed so hard her small Oriental eyes became mere slits.

What other construction could such a lonely soul as Braindele Kozak have put on Holtzman's invitation that they go on together "hand in hand" than a romantic one? At the time when Holtzman was Hotzmach, Shchupak's handyman, his suit might have been spurned. But now, as Bernhard Holtzman, with a troupe of his own, a treasure like Rapalesco over whom everyone fought, and a little

123

capital besides, it was quite different. "To go hand in hand," as he put it, after she succeeded in "snatching that pretty little heifer," Henrietta, from Getzel ben Getzel, the four of them, she and Holtzman, Rapalesco and Henrietta, could set out into the world—with her on top of the heap, as the saying went.

With this pleasant prospect in mind, Braindele went to work. The flighty Henrietta let herself be talked over at once, with Rapalesco dangling in front of her. To the blushing girl Braindele said: "What's there to be ashamed of? It can happen to anybody. It's as plain as the nose on my face that you're crazy about the boy and he about you."

Henrietta's long lashes fluttered. "He crazy about me? How do you know?"

Oh, she knew. Don't ask how she knew. Madame Cherniak knew everything. And just give her a chance, and one-two-three, they'd be smashing glasses at a wedding.

"Braindele. Darling, precious," said Henrietta, and she embraced Madame Cherniak.

Braindele smiled in quiet triumph. Each person has his own lucky star, and every dog has his day. Braindele's day had come. The time had arrived for her heart to awaken from its long sleep and to flutter with joy and anticipation. The time had come for her to taste of that heady draught which every living person must sip at least once.

But even the sweetest elixir has its bitter ingredient. Braindele's bliss had one flaw. This wasn't her first romance, and perhaps not her last. If we wished to be modern and cynical, we could psychoanalyze Braindele's character in terms of rejections and repressions and sublimations. But in simple human terms, how many times she had burned herself! How many blows she had received from "those brutal, false, double-dealing men!"

There had been a time when Shchupak himself, needing her help, had paid court to her, and she had believed him. Later she had torn her hair in anguish. To this day she couldn't bear to hear his name mentioned, and yet she spoke of him three times a day.

After Shchupak, his lieutenant Sholom Meyer had tried to butter her up. This creature had ridden into her heart, as they say, with boots on. The affair had gone so far they were speaking of marriage. But at the last moment Sholom Meyer had balked. He had become deaf and blind. An actor hates marriage. A flirtation, a walk, a gift, a supper, a joke, a dance—anything but marriage. "The best marriage is the worst death."

124

As with Braindele's other romances, the one with Sholom Meyer began with a loan, then another, then another, and ended with a quiet scandal, a heartache and renewed hatred toward "those brutal, false, double-dealing men." Sordid as it had been, it had wrenched her heart and crushed her spirit almost beyond repair. But only almost.

Braindele never lost hope. Sooner or later, she believed, "He" would appear. He had to appear. And he would understand her and recognize her true worth. She would take him in, and open her coffers to him. He would see her linens. He would see her wardrobe. He would see her jewels. Everything lay ready, everything prepared just for him. And she would bare her soul to him. She would open up her heart. What if she were not as beautiful as some women? What if she were no longer young? In lieu of that, how much devotion and tenderness her heart contained. How much adoration and love she was capable of!

Whenever an actor had nothing left to pawn, he would come to Madame Cherniak for a loan, humbly and with compliments on his lips. She knew it meant nothing, that next day he would run from her as from the plague. But each figured as a potential lover. Deep in her heart she thought, "Who knows? Maybe he's the destined one."

And now it was Holtzman. He had entered her heart and reigned there supreme. She did his bidding as long as he needed her.

But the time of reckoning came and it turned out that they had misunderstood each other. For him "to go hand in hand" meant merely a share in his business, putting her money into his theater.

Put in her money? This was not what Madame Cherniak had dreamed of. "Those brutal, false, double-dealing men!"

20   FAREWELL TO LEMBERG

Another of Holtzman's plots involved the Lemberg Maecenas, Dr. Levias-Leviathan and his half million. He would set Rapalesco on this German. The "kid" would give him a going-over.

He coached Rapalesco on how to approach Dr. Levias, what demands to put before him.

"First of all, my dear songbird, let him pay our expenses to Vienna and back, to that Rosenthal . . ."

"Zonenthal," Rapalesco corrected him.

"And let him guarantee the expenses of our troupe, I don't say for long, just for a year, until you get somewhere with this Rosenthal."

"Zonenthal."

"And let him fit us out with clothes for the winter, and do it right. Let him buy you a good fur coat, of marten's fur, and a fox for me. We can't present ourselves before this Rosenthal looking like ragamuffins."

"Zonenthal."

"Why do you keep correcting me all the time, you imbecile?" Holtzman began yelling, but checked himself and finished in a softer tone. "Rosenthal, Zonenthal, what difference does it make? He can rot in the ground for all of me. The point is we can't let this German slide out like a greased pig from between our hands. Not before he comes across with some sugar. What do you say, kitten?"

The "kitten" had nothing to say to this. Holtzman and Rapalesco had entirely different views of life. What was all-in-all to one meant nothing to the other. And yet they lived together in perfect harmony. What was there to quarrel about? Holtzman still looked upon Rapalesco as a "kid," a snotnose, a child not dry behind the ears yet. And Rapalesco regarded Holtzman as a devoted friend who had only his good at heart. And if Holtzman sometimes lost his temper, one had to bear with a sick man.

"I am, as you know, temperamental, and not so much temperamental as hot-tempered, and not so much hot-tempered as plain crazy. And it's all because of this blasted cough of mine, may a cholera take it together with Shchupak." Thus Holtzman apologized after every outburst, and they became friends again.

Luck favored Holtzman. Dr. Levias had extended to him and Rapalesco an invitation to dine at his home. For Holtzman this visit was an occasion to prepare for with care. "The devil take it, when you go to dine with such a Maecenas, you have to go in style." And he fitted deed to word by buying a new suit, at a bargain for which he congratulated himself so: "May the director Yokel ben Fleckel have so many boils, how much more we would have to pay for such a suit at home."

126

In high spirits they prepared for the evening. Holtzman shaved closely, leaving only a narrow fringe of hair on either side of his sunken cheeks. He put on a stiff, snow-white collar and a smart bow tie. Patent-leather shoes and a tall top hat completed his costume. Rapalesco remarked that Holtzman was getting handsomer and younger every day. "Handsomer maybe, but younger? God knows." And Holtzman bent his head toward Rapalesco. "See these gray hairs, my songbird? A cholera on Shchupak. I have him to thank for them."

Rapalesco, too, was fashionably attired, only his wrists stuck out from the sleeves of his evening jacket which got tighter as he grew. His white shirt front bulged from the tight vest. But his whole figure displayed so much freshness and youth, it was a pleasure indeed to look at him. No wonder the prima donna, Henrietta Shwalb, had thrown over all her admirers to devote herself exclusively to him, though he had either the heart of a Tartar or eyes in the wrong place, or he was simply, as she put it, "a green cucumber."

Accustomed to having men swoon at her feet, she couldn't understand what ailed this young fellow. How could she know that his mind and his heart were elsewhere. At night in his dreams and in the daytime in his reveries he saw only one place, Vienna, where two people drew him like a magnet.

That Reizel was now in Vienna he firmly believed. When he got there, all he would have to do was find out at which theater "the famous Rosa Spivak" was singing. Then he would buy a ticket and sit down in the audience and listen to her. What was so unusual about that? A famous diva sings, let her sing. But, ah, what if he couldn't sit still? What if his heart almost leaped out of his breast? Calm yourself, Rapalesco, calm yourself. Things are not as they were. This is Vienna, not Holeneshti. You are no longer Leibel Rapalovich of Holeneshti, but Leo Rapalesco of Bucharest. She is not Reizel, the Cantor's daughter from God's Street, but the famous singer, Rosa Spivak of Vienna. Now you are an artist yourself, and you must sit still and listen. Calm yourself, Rapalesco. Later, during the intermission, you will go backstage and say to her, "Can you guess who I am?"

But no. This plan didn't please him. He would write her a letter instead. He would tell her that an actor of the Yiddish Theater of Bucharest, by the name of Rapalesco, wished to meet the renowned singer, Rosa Spivak. He begged her—no, he didn't beg—he requested her to come to the theater and visit him between acts, for he had greetings for her from Holeneshti. The mention of Holeneshti would surely bring her. He would pick her out in the audience at once by those black, glowing, gipsy eyes. How could he go on acting after that? How could he control his voice, his motions? Ten minutes, five minutes, one minute more, and the curtain would descend, and she would be in the wings, running toward him, arms outstretched. From her shoulders would slip the red scarf. Miraculous. The same scarf she wore the night of the fire in Holeneshti. And her eyes, her dark beautiful eyes are veiled with mist. Is she crying? Yes. Doesn't he feel his own heart crying inside of him? Aren't tears rolling down his cheeks? She comes close and they fall in each other's arms. Each calls the other's name. *Leibel. Reizel.*

The scene shifts. In Vienna, he asks a passerby, "Can you tell me where the great Zonenthal lives?" The passerby laughs. "Who doesn't know where Zonenthal lives? Do you see that crystal palace with the gold roof? This is where Zonenthal lives." With beating heart he mounts the steps of the palace. A dazzling figure hung with diamonds from head to foot comes to meet him, Zonenthal himself, with a face like an angel's and a smile like the sun on a fine summer's day. "Welcome," he says. "Is this the young artist of whom I have heard so much?" How sincere he is, how kindly and simply he talks, just as though he weren't the great Zonenthal himself, but an ordinary human being. He takes Rapalesco by the hand and leads him into the palace and seats him on a golden chair. He listens to Rapalesco declaim and his praise falls on Rapalesco like golden rain. "No," says Zonenthal gently, in words and tones just like those of Dr. Levias, "you must not act in such common roles. A God-given talent like yours," he says, "must find an outlet in more serious, classical roles. . . ."

"Dr. Julius Levias."

Rapalesco and Holtzman stopped in front of a tall iron gateway and read the gold-letter inscription on a white card. Within the spiked iron railing stood an imposing residence surrounded by poplar trees. The spacious, tree-shaded grounds and the substantial house seemed to say to them, "Here is wealth, here is comfort, here is repose."

"The devil take money!" Holtzman exclaimed, as he whipped out a crackling white handkerchief from his pocket, blew his nose vigorously, and pulled at the bell.

There are people whose appearance changes with their surround-

128

ings. When you meet them abroad the face they present to you is very different from the one they show at home. Entering Dr. Levias' mansion, Holtzman and Rapalesco barely recognized their host. Where was his ingratiating smile? His genial manner? His loquacity? At home Dr. Levias was stiff and formal, and seemed to have shrunk in size a head shorter.

Not that he didn't receive them graciously. On the contrary. He himself helped them off with their wraps, and led them into a library lined with books from floor to ceiling. He sat them down in two soft armchairs and engaged them in polite conversation. How did they like Lemberg? What did they think of the weather? With that sort of constrained chit-chat the interval between their arrival and the serving of dinner passed.

After a half-hour of this Dr. Levias rose from his armchair and conducted his guests through a succession of rooms hung with heavy portraits and handsome mirrors, and led them to a sumptuously set table, where they were confronted by a wizened old crone with a face like a sour apple.

"My *muterchen,*" said Dr. Levias, kissing the wrinkled crone's hand.

The *muterchen,* an old woman with an orthodox wig on her head, a flowered silk dress, diamond earrings, and huge pearls, gave them a look which chilled their bones to the marrow. "An old witch," Holtzman's look said to Rapalesco. And both of them, almost faint with hunger by now, sat down at the table and fell to without waiting to be urged.

There was little conversation. Mother Levias looked at them with frank distaste as though to say, "What brought those *schlimazls* here?" She said nothing in words, and when the others spoke, one remark didn't adhere to the next. Finally, all four gave up, and if it weren't for the clatter of forks and knives, every gulp and swallow with which the guests choked down their food would have echoed through the room. It brought distinct relief to everyone when Dr. Levias rose from the table, kissed the *muterchen's* hand again, and led the guests back to the library.

Here the host unlocked a drawer of the desk and took three cigars from three different boxes. Holtzman's sharp eye noted the three different brands, best, middling, and vile. The best cigar Dr. Levias took for himself, the middling one he handed to Rapalesco, and the vile one he offered to Holtzman. When they lit up, Holtzman demonstrated at once his fine judgment of cigars, for he choked on the

129

first draw. If he hadn't come here with an ulterior motive, he wouldn't have hesitated to tell this Maecenas off. He would have asked him right out where he got these stinking cigars—from a street peddler? They were fit for poisoning flies. But with so much at stake, Holtzman kept his peace. He forced himself to smoke the vile cigar, coughing all the time, and listening to the Maecenas discourse on "art."

"He's singing the same song over again," Holtzman thought. "It's enough to make you throw up. Art and more art and classic drama and the State Theater in Vienna. Our Vienna. And Zonenthal. Our Zonenthal. At last he's getting to him. And the stupid 'kid' is hanging on to every word as though it were Holy Scriptures. This will go on all night if I don't whip my horses and drive into the gate."

"Forgive me, sir," Holtzman broke in, "I'm a plain person and I don't understand such things. You say the boy shouldn't act in the melodramas he's been doing up to now. You say he must go to Vienna. No doubt you're right. You know more about such things than I. But the question is: how does the cat cross the river? You must have heard the proverb, 'Without fingers you can't thumb your nose.'"

Dr. Levias started up as though he had been scalded. "Pardon, you must mean the letter I promised to write to Zonenthal. Just one moment, please."

In vain Holtzman tried to head him off, to tell him the letter could wait. In vain he hinted that the trip was expensive and they were running out of "thread." Dr. Levias was deaf to these innuendoes, as deaf as a post.

Getting nowhere with hints, Holtzman decided to come out with plain talk. But no sooner did he mention money, than Dr. Levias handed him the letter, sealed and addressed, pressed his hand warmly, rang for the servant, and indicated that the two gentlemen were ready to leave. Then he hospitably escorted them to the door.

The last guest performance in Lemberg went off with even greater *éclat* than the first, without a hitch. The pacing was perfect, no actor fumbled a cue; the stage manager didn't have to sweat. The two troupes worked in perfect rapport with each other, the whole raised to a high level by the inspired acting of the great artist from Bucharest.

Tonight Rapalesco felt himself in his element. No matter that the play itself was silly and inconsequential; the actors breathed life into it. The entire audience went wild at the end, shouting, "Rapalesco, we want Rapalesco!"

130

And Rapalesco took curtain call after curtain call. And not alone, but with the lovely prima donna of the Lemberg theater who shared in the triumph. Each time Rapalesco took her hand, she felt a shiver run down her spine. "He's mine!" So thought Henrietta and smiled, flashing all her white teeth and imitation jewels.

Taking a cue from his sister, the tragedian Isaac Shwalb also swelled with rapture. Fortune had smiled on him at last. First, he would be rid of this bloodsucker, Getzel ben Getzel, for good. Second, he had entered into partnership with Holtzman. From now on the troupe would be called Holtzman, Shwalb & Co. And his sister Yentel had the young man in her hands. Not a bad match. His colleagues would burst with envy, and Yokel ben Fleckel would have an apoplectic fit.

"What are you peeking through the cracks for? Whom are you looking for?" Shwalb asked his new partner Holtzman, who paced restlessly up and down behind the drawn curtain, pulling the folds aside every minute to peer into the audience.

"Last winter's snow," Holtzman replied, pulling the curtain aside once more and raking the audience with his eyes, looking for Dr. Levias, who had promised to come to the theater tonight. Holtzman began cursing all doctors, all Germans, all patrons of the drama, with deadly curses. "Whom are you blessing?" the actors asked curiously.

"I just remembered an uncle of mine, a tailor who remained a pauper all his life though he stole the customers' cloth. He's now in the next world by grace of all the patches he sewed during his life."

For the actors this was no alibi. Swiftly they carried to their director the information that Holtzman was raving like a maniac on the stage, in other words that he was in a great dither about something. What could it be?

Getzel ben Getzel heard them out quietly, his eyes lowered, barely restraining a smile. Let him rave, he thought. Much good it will do him. He'll start foaming at the mouth when he gets ready to leave tomorrow. He'll get the surprise of his life.

But it was Getzel ben Getzel who got the surprise of his life. Something occurred which had never yet happened in the annals of Lemberg. The monopolist was undone. His prima donna absconded. And such a prima donna. And with her went the villain, her brother. And another actor, Benny Gorgel, an excellent prompter. And even Madame Cherniak, known as Braindele Kozak.

131

"What's to be done?" Getzel wept and wailed in front of the remaining actors. "I might as well lock the doors."

"Not otherwise," the actors comforted him, and went off to the Café Monopol to sink their sorrows in a game of cards. And the director, Getzel ben Getzel, girded his loins, and tucked his feet over his shoulders, as the saying is, and set out after the runaways to Vienna, to Bucharest, to the ends of the earth if need be. "Let my name not be Getzel ben Getzel if I won't catch them yet," he swore, "unless there's no justice left on earth."

Part III

21 VIENNA

The Holtzman-Shwalb partnership was signed and sealed in the gay and carefree city of Vienna. The ceremony took place in one of the café-restaurants for which Vienna is justly famous. Though far from being a first-class café, still one could pass a tolerable evening in one of its secluded rooms, over a glass of Pilsner and a plate of sausage. The terms arrived at were as follows:

1. Holtzman and Shwalb would conduct a theater under the name, "Holtzman, Shwalb & Company."

2. Its joint directors would be Bernhard Holtzman and Isaac Shwalb.

3. Each would put into the partnership the following: Shwalb, his sister Henrietta as prima donna. Holtzman, the famous artist Leo Rapalesco as leading man.

4. All profits over and above expenses to be divided equally between the two partners, share and share alike.

5. Neither of the directors would be obliged to act, except to fill in during an actor's illness. In that event the sick actor's share would go to the directors.

6. All actors would work on shares. Of the net profit of the evening's receipts half would go to the directors, the rest to the actors.

Of the actors' half, Henrietta and Rapalesco each would receive a double share.

7. It was none of the actors' affair what the directors earned, or what they, God forbid, lost.

8. The treasurer of the business would be . . .

Here a sharp disagreement took place. Each partner wanted to be closest to the trough. The dilemma was resolved by Holtzman, who proposed that Shwalb sit at the cash-box, since he was weak on high finance, while large accounts would pass through Holtzman's hands. Trust Holtzman to know how to work out a business deal. He had been trained by a good teacher, Shchupak, may his name and memory be erased forever.

The terms agreed upon, Holtzman rang for the waiter, called for pen and ink and a sheet of paper, and turned them over to Shwalb with an expansive gesture.

"Well, let's get it down in writing."

"Who, me?" said Shwalb innocently, pushing aside the pen and ink. "I have never in my life held a pen in my hand."

"Is that so?" Holtzman asked in feigned wonder. "How can a person not know how to write a few words at least in our own tongue, in plain Yiddish?"

"Where would I learn?" Shwalb defended himself. And since he was on his third glass of beer, his tongue became unloosened and he began to relate his biography.

He was born he didn't know where, and he was raised an orphan, he didn't know by whom. That is, actually, there were three orphans: he and his older brother Nissel, who was in London now, and their young sister Yentel, known as Henrietta. Each of them wallowed in a different mudhole, until certain good people took pity on them and placed them out. He and his brother Nissel were apprenticed to a baker. But there was more money selling tobacco than bagels and they turned to that. But peddling cigarettes was no bed of roses either. Luckily Isaac discovered he had a talent for play-acting. When *Purim* came, he shoveled in gold. Somehow they got by. They went naked and barefoot and hungry, but they thumbed their noses at the world.

The problem was, what to do with their sister? A girl is only a girl. They hired her out into service, for room and board, just to get a load off their shoulders. But every three weeks she changed jobs. For on top of being a girl, she had been gifted since childhood. Not with brains, you understand, but with looks. And most employers have this failing in common—when they see a pretty girl, they can't keep their hands off her. If only his older brother Nissel had stayed home, he could have handled that problem. He had a fist, Nissel had. "Do you see me?" said Shwalb, squaring his shoulders. "Well, I'm a weakling next to him." But Nissel had taken a notion to run off to London. And on foot, if you please. He had promised to write every week, but when had he written? Years later, when he, Shwalb, was already established as a tragedian and Henrietta was a prima donna for this Yokel ben Fleckel. "Now tell me," Shwalb concluded, extending both hands in a helpless gesture, "when did I have time to learn to write?"

Having heard out this candid tale, Holtzman had to agree. He confessed to Shwalb in a burst of frankness that he, too, could write only when no one was looking. But what did they need writing for, anyway? "To the devil with contracts," said Holtzman. "It isn't the note that pays, but the man." And he tore the clean sheet of paper in half and jovially extended his hand to his partner. "Let's shake hands instead and give each other our word that everything we agreed on will be as holy as Scripture. Let's take another glass of beer on it. Here's how. *L'chaim*. May God grant us fortune and luck."

"*L'chaim. L'chaim.* To our success."

The partners' next step was to explore the city of Vienna for a suitable theater location. They soon decided that their efforts were useless. Vienna was no city and the Viennese Jews were not Jews. "Jews," said Holtzman, "who can get along without a Yiddish theater, who either run to see the great Zonenthal, or are satisfied with a cabaret or a beerhall where they listen to songs like *Eve* or *Friday in the Evening*, and yell *bravo* and lick their chops—such Jews deserve to be strung from a tree or to be shot with a gun."

And Holtzman decided, with his partner's approval, to spit on this brilliant Vienna and go back to the provinces, take a run through blessed Galicia, Bukovina, Rumania, Hungary, where Jews hadn't yet tasted of the fruit of the tree of knowledge, where the public still ran to gape at Yiddish actors as at a bear or an elephant or a monkey. . . .

The only thing that kept Holtzman in Vienna was Zonenthal. An artist who possessed a round million deserved to have an extra day spent in Vienna for his sake. It wasn't, said Holtzman, that he was so impressed by wealth. Heaven forbid. He had known millionaires in his day. He had talked to them, ridden in the same carriage with them, and if you must know, he had dined at the same table with them. No, plain millionaires had no attraction for him. Holtzman only submitted that an actor, like Zonenthal, who had worked himself up to a million, without gambling or boozing or frittering it away, was worth a look.

And Holtzman spruced himself up, smoothed the dents in his top hat, bought a new pair of patent-leather shoes, fresh gloves, and an imitation-silk umbrella, took up the letter from Dr. Levias and said to Rapalesco, "Well, my dear songbird, with the right foot."

Here his partner Shwalb put in that he would be pleased to go along with them to see Zonenthal. "Since we're partners, it's only right." But Holtzman clipped his wings. "Nothing doing. Partnerhood is not brotherhood. You can talk about the rights of a partner, but you have to know who is suited for what."

Shwalb took exception to this. Would it cost any more if the three of them went? He wouldn't bite a piece off their precious Zonenthal. But Holtzman gave him to understand that every man must know his station. When something else came up, then he could climb on the table. Shwalb didn't understand this rebuff. He let *him* know that first of all the prima donna Henrietta was his own sister and he was her brother. Holtzman on his side flared up and began coughing and spouting Biblical texts, which he translated forthwith into plain Yiddish, "Don't climb into my attic and don't crap on my ladder."

From this last quotation we can gather that the two partners had reached the most intimate terms. Shwalb did not join the excursion.

Neither Holtzman nor Rapalesco could understand why such a great man as Zonenthal didn't have his own residence but lived in a hotel like any common actor. "If a *nash brat,* one of our own kind, chooses to splash in a mud puddle together with chickens and ducks, and become acquainted with landladies and bedbugs, that's his affair. For that we are poor Yiddish show-players. But Zonenthal! In Vienna! That's something else again."

So complained Holtzman as they rode in a fine carriage to Zonenthal's address. But when the carriage drew up in front of an imposing hotel and a lackey in gold buttons came out, Holtzman changed his tune. "The devil with money!" he informed Rapalesco. Then he announced that they wished to see Herr Zonenthal. Whereupon Gold Buttons surveyed the two from head to foot, and told them that they couldn't see Zonenthal. "And why?" Holtzman asked. "Herr Zonenthal isn't receiving," said the lackey. "What do you mean, he isn't receiv-

138

ing?" Gold Buttons was about to turn away, when Holtzman haughtily announced that he had a letter to Zonenthal from an important personage who was perhaps as rich as his employer. He needn't think, he added, they were just nobodies; they, too, were artists.

Here Holtzman took off one glove, removed his hat, put it on again, then gave Gold Buttons a hearty slap on the back. The disconcerted Gold Buttons took the letter and walked off. A good quarter hour passed before he returned with the answer. Herr Zonenthal regretted he was busy; if they wished to speak to him, let them come to his dressing-room tonight during the first intermission.

That was all the information they could extract from the lackey. Before Holtzman could open his mouth to speak, Gold Buttons had shown the visitors that he wore the same buttons in back as in front.

Returned from their mission, the two envoys met an eager chorus. "Well?"

"Well, what?"

"What's new with the great Zonenthal?"

"What should be new?" said Holtzman blandly. "You can imagine, he's the same Zonenthal."

And Holtzman began "knocking the teakettle" about the marvels they had seen, in what luxury Zonenthal lived, what a charming man he was, how graciously he had received them, how he had treated them to tea, beer and cigars, "this big," demonstrating the size by stretching out his arms and driving his fist straight into Shwalb's red face.

Holtzman decided then and there to hire a box at the State Theater that very evening to see Zonenthal perform, the party to consist of the two directors, Rapalesco, Henrietta, and Braindele Kozak.

In a word, Holtzman showed no sign of despondency. If anything, livelier and more talkative than usual, he performed all sorts of antics, told jokes, sang bits of songs, and kept everyone in stitches. But if Holtzman acted as though a great piece of good luck had befallen him, Rapalesco presented the other extreme. He went about gloomy and dejected. And no wonder. For in a brief space of time both of his dreams had been shattered.

At the very outset his search for Marcella Zembrich, with whom, according to Braindele Kozak, Reizel was living, had proved fruitless. Madame Cherniak, who had promised to find Rosa in Vienna, had changed her tune once they arrived in the big city. Every day she brought him another piece of news: Rosa Spivak had parted company

139

with Marcella Zembrich and had suddenly gone off with another artist to Berlin; she was in a musical conservatory in Paris, studying at the expense of a certain rich patron by the name of Jacques Reszko, a Gentile who had fallen head over heels in love with the Yiddish singer; she was now in London giving concerts with a certain young violinist, a Jewish boy named Grischa Stellmach, a sensation in musical circles. Gossip had it that this Grischa was engaged to Rosa, if not married to her already.

"A complete falsehood!" Rapalesco burst out.

The truth was Braindele had changed her course of action. It now suited her own purpose better to wean Rapalesco away from Rosa. To the young artist her change of heart was a great blow. And the visit to the great Zonenthal was another.

Each of the five people who sat in the box of the State Theater that evening saw the play in a different light. Holtzman's sole interest lay in the decor and the audience. "This is what I call theater!" If he could work himself up, with God's help, to a theater like this in three years, he would show the world! For let us not fool ourselves. Holtzman, in his own opinion, had as much brains as any of these Germans.

As Holtzman's eyes swept the sea of faces below him, the usual oath tore itself from his lips. "A cholera take it!" It was hard to tell for whom the oath was intended—the Germans who packed the brilliant theater or the Jews who would sooner run to see Zonenthal than go to the Yiddish theater Holtzman would have set up in this cursed city. "Tfui," he spat. "Vienna. Call that a city? I'd better run off as fast as I can to some little Yiddish town like Holeneshti. This whole audience with its thousand baldheads isn't worth one Holeneshti Jew."

Madame Cherniak's thoughts ran along the same lines, though with a different twist. She was thinking of the time when Holtzman would declare himself ready to go "hand in hand" with her, meaning under the marriage canopy. Then, oh, then they would set up a theater that was really a theater.

And her thoughts carried her away from Vienna to some town in Galicia or Bukovina. She saw herself as Madame Holtzman. They were already, with God's help, owners of a theater, with their own properties and decorations, and their own troupe of players, among them Rapalesco and the prima donna Henrietta, who was now Henrietta Rapalesco. Madame Cherniak would attend to that little matter. For

140

then Holtzman would stop casting sheep's eyes at the prima donna, the plague take him. That meant she must knock Rosa Spivak out of the young fellow's head.

Shwalb watched the stage with great absorption, but his soul roamed elsewhere, to a table with "a good glass of beer and a chunk of salami," the buffet temptingly spread with a white cloth and knives and forks and plates. There were other good things to eat, and his mouth watered.

Henrietta, too, while her eyes were on the stage, had her mind elsewhere. She watched to see what impression her new coiffure, gown, and jewels were making on the young man who would soon be hers. First, she thought, she would tease him a little, play hard to get. Then when he came crawling to her, ready to eat dirt like the others, she'd know what to do.

But it wasn't working that way. Oblivious of her, he hung over the rail of the box, trembling all over, his face aflame, his eyes burning like coals. Henrietta couldn't understand it. He hadn't looked at her or uttered a word to her since the curtain went up. As soon as the act ended, Rapalesco sprang out of his seat. He seemed to have gone out of his mind. He was shaking hands with everyone in the box. There were tears, actual tears, in his eyes. And when he shook hands with her brother Isaac, the tragedian, he embraced him with both arms and burst out, "That's what I call acting. That's real art."

Henrietta looked at him askance and thought, "The boy must be touched. He's out of his mind."

The first act over, Holtzman began dickering with the ushers of the State Theater to let him go backstage to see Zonenthal. It turned out, however, that Zonenthal would receive only one of them, the younger one, about whom Dr. Levias of Lemberg had written him.

"Good morning to you! May all the nightmares I dreamed last night and the night before and all the nights of my life . . ."

Holtzman stopped, abashed by the stares of his companions. If a hole had conveniently opened under his feet, he'd have jumped into it. They were exchanging meaningful glances among themselves, and Shwalb looked him in the eye as though to say, "What, after such cigars?" But time didn't stand still. The minutes were running out, and the usher stood waiting. Holtzman took Rapalesco aside and told him a piece of news he had just learned in the theater this evening. "This Zonenthal has a young son, a regular scapegrace. A wastrel.

141

The boy keeps signing checks and the old man keeps paying. So you have to see to it," Holtzman warned, thrusting his sharp chin into Rapalesco's face as though to drive the point home the better, "you have to see to it, that the same thing that happened with the Lemberg Maecenas doesn't happen here. Talk to him point-blank, in round numbers—eighteen and thirteen. Do you understand? Don't let him slide out from under. If we eat pork, let the grease run over our beards. Understood?"

Here something happened to Rapalesco which Holtzman could never have foreseen. Whether provoked beyond endurance by Holtzman's blunt "eighteen and thirteen," or wounded by Zonenthal's refusal to see them that morning, or simply overwrought by the evening's excitement, as he was about to follow the usher, he turned sharply on his heel and said to Holtzman, "I'm not going."

"W-what?"

"I'm not going."

"What do you mean, you're not going?"

"Just what I said."

Holtzman rubbed his eyes and looked at Rapalesco in the bright glare of the electric lights. The "kid" had never disobeyed him before. This was the first "no" he had ever heard from his lips. In his words, and more than that, in the tone of his voice, Holtzman heard such resolution he didn't dare persist. He felt like Balaam when the ass under him suddenly spoke,

"*No* is *no*," said Holtzman with a smile which sat oddly on his lips. In this brief interval he had aged visibly. His sharp nose had become sharper, his shoulders sagged, and he was seized by a racking cough. In the meanwhile the bell sounded and the audience began to drift back to its seats. Without a word the two returned to their box.

Leaving the theater, the five actors were joined by the rest of the company from the gallery, and they marched in a body through the streets of Vienna. On the way they talked and laughed in loud voices, exchanging comments, passing judgments, each trying to outshout and outgesticulate the next one. You could hear such gems as "Oaf," "Stick," "Imbecile," "Oxtail," "Chunk of wood," "Braggart," "Psalm-chanter," "Potato-eater." Whom these epithets were intended for is hard to say. But their spirits ran high. The shouts carried far into the surrounding streets, and the laughter even farther. It was as though a strange, turbulent current had flowed into the placid stream of the city, startling the stolid Germans.

142

Only two of this company didn't take part in the merrymaking, the director, Holtzman, and the leading man, Rapalesco, both sunk in their own thoughts. Holtzman, walking arm-in-arm with Braindele Kozak and ostensibly listening to her chatter, thought about the "kid's" defiance. The "kid" walked behind with Henrietta, pretending to listen to her chatter, answering one question in four. His thoughts, too, were elsewhere—studying new roles, those in which Zonenthal excelled. He imagined the world thrilling to his portrayal and predicting that he would soon outrank the great Zonenthal. He dreamed of being invited to the Vienna theater as a guest artist, and Zonenthal in the audience, leaping up on the stage, embracing him and proclaiming to the world that he had been outstripped by the young Rapalesco. . . .

That night was a difficult one for Holtzman. *What has happened to the kid?* he thought, coughing and tossing from side to side. A change had come over the boy since they had come to Vienna. He was as capricious as a spoiled child. This city was to blame, may it burn down to the ground. He was repelled and disillusioned by Vienna which everyone called gay and brilliant, but which to him seemed as dark as the grave. A miasma hung over it, a breath of the plague. In this city all his dreams had gone up in smoke. Its people were ugly, false, wicked. His friends plotted against him, to rob him of his most cherished possession, to tear Rapalesco right from under his nose.

"I have to watch the 'kid,' " he thought. "Who knows what thoughts Shwalb has in his mind? And what schemes Henrietta has in her heart? And what kind of viper lies in Braindele's bosom? One man alone among all those harpies!"

Holtzman sat up in bed, leaned forward on his sharp elbow, coughed dryly and spoke to Rapalesco in the next bed.

"Rapalesco, are you sleeping?"

"No, what is it?"

"I just had an idea."

"What is it?"

"Did you hear me cough?"

"Well?"

"I believe this is the end. I have to get ready. Make my peace with this world and get ready to join my father in the next . . ."

Rapalesco sat up with a start and looked at Holtzman with wide, frightened eyes.

"Have you gone out of your mind? Or are you raving in a fever?"

143

Pleased by Rapalesco's response, Holtzman burst out laughing. Then his laugh turned to a wheeze, and he began cursing.

"Fool that you are. May Shchupak suffer as many years as I will live yet. I was just figuring . . . maybe I should write to my mother and sister out there in the sticks to come and join me . . . my cough might get better."

22   "A MAN OF EDUCATION"

The only educated man of the troupe, Holtzman, Shwalb & Co., was the prompter, Benny Gorgel, whom Holtzman had spirited away from the Lemberg theater. Getzel ben Getzel himself used to boast that no one had such a prompter as he. For his prompter, you understand, was "a man of education." And for this very reason Holtzman had snapped him up along with the prima donna, saying, as though to justify his action in his own eyes, "I don't know myself what I want with this piece of carrion. At a glance he isn't worth a broken *heller*. But still, the ragpicker take him, 'a man of education' will always earn his keep."

Holtzman was right, as far as he went. At a glance you wouldn't have given a broken *heller,* or a groschen, or a brass farthing for this sallow-faced, emaciated individual with a long skinny neck, a huge bobbing Adam's apple, and a shock of unruly black hair. If he had at least smeared his hair with grease or combed it, he might have passed. But the prompter was not the man to bother with such frivolities. "A man of education" has better ways of occupying his time. You have to forgive him for wearing unpressed clothes and a battered hat. You must overlook the fact that his collar is grimy. Notwithstanding his awe for "a man of education," Holtzman crowned him with such nicknames as *"schlimazl,"* "carrion" and *"Kuni-Lemel."* According to axiom, the more learned a man, the more modest he is. And so the prompter, not offended by Holtzman's nomenclature, performed every menial task assigned to him without complaint. Holtzman worked according to the tenet that a man, though accomplished as Satan himself, as long as he worked for an employer, had to earn his bread in

144

the sweat of his brow. For wasn't Holtzman himself a cut above the common herd? And yet hadn't he, too, once starved and slaved and shined shoes for Shchupak, may his name and memory be erased?

Thus Holtzman justified his treatment of the poor prompter, and that "man of education" accepted his destiny quietly and without a murmur, as though it had been decreed on high.

But each man has his own star. And the time came when the prompter's star suddenly blazed in the heavens and he rose in every-one's eyes, even in those of his employer, Holtzman.

This happened when the troupe, Holtzman, Shwalb & Co., after forsaking "that cursed Vienna," had taken to the road again, putting on time-honored operettas, melodramas, and farces, as Providence had decreed.

One day during rehearsal, when it was time for Rapalesco to come on, he couldn't be found anywhere. A frantic search began. They looked for him one hour, two hours, three hours, to no avail. Rapa-lesco had mysteriously vanished—and the prompter with him.

It was a miracle Holtzman didn't have an apoplectic stroke then and there. He began imagining all sorts of contingencies, one more terrible than the next. After the "kid's" display of independence in Vienna anything was possible. A sharp pain gripped him in the belly and he began to shake as with an ague. His nose lengthened, the light in his eyes went out, and a corpselike pallor spread over his face.

Then one of the scouts arrived with the glad news that they had found the missing pair. Rapalesco and Benny Gorgel sat closeted in a room at the inn, reading a book together.

Holtzman, reviving, leaped up, clapped his tall hat on his head, snatched up his cane, and flew to the inn. He burst into the room where the two young men sat reading.

"What happened?" he shouted.

In reply Rapalesco caught him by the shoulders and embraced him. "We've stumbled on a find. A treasure."

Holtzman looked at him as though he had gone mad. "What treas-ure? What did you find?"

"*Uriel Acosta*. The same play in which we saw the great Zonenthal in Vienna. Benny Gorgel found it among his books, translated word for word into our language, into Yiddish. That's the end," Rapalesco declared. "I won't play any other part but Uriel Acosta. No more operettas, no more melodramas, no more farces!"

Just as he stood, in his top hat and with the cane over his arm,

Holtzman sank down on a bench, bathed in cold sweat. What kind of talk was this? What sort of language?

He tried to remonstrate. What did Rapalesco mean, not play operettas and farces? What about him, Holtzman, the director? Did he have no voice in the matter? What would become of their decorations? The costumes? The play scripts? The scores? The playbills? What was this? The end of the world?

And Holtzman wished he could tear the prompter apart limb for limb. Here was a fine how-do-you-do. And all because of this "man of education."

Once they put on *Uriel Acosta,* they had to repeat it again and again. Some places insisted on a straight run of this play. In Paris, for instance, where the troupe was booked for twelve performances, the public wanted only *Uriel Acosta.* As Holtzman put it, the Day of Judgment had come. The audience almost tore the theater apart. Gentiles came to see the Yiddish star Rapalesco and couldn't praise him enough. In the newspapers, Holtzman heard, critics compared Rapalesco to the great actors of the world, predicting he would outshine the great Zonenthal.

Naturally Holtzman strutted like a rooster and crowed in glee over the fact that a "piece of junk" like *Uriel Acosta,* may God not punish him for these words, brought in as much money as an operetta or a farce. The Day of Judgment had indeed come. "The world has been turned upside down," Holtzman said. "A half-crazed madman on the stage is dearer to them than the loveliest prima donna. Who would have thought it? And in the long run, who cares? Let it be from a Cossack, as long as we make a living. You never bite the hand that feeds you. Long may he live, this *schlimazl,* the prompter, who scraped up the book. When you're dealing with 'a man of education,' anything can happen. I'll have to give him one of my old suits, see to it that the *Kuni-Lemel* puts on a clean collar and a fresh tie, and while I'm about it I'll take him to the barber. He's getting to look like a country priest."

And so Holtzman raised the prompter's wages, gave credit where credit was due, and stopped calling him "Carrion," "*Schlimazl*" and other such names. Holtzman had prospered. He went about these days with his mustache turned up at the ends á la Wilhelm II, his hands in his pockets, and a heavy gold chain spanning his white vest, thanking God every day that he had made good without benefit of patrons or

146

renowned artists, let them all sink into the ground together with Shchupak, amen.

Only one thing Holtzman lacked, and that was a woman. Though in a manner of speaking, he had that, too. And it didn't cost him anything. Madame Cherniak had appointed herself his housekeeper and hostess. She watched every groschen and looked after his comfort with utter devotion, mending his clothes, darning his socks, cooking his dinner, and whipping up eggnogs to ease his cough. It reached the stage where the actors called her Madame Hotzmach behind her back. Luckily Holtzman knew nothing of this. He would have had a double heartache, first because they had remembered his old nickname, second because they had wished such a match on him. Holtzman hankered after something else, a young girl, a "tender little citron" like the prima donna. I ask you, why not? If she wasn't so clever, she made up in looks what she lacked in brains. The only drawback was she was too giddy, talked too much, giggled too much, pranced around like a circus pony. But wait till he put a ring on her finger. Then he would lay down the law to her.

However, his suit made no progress. He had drunk more than one glass of beer with the prima donna's brother, Isaac Shwalb, and had given him to understand what he wanted. Isaac Shwalb, that glutton, ate, drank, stuffed his face, promised him everything under the sun— and in the end, nothing. . . . Holtzman resolved to approach the girl himself. "Once for all," he said to himself, "I have to find out where I stand, whether I'm fish, flesh or fowl."

One day, a Saturday and therefore a holiday, Holtzman dressed himself up like a French boulevardier. He had become quite Frenchified of late. "Decked out like a corpse," the actors said. He shaved his face, waxed the ends of his mustache, picked up his cane, and proposed to the prima donna that they go for a stroll. Looking him up and down, she said, "When I get lonesome for you, I'll send for you."

On another occasion he talked to her seriously about marriage. It was time, he told her, to stop prancing around, and begin to think of settling down. Henrietta answered him rudely. "Why worry about others? Keep your phiz out of my biz." He swallowed the elegant rhyme and asked, "How do you know I'm not thinking of myself? Maybe I'm figuring on getting married soon." "Is that so?" she asked with an insolent laugh. "To whom? To the angel of death?"

Holtzman began racking his brain again. Who stood between him

147

and Henrietta? Who could his rival be? For a rival he must have. At this juncture Braindele Kozak came to his aid. She opened his brain for him. He was an old fool, she said. If he had eyes in front of his head instead of in back, he could see who his rival was, which cat was stealing the butter.

This subtle allusion opened Holtzman's eyes to the romance between Henrietta and Rapalesco. The knowledge dealt him a double blow. "The tender little citron" stood out of his reach, and a threat hung over a new plan he had had recently hit upon.

This plan had sprung full blown from his brain one fine morning after he had received a letter from his mother, Sarah-Brocha.

To my dear, beloved son, Hirsch-Bear Holtzman, Greetings! I am writing to you, my beloved Hirsch-Bear by the hand of Itzik the *Melammed's* son. First of all, I want you to know that I am, God be thanked, in the best of health, hoping to hear the same from you in the future. Amen. Second, I want you to know that I haven't heard from you in a long time, and I don't know what to think any more. I beg you, dear Hirsch-Bear, write me about your health and how you are doing. Your sister Zlatka sends her regards. I wish you could see what a fine young woman she has turned out to be, you wouldn't know her, she has grown so, and she is as pretty a girl as you will see anywhere, and a heart of gold. I don't say this because I am her mother, that's what everyone says. When I look at her, my heart aches, it's time to think of her future, she can't sit with a needle and thread stitching shirts all her days. It's time to think of a match. I have suitors aplenty for her, not one but a thousand. But they're all fit for kindling wood. One is Yossel the Carpenter's son Fishel; the other is a butcher boy, his name is Rueben, but she won't have him, she says he smells. Yossel the Carpenter's son is crazy for her, but he's a no-good, a charlatan, doesn't have a pair of shoes to his name, and jumps around like a grasshopper. I've told him more than once to forget what my daughter's name is or I'll show him the gate, but young men these days are worse than pigs, if you drive them out of the door, they crawl in through the window. If your Uncle Zalman were only alive he'd make short work of him, but what can I do, a widow alone, and poor besides? If I had a dowry to give her, if I could stuff some young fellow's mouth with at least a hundred and fifty rubles, she'd have been a bride by now. She has suitors aplenty, not one but a thousand. I wish I had as few worries about money, as I have about that, she is getting prettier every day, if you saw her you wouldn't know her. She sends her regards and I beg you, dear son, write at once and tell me how you are and especially about your health. I don't know what to think any more. Keep well, dear son, with

148

best wishes from your mother who hopes to hear good news from you.

Sarah-Brocha Holtzman.

The words, "You wouldn't know her, she's getting prettier every day," inspired Holtzman's latest plan.

"If she's really as my mother says, it would be an idea to have her come here and put her next to the 'kid.' If she takes his fancy, who knows?" And Holtzman locked himself up in private with his new secretary, the prompter, and dictated this letter to his mother:

> To my dear mother, Sarah-Brocha, many blessings, and to my dear sister Zlatka, many blessings—
> Be informed, my dear mother, that I am, thank God, in the best of health and I am not an actor any more. I have, God be praised, a theater of my own and a troupe of actors. I have prospered and I live like a human being, dress like a human being, hold my head up, and walk out among people like a human being, and I have made myself a name in the world. One thing only I lack—I have no home. And so I have resolved on this: that you take Zlatka and come here to me without any delay. You will make a home for me, and you will be mistress of it. You've stood at strange ovens long enough. It's time you rested your old bones and get a taste of what life is like. And about Zlatka, don't worry at all. I have a finer match for her than Yossel the Carpenter's son, finer even than Rueben the butcher. So do not delay and come right to me, together with Zlatka.
>
> Your devoted son, Bernhard Holtzman.
Director of the Theater, Holtzman, Shwalb & Co.

His mother's answer was to the effect that she was, thank God, in the best of health, and Zlatka also, who had grown to be such a fine young woman he wouldn't know her; and about their coming to him she would have flown to him at once if she had wings, but how could she come when it cost money, people's traveling expenses, and the border to cross. If she only had what the tickets cost, she would have married off her daughter long ago, there were suitors aplenty, not one but a thousand. A beautiful girl, if he only saw her, etc., etc.

Holtzman sent her money at once, warning her not to dare marry off Zlatka, but bring her along. This letter was followed by another and another, until God finally came to his aid. One mild evening late in summer—the troupe was then playing in a small town in Galicia— a commotion was heard outside the theater just before curtain time,

149

and Holtzman got word a poor old woman and a young girl were asking for him.

"A curse on you, bastards, those are my guests," yelled Holtzman, rushing outside.

"Your guests? Then we wish you a *maz'l tov*. May you enjoy their company," said his colleagues, and followed him outside to take a look.

It was a cool, clear September night. The moon had not yet risen, but the sky with its few trembling stars held enough light for Holtzman's colleagues to discern a tall, bony woman with the look of an overworked nag, hung with bundles and baskets and surrounded by quilts, pillows, and featherbeds, and beside her, like a timid colt, a young girl with rounded cheeks, a childish turned-up nose, and downcast eyes fringed with long lashes. Her short, tight jacket strained across her young breasts.

The old woman went up to each actor in turn, gazed into his eyes anxiously, then turned away shaking her head, until she came to Holtzman. Then she lifted up her voice in a loud cry, half-joyous, half-keening. "Ai, ai, thunder strike me. A plague take me. Woe to a poor mother. Is this you, Hirsch-Bear, my beloved son?"

Actors, always playing dramatic parts on the stage, recoil from emotional scenes in real life. They turned their backs on the old woman to inspect the young girl in the faded dress and tight jacket, who stood shyly aside. They took in with silent approval the swell of her young breasts, the curve of her cheeks, and the sweep of her lashes. The only one to speak was Isaac Shwalb, who muttered under his nose, "A little apple!"

His remark passed unnoticed this time. When people who are in the habit of gazing daily at bloodless, wrinkled faces covered with paint, at false teeth, pencilled eyebrows, dyed hair, painted smiles, and corseted figures with unnaturally high busts, are suddenly confronted by a face and figure breathing natural freshness and charm, they can only stand and gape. They calculate, wonder, appraise, and remember that once they, too, were young and unspoiled. And involuntarily a sigh of envy toward the newcomer and of vindictiveness against the whole world escapes from their lips.

Though his young sister had made such a dynamic impression on the actors, Holtzman himself felt put out. It went against the grain that he, director of the theater, who lived like a human being, dressed

150

like a human being, and held his head up among his fellows, should be related to such paupers. He gave vent to his irritation by cursing the actors roundly and chasing them off, and by the same token, showing his guests who was master here. He could not only chase the actors out; he could give his partner a tongue-lashing too. "Listen, you water-ox, you potbelly, you glutton, why are you hanging around here with the rest of the riffraff?"

Holtzman then turned over the management of the evening's performance to Shwalb and took his guests, along with their featherbeds, pillows, quilts, and bundles of rags, to his lodging.

The next day, after the evening's performance, Holtzman assembled the whole company and treated them to beer in honor of the guests. The two women now looked more presentable, Sarah-Brocha in her Sabbath shawl, like a mare draped in a blanket, and Zlatka, with her hair washed and braided, charming the entire company anew.

"A little apple," Shwalb rumbled once more. This time the entire company heard and roared with laughter.

Henrietta Shwalb and Madame Cherniak laughed along with the rest. But their laughter had a strained sound. They had been in an ill humor all day, Henrietta disgruntled because there was another pretty girl in the world, at whom Rapalesco had already glanced. She tried to find fault with the newcomer's looks, noting her red, chapped hands and her pointed nose. So she laughed along with the actors in a high artificial voice, which the actors called "laughing out of the wrong side of the mouth."

But it was Madame Cherniak who was really to be pitied. Ugly red splotches appeared on her round moonlike face; unshed tears glittered in her small Oriental eyes. Yet she held her head high and laughed as loudly and as frequently as the others. The actors dubbed this "the laughter of an unwashed corpse."

Madame Cherniak sensed that now she would have to yield her place to the old witch, on whom she wished, with all her heart, a sudden illness and a quick death. Braindele knew very well the taste of exile and banishment. This wasn't the first time she had been thrown out like a broken dish. "Now, this wily Holtzman," she thought, "will pretend to play dead. He'll forget everything we talked about, and if I try to remind him, he'll fall into a coughing fit that will last half an hour."

Poor Braindele Kozak. Everything turned out just as her heart

151

foretold. Holtzman didn't so much as acknowledge her services, or thank her for running his home and guarding his health. And when he saw her open her mouth to speak, he doubled over in a fit of coughing.

Quietly, without any formal farewells or a single tear, Madame Cherniak moved that same day to a new lodging. Having packed her trunks, she smoothed her dress, composed her features, wrapped the voluminous red cape around her, and smiling and with her usual dancing step, she left Holtzman's household and his employ.

"He who changes his place changes his luck," the jesting actors callously called after her.

"I'll pay Holtzman back for this, unless I'm first laid in the ground and the grass grows over me," Braindele vowed to herself.

For the first few days, while Sarah-Brocha and Zlatka were still guests, Holtzman treated them as such. He saw to it that they ate, drank, and lacked for nothing. He showed them all his "splendor and wealth" and didn't leave them alone for a moment. Every evening he gave them choice seats at the theater. Zlatka, as might be expected, was enraptured by all she saw. Even the old woman, who despised the theater and everything about it as a good Jew despises pork, pretended to enjoy it. She watched the stage with one eye and the audience with the other, laughed at the "comedians" and cursed them in a loud voice that carried all through the theater, until Holtzman had to shush her from the wings. In a word, mother and daughter bathed in milk and honey.

But the welcome wore out and Holtzman took his mother and sister in hand. He began teaching them manners and deportment, how to stand, how to walk, how to behave among people. He put gloves on Zlatka's hands to hide their roughness. He bought her a hat with a curling feather almost like the prima donna's and a dress like a princess's in which she felt cramped and constrained. The hat hurt her head, the corset made her gasp for breath, and the thought of people watching her made her giddy and self-conscious. She would gladly have changed back into her old dress and jacket and her comfortable old shoes.

Comparing his sister in her new attire to the prima donna, Holtzman found her not a bad-looking girl. The only trouble was that she was bashful and tongue-tied in company. She had to be livened up, made more "civilized." He watched the "kid" talking to Zlatka and saw her blush and lower her eyes. He motioned to her to lower her hands and raise her eyes. She blushed even harder. When they were alone, Holtzman lit into her. "Why are you afraid to look a person in the eyes? Did you steal something, or what?" When he caught her without her gloves, he bellowed, "Are you showing off your little rosy fingers?"

He got into worse difficulties with his mother. "Why should the director's mother go around looking like a ragpicker?" he asked. If he was ashamed of his old mother, she replied, she would just turn the shafts of her wagon around and drive straight back home where she came from. Without further ado she began throwing her featherbeds and pillows together, and called out to Zlatka, "Come along, daughter. Why should we ragpickers stick around here with the gentry? We might brush against them and soil their fine clothes."

Holtzman had to eat his words. And he got it even worse when he set out to make an actress of his sister. The old woman stood her ground like a balky old horse. "Once for all, no. I'd sooner drop dead than let my daughter dance on a rope with all those comedians. Only after I am dead and they put coppers on my eyes . . ." Holtzman was bathed in a cold sweat and he actually began spitting blood.

Then the old woman became frightened, and wailed aloud, "Woe is me, woe is me. A plague take me. Thunder strike me." And she gave her consent, but on one condition. Holtzman made an oath before two witnesses that he would find Zlatka a husband within half a year.

The witnesses were Holtzman's new confidant, "the man of education," and his partner, Isaac Shwalb, who himself hankered after "the little apple." He declared himself willing and ready to marry his partner's sister, thinking Holtzman would grab him with both arms. But Holtzman acted indifferent. He had something else in mind. Neither Sarah-Brocha nor Zlatka knew. It had never occurred to the mother to think of Rapalesco as a suitor for her daughter, and Zlatka didn't permit herself to think of such happiness, except perhaps in her dreams.

After many months of touring, the troupe of Holtzman, Shwalb & Co. arrived in Chernovitz, ancient capital of Bukovina. There we left them, as the reader will recall, at the famous hostelry, "Under the Black Rooster," deep in a game of "tertel-mertel." The banker, Isaac Shwalb, dealt out cards feverishly. Rapalesco was winning, and the crowd envied him openly.

"What a run of luck! Three times in a row he breaks the bank."

"A naked man must have crossed his path."

"He was born with a caul."

"Rapalesco again! He's raking in the whole pot."

"Every last copper."

"Shwalb, you're a corpse. *Yiskadal, v'iskadash.*" They quoted in mockery from the mourning prayer.

Each time Rapalesco swept up a heap of coins, he took the winnings to his partner, Zlatka. As he poured the coins into her open palms, he looked into her starry eyes with an expression which seemed to say, "I know why you're so blissful, my girl. It isn't the money, but something else that puts those stars into your eyes."

Nobody noticed it except Holtzman, who could see everything without looking, and hear when no one spoke. He thought in his heart, "May no evil eye fall on the 'kid.' He's walking right into our stable. If God wills it, we'll soon show the world what's what."

"Water-ox, why are you gaping? Deal out the cards!" Holtzman shouted at his partner, Shwalb.

"I'm dealing, I'm dealing," answered Shwalb, picking up the deck. Just then there was a knock at the door, and a messenger came in with a telegram. "For whom?" shouted the actors. "For Isaac Shwalb. "From where?" "From London." "What's it say?" "Wait, let him read it." "How can he? The poor fellow can't read."

Shwalb wound up the game and paid off his losses. This took time, for you needed the head of a prime minister to remember how much each one had put into the pot.

Then he ran outside to have the desk clerk read him the telegram, while the crowd waited impatiently. What secrets could Shwalb be keeping from his partner, Holtzman? Holtzman himself sat like a whipped cur, cursing the day he had tied himself to this gross creature. "A cholera take this cigarette-twister," he was muttering under his breath when Shwalb returned with a shining face and announced to the company, "Children, we're going to London."

Pandemonium greeted this announcement. One actor leaped on the table, raised his right arm aloft and shouted, "London! Long live London!" Another slapped himself on the thigh. "London's just where I want to go, the devil take me." A third, a long, skinny creature in checkered trousers, showed off his English, rolling his eyes and drawling, "Oh, yes, yes. You hear my dear. I like I strike. My ring my king." Others slapped each other on the back, danced, and sang.

154

"Be still, you bastards!" yelled Holtzman, pounding on the table. "Look at them going crazy. You'd think it's their grandmother's golden wedding. Show respect for your elders and betters."

Then, turning to Shwalb, he said in a low voice, but with a hint of menace in it, "Show us the telegram, Shwelbele."

Shwalb began hemming and hawing. "Show you the telegram? Certainly. Why not? You think I won't show it to you? I'll show it to you, I'll show it to you. Not now, a little later. First I have something to tell you. Come with me to the Cellar. I'll show it to you there."

And Shwalb said to the company, "Who's going to the Cellar with me?"

A chorus answered, "What do you mean, who? All of us."

"To the Cellar. To the Cellar."

And the horde of actors burst out of the Black Rooster and made their way in a body to the Cellar.

The Cellar was not actually a cellar but a whole building; and not a building but a wine shop; and not just any wine shop, but Meyer Beshel's. In Chernovitz, when you said you were going to the Cellar, everyone took it for granted you meant Meyer Beshel's.

Meyer Beshel himself passed for a German. He spoke German, wore a top hat and was clean-shaven. But that was beside the point. If you wanted a glass of Yiddish wine, and Muscatel at that, made in Rumania, you had only to ask for it. And if you were hungry and wanted a piece of meat, you got a good piece of kosher veal, too. (If you preferred to call it *wiener schnitzel,* that was your privilege.) Or if you wanted to, you could have a genuine home-made pot roast. (If you preferred to call it goulash, it became goulash.) With this roast or goulash Meyer Beshel's served genuine kosher dill pickles, or if you preferred, German salt cucumbers. It wasn't the name that mattered, but the flavor. And at Meyer Beshel's everything had the genuine Yiddish flavor. If you craved a carrot *tsimmes,* the Sabbath pudding, in the middle of the week, or a potato *kugel* or noodles and cheese, you got those, too. As long as you had the money, Meyer Beshel was an excellent host and a good fellow, though he was as fat as King Og and had a sinister, cross-eyed look.

In the Cellar, noted not only for its food and drink but for its convivial atmosphere, no one could get bored or lonely. If there was nobody else to talk to, there was always Meyer Beshel himself. The moment you crossed his doorstep you became his guest, whose visit he

155

had to make a pleasant one. He regaled his clients with all the gossip in Chernovitz. His tales about his townspeople, all told, of course, in strict confidence and all accompanied by the sweetest of smiles, could make your hair stand on end. Listening to him, you wondered, "Am I asleep? Is this a dream? Or is the man a consummate liar?"

In spite of this, you could find among Meyer Beshel's patrons the finest citizens of Chernovitz, community leaders, businessmen, officials. Though they were used to speaking German elsewhere, when they descended into Meyer Beshel's Cellar, they descended a step further and spoke Yiddish, and a Yiddish unheard since the Diaspora began.

To this Cellar, then, the actors repaired in a body. Some ordered a *tsimmes,* others a pot roast with pickles, or only pickles, depending on the state of their pocketbooks after the game of "tertel-mertel."

"Today it's my turn to stand drinks," Isaac Shwalb announced, and ordered glasses of wine all around. He and Holtzman took a small table apart as befitted directors with important business to discuss.

His first glass of wine loosened Isaac Shwalb's tongue and he began telling his story to Holtzman from beginning to end, every word of it true, may God punish him if he lied even this much. In brief, he had long ago come to feel himself in Holtzman's way, a hindrance and stumbling block. Yet he had stuck with him. Because of whom? Because of his sister, the prima donna. But recently the prima donna had gone out of style, so to speak, after they had discarded their fine operettas and farces for such trash as *Uriel Acosta.* Since then it had been Rapalesco and nothing but Rapalesco. For himself he didn't care. They wanted *Uriel Acosta?* Let it be *Uriel Acosta.* But what to do with his sister? She ate him up alive. She, too, had a soul, she said. She too craved applause. So he had written a letter to his brother Nissel in London, telling him thus and so. He, Isaac, was in the habit of doing this. When he had a problem, he wrote straight to his brother Nissel in London. And he got a reply. "Imbecile that you are," wrote his brother Nissel from London, "how much longer will you drag yourself over the provinces? Take our sister with you and come to me in London. I have an excellent opportunity for you. We have a fine little theater here called the Pavilion Theater. The artists are nothing but sticks, one worse than the next. And yet they shovel in gold. For the public here hasn't been spoiled. Whatever you throw to them they swallow down and lick their fingers. I have talked with the right people, and they told me, 'Just write your brother to come here and bring your sister, the prima donna. We've heard about her and

156

read of her in the papers. Good news travels fast.' " And so on in the same vein. So Isaac sent a letter to his brother Nissel in London, telling him thus and so. "It's easy to say, 'Pick up and come! but you have to know what you're coming for. You need conditions, guarantees, contracts." An answer came from his brother. "You ox, when I tell you to come, ask no questions, but come. We are ready with everything—conditions, guarantees, contracts." Isaac wrote back: "I have so much and so much and my sister has so much and so much. Send us a telegram and we'll come." And so the telegram came.

"Well, what do you say about my brother?" said Shwalb, thrusting his red face under Holtzman's nose.

"What should I say?" answered Holtzman coldly, examining the tips of his fingers. "I told you long ago you aren't worth the scrap of leather in your brother's bootsoles. It's good to be here in Chernovitz when you have a brother like Nissel in London. That goes without saying. But I'd like to take a look at that telegram."

Shwalb took a gulp of wine. "Why, can you read it then?"

"I don't have to read it. I just want a look."

"There's nothing to look at. A telegram like all telegrams." And Shwalb held the paper up against the window. In that instant the telegram was in Holtzman's hands.

He called over his secretary, "the man of education," who read it aloud: "Don't dare come to London without Rapalesco."

Holtzman gave his partner no time to speak. Tearing the paper out of the prompter's hands, he slapped Shwalb smartly across the face with it.

23 **SAD NEWS**

The famous troupe, Holtzman, Shwalb & Co., was preparing to leave for London. Nissel Shwalb had already sent them a clipping from a London Yiddish newspaper with these headlines:

SENSATIONAL! STUPENDOUS!

Leo Rapalesco, the great Yiddish star, who has taken the continent by storm, will soon appear in London at the Pavilion Theater.

157

The company's last engagement in Chernovitz was sponsored by a certain youth organization made up of dissidents of the Chassidic population. Young people poured into Chernovitz from the surrounding towns of Ostritza, Sitzka, Shifenitz, Novoseletz, Sadegoro, Boyair, Shotz, places into which a Yiddish theater had never penetrated before, since the majority of the population, fervent *Chassidim,* eschewed all worldly pleasures. Apparently the name "Rapalesco" had even reached this wilderness. The youthful dissidents had defied their elders to come to Chernovitz to see *Uriel Acosta,* a play about a young heretic.

That evening Rapalesco surpassed even himself in his portrayal of Acosta, a quiet, withdrawn, lonely philosopher, a true Spinoza. With spontaneous, intuitive understanding, earnestly and simply, he showed the meaning of true courage, that the true hero was not the armed conqueror of his fellowmen, but he who fought and won victories over his own soul.

Nowhere else had Rapalesco's acting caused such a sensation. The young men in the audience, still dressed in Chassidic garb, with curling earlocks, long gabardines and fringed shawls, themselves stood for revolt against authority. They, like Acosta, waged a war against superstition. They, too, though they had won over themselves, were the victims of reaction; they fell, as Acosta had fallen. . . . They saw mirrored on the stage their own heroism and their own anguish. And they responded with thunderous applause, and gave Rapalesco an ovation such as he had never had before. Long after the lights went out and the hall was empty, a crowd still milled about the doors eager to see Rapalesco once more and to touch the hem of his garments, the theater attendants helpless against the mob of zealots. But Rapalesco had gone.

Here is what had happened. Right after the first act, Holtzman, who stood guard over his protégé at all times, had seen among the Chernovitz youth pushing backstage an older man with a luxuriant beard, bulging eyes, and a lugubrious face. Instantly suspicious, Holtzman had told him to step back. "Uncle," he said mildly, "don't imitate that which squeals and don't crawl where you're not wanted."

After the second act, the bearded character with the bulging eyes reappeared. Holtzman now told him in more pointed language to make himself scarce. "Look at the hog. I tell him to stop shoving and he plays dead."

After the third act Holtzman caught him three steps from Rapalesco's door, picked him up by the collar and threw him out bodily,

158

cursing him and all other vermin who tried to crawl in underfoot. But while the actors were changing their clothes, Holtzman saw the lugubrious character squeeze himself into Rapalesco's dressing room. Like a roused tiger, Holtzman rushed in after him, only to find him and Rapalesco embracing each other like long-lost brothers.

Holtzman's mouth fell open. If his dead father had appeared to him from the other world, he couldn't have been more thunderstruck. He stood like a clay image, like a half-finished statue of fear. His pockmarked face, pitted with dark holes, and his narrowed eyes seemed to say, "Help, people, help! Tear me to pieces. Throw my flesh to the dogs. But tell me first who's this creature who has fallen on the 'kid's' neck."

The reader might have guessed by now that the bearded individual with the bulging eyes was none other than Ben Rapalovich's cashier, Simcha, from Holeneshti, whom Leibel had once nicknamed Joy-and-Gladness. He and Rapalesco left the theater quietly by a side entrance and went straight to the Black Rooster, Holtzman trailing after them. There Rapalesco asked Holtzman pointedly to be left alone with his guest for the evening.

"With the greatest pleasure," said Holtzman, while his eyes glared balefully at the intruder. Holtzman called out in a loud voice, so that the whole company might hear, that Rapalesco was not to be disturbed. He himself, may it not be counted to his discredit, went to his own room, next to Rapalesco's, and put his ear to the keyhole.

Joy-and-Gladness, when we left him in Bucharest in the company of Anshel, was a gloomy-looking youth with a growth on his lips covered by a mustache. Now, God be thanked, he was a married man, with two children, and a full beard. But if anything, he looked more sleepy-eyed and lugubrious than ever. And the beard which had spread the length and breadth of his face gave him the appearance of a man well along in years and burdened with the troubles of the whole world.

Alone with Rapalesco, he began his story. "Listen to me, Leibel," said Joy-and-Gladness. "Your brother and I—do you hear me?—went out into the world to hunt for yesteryear's snow, meaning Shchupak and his gang. For when the witnesses were cross-examined by the police, the truth rose like oil upon the waters, and we knew it had all been Shchupak's doing. He had no other road but to Rumania, and so we set out for Rumania. When we got to Jassy—do you hear

159

me or not?—we began asking the people there if they had seen some
Yiddish actors, *schlimazls,* one tall and the other short, who walked
with a skip and a jump. They told us that they had seen many actors,
tall and short, but whether they walked with a skip and a jump or
skipped and jumped as they walked they had forgotten to notice.
Next time they promised to look more closely. What do you think of
those Moldavian wits? We saw there was nothing to be gained by
staying in Jassy. Bad luck—what to do next? We kept on traveling—
do you hear me or not?—until we came to Bucharest. On the way
Anshel says to me, 'Let my name not be Anshel if we don't nab them
there.' 'From your mouth,' I told him, 'into God's ears.' When we
came to Bucharest, your brother—do you hear me or not?—began to
live like a prince. May heaven protect all Jews from such debauchery.
We had brought a sackful of money along and he began throwing it
around. There wasn't a theater, a wine shop, or a cabaret he didn't
visit. I argued with him, 'Anshel,' I said, 'in God's name,' I said,
'what are you doing? You're burning money.' 'It's none of your business,' he tells me, 'Keep your mouth shut.' Bad luck—what could I
do? I kept my mouth shut. A day passed, two days, three days. Our
money is melting like snow, there's almost none left. Says he, 'Write
to my father to send more. Tell him we're hard on their trail, we're
working day and night, and it takes money.' I pleaded with him.
'Anshel,' I said, 'for God's sake, what will the outcome be?' 'It's none
of your grandfather's business,' says he. 'I tell you to write, write.'
Bad luck—what could I do? I wrote. In the meanwhile we are sitting
one night in a sort of theater or café called the 'Paradiso.' Girls all
around us buzzing like flies, some singing, some dancing, some playing on harps. And one they called Marinesco-Malinesco, not a girl
but a good-sized woman—do you hear me or not?—and a regular
gipsy for going through your pockets—is sitting with us. (Here Simcha
bared his teeth in a half-smile.) Suddenly I take a look—do you hear
me or not?—and right in the door I see two faces and I could have
sworn one was you. And I called out to Anshel, 'It's him, as I live and
breathe, it's Leibel.' 'You're dreaming,' says Anshel. I say one thing,
he says another. By the time we started to follow, it was too late.
Bad luck—what to do next? Meanwhile a letter arrives from Holeneshti that your mother is very sick and for Anshel to come straight
home. I asked Anshel, 'Are we going?' And he says, 'Write them we're
right on their trail and to send more money.' 'For God's sake, Anshel,'
I say, 'either let us go home or travel on.' And he, 'It's none of your
grandmother's business. I tell you to write—write.' Bad luck—what to

160

do next? I write. But in a disguised fashion—do you hear me or not—like a diplomat. Here is what I told your father. I told him our trip was a failure, a waste of money, pure and simple. What I had written him up till then about hunting for you night and day and how we were hard on your trail was a lie. I had only written it because Anshel had ordered me thus. What else could I do? I said. I'm only an employe. He tells me to write, so I write. 'But don't send us any more money,' I wrote. 'If we run out of funds, we'll have to come home.' That's how I wrote—do you hear me or not—like a diplomat. Maybe you think I was wrong. But what else could I do? Listen to this: a week passed, and we get a telegram from Holeneshti, 'Come home at once. Mother passed away.' "

When Joy-and-Gladness uttered these words, Rapalesco caught him by the shoulders. "What did you say? My mother . . ."

"May she rest in peace. How else could it have been, my child? Didn't she have enough sorrows to bear? She was always—may she forgive my words—nothing but skin and bones. Her body and soul barely held together. And you must remember the fine life your father led her. And on top of it one misery after another. I don't know whom she loved most—you or Anshel. And as long as Anshel stayed in Bucharest, she had hopes he would find you. But when she heard—do you hear me or not? . . ."

Rapalesco didn't hear. He put his head on his arm, and was weeping like a small child. Joy-and-Gladness began wringing his hands and muttering to himself, "Bad luck, bad luck. What shall I do?" In the meanwhile others had heard Rapalesco weeping and broke into the room. Holtzman came, and after him his mother and Zlatka. Cries and laments filled the room. "What is it? What happened?"

"My mother died," Rapalesco cried, and fell on Holtzman's neck. Holtzman made a grimace as if to cry and, looking at him, Zlatka burst into tears. Sarah-Brocha wrung her dry, bony hands and raised a lament, "Woe is me, woe is me. Thunder has struck. A mother of tiny children, of infants, of nestlings, gone from the world. Who will look after the poor orphans? Who will watch over them? Whose head will ache for the poor bereaved babes, all alone in the world. For as long as a mother is a mother, a father is a father. But when the mother goes . . . woe, woe. . . ."

"Stop this howling," roared Holtzman, then turned on the cashier in a rage. "You crazy loon, who told you to come here? Who invited you? Who tickled your tongue to speak? Such news you send through an enemy."

Joy-and-Gladness looked crestfallen, but Rapalesco came to his defense. He let Holtzman know Simcha was his guest and that he wished to be left alone with him. Holtzman disliked leaving the "kid" alone with the crazy loon, but there was no help for it. Gone the time when he could tell Rapalesco what to do. Nowadays when Rapalesco spoke, the matter ended. Holtzman vented his bitterness on the two women. "Who the devil sent for you two? Look at them blubbering. We don't need any hired mourners here." He drove them out, and followed them, only to resume his post at the keyhole.

Neither Simcha nor Rapalesco slept that night . . . nor did Holtzman. The cashier's monotonous voice droned like a hollow bell with its reiterations of "Listen to me now" and "Do you hear me or not?" and "Bad luck—what to do next?" Poor Holtzman couldn't move from the keyhole. He couldn't rise from the stool, lest in the next room they hear its scraping. With an almost superhuman effort he managed to hold back his cough. Miserably he sat through the night hearing the news of Holeneshti.

So Beilka died, while the old grandmother who shook with palsy lived on. In her dotage and blind in both eyes—she lived! Go ask questions of God! Now all the family had scattered. Ben had married off Anshel to that girl from Beltz, a homely girl but of good family. But Anshel wasn't allowed to show himself before his father. Ben never forgave him for his behavior in Bucharest. Anshel lived in Beltz and kept a tobacco shop. Pearl had divorced her husband. Judith had married, against her father's wishes, Yechiel the Musician's brother, also a musician. The youngest, Bathsheba, wanted to study midwifery, but Rapalovich forbade it, and married her off, to him, Simcha. Here Simcha lowered his eyes in embarrassment and began to defend himself. He had long had his eye on Bathsheba, but had never dared aspire to such a match. Still, wherein was Yechiel the Fiddler's brother more exalted than he? At least he, Simcha, was a member of the family, though distantly connected. Bathsheba wasn't eager for the match at first. She made scenes and wept and carried on and threatened to do away with herself. He, Simcha, wasn't happy, either. Bathsheba was a fine girl, the best of the lot, but he didn't want to take her by force. But old Rapalovich put his foot down, and the marriage went through. And it had turned out for the best. They had two children now and a third was due any day. They would be contented enough, if it weren't for another calamity.

"What other calamity?" Rapalesco asked, frightened, and Simcha calmed him. "Nothing, nothing. Just a way of speaking. Your father,

162

in his old age, and perhaps from all the grief he had been through, has turned to religion."

"Is that all?" mumbled Holtzman behind the keyhole, and spat. "Tfui, tfui, you sleepy-faced loon, may you be a scapegoat for all the Jews in Chernovitz."

And Simcha's voice droned on.

"Listen further to what I will tell you. Your father turned to religion, and not in a small way, but with full devotion. Day and night, night and day, he prayed and read psalms. Well, prayers and psalms we could put up with, if it wasn't for something much worse. He became—do you hear me or not?—a Chassid, and took up first with one rabbi, then another, first to the Rabbi of Stepanich, and then the Rabbi of Boyan. Now he's a disciple of him of Boyan. He lives there and won't come home at all. I've written him letter after letter. 'Father, for God's sake, what will the outcome be? The farm is going to wrack and ruin.' Does the wall answer when you pound on it? That's how he answers. He only keeps writing—do you hear me or not?—to send him more money. Have I got a spring that gushes gold? Or a well in my backyard? A well goes dry, too. Bad luck—what to do next? I thought it over and decided to run down to Boyan to see for myself. I can't disown the old man completely. So I come to Boyan. When I took a look at him, my heart sank. I wept—do you hear me or not?—like a child. You wouldn't have known Ben Rapalovich. His belly hangs like a sack. His cheeks are sunken, his eyes burn as with a fever. He is old and grey. I tried talking to him, but go talk to a man who is half out of this world. He only wants to take me to the rabbi. All he knows is the rabbi, the rabbi, and once more the rabbi. On the Sabbath, when the rabbi sits at the head of the table, he sits with the other disciples at the foot and picks up the leavings. When they sing, he sings with them. In the evening when the Chassidim get in a ring and dance, he dances with them. I try to talk to him and he won't listen. Tomorrow, he says, tomorrow. And so from day to day. You can't mention business to him. You can't speak of the children. Especially Anshel. Anshel, he says, is the angel of death. He murdered his mother in cold blood. If it weren't for Anshel, he, Ben wouldn't be a widower now. In the meanwhile, at the inn where I'm staying, I hear some young people talk about going to Chernovitz. There's a Yiddish theater in Chernovitz, they say, and a young actor from Bucharest by the name of Rapalesco, who will put on a play just for them. The words, *Yiddish theater, Bucharest,*

163

Rapalesco—do you hear me or not?—sank into my brain. Could this Rapalesco of Bucharest be our Leibel? And I thought it over; the journey has cost this much. Let it cost a little more. I will run down to Chernovitz and see for myself. But first I will speak about it to Father. When he heard the words, *Yiddish theater*—do you hear me or not—he grabbed a stout stick, and told me he'd split my head open if I said any more. Bad luck—what to do next? I went out and hired a wagon to take me to Chernovitz—and paid through the nose. For let's not fool ourselves—if it cost ten times as much, and if I had to make the journey on foot, would that stop me? It's been worth all that to see you alive and well. And to see the honor in which you are held. Will you believe it or not—last night when they began shouting *Rapalesco* and when the crowd lifted you on their shoulders, tears stood in my eyes. I thought—do you hear me or not?—this is the same Leibel who slept in one room with me, right in the next bed."

Joy-and-Gladness wiped away a tear and suddenly his voice and expression changed and he spoke in a coaxing tone. "Do you remember, dear soul, how we slept in the same room? I always kept my trousers with the keys in them under my pillow. That Saturday night I also put them under my pillow. Do you think I didn't hear someone moving about my bed and rustling at the desk? I heard—may I hear nothing but good news from now on as I heard that. But I couldn't pry my eyes open. What happened to that money, dear soul? I mean who kept it? The one with the ugly puckered face? Or the short fellow with the hopping step and the shifty eyes? Or that pockmarked creature who used to be called Hotzmach and who is now called Holtzman?"

A scraping sound was heard suddenly behind the wall, and both Simcha and Rapalesco started and listened. But the sound was not repeated. Rapalesco got up from his seat and began pacing back and forth. Suddenly he faced Simcha.

"And what's happened to my old teacher, the Cantor?"

"You mean Israel the Cantor? He's a big man now."

"What do you mean?"

"I mean he's rich."

"Israel the Cantor a rich man!"

"That's what I said. A rich man. He's not a cantor any more. And he doesn't teach, either. My, my. Not the same Israel at all. And his wife Leah—do you remember Leah the Cantor's wife? She wears pearls on weekdays and goes about dressed—do you hear me or not— like a rich man's wife, and boasts about her daughter wherever she

164

goes. It's 'my Reizel this' and 'my Reizel that' till everyone in Holeneshti is sick and tired of hearing about Reizel. She isn't called Reizel any more, but Rosa. She's a famous singer and gives concerts all over the world. She's in London now, they say. Not so long ago she paid us a visit in Holeneshti. She came with a whole crowd of hangers-on, singers and musicians, and they flew around Holeneshti in carriages and automobiles, raising the dust and scaring the chickens. May we both earn in a year what the journey must have cost her. Tfui. Tfui. They say she's betrothed to a fellow who has a million—do you hear me—no less than a million. All Holeneshti went crazy for her. They followed her around in the streets. She's turned out to be a real beauty and they say when she sings they all fall at her feet. And rich! You will see for yourself when I tell you what she wants to do. She wants to buy our house, that is your father's house, and for whom? For herself? No, for her parents. The Cantor won't hear of it, nor his wife. They tell her what do they need such a big hat for? It will fall over their ears. They would rather buy the widow Necha's house. But the daughter Reizel—do you hear me or not?—has put her foot down. She wants Rapalovich's house or nothing. And not just the house, but the whole farm with its barns and outbuildings. What more do you want—even the old dog Terkish—you remember him?—she wants, too. If she buys, she buys the whole business, lock, stock and barrel. What do you think of that for a cantor's daughter?"

Simcha laughed for the second time that night, but seeing Rapalesco's face, he grew sober and began to defend himself. "I wouldn't consent to selling the house on any condition. But when God sends such a buyer! I thought it over—do you hear me or not?—and decided to let her have it for a stiff price. Why not? Do you think I was wrong? If a cantor's daughter has the nerve . . . What's wrong, Leibel? Why do you suddenly look so . . .? Are you sad because we're selling the house? Believe me, my dear boy, my heart ached, too, as much as yours, and maybe even more. But what else can I do? The property is going to wrack and ruin. Your father won't stir from the rabbi's. All the children are scattered, like the sands of the ocean. Who is left at home? Only your old grandmother in her dotage, and my Bathsheba and the children. I don't count myself. What do I need? I, as you see me here, need nothing at all. I live—do you hear me or not?—as I always lived. Another man in my place—eh, eh." He drew out the last few words like the refrain of a chant, and made a sweeping gesture with his two hands to show what another man would have done in his place.

Simcha's self-justifications fell on deaf ears. Rapalesco's head whirled and his heart overflowed with conflicting emotions. Pangs of conscience, homesickness, longing, regret, eagerness, and love fought for mastery. Never in his life had he lived through such a night. In one short night he had lost both mother and father, brothers and sisters, the home in which he was born and the town in which he had grown up—all lost to him forever. An eternity suddenly separated him from his past life. Everything turned as dark as a starless night and was as full of mystery; and from this impenetrable darkness one tiny pinpoint of life beckoned to him, Reizel. The dreams they had once dreamed together had come true for her. Not for him . . . Did he envy her? No. He only grieved that for him no one remained in Holeneshti. For him Holeneshti held a graveyard.

Rapalesco wondered about one thing. What drew Reizel to Holeneshti he could easily see. She hadn't lost everything as he had. But why did she want to buy his old home for her parents? Why that house only and not another? Did his home have a special meaning for her? Was the house dear to her because he had been born and raised in it? Could it be that she still loved him?

And he recalled that night of beauty and fire and grandeur on God's Street; of terror and enchantment, when Reizel had stood before him in an aureole of fire, herself a princess of darkness and fire. Ah, youth, youth. Where are the tears you cannot dry? Where is the grief you cannot console? How deep lies the wound you cannot heal? Leibel forgot in this moment the whole ruin of his home, the loss of his heritage, and thought of only one thing: to get to London as quickly as possible and renew his search for Reizel.

Outside, dawn flicked across the sky. The market place opposite the Black Rooster began to show signs of life. And still Rapalesco and Simcha talked, that is, Simcha talked and Rapalesco listened. And behind the door Holtzman, drooping with weariness, his ear to the keyhole, listened too. When Rapalesco questioned Simcha's recital once or twice, and Simcha began swearing by all that was dear to him, by his wife and children and his hopes of returning to them alive, that all he said was gospel truth, Holtzman almost choked with laughter. But when Simcha inquired about the money stolen from the desk, Holtzman started so suddenly, his stool scraped the floor. A silence followed during which Holtzman held his breath painfully. Did they suspect him of eavesdropping? He waited for a knock on the

166

wall, but when none came, he relaxed and listened again. How would the "kid" answer this question?

But next he heard the words: "And what's happened to my old teacher, the Cantor?"

"The kid's no fool," thought Holtzman, hugging himself in glee. "That one asks about money and he answers with an old teacher. If so, I can afford to go to sleep. It's almost day. That sleepy-faced loon—the ragpickers take him—has almost put me to sleep with his droning."

When Holtzman awoke several hours later, it was broad daylight. He got up and knocked briskly on Rapalesco's door.

"Who is it?" a sleepy voice called out.

"It is I, Bernhard." And Holtzman pushed open the door and strode in, bringing with him a gust of fresh air.

He glanced at Rapalesco, who lay stretched out on the sofa, fully dressed, but strangely flushed and disheveled, then at the gloomy guest, who looked like a sleepy small-town sexton during penitential week. Holtzman had an almost overpowering impulse to haul out the intruder by the scruff of his neck; but he said with a forced smile, "Just take a look. You didn't sleep at all."

"No," said Rapalesco. "We didn't sleep."

Holtzman glanced at the untouched bed and smiled again. "You didn't even lie down."

"We didn't lie down," said Simcha, stifling a yawn.

"You sat up all night blabbing?"

"All night." Simcha nodded.

"Well, it's time to get ready for our journey," said Holtzman with a sharp look at the "kid."

"I'm ready," said Rapalesco, jumping off the sofa, his face shining with eagerness.

"A kid remains a kid," thought Holtzman. "Thank God he didn't take it into his head to sit down and mourn for his dead mother for seven days and seven nights. Or what if he'd suddenly taken a notion to run down to the Rabbinical Court at Boyan to see his father?"

All morning Holtzman didn't let Rapalesco and his guest out of sight. But he needn't have worried. Rapalesco himself breathed easier when he had helped his new brother-in-law climb into the wagon for his journey home. The wagon overflowed with Chassidic youths returning from Chernovitz, going back with heavy hearts. God alone knew when, in their circumscribed lives, they would again have the opportunity to behold an artist like Rapalesco.

167

"With your heads sunk in the ground!" Holtzman blessed them, and turned to the actors. "Now, children, to work."

The actors started packing and loading the wagons, while over them stood their director, his hat shoved back on his head and sweat pouring down his face, ordering them about as Shchupak had once been ordering him.

"Not that way, this way. The small box first, then the big one. I mean the other way around. First the big one, then the small one. Hey, you, why are you standing there like a clay image? Grab hold of the right end, and he'll grab the left. I mean the other way around, you take the left and let him take the right. What are you watching me for with that dumb look? Better watch how you're carrying King Solomon's throne, may you be carried out feet first. Easy with that crown, you bastard; if you break the crown, I'll break your head for you."

For every question Holtzman found a fitting curse in answer. If someone told him they were short of rope, he said, "May you be short of breath." If an actor asked, "Where shall I put this?" he said, "Put yourself in the grave." "Shall I tie up this trunk?" "Tie yourself into knots." "We need another wagon." "What you need is a brain stroke." "He wants us to give him more money." "May God give you a new soul."

He invented a brand-new curse on the spot, a longish one, but effective for all that. "May you get as many pimples on your tongue as the number of holes that have been punched in all the matzos the Jews have eaten since their exodus from Egypt."

Into the midst of all this Sarah-Brocha advanced with her bundles of bedding.

"So you're here, too, with your rags!" Holtzman shouted at her. "I'll rip open your featherbeds and scatter the feathers to the four winds."

"May God help you in your work," said the old woman without rancor. She was the only one of those about Holtzman who wasn't afraid of him.

Holtzman spat in reply, and the old woman went off. She was back almost immediately. What now? Nothing. She only wanted her son to step into the house for a bite. "Look at him" she said. "Nothing but skin and bones. His clothes flap around on him as on a scarecrow. A corpse has a better-fed look. His cheeks are so hollow you can hear his teeth rattle. Health and joy are to be found at the table. Eating, unlike dressing, is no vanity. . . ."

Sarah-Brocha would have gone on pouring out her stock of folk-

168

sayings but Holtzman, in no mood to listen, interrupted. "Will you stop jawing or not? Don't you ever run out of words?"

Then he was seized with a fit of coughing, and the actors looked on, tittering behind their hands.

No. Holtzman was not in good spirits today. The journey to London stuck like a bone in his throat. He could neither swallow it nor spit it out. He didn't know why, but his heart felt heavy. He had dreamed of old women last night. A bad omen. May all the bad luck fall on their heads.

24 MR. KLAMMER

Now that the wandering troupe, Holtzman, Shwalb & Co., has safely embarked for London, we shall forsake the hero, as the romances put it, and turn to the heroine. But first a digression, a brief visit to Whitechapel, the London Jewish quarter.

At the time of our writing, Whitechapel was a sort of Berdichev or Vilno or Brod, or all three rolled into one, with maybe Jerusalem thrown in. Nowhere did the pulse of Yiddish life beat so hard or fast. Nowhere could a Jew feel more at home. The sights and sounds and smells were East European, the language our language, the tumult, the running, the shouting, the whole tempo of life our own. Even the ways of making a livelihood.

What I am trying to say is that the Jews of Berdichev or Vilno or Brod had accomplished nothing new in Whitechapel. They lived off each other just as before, tore the food out of each other's hands as they always had done. Did I say hands? They literally tore the bites out of each other's mouths. In a word, if a Jew came to Whitechapel, he had come home. He had no trouble at all finding a Jewish lodging, a Jewish synagogue, or a Jewish meal.

And speaking of meals brings us straight to Whitechapel's foremost restaurant, a place known as the "Café National." This was not only a restaurant but a club, a gathering-place for both natives and stragglers passing through London. On entering the Café National, day or night, you would find a conglomeration of Jews of every type and occupation and political creed. Stockbrokers, doctors of philosophy,

169

traveling salesmen, missionaries, peddlers, actors, diamond merchants, office workers, journalists, chess players, clerks, Zionists, Territorialists, and young men of indeterminate background and calling who filled the club day and night with argument and smoke. The noisiest, the most argumentative, and the one who blew most smoke was Mr. Klammer, the proprietor of the restaurant.

Mr. Klammer was a Galician Jew, a man of distinguished appearance with a trim beard like Theodore Herzl's. By virtue of this beard and his stately appearance, Mr. Klammer counted himself a Zionist, though by conviction he leaned somewhat more toward Territorialism. Actually he did not belong to any party or faction, for Mr. Klammer, you understand, something of a skeptic, believed in nobody but himself. But since people often told him that his beard matched Herzl's like a twin, he enrolled himself in the ranks of the Zionists, with one reservation. If Mr. Zangwill happened to find a suitable territory for the Jews to migrate to, he, Mr. Klammer, would not oppose him. Dr. Herzl was certainly a great man and a gentleman, but then Mr. Zangwill was no "*boychik*," either.

Live and let live—that was Mr. Klammer's motto, his guiding principle. For Mr. Klammer was, above all, a man of principle. He prided himself on his fluent English and considered himself a man of the world and a scholar. There was nothing he did not know something about, nothing he wouldn't venture an opinion on. His business, the restaurant, was as abhorrent to him as pork to a devout Jew. He ignored all the details of running it, except one: he always accepted money willingly. But when no money came in, he resigned himself to that, too. He followed the principle, "All ye who are hungry, enter and be fed." Which meant that if a Jew came to his restaurant, ate and drank his fill, and went off to America, could he go chasing after him?

A worthy principle. The only trouble was Mr. Klammer repeated it again and again in a loud voice, taking credit for both worldliness and generosity. He talked about himself constantly, having no other occupation but talk. His wife did all the work in the restaurant, not seeing the light of day till Saturday afternoon, when she put on her Sabbath dress and hat and became transformed into a "lady." Even then she first saw to it that her husband had his breakfast and dinner properly served to him. Most of the day you could see Mr. Klammer stalking about the club fingering his Herzl beard, or at a table having a beer with a guest, to whom he lamented his hard luck. "Woe is me, that I, Mr. Klammer, must sell noodles! But what can I do

170

when I have to eat, too? Or as the Englishman says, 'You must work for a living.' "

Mr. Klammer loathed the restaurant business. His great desire was to take part in community affairs, to stick his finger into the doings of London's charitable organizations, to give opinions about the Russian immigrants, whom he invariably called *"Katzaps"* or *"Schnorrers,"* and who, according to him, should all hang on one rope. If you conclude from this that Mr. Klammer was a hard-hearted man, or that English Jews were dear to him, you are sadly mistaken. He could berate the rich London Jews as well, though he took care to do it behind their backs.

Mr. Klammer was a touchy man. Cross him once and you remained in his bad graces forever. All too eagerly he jumped into any discussion feet first. "Friends, let me tell you, you haven't the least notion of what you're talking about. It costs nothing to throw words around, or as the Englishman says, 'Talk is cheap.' " Saying which, he fingered his Herzl beard and threw a sharp look around him. "What, actually, is the subject of your conversation?"

This was Mr. Klammer, proprietor of the "Café National" where every visitor to Whitechapel landed sooner or later. And here, among others, came a certain Yiddish actor, a *schlimazl,* of short stature, and queer hopping step, a hoarse voice, and shrewd eyes. He ate and drank on credit for two weeks, assuring Mr. Klammer he had a friend in London, a young woman who was a famous singer or musician, he didn't make it clear which. It was difficult, said this actor, to approach her, but when he did, he would be showered with gold as a bridegroom is showered with rice. One day this actor, this *schlimazl,* came to Mr. Klammer and asked for the loan of a few shillings for a run over to Brighton, the swanky resort, to see this singer or musician. In the meanwhile he entrusted to Mr. Klammer's keeping a satchel which he asked him to put under lock and key, since it contained valuable documents. "All right," Mr. Klammer said. "If you say so, it must be so, or as the Englishman puts it, 'Seeing is believing.' " Mr. Klammer lent the actor the few shillings and locked up the satchel in his desk. He waited a day, two days, three days, a month and even a year, but the *schnorrer* never showed up. One day Mr. Klammer took it into his head to look into the bag and see what valuable documents were in it, or as the Englishman says, "What trash it holds." He looked. There was a packet of letters, written in Yiddish, unsigned, each with a salutation, "Dear friend," or "Beloved," or "Dearest." Mr. Klammer was properly disgusted. "All

171

right," he thought to himself. "May all the nightmares fall on his head, the *schlimazl* who left these 'documents.' What do I need them for? I'll throw them out, or as the Englishman says, 'Get rid of the rubbish.' "

But when he started reading these letters, left by Sholom Meyer, whom you have surely recognized by now, he could not put them down. And such letters. They take you as on wings back to God's Street, where at midnight Reizel waited for Sholom Meyer, her "deliverer.". . .

Each minute was like an hour. An hour? It was more like a day, a year. When the town clock finished striking twelve, Reizel raised herself slowly from her bed, cautiously opened the window, and leaned out. The night was pitch dark. Nothing stirred. There was no sound. Then suddenly she heard the signal agreed upon. Her legs and arms trembled. She said to herself, "Reizel, shut the window. Reizel, pull the covers over your head and say good night." Then she remembered Leibel and their pledge. And she took courage.

"Goodbye, dear Father and Mother. Goodbye, Holeneshti. The Cantor's daughter bids you farewell. No more Reizel. 'The bird has flown from the cage.' " What would her father say when he found out she had run off? But she was already out the window. . . .

When, after crossing the border, she discovered they were not in Rumania at all, she became hysterical with anguish. She tore her hair and screamed and wept till she scared her companions out of their wits. The director became alarmed and got away as soon as he could.

Left alone with Sholom Meyer, she began weeping as though her heart would break. He tried to console her and swore by heaven and earth no harm would come to her, and he would tell her the truth. They had actually intended to go to Rumania, but at the last moment they changed their plans because the director, Shchupak, it turned out, had two wives. He claimed that he had divorced the first long ago and had witnesses to prove it, but she denied it. The second demanded a divorce, which he wouldn't give her until she returned the money and clothes and jewels he had given her—a small fortune. She, on the other hand, claimed she had spent far more on him. Sholom Meyer said all three were right, and since all three were right, they shouldn't be allowed to meet, or they'd tear each other to pieces.

A short time before that Shchupak had received a letter from a friend warning him that his first wife had found out where he was and meant to come to Holeneshti. He had long been wanting to go to

Rumania, to Bucharest, and this bit of news gave him the push he needed.

Then go, simpleton, and be quiet about it; but no. He had to write a letter to his second wife, the undivorced one: "I am letting you know, thus and so. I am off to Rumania. It's time we put an end to this thing, once for all. If you want to come back to me, join me in Bucharest." So what does she do, this second wife? She sends him an answer: "Put an end to your first wife before you deal with the second." And she also writes to the first wife: "If you want to settle with Shchupak, come as quickly as you can to Bucharest." Shchupak learned about this half an hour before the departure of the theater troupe, in Henich the Vintner's cellar!

When Reizel asked what would happen to Hotzmach, Sholom Meyer said, "Why Hotzmach? Are you lonesome for him?" Reizel made the excuse that until the whole company was together again, she couldn't be happy. If he wanted to please her, he must see to it that every one of them came, that clown Hotzmach, too.

Sholom Meyer promised he would arrange this. Then he ran off to town and came back with a bundle of clothes for her to choose from. Then she bathed and dressed and arranged her hair, and when she looked into the mirror, she didn't recognize herself. Her tears had dried. Her eyes shone. She suddenly felt hungry. She wanted to eat, and not only to eat, but to sing. And she began singing and sang and sang like a nightingale, just as though she didn't have a care in the world. . . .

But it didn't take long for her to learn what they really had in mind. And then, the tears, the homesickness, the shame, the disillusionment!

She made her debut with a song Shchupak boasted he had written himself. But Sholom Meyer said, "You can spit in his face. Who wrote the song nobody knows." It began with the words:

"Friday in the evening
Every Jew is King."

The important thing was not the song itself, but the way you sang it. And not so much the way you sang it as the costume. They dressed her up as a young man, a *Chassid*, with earlocks pasted on her cheeks, a cap with a visor, a silk *caftan,* and tight satin pants. When she sang the song, dancing to the music at the same time, she thought the ceiling would cave in on her. The shouts of "Bravo!" "Rosa Spivak!" almost split her eardrums. The boards shook under her. The footlights swam in front of her eyes.

Shchupak and Sholom Meyer took her between them and pushed her out again. She repeated the song and dance. And when she was done, she ran backstage, threw herself on the floor, and wept.

"Kitten, you're crying. You ought to be happy. You made a hit, you made!" said Sholom Meyer. "Patti isn't worth your foot, may God grant me fortune and luck." And the director, Shchupak, stood at a distance and swelled with rapture. "Ahh, her voice is sweet, sugar-sweet, let my name not be Albret."

Overnight she became a success. Night after night, after the play was over, they served her up as a sort of dessert. And she heard people shouting, "When will they end this circus and bring on little Rosa?" She could sink into the ground from such compliments. And the way the men peered under her blouse, undressed her with their eyes, and the angry looks of their wives. She cursed the men and their wives and the Yiddish theater, and herself and the day she was born.

For a long time she believed Leibel and the others would soon arrive. But the only one who showed up was Braindele Kozak. From her Rosa learned that Sholom Meyer had never written to the other actors. "What about Hotzmach?" Rosa asked. "Hotzmach disappeared, as though into the grave."

But one day she told Rosa she had heard from a friend, a Yiddish actor, that he had seen Hotzmach strolling about Bucharest with a young fellow. Rosa's heart leaped. She could have kissed Braindele Kozak. And now they became like two sisters. Braindele opened Rosa's eyes to Shchupak and Sholom Meyer, and she taught her how to behave toward them, even if she also taught her some things Rosa could have done without. . . .

One hot summer day during rehearsal (Rosa had by then begun to do leading parts), the director received a message that a stranger wanted to see him. Whenever Shchupak heard someone was asking for him, he grew pale—because of his wives (Braindele Kozak said he had not two but three). Now Shchupak began yelling for his adviser, Sholom Meyer, who was nowhere in sight.

Meanwhile the stranger, apparently tired of waiting, broke in on them. When he and Shchupak saw each other, they fell into each other's arms. "Stellmach!" "Shchupak!" When Sholom Meyer appeared, the kissing and hugging began anew.

Stellmach was a short, stocky, dark-compexioned man, well along in years, but frisky as a youngster, with quick eyes and an oily smile.

174

He looked pleased with himself, with God, with the whole world. One virtue he had, which he himself called attention to. Though life had been good to him, and he was now a rich man, he detested putting on airs, and liked to tell everyone of his humble beginnings. While he talked, he stroked his listener's hand, or held fast to a button of his coat, so he wouldn't escape. And his tale unwound itself like a ball of yarn, full of snarls and kinks, of ups and downs, of miracles and luck, like a tale from the thousand and one nights.

Once upon a time he was—may it never happen to you or to any of our people or even to the stranger in our midst—a poor man, a pauper, burdened with a large family. . . . Not a crust of bread in his house. He lived by making lambskin caps in a small God-forsaken townlet near Berdichev, a place called Machanevka or Achanevka. He walked miles on foot to the country fairs, with his merchandise on his back, in the heat of summer and the cold of winter, his boots tied with string so the soles wouldn't fall off, and his coat full of holes like a sieve. The frost burned his face, the wind whistled through his rags, his belly rumbled with hunger, and there at home lay his sick wife surrounded by hungry children, the oldest, Herschele, not quite six.

Ever since he could toddle, Herschele had gone about beating two sticks together. "Herschele, what are you doing?" "I'm playing a fiddle." One day the father brought him a fiddle he had got from a peasant, and at sight of it the child burst into tears of joy. Where had he seen a fiddle? Who had taught him to play it? Nobody knew. But soon he was drawing tunes from it.

God willed that in the vicinity there lived a nobleman, a count or a prince, who owned the townlet and everything around. Learning about the poor Jewish capmaker who had a son said to be a musical prodigy, the count or prince or whatever he was summoned the Jew and the child and the fiddle. And when a nobleman gives an order like that, you can't be a hog and refuse. So they came.

The child was put on a table and told to play. Hearing him, the nobleman, and his wife as well, were beside themselves with rapture. "Sit down!" said the count to the father. "Why do you stand? Do you know what you have there? You have a treasure, a jewel, a diamond. You are," says he, "a millionaire. You'll be the lowest of the low if you let such a talent go to waste. Take your child to the city to study music." Says the poor father, "Your Highness, it is easy to say, 'Study music,' but I am a poor man and burdened with children." "Don't worry," says the nobleman. "You just put him in my hands and

I'll make something of him." But Stellmach wasn't the kind you pick up ten for a kopek. He thought to himself, "By the time the count makes something of him, the father will be less a child and the Jewish folk less a Jew." "No, my dear count," he says, "that's not the way. You'd better have horses harnessed and lend me a few rubles and I will take the child to Berdichev myself. It's a big town, with rich Jews. Perhaps they will help."

And so it came to pass. He arrived with the child in Berdichev. There he stopped one person after another. "What shall I do, Jewish children? I have a treasure, a jewel, a million." They looked at him as though he were out of his mind. A man in rags, dragging a barefoot child by the hand, prattles about millions, tells them a nobleman said so, and wants them to stop everything they're doing to listen! They laughed at him, cursed him, and drove him away. Some young people finally did listen, and one of them said, "Here's what we'll do. We'll get up a concert for you." The father gaped. What in heaven's name was a concert? But if they said concert, let it be concert.

Well, they rented a hall, had posters printed, and began offering tickets that nobody would buy. "Don't worry," they said, "there's time till the night of the concert." Came the night of the concert, eight o'clock, nine o'clock, half-past nine. Around eleven o'clock a few people straggled in, out of curiosity, not even a *minyun*, not enough for prayers. They looked around. Where's the child? The child is asleep on a bench. They wake him, put him up on a stool, and give him his fiddle. The child begins playing. Well, well. What a concert that was!

The little audience went wild, surrounded the child, kissed him, fondled him, almost smothered him to death. But that didn't pay for the hall or pay for their keep. When they got back to their lodging, worn-out and hungry, they were served no supper, and the landlord wouldn't give them a bed. So they spread their coats on the floor and bedded themselves down with their fists for a pillow. The child fell asleep—a child is only a child—but the father lay awake thinking. His brain was splitting. His heart told him next to him lay a treasure, a million. But what to do with it? Shout to the heavens?

With these thoughts he fell asleep and had a strange dream. In the middle of the town stood a plum tree loaded with fruit. On the very topmost branch stood his son, shaking the tree, and down fell not plums but millions. The father was stuffing the millions into his pockets when suddenly he heard a tumult. The room is full of people; the landlord stands frozen with terror; the landlady is wringing her

176

hands and wailing, "My pearls, my pearls." He is seized and searched because during the night the landlady's pearls had been stolen. . . .

After many adventures, the boy, no longer Herschele, but Grischa, received a grant to study in St. Petersburg, where the father and son were much feted. Students, professors, noblemen, ladies—all came to see Grischa Stellmach. The years passed. The child grew and his name grew with him. His St. Petersburg teachers had nothing more to teach him. Time to think of the future. The grant couldn't go on forever. Stellmach must take the child out into the world and as quickly as possible. As a child he was a prodigy, a nine days' wonder. But what when he grew out of his short pants? Better cash in on him while there was still time. He began looking around for a partner. Your money, my merchandise.

God brought him a German by the name of Schultz, but this German, this partner, wanted him to sign a contract for ten years. German, are you crazy or out of your mind? Why ten years? One year, two years, even three. But ten! The German couldn't be budged. In the meanwhile Stellmach keeps getting letters from home, asking for money. In the end he got the German down to five years. They toured the Continent, and God be praised, luck was with them. Like the sands of the sea, like the stars in the sky, wealthy men, generals, princes, fine ladies poured in to hear Grischa play—and the money rolled in. But why should the German get so much of it? What had he risked? His father's inheritance? Or his great wisdom? Stellmach, God be praised, knew the concert trade by now, too. You didn't have to be a Solomon. You came to a town, sent notices to the papers, for which you paid, of course. GRISCHA STELLMACH WILL SOON ARRIVE. GRISCHA STELLMACH IS ARRIVING. GRISCHA STELLMACH HAS ARRIVED. Then you rent a hall, or a theater, paste up the billboards, print tickets, and it's done. The only heartache is that German. But never mind. The five years will soon be up and the contract will run out, and the devil take the German.

Having finished his tale, Stellmach asked Shchupak what was doing in the Yiddish theater. For Yiddish theater, he would have them know, was his real love. His son's concerts—they were business. When he wanted to enjoy himself, he went to the Yiddish theater. When he came to a new town, his first question was, "Where can I eat kosher, and is there a Yiddish theater in town?" Jewish fish and Jewish plays—what could be tastier? He had heard that Shchupak had something new to offer, a morsel by the name of Rosa Spivak. "This is she," said

Shchupak, pointing to the girl. "She's a niece of mine from Warsaw, an orphan, without father or mother."

"Poor child," said Stellmach, and pressed her hand with his soft, hairy one and promised to come that evening to hear her sing. "With the boy?" asked Sholom Meyer. "God forbid!" said Stellmach, jumping as though he had been scalded. "What do you mean, I'll take my Grischa to the Yiddish theater? Just let him show his face among Jews, and the whole game is up. Both the cow and the rope are lost. Not that I haven't brought him up as a good Jew. On the contrary. But you have to understand this—it's a delicate matter." And he rubbed two fingers together as though he were handling a piece of fine silk. "You are playing with my Grischa? When my Grischa goes abroad, he travels first class, where Jews aren't allowed. And we stop in exclusive hotels. When we go to a concert, let it be three steps away, we ride in a covered carriage. Nobody gets a look at him without paying. Ha ha. And if you want to see him privately, to ask a favor, or just to get acquainted, you have to go to the German first. Though between you and me and the wall, the German Schultz is no more a German than I. But he doesn't want it known. Bad for business. Ha ha."

Rosa recoiled at his words, and the ugly little laugh that went with them. Yet through him she was to meet Marcella Zembrich. . . .

That lover of Yiddish theater, Meyer Stellmach, couldn't stay away from Shchupak's theater. Night after night he came, saw each play three times over, sat in the best seat—naturally, without paying. "A lover of Yiddish theater" never pays money, only applause and compliments. The first night he heard Rosa sing, he rushed backstage and embraced Shchupak with tears in his eyes.

Still, one thing has nothing to do with another. Though the director hinted that he would like to hear Grischa play, Stellmach made himself deaf and dumb. Finally Shchupak's hints became so broad that he couldn't ignore them any longer. He appeared one Sunday with three matinée tickets, for Shchupak, Sholom Meyer, and Rosa. Grischa would play, the German would accompany him, and Zembrich would sing—"the famous Marcella Zembrich, a second Patti. Ten times, a hundred times, a thousand times greater than Patti. The first time Patti heard her, she fell on her neck and exclaimed, 'We are two stars. I am the star that is sinking, and you are the star that is rising.' Zembrich, you understand, wouldn't share a concert with anyone but my Grischa."

And so, finally, Rosa saw Grischa, that is, two Grischas. For she saw

178

one, and heard another. The Grischa who stepped out on the stage, an overgrown boy in short pants, round-faced and pimpled, with mere slits for eyes, you wouldn't look at twice in the street. But when he put the fiddle under his chin, he was somebody else. You saw his eyes for the first time, deep blue, like pieces of sky. And his whole face became transfigured. But the moment he finished and his hand dropped to his side, there stood the same awkward boy.

Then out came Marcella Zembrich. Her singing pierced Rosa through and through. Where did such smoothness, such sweetness, and strength come from? Not from a human throat. After her came again that pimply-faced boy; again he raised his bow; and again his fiddle sang and wept. He finished, and the magic was gone. Rosa couldn't tell who enthralled her more that day, Grischa or Zembrich. . . .

Rosa walked out of the concert-hall like a creature born anew. She waited with other people on the sidewalk for Marcella and Grischa to come. She joined in the fresh ovation they received as they got into their limousine. She wondered: Would she some day be another Marcella Zembrich? Would she, too, be sped on her way with applause? She resolved then and there to approach Zembrich, no matter what, ask her for an audition, and find out what she must do to become like her.

Just then up came Rosa's watchdog and guardian, Sholom Meyer. "We're going out for a bite to eat," he said, "Shchupak and you and I, and old Stellmach, who's coming with us for a bite of *gefilte fish* and horseradish." The lover of Yiddish theater was also a lover of Yiddish fish, especially when someone else paid for it. "This is my chance," thought Rosa. "I must ask him to introduce me to Marcella Zembrich. But how to do it without Shchupak hearing?"

Even when the lover of Yiddish theater had his mouth full of fish and horseradish, he didn't stop talking about Grischa and Zembrich, who had sung for Emperor Franz Josef himself. And yet she herself had proposed the joint concerts with Grischa.

While Shchupak and Sholom Meyer were settling the check, Rosa spoke to Stellmach. "I have a favor to ask of you." When he heard the word "favor," his jaw fell, his red face turned yellow and green, and his eyes became glassy. She took pity on him. "A very small favor," she explained. "I want you to introduce me to Marcella Zembrich so that she can hear me sing." His smile reappeared and the color returned to his cheeks. "Oh," he said, "why not? With the greatest pleasure." "But one thing," Rosa added. "None of my people must know. Do you understand?" "I understand, darling, why shouldn't I?

179

Tomorrow, around eleven, come to my hotel, and I will arrange it. Not a bird will know."

To visit Stellmach at his hotel without Shchupak knowing, was no easy matter. When Shchupak had to let Rosa out of his sight a moment, his lieutenant Sholom Meyer took up the watch. But when you need a thief badly enough, you cut him down from the gallows. Rosa told Sholom Meyer, as innocently as she could, that she wanted to know what a great singer thought of her voice. That worked. "Kitten," he said, "is there anything in the world I wouldn't do for you? I'd go through fire and water for you. May God grant me fortune and luck. . . ."

The morning after the concert Sholom Meyer told Shchupak he was taking Rosa to town to buy a few things. "What kind of things all of a sudden?" asked Shchupak. "Who knows?" said Sholom Meyer. "Ribbons, trinkets, foolishness." "What sort of ribbons, trinkets, and foolishness?" Shchupak wanted to know. Sholom Meyer gave him a look. "When I say I'm going, I'm going, and that's all there is to it."

A queer thing about those two. The director was boss; he ordered Sholom Meyer around, cursed him, treated him like a flunkey. But let Sholom Meyer raise his voice in a certain way and Shchupak crumpled up altogether. And so, without any more questions asked, Rosa and Sholom Meyer went to Stellmach's hotel.

There Stellmach began telling them his biography all over again, for a good three hours. Finally Sholom Meyer could stand it no longer. He said they had very little time left, and could Mr. Stellmach please introduce them? Now Stellmach began to hem and haw. The German was with Zembrich and also his Grischa. He didn't know what to do. Sholom Meyer said sweetly, "You don't know what to do?" "No, what should I do?" "Drop dead on the spot."

Stellmach chose to receive this as a jest. But Rosa's guardian and protector didn't let him get away with a laugh. "Mr. Stellmach, throw away your bag of tricks, and tell us in plain language, yes or no. Don't worry about your Grischa. We won't bite a piece off him. And as for that imitation German from Berdichev, he can go to hell. If you don't take us in to her, we'll walk in by ourselves, may God grant me fortune and luck."

The lover of Yiddish theater shriveled up, licked his lips, sat down, stood up, buttoned then unbuttoned his coat, and finally walked up to a door, put his ear to the keyhole, rapped on it, saying, "It is I, Stellmach. . . ."

The details of how our heroine was received by Marcella Zembrich remained a mystery to Mr. Klammer, for here the letters broke off. When next we run into the name Rosa Spivak, it is printed in huge letters, along with that of Grischa Stellmach, on large billboards in the West End of London. At the same time, in the East End, in White-chapel, we see billboards announcing that the Pavilion Theater is about to present the great star imported from the Continent, Leo Rapalesco of Bucharest, and the beloved prima donna, Henrietta Shwalb of Buenos Aires.

25 NISSEL SHWALB

The wandering troupe, Holtzman, Shwalb & Co., arrived in London in a darkness such as had reigned in plague-stricken Egypt. The director, Bernhard Holtzman, felt as though he had fallen into a dark pit or a boiling cauldron. Everything looked black and desolate to him. The people appeared insane and their talk gibberish.

The troupe almost had to feel their way with their hands. This city, which God had cursed by denying it the sun, was once more cursed by Holtzman. He echoed Heinrich Heine's wish that the sea swallow it up and spew it forth again.

Yes, Holtzman felt miserable in London. More miserable even than he had once felt in Holeneshti. Not in vain had he been visited by dark omens and premonitions on the eve of his departure from Cher-novitz.

His very first encounter in London was an unhappy one. The troupe was met at the railway station by Shwalb's brother, Nissel, and another personage, whom Nissel Shwalb introduced as Mr. Hotchkiss, inform-ing them, in a whispered aside in Yiddish, that he was the Gentile owner and manager of the famous London Yiddish Pavilion Theater. From the first this personage struck Holtzman more like a fellow who carries around oranges and ice-water between acts than the owner and manager of a theater. He was smooth-shaven and expressionless, like a peeled onion. His frock coat was a poor fit, his checked trousers too wide on top and too narrow at the ankles, the heels of his polished shoes too high. From his scrawny red neck protruded a huge Adam's apple. Hotchkiss extended two fingers of his right hand, bared three gold teeth and languidly uttered two words, "All right," then turned to his guests that part of his anatomy which nature had intended to remain in back, beckoned to some unseen person with his finger, and a splendid automobile drew up to his side, into which he jumped, vanishing in the fog.

Shwalb's brother Nissel presented a different appearance. Wide as a barrel, twice as tall as his brother Isaac, dressed in the height of fashion, with a cigar between his teeth, he looked like a man of the world, a prosperous merchant. He seemed pleased with himself, with his guests, with the whole world. He at once assumed command. First he embraced each guest heartily, then began lifting the luggage off the wagon with his own hands, disposing of it as he saw fit. Finally he ordered a carriage and began seating the guests. "You, Isaac, sit right up there with Rapalesco. Your partner and I will sit opposite."

As he spoke, his broad palm descended heavily on Holtzman's thin shoulders. "What a paw," thought Holtzman. "May it shrivel up this Thursday night and drop off. The way he orders us around. You sit here and I sit here. And where am I? I'll have to clip this bird's wings. A hog like that has to be slapped on the jowls."

To his partner, however, Holtzman said only, "Look you, Itzikel, that brother of yours, may no harm come to him, has grown both wide and tall."

Isaac looked up at his brother with love and admiration, his face glistening like a pudding just out of the oven.

"You don't find a build like that often," he said.

"That we can see," said Holtzman, and thought to himself, "Where were all of you during the great plague?"

The water-ox, as Holtzman at once dubbed Nissel Shwalb, took charge again when they arrived in Whitechapel. He helped each one out of the carriage personally, almost lifting him off with a hearty "hoopla" and a laugh which made Holtzman wince with pain.

Yes, something told Holtzman that here, on the narrow horizon of the grey London sky, his star, which until now had shone bright and clear, was about to go under.

Though Holtzman couldn't stomach Nissel Shwalb, Rapalesco found him entirely to his taste. He was delighted with the older man's high spirits, with his incessant flow of talk and his hearty laugh.

Rapalesco had always liked gay companions. In the early days in Holeneshti, when Holtzman was Hotzmach and under Shchupak's

182

thumb, he had been such a gay companion. Since he had become director of his own troupe, he had grown subject to fits of depression, suspicious of everyone he thought might be sharpening his teeth to snap up the "kid." Here, in the bustle and roar of London, his suspicions increased. He felt himself losing his hold on the "kid." The more Holtzman ridiculed and reviled his partner's brother, the more Rapalesco was drawn to Nissel Shwalb.

Nissel talked so fast that before one word was out of his mouth the next one was on its way. By nature no mean liar (he was a salesman and most salesmen, may they forgive my words, are great liars), he buttressed each story with an oath such as, "May I have everyone's good at heart," or "As you see me swimming," or "If I'm lying, may you choke to death." These oaths tripped off his tongue so fast you couldn't absorb with your brain what your ear hadn't caught.

No sooner were the newcomers settled than Shwalb undertook to show Rapalesco the sights, promising to cover all London in one day. True, to show that city in one day was a slight exaggeration. But what then? Wasn't tomorrow a day, too? And the day after tomorrow? All that really mattered was that Nissel Shwalb knew the city by heart, and if you went sightseeing with him you were never bored. His mouth didn't shut for an instant. About every street, every house almost, he had a piece of history to relate. Not the kind of history you find in books, or tales and anecdotes you gather by hearsay, but actual incidents in which he himself had been involved. And he was so convincing, and his laugh so infectious, you began thinking, "The devil take him, maybe he *is* telling the truth."

In this fellow's company Rapalesco saw every alley and rathole in London, all the theaters, operas, and music halls. They had plenty of time on their hands, for the troupe, Holtzman, Shwalb & Co., appeared in the Pavilion Theater only two nights a week. Rapalesco would have enjoyed these excursions more had Nissel Shwalb not taken it into his head to take his sister Henrietta along. He wanted her to get a taste of the big world and to hear music. "It will come in handy," he said. However, he had another motive. His brother Isaac had given him to understand how things stood with their sister. "We have to get those two married to each other," he said. "If not, that asthmatic Holtzman will grab her off."

"Who did you say? That green gooseberry?" Nissel exclaimed.

"A green gooseberry did you say? A sour apple," said Isaac Shwalb.

"Gooseberries, sour apples, they're all the same. You chew and you spit," answered his brother.

183

Nissel Shwalb was a man who specialized in combinations. As a salesman you don't make a living in London. So you have to scheme and contrive, manipulate and combine. And Nissel combined everything that allowed itself to be combined. Honesty demands that we give credit where credit is due. Though some of his combinations might, at first blush, appear fantastic, in the end they turned out all right. And if occasionally one of his combinations fell through, he was only human.

Nissel himself used to tell how, as a result of his combinations, more than one firm had gone broke. But the blame wasn't his. If his advice had been followed to the letter, everything would have turned out differently. The trouble was nobody listened to him. People, he said, were nothing but asses, donkeys, dumb oxen. Nobody understood the tactics of business; nobody appreciated the art of combination as he did.

That the Yiddish Pavilion Theater had fallen into the hands of a Gentile was the result of one of Nissel's famous combinations, just as it had been Nissel's contribution that at one time the only Yiddish language newspaper in London had been published by a Gentile, instead of a Jew. What was the reason behind it? None whatever. Nissel Shwalb had conceived the idea, and that's how it turned out.

True, *The Yiddish Courier* had been nothing but a rag, and its Gentile publisher had gone broke. But who was to blame? The stubborn fool of an Englishman wouldn't take Nissel's advice to print the *Courier* twice a day, morning and night, like English papers. You might pose this question: If the Jews of London weren't willing to buy a paper once a day, would they buy it twice a day? The answer is: Certainly they would, just out of curiosity, to see what a Yiddish paper could find to print twice a day.

Here is how it came about that the Pavilion Theater fell into the hands of the Gentile. Nissel Shwalb, like his brother Isaac, had always been a lover of Yiddish theater. It must have been a family trait. A habitué of the Pavilion Theater, he almost, one might say, lived there. But while the London public sat night after night in the theater, like so many sheep, watching the antics of the players with relish and drinking in the songs and music which would have turned the stomachs of a more discriminating audience, Nissel's head buzzed with schemes. Why shouldn't the Yiddish public have a real theater, he thought? And not one theater, but three? One for drama, one for operettas, and one for grand opera? To such a theater even the "aristocracy" from the West End would come. All you needed was a fine house and artists who were artists. The house was no problem. You didn't need a finer building than the Pavilion Theater. As for artists, that was no problem. Where was America? Weren't there enough "stars" in America? For money you could bring not only Adler from America, but Sarah Bernhardt from Paris. And if the worst came to worst, they could get along with their local talent. Throw in his sister Henrietta from his brother's troupe, Holtzman, Shwalb & Co., and that young artist Leo Rapalesco, and you had a theater fit for the king.

Nissel threw aside all his other business to promote his three theaters. Letters flew back and forth between him and his brother in Austria; letters flew to America, to Russia, and even to Johannesburg and Buenos Aires. Nissel Shwalb didn't overlook a single Yiddish theater or a famous personage. And from everywhere came heartening words. The road was wide open. Only one obstacle remained. Where to get money?

But Nissel Shwalb, that master of combinations, was not one to stop halfway. He was a man who didn't choose and pick, but went straight to his goal. And he was blessed with luck.

One foggy day, when the London street lamps, burning at midday, weren't enough to keep the pedestrians from bumping into one another, that genial promoter, Nissel Shwalb, set out for the City, as London's business section is called. He went straight to the firm, Hotchkiss Bros., Ltd., for whom he held an agency for selling sewing machines, bicycles, and automobiles.

Hotchkiss Bros., Ltd. belonged to two wealthy Englishmen, the Hotchkiss brothers, of whom the elder spent most of his time in Switzerland risking his neck climbing the Alps, leaving the younger to run the business.

After bidding the younger Hotchkiss good morning, Shwalb begged him to lay aside what he was doing and give him his attention. He had brought him a proposition which comes only once in seven centuries. Mr. Hotchkiss forsook his correspondence, hitched his checked trousers over his meager calves, and gave an ear to this proposition that comes only once in seven hundred years.

Nissel Shwalb painted for his employer the lurid state of the Yiddish theater in general and the Pavilion Theater in particular. Then he unfolded his plan for three theaters, one for drama, one for operettas, and one for grand opera. Then he spread out a sheaf of letters and cablegrams from artists all over the world together with clippings from a dozen newspapers, translating them from Yiddish

185

into English, and winding up his monologue with a detailed account of how many pounds sterling one had to put in and how many pounds sterling one could expect to take out.

As Nissel Shwalb talked, Mr. Hotchkiss sat looking out of the window and tapping his three gold teeth with his fingers. Then he arose, stretched himself, scratched his Adam's apple, and said languidly, "All right." He presented two fingers of his right hand to his agent and told him to return for his answer tomorrow at quarter past eleven.

The answer he gave to Nissel Shwalb was already known. Only a man of such sanguine temperament as Nissel Shwalb could have dreamed up such a combination, and only a man blessed with his luck could have put it over.

26 THE MUSICAL FAMILY

"Tonight we're going to the cantor's," said Nissel Shwalb to Rapalesco.

At the word *cantor* Rapalesco started. His one-time teacher, Israel the Cantor, rose before his eyes. He asked with a beating heart, "Which cantor?"

"The cantor from Lomzha. The one I introduced to you at the theater the other night; he has his whole family with him. Don't you remember?"

Rapalesco vaguely recalled Nissel Shwalb bringing backstage a man with a red beard and cotton wadding in his ears, with a cluster of children, boys and girls of all sizes and ages, around him.

Nissel had extolled this family to the skies, and told Rapalesco anecdotes and scandals about them right in front of their eyes. In the din of the theater the stories had gone in one ear and out of the other. Now, on the way to the cantor's, Nissel repeated these tales. They were a family of accomplished musicians, he said, every last one of them, from the cantor down to the youngest child.

"And do you think anyone taught them to play?" Nissel laughed. "Not on your life. The cantor's children came out of their mother's belly full-fledged musicians. May I choke on my words, if I'm lying."

186

Nissel Shwalb stopped at a Jewish food store to load up with rolls, sausage and pickles, and other delicatessen. "Tidbits for them," he explained. "They're paupers, such paupers. Ha ha. Without a helping hand now and then, they would have starved long ago, right here in London. A big family of eaters like that, and not a breadwinner among them. But as soon as they get on their feet, they'll shower the house with gold, as you see me swimming."

Nissel Shwalb lit match after match as they descended some rickety stairs into a dark hole in the ground. They walked into a room filled with beds like a hospital. On the walls hung all kinds of instruments. In the middle of the room stood a large broken-down piano, at which sat a girl of about six or seven or maybe eight (Nissel Shwalb swore she was under four, and we might as well humor him) drawing unearthly sounds from it. The fault was that of the ancient instrument, which should have been scrapped long ago.

When she saw the guests, the little girl left her piano, and cried out, "Uncle Nissel! Uncle Nissel is here."

Like characters in a play there appeared one after the other from behind a closed door the assorted children of the family. After them appeared their father, the Lomzha cantor, a man along in years, his red hair and beard shot with grey. His strangely glittering eyes and trembling hands attested to the fact that he didn't eat often or well. Yet he looked scrupulously neat and carried his shoulders erect and his head high. A plague on it, his look said, the face needn't show what the stomach feels.

"First of all," said Nissel Shwalb, "let's have a bite to eat. I'm dead hungry, as you see me swimming." And he undid the packages of food and began eating as though he had, indeed, just ended a fast.

"Why do you sit around like uninvited guests?" Nissel shouted at the family. The cantor with the hungry eyes and trembling hands advanced first and took the proffered food delicately. After all, when you're invited to eat, you can't be a hog and refuse. But the children were not so backward. The food vanished at great speed. Watching them, Rapalesco suddenly discovered that he too was famished.

"Sit, take, break, cut, chew, make yourself at home, you're among friends," Nissel Shwalb urged him on, and the children regarded him with such eager, friendly glances that he began to feel as though he were at home among old friends. Where had he suddenly acquired such a tremendous appetite? Why did he all at once feel so warm and relaxed, so free and light-hearted? A wonderful family.

While they ate, Nissel Shwalb didn't stop talking. He had a special story or joke for each child, for whom he had a separate pet name. When the meal was finished, the cantor wiped his lips for the last time, changed the cotton in his ears, and called on the children to take down their instruments and treat the two guests to a "bit of concert."

The "bit of concert" lasted all evening, an evening one couldn't forget. Here was every kind of musical instrument, fiddle, flute, cello, piano, viola, cymbals, harp, and drum, and each played in a masterly way by a half-naked child. Rapalesco was moved almost to tears. During the course of his wanderings he had seen many such talents lying on dung-heaps. "God in Heaven," he mused. "Are there no patrons of the arts left among us?" And he thought of the Lemberg Maecenas, Dr. Julius Levias, whose love of art had evaporated when put to the test. "If I had a little money of my own, I would take a family like this out of their mudhole and show them the light of day."

It was late when Nissel Shwalb and Rapalesco walked home from the cantor's. The streets of Whitechapel were gay, but except for a tall policeman on the corner, not a soul was in sight. Rapalesco, by habit quiet and restrained in his speech, was unusually talkative and elated. "Lord in Heaven. Such gifted children! Such blessed hands. And they lie buried in that stinking hole under the ground. How can it be that in all of London there isn't a single Maecenas to help them?"

"Maecenas did you say? There's a man here, a Russian Jew, once a pauper and now a millionaire, a man named Stellmach—and this Maecenas of ours . . ."

"Stellmach?" Rapalesco stopped. It seemed to him he had heard the name in connection with Reizel . . . he couldn't remember where.

Seeing the look on his face, Shwalb said, "Just look at him. I haven't started on my story and he's already beside himself. . . . Now Stellmach is a great lover of Yiddish theater and music. His son Grischa is a famous violinist, a child prodigy, who's played command performances at the English Court many times. And it's through this son that Stellmach has grown rich."

Now Rapalesco remembered. Eagerly he asked, "Well, and where is he, this famous violinist?"

"Don't rush me." Nissel raised his hand. "I haven't got to the son yet. I'm still talking about the father. I met him at the buffet during an intermission. I see a man standing there, chewing away, and giving me the eye. So I gave him the eye. 'Where's a Jew from?' I asked. 'You look familiar to me.' 'I'm Stellmach,' he says. 'So, you're Stellmach, himself. Tell me, Mr. Stellmach, of which Stellmachs are

188

you?' He looks at me as though I was a fool and says with an injured air, 'What do you mean, which of the Stellmachs? Haven't you ever heard the name Grischa Stellmach? A man lives in London and doesn't know there's a Grischa Stellmach in the world who plays at the King's Court.' 'That there's a Grischa Stellmach in London who has played for the King I know, though I'm not a frequent guest at Court. But what has that to do with you?'

" 'Ha ha,' he laughs, 'I'm his father.' *'Maz'ltov,'* say I, 'lucky the son who has such a father.' Well, one word led to another. That is, he did most of the talking. He's not one to listen. And when he starts on his Grischa, you can't stop him with ten horses. Tra-ra-ra Tra-ta-ta. Grischa this, Grischa that. I cut him short. 'I see you're a great lover of music,' I said. 'If you want to hear music that is music, I'll take you to a certain place, and you won't have to pay, either.' Says he, 'With the greatest pleasure. Yiddish theater, music, and such things are so dear to me, I would walk three miles on foot.' 'Excellent,' I think to myself. 'Then you're my man. Maybe it's fated that through you this poor family will be delivered from bondage.' Well, we set a date, and I took him to the cantor's. He comes once, twice, three times. My Stellmach is beside himself. When he comes to the cantor's, he forgets to go home. He sits there, and eats and drinks and talks about his Grischa. I thought to myself, 'You're such an admirer of the cantor's, the time has come to talk turkey.' And I said to him, 'These gifted children must be given a chance. They have to be stuck around in conservatories.' He gives me a blank look, as though he didn't understand. So I put it to him point blank, 'Mr. Stellmach,' I said, 'they need money.'

"At the word 'money' his face turned—what shall I tell you? Better-looking people are put into the grave. He got up in a hurry, said goodbye and went like a shot. I haven't seen him to this day. But I thought to myself, 'Nobody slips out of Nissel Shwalb's hands so easily.' I found out where this weasel lived and went to his address. I knock on the door, and I hear a voice from inside, his voice, saying, 'Take a look who's knocking. If it's a tall, stout man, say I'm not home.' When I heard this, I said to myself, 'Aha, you're wise to me. Well, if you want to twist yourself out of my hands, it will cost you dear.' And it will cost him dear, as you see me swimming, I promise you that."

Shwalb finished in triumph and looked to Rapalesco for approval. Rapalesco nodded absently. He had heard little of the tale, except the name Grischa Stellmach. This must be the same Grischa rumored to

189

be engaged to Reizel. Now one thing remained—to get acquainted with this Grischa Stellmach.

There is a quaint saying among us: "Play the bridegroom a lament, he takes it for a nuptial song."

Not only did Nissel Shwalb's scheme for three theaters fall through, but even the one Pavilion Theater wasn't doing any too well. It's true the people of London flocked to see the much-touted Leo Rapalesco of Bucharest and the beautiful Prima Donna Shwalb of Buenos Aires. The theater was packed but alas, with the same pregnant women with nursing infants, the same boys and girls who pelted each other with orange peels. The Pavilion Theater still looked more like a synagogue yard in a small town during the high holidays than a metropolitan theater. The wealthy and refined Jews from the West End, on whose patronage Nissel Shwalb had staked the venture, didn't stick their aristocratic noses into the Whitechapel theater any more than they had in the past or would in the future until the Messiah came. . . .

The revenue that came in was eaten up by the guest troupe, Holtzman, Shwalb & Co., nothing was left for the local actors. The capitalist, Mr. Hotchkiss, having paid out the last sum he would risk on the enterprise, was ready to close in the middle of the season.

Nissel Shwalb cursed Mr. Hotchkiss for a stubborn fool who wouldn't subscribe to his theory that "the larger the head, the wider the hat, and the bigger the pot, the more kindling it needs." Just because business was bad, said Shwalb, they should expand, bring Adler from America, send the troupe on tour through all England, spare no money, and in time, for every pound sterling Mr. Hotchkiss put in, he would take out two, three, ten, twenty, *ad infinitum*.

Mr. Hotchkiss heard Nissel Shwalb out to the end, tapping his fingers over his three gold teeth, and looking out of the window. Then he rose, stretched himself, extended two fingers of his right hand to Shwalb, and said languidly, "All right. Not another shilling."

What could Nissel Shwalb do? He couldn't graft his own head on the Englishman's shoulders. He hit on a new combination. This new combination consisted of one word. One single word. But this word had such drawing power, such magnetism, such magic, that if you let it fall from your lips, the sleepiest among our people became wide awake, the slothful turned industrious, and the most despairing and skeptical were filled with new hope and faith.

This word was *America*.

190

If I were to make a parallel, I would say that America was a great sea into which all rivers flowed. A beautiful dream which did not always come true. The farthest point on the horizon to which a human being could reach. A last refuge for the dispossessed of the world. A final remedy for those whom all other remedies had failed.

Long drawn to this "golden land," all of Nissel's previous combinations had held him back. This time, however, nothing short of a catastrophe from heaven could stop him. And not even that. For God Himself had ordained it.

The plan, America, was born in the cellar of the musical family of the cantor from Lomzha. The cantor had received a letter from friends across the ocean telling him he and his family must come to America without fail. Musical talent, the writer said, was a scarce article in America, which had to be imported from Europe. Any paltry little fiddler, the letter said, who in the old country had gone about with holes in his pants, became, the day after he arrived in America, a professor of music.

Having seen the letter Nissel Shwalb leaped up as though scalded. He gave himself a smart slap on the forehead and the cantor another slap on the back.

"We're going to America. As you see me swimming, we're going to America. I've thought of a combination. We'll see each other tomorrow or the day after. All will be well. Leave it to me. Goodbye."

In another moment Nissel Shwalb, out of the cellar, joyfully strode through the streets of Whitechapel, his derby tilted to the side of his head, and whistling a gay tune. "What a city," he thought. "What a marvelous city. It's a joy and a delight to be alive in the world. May I have everyone's good at heart."

27   BRAINDELE'S REVENGE

The reader must know by now that we are not given to moralizing and that we are not here to preach sermons. But we must bow to Truth, and the truth is that both good and bad actions are often repaid in kind, and in this world. It isn't worth while to make foes. Ten friends are better than one enemy. And a cat, they say, can cause mischief too. Of whom are we speaking now? Braindele Kozak.

When Braindele left Holtzman's employ, she swore to get even with the "D'rector." But what means of revenge could she find, a poor, homeless, wandering soul who had been created for the sole purpose of being used by others and then cast aside? She wandered over Europe, caught a few more blows from "those false, heartless double-dealing men," and was finally cast upon the shores of the New World. And, God be thanked, she did not regret it. Here she was no longer known as Braindele Kozak, but called by her proper name, Madame Cherniak. She had a good job, as she informed Henrietta Shwalb in a letter written in large, round characters like bagels. True, she was no longer an actress, for here in this blessed land of Columbus every trade had its union and Yiddish actors had a union, too, and wouldn't permit a strange actor to join. She had a different occupation now, also an honorable one, and also in the Yiddish theater.

What this occupation was she didn't write. But she made a living. She rounded out this bit of information with the blessing, "May a quick death come to all men, and especially to that asthmatic director, Holtzman—is he still alive?"

"You can't imagine, my friend," wrote Madame Cherniak, "how delighted I was when I found out you were in London, that last station of Europe, before America. How wonderful, I thought if you could only come here. For America is the place for you. I took the liberty of speaking to several theater managers about you and showed them your picture. And they almost went wild. They begged me for your address. They will surely write, or have written already, to engage you as prima donna. My advice is, don't sign any contracts, don't even answer their letters, but come here at once. For the other actors I can't speak. It's difficult because of the union. But stars like you or Rapalesco would quickly find a place here. One warning: keep this a secret. Aside from your brother and Rapalesco, not a soul must know. Especially that asthmatic director, who will lead you astray if you let him. Remember, don't write and don't speak to anyone. Just come. I told a few people you were coming, and they printed the news in the paper together with your picture. I send you the paper and I want you to know you have on this side of the ocean a devoted and loyal friend whose name is,

Braina Cherniak"

Thus Braindele dug a quick grave for her old enemy Holtzman. She was not content with luring away the prima donna, she had to tear away from him the goose that laid the golden eggs, his Rapalesco.

192

Thus Braindele Kozak schemed, and God Himself came to her aid.

Braindele Kozak had always been a great reader. But she hadn't read a tenth as much in her whole life in the old country as she read here in the blessed land of Columbus. There, in her old home, she had also loved the printed word. But when did she have an opportunity to see it? Once in a blue moon she would get her hands on a book, "a highly interesting romance," over which she would weep quietly to herself. But here, in the blessed land of Columbus, she was spared the trouble of looking for books. All you had to do was to step out into the street and a paper was shoved under your nose, then another paper and another, each as large as a bedsheet, yours for a mere penny, and full of dove's milk. What couldn't you find in the papers? The latest news from home and from all over the world, every item under a huge headline you could see a mile off. And the serials the papers ran! In every paper ran two serials, one more enchanting than the next!

In one of the papers Braindele Kozak read, under the heading, "Drama, Art, and Music," a startling piece of news. "Uptown," in the fashionable quarter of New York, two guests were expected from Paris, two great stars, the famous violinist of the English Royal Court, Grischa Stellmach, and the greatest singer in the world, the successor to Patti, the well-known Rosalie Spivak.

Rosalie Spivak! Braindele slapped her skirts with both hands. Heavens above! That must be Rosa Spivak.

Rosa Spivak was coming. What rapture, what joy! First of all, when they met, they would fall on each other's necks. Then Rosa would ask her how she was doing. Had she been long in this country? In which theater did she work? What roles did she play? Ahh. What roles. She worked in the theater, but she played no more roles. Here they had a union and the union . . . But she had another job in the theater. She helped the "Misses" with their dresses and coiffures. What did it matter? As long as she made a living. Rosa would nod and look at her with those melting black eyes. Madame Cherniak understood the look. She knew the girl through and through. She was thinking, "Why shouldn't Madame Cherniak come to me?" Why should she work for strangers when she can work for a friend once like a sister to her?

So poor Braindele Kozak wove her fantasies. She could hardly wait until dawn, when she threw a robe over her shoulders and sat down to write a letter to Leo Rapalesco in the Pavilion Theater, Whitechapel, London, in the same huge round characters that looked like bagels.

My dear Leo Rapalesco,
    I'm sure you have not forgotten your old acquaintance and devoted friend Cherniak, who once roamed over the world with you. Ah, what happy days those were. Though, to be sure, none of us lacked troubles. Each had his pack to carry. But let us not speak of that which is past. Let us better speak of the present. I have read in the local papers that your troupe is now in London and you are having a great "success." This gave me so much joy that I sat down at once to write you a letter and send you warm greetings from that faraway land where I now find myself, and where I make a living. I do not regret having left Holtzman and his company, and I pray to God that I will never regret it. America is the true home of the Yiddish theater. Come here, and you will be exalted. Not any actor, because here in this blessed land of Columbus every trade has a union and actors have a union, too. They do not allow a stranger on the stage unless he is a star. So if you came there would be no question of a union. I have proof. I mentioned your name to several theater managers and they told me, "If Rapalesco comes, we'll sweeten him up." I give you their very words. London is not the place for you. Your place is here, in this golden land. Here you will be a great star forever and ever with hosts of admirers, among whom am I,

Your devoted friend,
Braina Cherniak

P.S. I forgot to mention—any day now my old friend Rosa Spivak —do you remember her?—is due to arrive here from Paris. In the papers, where I saw her picture, she is no longer called Rosa Spivak, but "Miss Rosalie Spivak." And she is more beautiful than ever. I send you a clipping with her picture. It goes without saying my letter to you must remain a dark secret. I send my address, so you can answer my letter.

Braina Cherniak

Luck favored Braindele. Her letters to Henrietta and Rapalesco arrived just at the time when the London Pavilion Theater was about to close, and the troupe, Holtzman, Shwalb & Co., was about to fall apart.

A few days before, while strolling about the West End of London with the prompter, Benny Gorgel, Rapalesco's glance had been arrested by a large theatrical poster. When he saw it, he stopped, and his hand flew to his heart.

"What is it? God be with you," the man of education exclaimed. "What did you see? A torn old poster from Khmelnitzky's time?"

194

"Stop a moment, let's see what it says." And Rapalesco read that, at a certain date about two months ago, Rosalie Spivak and Grischa Stellmach had given a concert.

A storm broke out in our young hero's breast. On that same day he, Rapalesco, had been in London. How could he have missed it? Who knows, maybe Reizel was still in London?

And he began asking around. The first person he approached was his new friend and guide, Nissel Shwalb. Instead of asking his question point-blank, he took a roundabout approach. He asked Nissel Shwalb to enumerate the names of famous singers and musicians he had heard in his life.

Nothing loath, Nissel Shwalb reeled off an astonishing list, many of them names from the *Haggadah*, that is, invented on the spur of the moment. It turned out that Nissel Shwalb had been on intimate terms with many famous people, for instance Patti. . . .

"Forget Patti," said Rapalesco impatiently. "Have you ever heard the name Spivak?"

"Which Spivak? There are two Spivaks."

Two Spivaks! Rapalesco hadn't been prepared for this. His brain reeled. "Rosa Spivak," he said, "or Rosalie Spivak."

Nissel Shwalb burst into a loud laugh, which meant one of two things: Either he knew Rosalie Spivak like his own sister, or she wasn't worth knowing. Then he began a long spiel about Patti that wound up with a near-scandal concerning Patti's grandchild.

"With Patti's grandchild?"

"Oho, she has great-grandchildren, and even great-great grand-children."

That day Rapalesco couldn't rest. He couldn't sit in one place. He kept disappearing on mysterious errands. He didn't hear what anyone said to him.

"What's happened to the 'kid'?" Holtzman asked his partner, Isaac.

"He's your 'kid,' why do you ask me?"

Holtzman went to his mother.

"What's wrong with the 'kid'?" he asked her.

Sarah-Brocha was on her way to the kitchen to pluck a chicken for dinner, and she didn't want to be bothered. She told him so in a few words. Holtzman spat and grabbed hold of his sister. "What's wrong with the 'kid'?"

Zlatka turned so pale he forgot about the "kid" and became alarmed for her. He locked the door and, taking her hand, looked deep into her eyes. "Zlatka, what's the trouble?"

"Nothing." Zlatka sobbed. "N—nothing." And she dropped her head on the table and burst into a flood of tears.

Mr. Hotchkiss kept his word like a true Englishman. He drew a line under the last sum, figured out how many pounds sterling he had lost in the business, and presented his agent with a languid, "All right." Then without bestowing on him his two fingers as usual, he turned his back, jumped into his automobile, and was off. At any other time Shwalb would have been deeply offended. But, as things stood, he didn't give it another thought. He was too deeply involved in his new combination to take it to heart that another Englishman had turned out to be a dolt. Who ever said Englishmen understood business? And do you think Nissel Shwalb didn't tell him so? He told him, as you see him swimming. "Mr. Hotchkiss," he said to him, "may I have as many blessings how much more brains I have in my left heel than you have under your hat." Those were his very words, may he choke if he weren't telling the truth.

Thus said Nissel Shwalb improvising aloud. He went on to tell how he would arrive in New York with his company of "true believers," the very *élite,* among them the greatest artists, meaning Rapalesco; the finest singers, meaning Henrietta Shwalb; the foremost musicians, meaning the Lomzha cantor and his family. And he, Nissel Shwalb, himself? You think, perhaps, he had no connection with the Yiddish theater? And what a connection! Nissel Shwalb had once been an *usher* in the Pavilion Theater. And he went on to describe what it meant to be an usher.

"His work, you understand, is more outside than inside. But you can't get along without him. He's stationed at the entrance, he takes up the tickets, shows people to their seats, and keeps order. On his shoulders rests the whole theater, just as, for instance, all of London rests on the shoulders of the police.

"I was, you must know, the head usher, as you see me swimming. When I was in charge, nobody threw orange rinds down from the boxes, and the nursing babies in the pit didn't cry, either. Let anyone start something—I grabbed him by the collar, and one-two-three, out he marched. . . ."

Nissel Shwalb then went on to paint the wonders of America, where their life would be paradise. How could it be otherwise, with a company which had its own orchestra, its own artists and singers,

196

and even its own ushers! And whatever they earned they would divide equally among all their members. Nobody would earn more than another. They would be a cooperative. Right?

This discussion took place in the cellar of the musical family and the cantor himself was the first to speak up, expressing willingness, this very moment, to sign a contract with both hands for as many years as they liked, even forever. "You can put it in the contract," he said, "that my children will play whenever they are wanted, and wherever they are wanted, and as much as they are wanted, and whatever the earning will be, we'll divide equally among all."

Here Isaac Shwalb entered a protest. He argued, and his red face sweated at every pore, that the plan was not altogether just. How could you put Rapalesco and his sister, the prima donna, in the same category with just anybody? There was a limit to everything.

Nissel Shwalb jumped up and went at his brother with both barrels loaded.

"You are nothing but a slave and a dupe. A miserable serf. I can see you've been enslaved by the exploiters, your Getzel ben Getzel, your Bernhard Holtzman. Well, I'm no Getzel ben Getzel or Bernhard Holtzman to ride on the backs of others. I believe, above all, in justice, equality, humanity. I would just as soon, as you see me swimming, labor in America a year and two and three and five and even six years in the behalf of others. May I have everyone's good at heart."

It goes without saying that Nissel Shwalb won out. And thus, by the consent of the majority; a new cooperative of Art, Music, and Theater was founded.

One problem remained, where to get money for transportation to America. This was resolved much more quickly and easily than could be imagined. Money had never been a source of worry to Nissel Shwalb. The important thing was to find the right combination. With that, Nissel Shwalb never had to go looking for money. Money sought him out.

This time it happened at the "Café National," headquarters of our old acquaintance, Mr. Klammer, who, as we know, was everyone's friend, and, above all, humanity's. Nissel had no secrets from Mr. Klammer. Whenever a new combination was brewing, he confided it first to Mr. Klammer, from whom it speedily reached the rest of the world.

Over a glass of beer he told Mr. Klammer of his plan, America and of what held them back, money for tickets and traveling expenses.

Mr. Klammer sat with his eyes shut, stroking the pointed beard which gave him his resemblance to Theodore Herzl. Hearing Nissel through, he said, "Well, Mr. Shwalb, have you any more to say, or is that all? If this is all, I have a question to put to you. If I found a capitalist for you, would you agree to divide your earnings in half with him?"

Nissel Shwalb by nature never reflected very long. He went by this theory, that if you spied a hare in the woods, you didn't stop to consider from which side to shoot. Piff-paff, and it was done. Still, for the sake of appearances, he paused long enough to rub his forehead as became a man reflecting on matters of high finance. Then he declared, "Most willingly, with the greatest pleasure, and with many thanks."

"All right, give me your hand, and let's wish each other good luck. The capitalist I am speaking of is—myself."

Saying this Mr. Klammer bestowed on his friend a smile of such sweetness and warmth and at the same time such dignity and self-congratulation that if Baron Rothschild had been in his place, he couldn't have behaved in a more stately and benevolent manner.

Nissel Shwalb had known Mr. Klammer for many years, as a Zionist and a Territorialist and a leader of the community and a good fellow and a restaurateur and a giver of free advice and what you will, but not as a capitalist.

Mr. Klammer must have guessed Nissel's thoughts, for he said, with the same benevolent and condescending smile, "Don't be so surprised at my entering into such a deal—how do they call it—a blind gamble. I'm not as rash as you think. I'm not risking my whole capital. My business I will leave with my wife. I'm weary of selling noodles. A person has to know what he's best fitted for. How does the Englishman say it? 'Everyone in his place.' Mr. Shwalb, give me your hand before I change my mind. I have a principle. When I do something, I do it at once. Or as the Englishman says, 'Strike while the iron is hot.' "

The news that the Pavilion Theater was about to close went like a shot to Holtzman's heart. He fell on his partner and began to berate him for having led him into this swamp. He unloosed a whole spate of curses at Isaac Shwalb's head.

Isaac Shwalb was by nature a mild man. When you cursed him, he kept his mouth shut. He merely looked at his tormentor with the eyes of a martyr and sweated profusely. But this time he couldn't endure Holtzman's insults in silence. His brother's good name had been touched. Holtzman called Nissel by a certain name—and when his brother's reputation was at stake, the usually gentle Isaac was ready to draw blood.

Disgruntled by the way business had gone in London, irritated by the city itself with its perpetual clatter and noise, its mists and fogs, its cold grey buildings and cold grey people, and harassed by his cough which had taken a turn for the worse, Holtzman lost his last shred of restraint. He cursed not only his partner, but himself and his fate.

"Would that London had sunk into the ground together with you before I set foot here. Would I had broken a leg or both legs and my neck and back. As though one partner wasn't enough, now I am saddled with two blood-suckers."

"Why are you always throwing up two partners to me?" asked Shwalb.

"You're right. Since the theater is no longer a theater, our partnership is no longer a partnership. I'm rid of you and your brother."

"It's all the same to us," said Shwalb, rising. "We're going to America anyway."

"So you're going to America!" said Holtzman, in a voice full of sarcasm. "Then go in the best of health. Straight into the ground!"

Shwalb, who had turned his back on Holtzman, now swung around. "My sister is going along with us."

Holtzman clasped his hands together, leaned his cheek against them, and made a wry face. "Well, well, and what do you want me to do? Rend my garments and sit down and weep right in the middle of Whitechapel?"

Shwalb turned from the door and threw a parting shot at his partner. "I'll have you know that one day soon you will weep from both eyes, for another goes with us. . . ."

At this Holtzman's face turned all colors and his eyes, always as sharp as flint, began to shoot sparks.

"He won't live to see the day, that brother of yours, 'the wild ox.'" He said the last words in Hebrew, denoting the legendary ox to be eaten by the faithful at the coming of the Messiah.

What was there about the epithet "wild ox," even in Hebrew, to rouse such ire in Isaac Shwalb's breast? Was it any worse than the names "weasel" or "water-ox" which Holtzman had called Nissel Shwalb to his face every day? But you could never predict what a creature like Isaac Shwalb would do. On hearing the words, "wild

199

ox," his scarlet face actually turned green and he advanced on his partner with a murderous look in his eye.

Fortunately Sarah-Brocha appeared at that moment. Placing her bony but strong frame between them, she pushed her son into the room, threw Isaac outside bodily, and locked the door.

When Holtzman was left alone, his partner's words again bit deep into his heart. "You will weep from both eyes, for another goes with us." Those were plain words, blunt words. He didn't need an interpreter to translate them.

Now he knew why the "kid" had been going about lately as though he were in another world. The Shwalb girl had turned his head. It was plain as day.

"Hotzmach," he said to himself bitterly, using the old name, as though to make his self-abasement complete, "Hotzmach, you ought to burn alive. Where have your eyes been?"

Angrily he kicked over a stool that stood by the wall. Hearing the clatter, his mother came running from the kitchen. She didn't come alone. In her hands she held a half-plucked fowl. The fowl, head dangling from its slit neck, turned up its gelid, film-covered eyes at Holtzman with what he imagined to be an accusing look. Everyone was against him. Everyone.

He was seized with such rage that he thought any moment his heart would burst. He leaped at the old woman with clenched fists and screamed hoarsely, "Back to the kitchen. The kitchen. The kitchen."

Sarah-Brocha looked at him, spat, then turned and went back to the kitchen to finish plucking her fowl.

From the day of their arrival in England, Holtzman had felt a catastrophe impending. Now he knew. He had been displeased from the first by the sudden friendship which had sprung up between Nissel and the "kid." But what could he do about it? The "kid" had grown out of control. Who would have expected that this innocent little lamb, who only yesterday, it seemed, hadn't been able to add two and two, and who didn't know the face of a coin, as the saying goes, would suddenly become a full-grown man with ambition, with a serious outlook on life, with his own will?

And who was to blame for this if not Holtzman himself? What devilish impulse had prompted him, that time in Lemberg, to snatch away not only the prima donna, but those two *schlimazls*, Braindele Kozak and the prompter, Benny Gorgel, whom the actors called "a man of education"? As for Braindele Kozak, as soon as he had learned that she was plotting with the "kid," he had given her the gate.

But Benny Gorgel was another matter. He had turned out to be the real menace. He had brought him more grief than anyone could imagine. That "man of education" had caused Holtzman's downfall. What sort of mentor could he, Holtzman, be to the boy, when the other knew so much more? The "kid" spoke several languages now, read books, and quoted Shakespeare, and dreamed of the wide world, as he called it, and the open sky. That "wide world and open sky" were Greek to Holtzman, along with the prattle about "self-expression," a "reformed theater," a "new repertory," everything new, new, new. And what, Holtzman asked himself, would become of the old? Should it be thrown to the dogs? Strange, outlandish talk, picked up from that "man of education," may a cholera take him this very day, together with that "wild ox."

Holtzman's gloomy thoughts then turned from the "kid" to his sister Zlatka. He could see Zlatka was unhappy, wasting away from day to day. And who was to blame for this, if not he himself? Who had sent for her, if not he? Who had torn her away from her home and her work, had made an actress of her, doomed her to a life of wandering, filled her head with false hopes? What would happen to his lovelorn sister if Rapalesco got up one fine morning and went off to America?

After torturing himself with these thoughts, Holtzman caught himself up sharply. Nonsense! How was it possible? How could Rapalesco desert them and go out by himself to America? Nonsense! He was too tender-hearted, too soft, too honest for that. If it came to leaving, they would all go together. How else? But from this comforting thought he reverted to his fears. "But my cough, may a cholera take it, together with that 'wild ox'!"

For Holtzman's illness had been so aggravated in London, God alone knew when he could make such a long journey. The doctors told him to leave England, and go to Switzerland or Italy. Clear air, they said, and warm sunlight. What fools! What was the good of clean air and warm sun, I ask, without a theater and without a stage?

From sheer wretchedness, apparently, Holtzman began laughing, and his laugh turned to a racking cough. His old mother came running again from the kitchen, with rolled-up sleeves, without a fowl this time, but with a huge bowl in her hands.

"That good cough again," she said.

A strong odor of garlic and onions emanated from her and it made Holtzman choke. He tried with all his strength to hold back his cough. Gasping, he told her to go back to the kitchen, back to her onions and garlic. He pretended to laugh, twisting his mouth into a

201

grimace, then spat into his handkerchief, and hid it deep in his pockets, so that the old woman shouldn't see the red-tinted phlegm. Nonsense. You couldn't deceive Sarah-Brocha. A mother had a quick eye. She saw her affliction too well, and began wringing her hands. "Woe is me. Miserable wretch that I am." And by main force she put her son to bed and sent Zlatka for the doctor.

And as she hurried through the congested streets of London, Zlatka thought, "So many horses, trams, automobiles, carriages. Can't one of them take pity on me and run me over so I'll be dead?"

Part IV

28 THE KISS ON SHIPBOARD

Of the passengers on the great ocean liner *Atlantic*, sailing from Southampton to New York, few remained on deck after their first taste of the ocean. Those who did strolled up and down or gathered in groups drinking beer, smoking cigars, laughing and spinning yarns.

Among these lucky few appeared Mr. Klammer of London with his Herzl beard, and his partner, Nissel Shwalb, one-time salesman of sewing machines and bicycles, now entrepreneur, manager, director, treasurer, strategist, and guiding star of the newly formed theater troupe, Klammer, Shwalb & Co.

Holtzman, Shwalb & Co., dear reader, is no more. This event touched no one but Holtzman and shouldn't disturb us unduly. The world is an army marching to war. The army won't stop when one soldier falls by the way. The fallen soldier has one of two chances: if God grants, he will rise again. If not . . . It is sad, we admit. But who was to blame if Holtzman had neglected his cough so long that now the doctors wouldn't let him stir from bed, and even forbade him to talk. Not talk! A fine business. If a man can't talk, wherein is the difference between him and a beast? But there's no help for it. We will have to bid Holtzman goodbye for the present, wish him a speedy recovery, and follow our new company as it journeys to that land toward which all eyes have been drawn from the day Columbus discovered it until the present, a matter of over four hundred years.

The above-mentioned pair, Mr. Klammer and Nissel Shwalb, sat like two turtle-doves at a table, drinking beer, smoking cigars, and talking. Their mouths didn't shut for a moment. What were they talking about? Nothing. Absolutely nothing. They were only seeing which could "outbluff" the other.

Mr. Klammer reminisced about the "Café National," about the Russian *schnorrers,* about the London charities in which he had been active; he also told mere yarns, spiced with witticisms and examples, "as the Englishman puts it."

But none of them was news to Nissel Shwalb. He had already heard every story of Mr. Klammer's. And not only heard it. He had been there when it happened. And to prove it, he told a juicy little scandal which had almost resulted . . . and Nissel Shwalb disclosed the near-scandal with "As you see me swimming," or, "May I have everyone's good at heart."

Another person on the deck of the *Atlantic* didn't drink beer or smoke cigars. He simply sat, or rather reclined, in a steamer chair, muffled to the ears in a heavy coat and with a robe over his knees, a handsome young man with fair hair and a drawn face. His pallor showed that he had long ago succumbed to the vertigo which had sent the others below decks. He lay with half-closed eyes, holding his head in both hands, staring at the sky which merged with the sea. The horizon looked clear. The sun shone. Then why couldn't he raise his head or move a limb? Why did he want to die. He had forgotten his own name. That he was called Rapalesco he knew. But his real name—if you chopped his head off, he couldn't remember it. Ai. His head, his head.

"You don't feel well? Why don't you go lie down in your cabin? Come with me."

Nissel Shwalb bent over him and looked into his eyes with concern. But Rapalesco returned the look with a vacant stare. He tried to sit up, to raise his head, but he couldn't move.

"Here's a glass of cognac. Listen to me, take a sip, you'll feel better," said Nissel Shwalb, holding a glass to his lips. Thunder rumbled and lightning flashed before his eyes. But it was not lightning, only a ray of the sun which had glanced off the waves.

"Listen to me, suck this lemon. It will revive you."

Now he knew who it was. It was Holtzman, Bernhard Holtzman. But why was his face so full and ruddy and healthy? In one hand he held a glass, in the other a lemon. "Just take this lemon into your mouth. Or give me your arm, lean on me like this, and I'll help you down to your cabin." He raised his voice. "Hey, Mr. Klammer!"

206

No one answered. Where was Mr. Klammer? He was gone. He had gone, like Nissel's brother Isaac, Henrietta, and the Lomzha cantor with his musical family, each to his own bunk, moaning and groaning and wrestling with the Angel of Death. Of them all only Nissel Shwalb remained on his feet.

When Rapalesco began to revive and his head started to clear, he felt, rather than saw, himself lying in bed undressed, and he became conscious of a hand on his forehead, a warm, delicate woman's hand.

That he was still at sea he could tell by the rocking motion under him and the slap of the waves against the porthole over his head. With an effort he gathered together the scattered fragments of his memory. How had he got to his cabin? He wanted to sit up, but was afraid to attempt it lest he fall back again. "My head, my head."

"Does your head still ache?" He heard a woman's voice, a familiar voice, but he didn't know whose it was. He felt a hand, a woman's delicate, warm hand stroking his forehead, smoothing back his disheveled hair. Whose hand was it? And he recalled that a short time ago, he didn't recall just when, he had also felt a woman's hand stroking his forehead and smoothing his hair back, in exactly the same way.

That time it had been Holtzman's sister, Zlatka.

It had happened one evening. Rapalesco lay on the sofa in his room spinning his dreams around their usual center, the Cantor's daughter, Reizel.

There was no one else in the house, he remembered, except Zlatka. He had been oppressed by a strange melancholy, which constricted his heart and brought him close to tears. Whether he wept or not he couldn't remember. He only remembered that Zlatka had suddenly appeared in his room—had he called her perhaps?—and sat down at his side and began stroking his forehead as someone stroked it now. And a curious warmth had spread through his limbs. He had felt endlessly grateful to her. He had put his arms about her, he recalled, and had pulled her down to him, had nestled his head on her knee and had wept for a long, long time. Then he had confided to her that there was someone whom he loved more than life, for whom he would go through fire and water, whom he couldn't forget waking or sleeping.

"What is her name? Where is she?" Zlatka had asked in a tremulous

207

voice, and he remembered how her slight body had trembled. What her name was he wouldn't tell her. And where she was—ah, if he only knew, he would leave the troupe, throw everything over, and fly there! For long ago they had vowed to each other that, no matter where they wandered or what became of them, they would seek each other to live together forever. He only knew she was famous and rich, and had become a great singer. "You've heard the name Patti?" he said to Zlatka. "Well, she's greater than Patti, there's no comparison!"

He remembered the satisfaction he had felt at having found someone to whom he could talk about his beloved. For who else would listen to him like Zlatka? Couldn't he tell that every word he uttered was hallowed and precious to her? Couldn't he hear her heart beating against his? Couldn't he feel her flutter in his arms?

What Zlatka was undergoing at this moment Rapalesco never knew. Having revealed his secret to her, he had gone on to tell her of his hopes and plans for the future. When he found his beloved, he would never again be parted from her. As he talked, he remembered now, he had held Zlatka close in his arms and had promised her, when he found his Reizel (he had let the name slip, no matter), he would send for Zlatka to come and live with them.

"You do care for me, like a sister, don't you?" And he held her tightly, much more tightly than a sister is held. Zlatka was silent. Was he mistaken, he wanted to know? Didn't she care for him?

"Not care for you!" And Zlatka threw herself on his breast and began kissing his eyes and forehead, while her tears wet his face.

"Why are you crying, silly?" he asked. "Why are you crying, why?"

From that evening on, he remembered, he had tried to be alone with Zlatka as often as possible to talk about Reizel. And it hadn't been difficult to arrange. For Holtzman, himself, had encouraged it, even seemed to be trying to throw them together. When the three of them sat together, he would suddenly walk out. Ah, Holtzman. Holtzman. How difficult it had been to part from him, how difficult and how painful.

"Time to get up, dearest. Land is in sight. We're almost in America, my sweet. My darling, my sweetheart."

A familiar voice. A woman's voice. Who was calling him *dearest* and *darling* and *sweetheart?* He didn't want to know just yet. He didn't want to sit up, lest he fall down again. He sank back into his semi-conscious state and relived the painful moments of his parting from Holtzman. . . .

208

It had been a dismal London morning, chilly and grey. Rapalesco was all packed and ready for the journey, his cab waiting to take him to the station. He ran in to say goodbye to Holtzman.

"Goodbye, Bernhard. Farewell."

"Farewell," Holtzman answered with his eyes, for he was forbidden to talk. Ah, if Holtzman could only have talked. If he had snapped back at him as he used to, if he had berated him as he deserved, cursed him as only he could, Rapalesco would have felt better. But Holtzman only looked at him mutely; and oh, what reproach, what infinite sadness there was in that look. He only stretched out his thin, wasted hand, and Rapalesco felt its feverish heat.

Never had Rapalesco wanted to escape from Holtzman as he did now. And the opportunity was there. He could have turned to the door after saying goodbye, run down to his cab, and been off. But he sat down on a chair by the bed where Holtzman lay covered by the famous stole, consumed by fever and surrounded by the nauseating smells of medicine and the undeniable odor of death.

Approaching death lay on Holtzman's lips, clouded his feverish, sunken eyes, and carved his always pointed ears to unnatural sharpness. The realization of it made Rapalesco want to run, run as fast and as far as he could, away from this room where Holtzman lay dying.

But he remained there, bending over Holtzman and speaking to him affectionately, offering him words of comfort and hope, promising to write him from New York, a letter every day. And as soon as Holtzman got up—and he was sure to get up soon—he must book passage on a ship to New York, together with his mother and sister, and join him there in America.

Rapalesco felt his face flaming, every word he spoke was a lie. Holtzman would never get well. He would never sail for America. And even if he were well and able to go, the new company would not take him. But having started, Rapalesco couldn't stop himself.

"Farewell, Bernhard," said Rapalesco, finally, for the last time, and he rushed out of the door and down the stairs, thankful neither Zlatka nor her mother was in sight. Should he wait for them? No, he must go. . . . He got into the waiting hansom cab and was wheeled swiftly away to the station. There the company fell on him with a clamor. "Where have you been? We might have missed the boat." He only breathed more easily again when he stood on the deck of the *Atlantic* and felt the ship swaying under him. A delicious warmth

209

spread through his limbs. He was free and on his way to his beloved.

But suddenly Henrietta appeared at his side, elegantly dressed, twinkling all over with real and false diamonds. She put her arm through his and took him strolling up and down the deck. Her coquettish laugh displayed her pearly teeth, and people turned their heads to wonder at this handsome couple. Were they brother and sister? Or an engaged couple? Or honeymooners?

In her heart Henrietta knew Rapalesco was indifferent to her, but she gave the impression that she was certain he was madly in love with her, that they were all but officially engaged. Everyone but Rapalesco thought so, and there had been talk among the Shwalbs of breaking plates and putting up a marriage canopy. But how to bring it about? The asthmatic *schlimazl*, Holtzman, wouldn't permit the "kid" to fall into their sister's hands. But God came to their aid. When Rapalesco agreed to accompany them to America, the brothers decided, "The kid must be really crazy for our Yentel." And they planned the wedding in America.

It stands to reason their secret was not a secret from everyone. From Mr. Klammer, for instance, Nissel Shwalb had no secrets. When the ex-restaurateur was taken into their confidence, he insisted that he had suspected it right along. He had nothing against the match but this: they mustn't dally too long. The marriage must be fixed up one-two-three, or as the Englishman puts it, "Slow at the start, fast at the finish." For those fellows, meaning the actors, were a fickle lot. Extricating his fingers from his beard, he waved them back and forth in the air, "Fi-fu-fa," to show what a fickle lot they were.

The third member of the company, the Lomzha cantor, delivered himself of the same opinion when Nissel Shwalb told him the secret, naturally behind locked doors. And since the room into which they had locked themselves was the kitchen, where the cantor's wife was at that moment preparing dinner, she too heard the secret. Pretty soon the whole musical family, from the oldest to the youngest, looked forward eagerly to a wedding.

Therefore the only person ignorant of all this was the prospective groom. All his thoughts revolved about Reizel. For her sake he had deserted his old friend Holtzman on his deathbed, and Holtzman's disconsolate sister Zlatka, who had been unable to bring herself to say goodbye to him. . . .

Now, as he lay in his bunk, slowly recovering consciousness, Rapalesco wondered how he could have sunk so low, how he could have thus misused his old friends. As through a kaleidoscope, his whole life passed before his eyes, one picture darker than the next, not a bright spot or a redeeming feature anywhere. Everything he had done had been to further his own ends, without regard for others. He had robbed his father; in a great measure he had been responsible for his mother's early death. Just recently he had lied to Holtzman and deceived Zlatka. Posing as a brother to her he had made love to her, and had broken her young, innocent heart. There was no doubt of it. He was low, base, and vile, worthy of hatred. And at this moment, he was filled with self-loathing. He beat himself on the breast as on the Day of Atonement. A groan escaped him. "My head, my head."

"Your poor head," cooed a familiar voice, and a woman's hand stroked his forehead and smoothed the hair back with gentle fingers. A whiff of perfume came to his nostrils—Henrietta's. He opened one eye cautiously, then the other, and saw close to his face the familiar pencilled eyebrows and rouged cheeks. Henrietta's face came closer to his, her cheek brushed his cheek, and the blue eyes, shadowed with mascara, looked tenderly into his. The ripe red lips whispered close to his ear, "Dearest, darling, lover."

At this moment all was forgotten. His self-loathing and his remorse vanished. He forgot that he had just been beating his breast in penance. He forgot where he was going and for whose sake. He even forgot where he was and who he was. He only felt the soft hand stroking his forehead, only saw the blue eyes gazing into his, and the red lips close, very close. Another moment and they became locked in a long kiss.

Rapalesco would not be able to brush off this kiss lightly. For if it was not a calculated kiss, it was certainly a kiss before witnesses and therefore as good as a pledge. For why else, at this moment, should the door open and three people enter, Nissel Shwalb, Mr. Klammer, and the Lomzha cantor?

They burst in upon them with a congratulatory air, and Nissel Shwalb said, "*Maz'ltov*. Get up, Rapalesco. We've arrived in America."

29 AMERICA! AMERICA!

Since Christopher Columbus discovered America in 1492, the same land has been discovered over and over by every new immigrant.

"America! America!" bursts out a fiery Italian with a glossy black mustache and a pair of strong arms.

"America. America," sounds the lilting voice of a Spanish woman, with melting black eyes and a silk mantilla, which the wind has blown off her head, revealing shiny black hair just combed and pomaded in honor of the new land.

"America, *prosze pana,*" says one Pole, bowing to another, while they both stroke their long mustaches.

"Ya. America," comes in guttural accents from a stout German, all of whose fat has gone to his beer-barrel belly.

"America, oh, yes," drawls an Englishman in checkered trousers with a shaven face the color of rare beefsteak.

"Hurrah, America!" a Russian hails the new land, waving his cap in the air.

"*Bonzai,* America," comes in the liquid tones of a little Japanese, holding a small yellow valise, a coat, and a folded umbrella, all his earthly possessions.

"America. Woe is me," wails an olive-skinned Jewess in a black wig, holding one child by the hand and another in her arms. Her face drained of all color, she stares into the distance, where the outlines of chimneys, then roofs, then many-windowed buildings begin to appear. She can barely see the city, and already her heart beats with fear and is filled with worries and premonitions. Who knows if they will admit her with her two infants? Who knows if she won't get the same reception as in Germany? Will her husband be there to meet her? Will she need a passport as at home? Who knows if her pillows and bedding haven't been stolen?

Of all the passengers who arrived that day on the *Atlantic,* none pushed and shoved so frantically at the gangplanks, none were in such

212

a state of feverish excitement, so harassed and worried, as our Jews. And this is easy to understand. For they came from a land which had treated them without mercy. To them America was a Messiah, land of promise and deliverance. Meanwhile they huddled together like sheep, their hearts pounding, their pulses racing. "Merciful God" . . . they prayed wordlessly. What awaited them here in this blessed land?

Few among them didn't have, in New York, a son or a daughter, a husband or a wife, a relative or a friend, or at least a townsman waiting for them on shore, ready "to take them off" the ship, to help them through the debarkation ordeal at "The Isle of Tears," Ellis Island.

Among the passengers crowding on deck to get their first glimpse of the Golden Land were the artists of Klammer, Shwalb & Co. It was a pleasure to behold this cheerful troupe decked out in holiday finery, each according to his taste and his circumstances.

The brothers Shwalb had shaved closely; their faces looked as bare as two platters. And yet there was not a shred of likeness between them, the older, Nissel, resembling a comfortable German *burger* in his Sunday best, and Isaac a Russian corporal just discharged from the service, who has sworn never to drink vodka any more, only beer.

Mr. Klammer outshone them both. He had combed his beard and parted it to right and left in the manner of the Russian General Skoboliev. His snow-white shirt front and white tie, under the tightly cut dress jacket, would have given him the appearance of a fine gentleman, if they hadn't been so reminiscent of the garb of a head-waiter. Passing through the mirrored dining salon he caught a glimpse of himself in a glass and stopped to look closer, pleased with what he saw.

The case was quite different with the fourth member of the company, the Lomzha cantor. Though he had been away from Poland for many years, and though he had no sign of an earlock, that hirsute symbol of piety, and though even his beard—but why should we speak slander of anyone? Suffice it to say that the cantor had unearthed his ancient Sabbath gabardine with the silken sash, had buttoned his vest up to his chin, and pulled such a long, pious face that the brothers Shwalb and Mr. Klammer exclaimed in surprise, "What's going on there?"

"America," answered the cantor curtly. But since the one word didn't seem to satisfy his audience, he went on to enlighten them.

213

"America, you understand, is not Europe, and New York is not London. America is a land of 'either-or.' Either you're one thing or you're another. If you're an artist, you're an artist. If you're a cantor, you're a cantor. Take that between your teeth and chew it."

Whether they chewed it or not is hard to say. But the Lomzha cantor had a practical turn of mind. He had figured out that it would be a while before his children began bringing in money in America, and some time before the actors started shoveling in gold in this Golden Land. In the meantime the High Holy Days were coming, and where was the harm in grabbing himself a pulpit somewhere with the help of his co-religionists from Lomzha?

And he had felt like singing and warbling all morning, ever since they had sighted land. Accordingly he had dressed himself as a cantor should. His wife had also dressed in holiday garb, her silk kerchief tied in sharp points under her chin, but she had left her ears exposed, in the first place to display her gilded earrings, which had dangled from her ears since the day of her wedding, and in the second place to show a few wisps of her own blonde hair under the red wig. She wasn't at all clear yet what kind of land America was. Who knew what was more acceptable there—piety or vanity? Maybe you needed a little of both. Go tell about America!

On the other hand all the children were got up in European fashion, the girls in long dresses and the boys in short pants, round white collars, and hats on their unshorn locks. Short pants, bare thighs, and long hair, those were the earmarks of child prodigies. Huberman, Fidelman, Grischa Stellmach—all dressed thus for as long as they could hide their beards.

The high spirits of the musical family were matched, if not transcended, by the obvious happiness of a handsome young couple who stood, arms entwined, at the rail of the ship. Henrietta Shwalb and Rapalesco. A discerning observer might have detected a slightly abstracted and pensive look on the young man's face, but that Henrietta was in her seventh heaven was obvious to everyone.

Henrietta's chase was ended. On board ship she had sprung her last trap and the prey was hers. Hers, hers, hers! What a triumph this was, she, and she alone, knew. Its glow was reflected in her eyes and radiated from her face. Every gesture and movement she made seemed to shout, "Do you see this handsome young man with the blue eyes and the noble brow and the fair hair—may no evil eye harm him! He is mine, mine, mine!"

214

She looked into his eyes and tried to interpret the fires that burned in their depths. Of whom was he thinking? Of her, of course. Of whom else? Look everywhere, from steerage to first class—can you find a girl as lovely, with such a fine complexion, such cherry lips, such starry eyes which she can open innocently wide or narrow coquettishly, such pearly teeth which she has only to display in a laugh to have men swoon at her feet? Can you find a woman on shipboard so elegantly dressed, with hair so elaborately coiffed, whose hat sits so smartly and whose collar encircles her throat so neatly and whose gloves sheathe her hands so perfectly? Or one who can boast more jewelry?

There might be women on shipboard with more expensive jewels, for example, that tall, thin Englishwoman with the gold teeth. But the woman herself! The less said, the better. A face like a horse's and a figure like a clothespole. What good are the emeralds to her? Now if Henrietta had those emeralds! But never mind. She will have genuine emeralds. And genuine rubies and diamonds. Let Rapalesco just show himself on the stage. Let him play a few guest performances. Let the public see him, and Henrietta will drip with jewels.

"What do you think of those emeralds?" Henrietta asked Rapalesco coquettishly, squinting at the Englishwoman.

"What emeralds?" asked Rapalesco.

"Silly, are you blind? Can't you see? Over there?"

No, he didn't see and he wouldn't even look. An absent-minded angel. Ha-ha. Henrietta laughed, not for merriment, but to show her white teeth again. And she treated Rapalesco to the near-sighted squint she had just perfected in front of her mirror.

She had picked it up, recently, in London from a near-sighted lady with a lorgnette. The lady had looked most provocative squinting through her lorgnette. Henrietta had taken over the pose, practiced it in front of her mirror for hours, half-shutting her eyes and drawing her brows together just so.

"Yentel, what's wrong with you?" her brother Isaac had asked her one day. "Why are you screwing your eyes up like that?"

Henrietta grew red, sent her brother to the devil, but didn't abandon her squint.

Lucky, lucky Henrietta. Who is her equal now? She is young, bursting with health, beautiful and provocative, and nobody owns such a treasure as her Rapalesco. He is hers, all hers.

There had been a time, not so long ago, when he hadn't been hers.

Zlatka had stood in the way. That wishy-washy kitchen drudge with her pointed nose and hands like a washerwoman's. Henrietta hadn't noticed until her brothers had pointed it out to her. Then she saw the way Zlatka's eyes lit up when Rapalesco came in, the way she blushed when he spoke to her, and how often they were together.

"Come along, blockhead," Isaac had said to her one day, "and I'll show you something." He led her to Rapalesco's door and told her to look through the keyhole. She saw something quite different from what her brother intended, Rapalesco pacing up and down the room with bent head and hands in his pockets, and that wishy-washy girl sitting on a chair weeping.

"Her brother," Rapalesco told them later, "is very ill. The doctors have given up hope." "Whom are they fooling?" snorted Isaac, who had been spying on them right along. "If her brother is ill, does it mean she has to sit on his lap to weep?" "You lie in your teeth," Henrietta had screamed and slammed the door. Just the same the worm of jealousy had entered her breast. Thank God they had left London behind them. Now she had him all to herself. Nobody stood in her way. Nobody.

The first thing they would do when they landed in New York would be to have photographs in all sorts of poses. Pose Number 1: She and Rapalesco promenading, he in his new grey topcoat, she with a boa around her throat, her small hat tilted to one side. Pose Number 2: Facing each other over a small round table, he holding her hand and looking ardently into her eyes, she squinting delicately like the lady with the lorgnette. Pose Number 3: Against a pearl-grey background, their two heads enlarged, close together. Here her eyes must be wide open, gazing upward Madonnawise. Pose Number 4: —But oh, when would the ship dock? How much longer did they have to wait? Her mind turned back to the photographs, though her brother Nissel said the first thing they must do when they landed was to put up a marriage canopy. If it weren't for what people might say, he'd have done it on board ship. Henrietta didn't agree. She wanted the fun and excitement of an engagement.

"Do you think we're almost there?" she asked, but Rapalesco was still lost in a reverie of his own. Soon, very soon, he would reach the goal toward which he had been striving nearly all of his life. Soon he would see her whom he hadn't forgotten for a moment. In his breast pocket he had the picture Madame Cherniak had sent him. Involuntarily his hand went to his heart. Henrietta caught the gesture, nestled up to him and purred like a kitten.

216

"We'll be landing soon, don't you think?" And she flicked her finger over his nose and burst out laughing.

Rapalesco looked down at her in amazement. He was thinking, "Why did I get mixed up with this flirt? Am I in love with her? At this late hour? I have jumped out of the frying pan into the fire." And in spite of himself Zlatka came to his thoughts, with her melancholy face and eyes swollen with weeping. He remembered Holtzman's last words, his last look. Try as he might, he couldn't wipe out his memories. They crowded around him, they dogged his steps, they weighed down his heart.

When America sees fit to crown someone or something with a nickname, you can rest assured it's through no accident. Every ingredient has been weighed and measured, ground to a powder, and compounded like a chemical formula. And it is no accident that the entrance to this Golden Land, once called Castle Garden, then renamed Ellis Island, became to immigrants "The Isle of Tears." The name is as accurate as a druggist's prescription.

As with the heavenly paradise, so with this earthly paradise called America, the gates do not stand open to all. For some it's as easy as eating a bagel; others have to sweat blood. Even those who have prepared for every contingency are anxious; their hearts beat fast for hours before the ship docks. They are shaken by hot and cold chills. Their teeth chatter, they yawn and they stretch. They scrub themselves within an inch of their lives; they examine each other for a spot or a blemish. And having done everything in their power to make themselves worthy of paradise, they throw themselves on God's mercy for the rest.

The artists of the wandering troupe, Klammer, Shwalb & Co., laughed at this folly. A big bargain—America! They could enter and leave, they said, three times over with the greatest of ease. Fools, they said, had dreamed up these difficulties. There was no difficulty at all, as long as you were young and healthy and cheerful, dressed like a human being, had a few dollars in your pocket, and could mention the names of an acquaintance or two in New York.

For example, what did a man like Mr. Klammer, who spoke English as though it were his mother tongue, and wore such an elegant dinner jacket, have to fear in America? Or a giant like Nissel Shwalb? Or even Isaac? Would that all immigrants had so much to recommend them. As for the young couple, Rapalesco and Henrietta, no use talking. There remained only the cantor and his musical family.

Some people, it seems, are marked out for trouble. On the face of it, the cantor had nothing to worry about. His children were all healthy, and their appetites, thank God, left nothing to be desired. If only he had enough to feed them. But an unforeseen dilemma presented itself, and the cantor was himself to blame. He should have known that the head of such a large family would have to show some money and should have asked his companions to provide him with a few dollars beforehand. But he thought America was America. In the end, it turned out to be—may God not punish him for those words—worse than Lomzha. How many paupers arrived in Lomzha every day, and did anyone ask them if they had money? A fine thing!

The cantor had never sweated in the pulpit on the High Holy Days as he did now. Imagine being asked, all of a sudden, out of a clear sky, to produce money. What kind of money? Dollars, they said, American dollars. English pounds would do in a pinch, or even Russian rubles, as long as he had them. He must show that he had some cash, they explained, to see him through his first days in America, and not fall back on strangers.

"Strangers!" The cantor grasped at the word, as a drowning man grasps at a straw. "God forbid, I'm not among strangers. I have my whole family with me." If so, they retorted with cunning, how did he expect to support such a big family?

The cantor tried to explain his prospects as best he could, in broken English and garbled German, aided by vivid pantomime. But he got more and more tangled up. It had reached the point where the officials were ready to escort him back to the ship. In vain the cantor signalled with his hands and his eyebrows to Mr. Klammer to come to his aid. Mr. Klammer pretended not to see. He was an expert at giving advice back in Whitechapel, at his own "Café National," but not here among all those accursed Russian *schnorrers* who drove a man crazy with their yowling and yammering. Mr. Klammer turned his back, adjusted his jacket, parted his beard to right and left, and made himself scarce, or as the Englishman puts it, "I disown you bag and baggage."

Luckily, his partner, Nissel Shwalb, wasn't too far off. When he saw the cantor being questioned at such length, that master of combinations sniffed trouble at once. He pulled the cantor's wife aside, whispered to her urgently, nodding and winking in her husband's direction, then pointed to her bosom. After which he caught her by the hand, and shouting to the children to follow, led her, at a run, to where the cantor was being questioned.

At any other time and under different circumstances Nissel Shwalb couldn't have got away with such high-handed conduct. The cantor's wife, in her ambiguous turnout, half-modest and half-rakish, was in a company of actors. True enough. But just the same she would have you know she wasn't one of those chorus girls. She was a married woman, the cantor's lawfully wedded wife, and a hare-brained fellow like Nissel Shwalb had better watch his step. But in this wild scramble, with her husband plainly in trouble, she didn't have time to demand from him the respect due her station. Before she knew what had happened, Shwalb had caught her by the hand, and was explaining:

"Gentlemen, allow me to present the wife of this man. Neither of them speaks a word of English. This is their family." And he pointed to the mob of children. "They are a musical family, very talented. Each one of them earns his own bread, and not bread but gold. Only one of them," and he pointed to the cantor's wife, "earns nothing. She is a good wife to her husband, a mother to her children, and she is also housewife and cashier. She keeps all the family money in a safe place. To get a cent out of this woman, I tell you, is like crossing the Red Sea dry-shod."

He delivered himself of the above in English, then turned to the cantor's wife and said in plain Yiddish, "Woman! Unbutton your blouse if you please, and out with your moneybags."

It wasn't until they were safely on shore that the Lomzha cantor saw what great danger he had been in and from what dire peril he had been saved. He embraced his deliverer, insofar as it was possible to embrace a man of Nissel's proportions, and thanked him profusely with tears in his eyes. "Dear friend! Little father! Such wisdom, such presence of mind. You're a Solomon, no less. An angel from heaven."

Nissel then turned to see how the others were faring. And he saw a strange apparition, in the shape of a woman, approaching their company. Short and round as a barrel, with a face like a full moon and flashing white teeth, she was enveloped, from head to foot, in a voluminous red cape. This apparition threw herself first of all on his sister Henrietta's neck. Then she embraced and kissed his brother Isaac. Last of all she fell on Rapalesco like a mother greeting her long-lost son.

"Who is this creature?" Nissel Shwalb appealed to the cantor, then to the cantor's wife. But the cantor and his wife were themselves in the clutches of townsmen and townswomen from Lomzha, among them some mellow Yankees who had lost every vestige of greenness,

219

others in the halfway stage, part Yankee, part greenhorn, and still others as green as the day they had stepped off the ship, who hadn't even taken the red kerchiefs from around their necks and whose wives still wore their old-country wigs. Each insisted that the cantor and his family come to her house for dinner or supper or breakfast. "To me first." "No, me first." "I asked them first." The cantor and his wife were like two people bewitched. Could all this be real or was it only a dream? In all the years since they had left Lomzha and knocked around the world, during all the time they had lived in Whitechapel, they had never been showered with so much hospitality. Even in Lomzha they had never been so cordially treated. On the contrary, in Lomzha, they had always loomed a bit large in everyone's eyes. There were too many of them. Even on board ship Mr. Klammer had more than once asked pointedly why they had taken their whole fortune along. Couldn't they have left a child or two behind them as a memento? And here, all of a sudden, the minute they landed, they were received like exalted guests, people actually fighting over them. Blessed be the land of Columbus. The cantor and his wife exchanged a look, and their eyes brimmed over with tears. As for the children, so many invitations to dine at once! They didn't know whom to answer first. They generously promised to go to everyone. Why not? One person can't tear himself into little pieces. But a family like theirs . . . they'd have no trouble at all dividing the honors.

Nissel Shwalb stood on one side watching this scene, and his heart rejoiced. Who knew better than he how lonely and forsaken and friendless this family had been in London? And here they had found so many friends at once. He wasn't surprised. Not a bit. He had known it would happen, as he had everyone's good at heart. That was America for you. Blessed be this land. He would have liked to go up to these good people and thank them in behalf of the cantor and at the same time get acquainted with them, start a little discussion about America, the land of Columbus, Yankee-doodle land.

But his attention was diverted by the strange apparition in the red cape who had greeted Henrietta, then Isaac, and was now busy on Rapalesco. Nissel Shwalb couldn't endure this any longer. He went up to Rapalesco and tore Red Cape away from him. Rapalesco looked relieved. He wiped his face, smoothed back his hair, recovered his hat, and introduced them: "My friend Shwalb, my old acquaintance, Brai— Madame Cherniak." By a slip of the tongue he had almost given away her old nickname, Braindele Kozak.

30 "WITH TRUMPET AND SOUND OF THE HORN"

The newly formed cooperative of artists and musicians, Klammer, Shwalb & Co., had picked an auspicious time for coming to America. It was the happy, the golden time, one might say the harvest time in the Yiddish quarter of New York.

This was the month when Jewish life, in the United States of America, begins to awaken after the long lazy weeks of summer vacation, when the Jewish ghetto, everywhere, becomes more consciously Jewish, when the Yiddish papers blossom out with huge headlines and burgeon with advertisements of synagogues, cantors, *shofars,* palm branches, citrons, holiday greeting cards, and other sacred things. In a word, this was the time of the High Holy Days, ushering in the New Year, as the 98th Psalm says, "with trumpet and sound of the horn."

Just as in the old country, so in the new, this is a period of transition from the old to the new year, from summer to winter, a time for the liquidation of all that is worn and used, and of ushering in the new and the fresh; a time of change of employment and occupation, of refurbishing of old clothing and footwear, of hiring of teachers for the young, and of moving from old quarters to new. This period of transition is known as "The Season."

"The Season" is a good time, a happy time, and a hopeful time for everyone in this land of equal opportunity. It is a good time for those who seek work, as well as for those who provide work, for those who are sweated and for those who sweat others, for those to whom a nickel is a round sum of money and for those to whom a dollar is a scrap of paper. For those who are looking for bread and for those who seek entertainment, for those who swelter on the "top floor" or languish in a damp basement, for those who have spent the summer at a resort in the Catskills, playing poker or pinochle from morning till night, or the game called "flirtation," which consists of seducing another man's wife or of exchanging wives openly.

221

"The Season" is also a time of renewal and rebirth of theater in general and especially of the Yiddish theater, which according to the press occupies a place of honor in the Yiddish quarter of New York. Under the heading of "News of the Yiddish Theater World," vagrant items are collected, picked up here and there, backstage gossip, unsubstantiated rumors, idle chatter—for example, that a certain theater manager is due to arrive from Europe with singers from the Paris Opera; that this-and-that manager has rented so-and-so's theater; that a certain director has enticed a famous prima donna from a rival theater; or that another prima donna has left the Yiddish for the American stage; or that this-and-that playwright, who has won undying fame with his musical-dramatic-comi-tragic works, has written, for this season, three surpassing realistic-musical-melodramatic-patriotic plays. Thus the star gets a tickle in the ribs, the prima donna is favored with a pinch on the cheek, the theater manager gets a pat on the back, and the "playwright of undying fame" gets a nod.

And how the little tidbits expand to a feast once the plays and their stars have been launched and the holiday season is on! What rapturous headlines! In the long columns of print flickering before your eyes, and embellished with fancy lettering, mellifluous words and ringing phrases hold forth the promise of heavenly joys for the worthy public. The unsuspecting reader can't tell whether he's reading a news article or an editorial or a rave review. Never in the world will it occur to him that he is reading an *affiche* or, as it is called in America, an advertisement, in which the theater manager at so much a line blazons forth his wares with "trumpet and sound of the horn."

The reader is called upon to enjoy the exquisite sorrow of *Broken Hearts,* or to split his sides laughing at *The Alrightniks;* or to feast his eyes on sumptuous modern scenery and lavish patriotic symbols in *The Essence of the Jew;* to watch magnificent dancing and decor at *The Four Sticks;* to discover the new classic *The Menorah.*

Or a manager, spreading out over the paper like a landlord after his Sabbath meal, takes the reader into his confidence about his recent visit abroad. In all the capitals of Europe he has sampled the best the way a bee samples honey from every flower. And he has put it all into his new show for the holiday season, to delight the theatergoer with the variety of hitherto unseen national costumes that will fill every Yiddish heart with pride and patriotism, combining the glories of ancient Jewry with twentieth century elegance, abounding in Biblical motifs, supernatural Yiddish melodies, American patriotic

222

songs and the latest Paris dances. And the name for all this? That was the hardest task of all. A musical drama must have a name that rings like a bell, plays like a fiddle, sings like a prima donna. And thank God he had at last found the right name for such a colossal musical-dramatic-national-patriotic-tragi-comedy—*Moishe*.

The whole Yiddish public, individually and *en masse,* is known as "Moishe." *Moishe,* the vernacular for Moses, is like the Russian *Ivan,* a symbol of simplicity, naiveté, and grossness. *Moishe* is the sort of man with whom you don't have to stand on ceremony. You can give him hay to chew on and he won't complain. *Moishe* has a strong stomach; he can digest anything.

They say—and what "they say" must be accepted without cavil—that the coiner of the word Moishe is—may he forgive me for exposing him thus—the late, sainted Goldfadden, the so-called Father of the Yiddish Theater. I say, "May he forgive me," for the word *Moishe* is usually accompanied by a suffix which is unprintable in Yiddish, rhymes with the word *kadoches,* and stands for a part of the human anatomy.

True, there have been those who have objected to the indiscriminate use of this suffix. One of the most heated of the objectors burst into print one day with a fiery tirade in the Yiddish press against this cheapening and vulgarizing of the most sacred and historic name the Jewish people can boast of. But his tirade helped to establish the name *Moishe* more firmly than before. And not only in America. The name *Moishe* rolled across the ocean, together with its suffix, so that whenever a Yiddish actor on either side of the ocean says *Moishe* everyone knows what comes after.

In short, the author of the national-musical-dramatic-patriotic holiday spectacle had aimed well and hit his mark. The high point of the play was a catchy song warbled by the prima donna herself, with such incomparable grace and charm that it melted the hearts of the audience. And the prima donna was aided and abetted by the whole cast, the chorus, and the worthy public in the rendering of this song, "Moishe."

The prima donna, a shapely young woman, her figure enhanced by a tight-fitting officer's uniform, pleaded in her lovely mezzo-soprano:

Who has seen my Moishe?
Moishe? Moishe? Moishe?

He's the man I'm looking for.
Help, Jewish children, Moishe!
Who has seen my Moishe?

Here the prima donna threw a searching look through the audience, from the orchestra to the boxes to the gallery.

A voice from the orchestra, the boxes or the gallery, claimed:

I'm Moishe.

The prima donna trilled melodiously:

No! You're not my Moishe.

Another voice called out from the orchestra, the boxes or the gallery:

I'm Moishe.

Whereupon the prima donna and the cast and the chorus and the whole audience took up the refrain.

Moishe here and Moishe there,
There's a Moishe everywhere.

The hit song "Moishe" spread like wildfire through the ninth district of New York. And it made the national-musical-patriotic drama *Moishe* a hit. The manager of the theater where *Moishe* was running was certain it would remain in his repertory as long as *Moishe* didn't get tired of singing "Moishe." Let the critics criticize for all they were worth. Let the pamphleteers crack jokes and dub the season "All Fools' Week." And if it was a question who perverted the public taste the most, the theater or the press, let the critics leaf through the pages of any Yiddish-American newspaper and take a look at the serials printed year in and year out for the uplift and edification of *Moishe*.

A fiery polemic took place. A bloody battle was joined between the two great organs of the largest Jewish community in the world, its press and its theater. And all because of *Moishe*. And *Moishe* shrugged his shoulders. Where had he the time in this land of "hurry up" and "help yourself" to engage in such foolishness? Worn-out from a day's toil in shop and factory the Moishes filled the orchestra, the boxes, and the gallery of the theater where the beauteous prima donna in the officer's uniform sang:

Help, Jewish children, Moishe!
Who has seen my Moishe?

And they lifted their voices along with the cast and the chorus:

Moishe here and Moishe there,
You'll find Moishe everywhere.

The holiday season was almost at an end—"All Fools' Week" almost over, and the Yiddish theater of New York about to embark on its serious dramatic repertory. On billboards and in newspapers there began to appear names well known to the Yiddish-American theater world. The press spoke of new dramas about to be launched—old plays from the Old World brought out under new titles and so cleverly adapted to the current mode of the Yiddish stage that it was hard to tell where they had originally sprung from. Their adapters were endowed with the names of the great dramatists. One was called Suderman, another Hauptmann, a third Ibsen, a fourth Shakespeare, the Yiddish Shakespeare, greater than Shakespeare himself.

Not all of the critics were in agreement, nor all of the reviews alike. Opinions differed, and differed sharply. What one critic praised to the skies as the inspiration of a new Shakespeare, another tore apart and stepped on with both feet. In a word, the theatrical season was going full blast. But *Moishe* still reigned. The manager of *Moishe* went about, hands in pockets, lamenting his fate. Things were bad, he wept. His theater was too small to accommodate the throngs. He had the helpless look of a Rockefeller distressed as the millions rained down on him.

It is easy to imagine the envy of the other theater managers. In vain they dusted off past successes and presented them to the public as new merchandise. In vain they proclaimed their theaters, on billboards and in the papers, as the true homes of the Yiddish Drama. *Moishe* stood unshaken. Suddenly a shower of manna descended on the other managers' heads. It opened their eyes, revived their spirits, and practically made the dead come to life again. This was the cooperative, Klammer, Shwalb & Co.

They had done nothing the first few weeks after their arrival, merely watching and marveling at what went on. A stranger, when he first comes to a new country, is like a swimmer in unfamiliar waters. He has to take his bearings, look around him, learn the language, in short, acclimatize himself.

But to continue to sit around doing nothing was no plan, either. They could eat up the money Mr. Klammer had brought from London in no time at all. At every pound Mr. Klammer exchanged for dollars, he groaned and reproached his partners. He informed them that any day it would be as the Englishman says, "No pay—no show." Or as the Russian peasant puts it, "No money—no lullaby." Naturally the partners resented such insinuations, above all the leader and guiding star of the cooperative, Nissel Shwalb. All eyes turned toward that master of combinations. Nissel Shwalb only asked them to have patience and showed them, in simple figures such as two plus two, how very soon they would start shoveling in gold, raking in fortunes greater than those of Jacob Schiff and John Rockefeller. Nissel Shwalb, with his quick eye, had caught on that in this new land called America the laws of the Old World didn't apply. What went in Europe was suicide in America. He concluded that to appear with the whole company at once, as he had formerly planned, would be to risk breaking his neck. Better to come forward one by one, each to make his own "sensation." He demonstrated that he was what is known in America as "a good businessman." A good businessman doesn't display his whole stock at once. Nissel Shwalb first sought to provide for his sister Henrietta and his brother Isaac.

As for Isaac, the erstwhile Purim player and "heavy villain" was pronounced by booking agents as more fit for a butcher or a milkman or an ice-cream vendor. Isaac, therefore, had to take a different job for the time being, but a job close to the theater.

With Henrietta things went better. Nissel had only to let her be seen to cause a sensation. Henrietta was at that time in the full bloom of her youth and beauty. Besides which her dress was so elegant, her hat so modish, her jewels, both real and false, so numerous, that Nissel had only to lead her backstage and introduce her to the actors, to start rumors flying through the audience of a rising new star in the firmament of the Yiddish theater. Who she was and whence she came nobody yet knew. But they didn't have to wait long for newspaper streamers announcing the scheduled appearance of a certain famous actress from Buenos Aires, by the name of Henrietta Shwalb, in so-and-so's theater. Her beautiful face and lithe figure, said the papers, would put to shame all the actresses who had ever trod not only the

Yiddish stage, but all the stages in the land, and of the whole world. And speaking of beauty, at last year's beauty contest in Paris Henrietta Shwalb had won first prize.

Enough said. There was a packed house the first night to look over the great star from Buenos Aires and winner of the Paris beauty contest. We might add here that, for once, the worthy public, so used to being bluffed, felt satisfied. It greeted the new star with the sort of applause only heard in a Yiddish theater.

It is easy to imagine the swaggering air with which Nissel Shwalb walked into the manager's office when, upon arriving the next day to talk about terms, he saw the sign over the box office, SOLD OUT. Forgetting that the tidbit about the beauty prize in Paris had sprung from the fertile imagination of the theater manager himself, he went into detail about the event, how world-famous beauties had openly envied Henrietta; how the judges made a turnabout on discovering that she was a Jewess, and almost took the prize away from her. If he hadn't threatened to cause a scandal and not only threatened but actually told them thus-and-so and so-and-thus.

Nissel Shwalb had to stop abruptly in the middle of his narrative. A foot as heavy as a guardsman's had descended on his own. It was Madame Cherniak's. You might ask, how did Madame Cherniak happen to be there? We can only counter with another question. Would Braindele Kozak, responsible for Henrietta's coming from London, and therefore in her own eyes her patroness, have stayed away from such an interview? Nissel Shwalb was not so much surprised at how far afield he had gone with his story as at how such a heavy foot could belong to such a small woman.

Lucky Henrietta. Never in all her career on the stage had she received such ovations. This was not the clapping of human hands. Such an ear-splitting noise could only be produced by pounding pillows together or beating rugs outdoors, or, at the very least, by handing people two pieces of board and telling them, "Knock, bang, thump, clap to your heart's content."

We must confess at last that high up in the top gallery sat a group of people with just such boards in their hands, issuing such claps of thunder every time the star from Buenos Aires appeared. The theater almost fell apart from the noise. The public looked up in fright, then augmented the noise by clapping their own hands and stamping their feet. This is the nature of a public, which needs only a signal to get it started. Who has to know where the signal comes from? Into whose head will it enter that up there, on high, sit men banging away on boards, among this claque the star's own brother, Isaac? This was the theater job his brother had found for him.

Sic transit gloria mundi, says a Latin proverb. If we permit ourselves to translate it somewhat freely we might say, "Thus a tragedian turns into a clapper."

Once a wedge had been made, the cooperative, Klammer, Shwalb & Co., won entrance into all sorts of places. They went, one might say, through gates and doors and even cracks in the wall. While "the star from Buenos Aires" was rising, there sang in the press the melodious notes of the Lomzha Nightingale.

The Lomzha Nightingale was, of course, the Lomzha cantor. In London he had lain buried in a cellar, unknown and unrecognized, permitted to starve three times a day. Here, in New York, he grew three heads taller and became famous overnight. That season you could read in all the newspapers and upon huge posters:

COME THIS DAY TO OUR THEATER TO HEAR THE LOMZHA NIGHTINGALE SING KOL NIDRE WITH HIS OWN CHOIR WHICH WON THE ACCLAIM OF KING GEORGE OF ENGLAND

How did the Lomzha cantor break into the theater? And what did poor unsuspecting King George have to do with it? The reader can spare himself the trouble of asking. He need only recall that our cooperative was not in Yehupetz, but in the golden land of Columbus.

You can say what you will about our brethren in this golden land; you can say that they are a little too immersed in "business"; that they throw themselves into American life a bit too avidly and try to become more American than the Americans, and other such things which to some are a fault and to others a virtue. But one thing we must grant them: they have not forgotten this precept of our holy Bible: "Honor the stranger in thy midst, for thou wert once a stranger thyself." And they will not forget it even when they have ceased to be greenhorns themselves. Without exaggeration we can say that when it comes to hospitality every one of them is a Father Abraham. A guest, whether a close relative or only a townsman, is sacred to them. Everyone once downtrodden himself, given a taste of being an immigrant, will never rest after he has worked himself up in America until he had brought all his relatives over from the old country. If he only could, he would bring over his whole town, with its rabbi and *shochet* and cantor. Let them all see what a fine living he is making in this golden land and let them make a living, too.

228

But let not this dithyramb set up all our American brethren as blameless saints. Human beings are still human beings. When a countryman arrives, they receive him with open arms, give him the place of honor, wine him and dine him, show him off with great pride, give him the best of advice, and even help him out with cash as far as they are able. But time doesn't stand still. There is a saying here, a harsh saying, "Time is money." When the first flush of excitement dies down, they tell him, "Now, mister, get to work."

And the newcomer, rested and refreshed, full of hope, goes out into the street and stands confused, not knowing where to turn.

What is the trouble?

The trouble is this. He hasn't been warned that in this turbulent, noisy, work-ridden, business-engrossed land of "hurry up," where no one has time, all busy from morning till night, a newcomer mustn't wait until someone stops him in the street, gives him a greeting, offers him a pinch of snuff, and asks, "What is your name, brother?"

No, this is a land of self-reliance with everyone his own master. A land which has hammered out an iron maxim, "Help yourself." In our tongue this is as good as, "Uncle, don't stand in my way. Bow your head to the yoke and pull for all you're worth." Or, "Uncle, you're welcome to starve if you have nothing to eat." In a land like this you can't wait for indulgence or expect miracles. You have to gird your loins and go up to the first stranger you meet and say, "Sir, I am So-and-So and I can do this-and-that. Can you use a pair of hands?" Hands, that's the nub of the matter. There are no people here, only hands. Hands speaking, hands supplicating. And the louder you shout, "Hands," the better it will be for you.

But you need not be so simple as to think that you yourself have to walk through the streets shouting, "Hands, hands." For that there is a press. For this newspapers have been created which serve the broad public and which are crowded with advertisements from top to bottom. Whoever wants to make a living in this golden land, and insure himself against starving quietly in this free America, must solicit the help of the press. He must, whether he likes it or not, advertise himself in all the papers, extol himself and his merchandise, ring all the bells, sing his own praises "with trumpet and sound of the horn."

The leader of the cooperative took in this situation at a glance. His keen sense of smell and his quick eye told him that delay would be fatal, that he must take the reins in one hand, the whip in the other, and be on his way. In the case of the Lomzha cantor both time and chance played into his hands. The time was that of the High Holy Days in America and the lucky chance was that, just then, a certain "society" found itself without a cantor. When the notice first appeared, "Wanted—a Cantor for the High Holy Days," cantors began pouring in from all sides, and the Lomzha Nightingale faced stiff competition. However, his townsmen from Lomzha put in a good word.

But this was only the prelude to his career. An American "society" needs a cantor only for the High Holy Days, and from the High Holy Days you can't make a year's living. Here Nissel Shwalb displayed his enterprise. He rented a hall and had the following notice printed in all the papers:

"A Man like a Nightingale. A Throat like a Clarinet. A Voice like a Fiddle. This is the world-renowned Lomzha Cantor with his own choir. He will sing *Kol Nidre* in the M— Hall accompanied by his own orchestra, composed of all instruments, which has performed for King George of England."

The first concert was also the last concert, for the next morning Nissel Shwalb and his financial backer, Mr. Klammer, sat over a glass of beer and Havana cigars with the manager of a Yiddish theater and signed an agreement for thirty performances in which the Lomzha cantor with his choir would sing *Kol Nidre* every night in the famous operetta called, by a strange coincidence, *Kol Nidre*.

After the agreement had been signed, Mr. Klammer regretted their haste and began reproaching Shwalb for having sold their merchandise too cheap. His argument proved a just one when, after the first few performances, the same manager signed another agreement at exactly three times the price. As the upshot of this, a bitter quarrel rose between the two partners. Sharp words led to name-calling, which in turn might have led to blows if the cantor and his wife hadn't interfered in the nick of time. They reminded the two partners of an important piece of business, if not the most important, still lying ahead of them. To wit, providing for Rapalesco. In the meanwhile the cantor's wife prepared a very fine supper to which she invited all the members of the cooperative, along with Madame Cherniak and several Lomzha townsmen, who promised to bring their wives and spend a convivial evening with their fellow countryman, the Lomzha Nightingale, and at the same time get acquainted with his colleagues.

31 THE KIBITZARNIA

"Providing for" Rapalesco was not as easy as the partners had imagined. In the first place, they hardly laid eyes on him now. He spent the days gadding about town with that grotesque creature, Madame Cherniak. When night came, he vanished again. He went to all the concerts and plays in aristocratic, Gentile "uptown" New York, just as though he had come to the Gentiles and not to the Jews, as though the Yiddish theater had no interest for him, as though he were not a Yiddish artist.

At first his companions paid little attention to this. A young fellow, they reasoned, in a strange land for the first time, has a right to gad about a bit. But after a while they began to look at him askance and lecture him for not attending to business. Why couldn't he stay downtown and study the Yiddish stage and learn something from famous Yiddish-American artists?

To which Rapalesco replied that he could spare himself the trouble of studying the Yiddish stage—he knew it from *a* to *z*. And as for learning something from his fellow-actors, he could learn more among "the nations of the world," meaning the American stage.

This, however, was an excuse. Rapalesco had business of his own in New York, however much he displeased the members of the cooperative, who wanted their paragon to appear before the New York public as quickly as possible and show them who he was and what he could do.

Naturally Nissel Shwalb took the first step. He sought out a newspaper reporter, to whom he gave an exclusive interview acquainting him with the life and background of Leo Rapalesco, who came of a historic Jewish family in Bucharest. His father, Samuel Rapalesco, one of the wealthiest bankers in Rumania, had received citizenship rights from the King, though naturally it had cost him a small fortune. Even as a child little Leo had shown remarkable acting ability and had dreamed of studying dramatic art, but his fanatical parents had forbidden it. One fine day young Leo decided to take matters into his own hands. He presented himself to the Queen of Rumania, the famous dramatist, Carmen Silva . . .

"Carmen Silva is a novelist," the reporter interrupted.

Nothing daunted, Nissel Shwalb went on, "But she's a connoisseur of the drama, isn't she? Well, our Leo introduced himself to her and recited several monologues, and the Queen was so impressed she sent him to study at her own expense in the best Rumanian theater school. But young Rapalesco had always aspired to the Yiddish stage. 'I am,' said he, 'a child of the Jewish people and I must serve my own folk in my own mother tongue and not in any other.' And one fine morning he ran off with a wandering troupe of Yiddish actors. The director of this troupe, a gifted artist, scholar, and writer by the name of Holtzman, author of the great work, *Uriel Acosta*. . . ."

Here the reporter found it necessary to interrupt again.

"Excuse me, Mr. Shwalb, the author of *Uriel Acosta* is not Holtzman, but Karl Gutzkow."

Nissel Shwalb, not easily embarrassed, explained patiently, "I know the author of *Uriel Acosta* is Karl Gutzkow. I mean the translator of that work into Yiddish."

"I beg your pardon," the reporter persisted, "the translator of *Uriel Acosta* is not Holtzman, but Joseph Lerner."

Nissel Shwalb went on blithely, "I know it is Lerner. Lerner was the first translator. But Holtzman wasn't satisfied with his translation. And so, one fine morning, he sat down, and in the space of a night he did a new translation especially for Rapalesco. You can understand for yourself when I tell you that once in Vienna, Zonenthal, the great Zonenthal himself, saw Rapalesco in the role of *Uriel Acosta* and burst into tears like a small child and vowed once for all, 'That's the end, I don't play Acosta any more.' And, what do you think? He kept his word. He never played the part again, may I have everyone's good at heart."

American reporters are no infants. They recognize bluff when they see it. And so the reporter produced his own version. He threw out a little, added a little, with remarkable results.

The next morning when Rapalesco opened the paper, he read his own life's story under the following captions:

A NEW STAR IN THE YIDDISH THEATER
CARMEN SILVA BESIDE HERSELF
QUEEN CROWNS YOUNG ACTOR
ZONENTHAL WEEPS

232

Rapalesco laughed so hard he began to choke, and his companions had to pound him on the back for half an hour to bring him to.

Kibitz is a word which sprang from American soil, in Yiddish-American literary and theatrical circles. It has had a variety of meanings. At that time to kibitz was to indulge in repartee of a special sort, to needle someone, tickle him in the ribs, pull his leg, gnaw at his vitals, sprinkle salt on his wounds, give him the kiss of death, and all with a sweet smile, with a flash of rapier-like wit, with whimsy and humor. Yet, all these expressions lumped together don't quite convey its flavor. Consequently it will be just as hard to explain what a *kibitzarnia* is.

Superficially, a *kibitzarnia* is a club or café, in the ninth district of New York, where the intelligentsia, affiliated with literature, theater, and politics, gathers to eat, drink—and *kibitz*. They belong to different camps and parties, mainly rivals, often competitors, and almost without exception sworn enemies. They loathe each other, they hate to hear each other's names mentioned. If one were, God forbid, to give up the ghost, the others wouldn't hesitate to dance on his grave.

At certain set times of day and night they gather in the *kibitzarnia*, each surrounded by his own partisans. They order a bite to eat or a drink, smoke cigars—and the kibitzing starts. The barbed compliments fly between the tables. Racy stories and witticisms are passed around, each calculated to step on someone's toe where the shoe pinches most. The raconteur watches his opponent squirm with ill-concealed pleasure, though he himself may wince with pain at the next round. And all in an atmosphere of good fellowship and cosy intimacy, with gay talk and resounding laughter.

The *kibitzarnia*, dear reader, is a sort of free Gehenna where people rake each other over the coals, a steam bath where they beat each other with bundles of twigs until the blood spurts. Here opinions are formed, reputations are made and destroyed, careers decided.

It was a rainy autumn day when the skies of New York, obstructed by towering buildings called "skyscrapers," and iron railways on stilts, called "elevateds," had almost the lowering aspect of London skies. The time was noon. Everyone was in a hurry, everyone buying and selling, running and yelling. In a word the kettle was on the fire and boiling over.

The *kibitzarnia* was packed to the doors. A screen of blue smoke hung in the air, so thick you could cut it.

At one of the tables sat three men drinking beer, so absorbed in

233

talk they didn't hear what was on everyone's tongue. All three talked at once. Two of them were the well-known blowhards from London, Mr. Klammer and Nissel Shwalb, the third a native American. You can tell an American a mile away. Everything about him, his expression, his bearing, even his diction and mannerisms are different. Where your Englishman is long-faced and dour-looking, an American is cheerful and good-humored, with shrewd, twinkling eyes, engaging manners and flashing gold teeth. Our Yankee was a Yiddish-American theater manager by the name of Nickel.

Nickel was one of the most popular personalities in Yiddish New York, a "good guy," or as we say in Yiddish, "a good brother." He was generous to a fault. He would give you the shirt off his back. His wide-open, perennially youthful face always wore a disarming smile. He had a kind word for everyone and was always good for a touch, if he only had the money and wasn't looking for a loan himself. For as everyone knew, his wife wore the pants in the family and controlled the finances. His competitors in the *kibitzarnia* made the most of it, and many were the stories they spread around about Nickel's henpecked state. But he laughed at them all. If Nickel had taken all that was said about him to heart, he would have been in the grave long ago.

Nickel knew he had the reputation of being the biggest bluffer in Greater New York. He knew that a whopper, in the *kibitzarnia,* was always challenged, "Who told you—Nickel?" But why take to heart what the kibitzers say? Hypocrites! Loafers! Blowhards and windbags, everyone of them. Let one try to match Nickel's exploits, take their troupes on the road for one week and give twelve performances in eight cities twice a day from Philadelphia to Chicago and back!

This feat of Nickel's was accepted by Nissel Shwalb and Mr. Klammer without the blink of an eyelid and they capped it with several no less remarkable feats of their own. The three were absorbed in a contest of bluff.

Bluff is also an American word which is hard to define. To bluff is not to tell an outright lie or fib, it is not to babble or rant, to spin yarns out of thin air. This is merely known as "knocking a teakettle," for which America has nothing but scorn. An American is too much the businessman for that. When an American tilts his head to one side, tucks his thumb in his vest, and tells you a lie, it is rounded out, just plausible enough to be believed, certainly hard to refuse, and above all, it sticks to the business in hand.

The frequenters of the *kibitzarnia* are not idle loafers, not like the "fireside sages" of the old country, who sat around the synagogue

234

stove warming their backsides and spinning yarns because they had nothing better to do. Kibitzing, which goes hand in hand with bluff, is a vocation in itself, or as it is called in America, "a business."

Nickel, Mr. Klammer, and Nissel Shwalb, as they sat that noon in the *kibitzarnia,* were doing business, and bluffing was part of it. Nickel had just engaged the young star Leo Rapalesco of Bucharest, whom the Queen of Rumania had crowned as the world's greatest tragedian. Klammer described how Rapalesco had bowled over the London public, even charming a man like himself who had never gone to see "those strolling gipsy players" in the London Pavilion Theater. Nissel interjected, "What more do you want? Not only the Jews, but the Englishmen couldn't praise him enough. Irving, they said, was a dog next to him. May I have everyone's good at heart."

Nickel paid no attention. With an affable smile that displayed his gold teeth, he invented new marvels about himself and his theater, which "occupied first place in the United States of America." In the end the two bluffers from London had to yield to this master of bluff, and they fell silent. What other Yiddish theater in America, Nickel asked, could boast that Teddy Roosevelt, the president of the United States, had sat in one of its boxes and had insisted on meeting the manager. "Nickel, you are all right," said T.R. and, in front of everyone, he had unclasped his gold watch and chain and presented them to Nickel as a keepsake. With these words Nickel pulled out a tarnished, nickel-plated watch from his pocket, and explained that he never wore the precious gold watch and chain on weekdays.

Nickel talked on, oblivious of the kibitzing that went on behind his back about him, about his Bucharest bird whose talents the kibitzers belittled though they had never seen him act, calling him "Green-horn," "Chaim-Yankel," "Smart-Aleck," "Rumanian shepherd," and so on. Most of them were partisans of rival theaters who hadn't succeeded in signing him up, or reporters who had missed the scoop of the season, or rival actors waiting for a part, resentful of this young whippersnapper just off the ship, this Rapalesco of Bucharest of whom no one had heard before, grabbed up like a prize package.

But kibitzing alone wasn't enough. A counterplot had to be organized against him. Poor Rapalesco didn't know what surprise awaited him in this golden land. He didn't go near the *kibitzarnia.* His thoughts flitted elsewhere, in that aristocratic part of New York known as Fifth Avenue, where lived the opera singer whose name rang all over America, Rosalie Spivak.

32   ROSA WANDERS

The patient reader will no doubt remember that we
left our heroine at the door of Marcella Zembrich's hotel suite. We
will not follow her changing fortunes step by step, but simply say that
the world-famous artist, captivated by her gypsy personality and singing, took the young girl under her wing.

According to newspaper stories, the young singer aroused such
enthusiasm at the Austrian Court that she was given a stipend by
Emperor Franz Josef for the study of music. Having acquitted herself
with great brilliance at the Vienna Conservatory, she next went to
Berlin to study at the expense of a Hungarian magnate, and then to
Paris, where she met a certain patron of the arts, Jacques Reszko,
through whose influence she joined the Paris Grand Opera. There
she made her debut in the new opera, *Electra,* under the conductor-
ship of Richard Strauss, with such success that she was immediately
engaged for three months at the salary of half a million francs. Shortly
thereafter we see her in Vienna and in Bucharest, where she commands
the fee of ten thousand crowns for an evening's performance, and in
London for a fee of two hundred pounds a night. Now, in New York,
she draws two thousand dollars a performance, a figure equalled only
by the famous Melba. . . .

When Marcella Zembrich heard Rosa sing and tore her out of
Shchupak's hands, she not only gave her the finest musical training,
clothes, and money; she gave her a home and became her friend, her
beloved *Müterchen.* But she also urged Rosa to remember her parents
in Holeneshti. And finally, after these many years, Rosa went back to
her native town for a visit.

She found her home just as she had left it. The same tiny, impov-
erished townlet. The same little people with the same petty interests
and narrow ideas. And yet her heart beat fast when she beheld the
familiar streets and houses. She was ready to fall down on her knees

and kiss the black earth of the fields and the grey dust of the unpaved, unswept streets. She would have done it if she didn't have her Maestro Salponini and her friends with her.

She wished now she had come alone. For, though she wouldn't admit it, she was ashamed before her friends when her parents came out to meet her. Her mother fell on her neck and wept and laughed and poured out a stream of words, and her father stood there as pale as death and his hands trembled. Rosa felt strangely ill at ease. Was it their shabby clothes such as everyone in the town wore? Or was it because they spoke no other language but Yiddish? There it was, at any rate. She was ashamed of her good, kind parents, who had suffered so much on her account.

True, she was a Lady Bountiful now. She helped them all she could. But what good was that? The little comfort and joy she could give them now wouldn't wipe out a tenth of the pain and disgrace she had caused them. Every penny she spent on them now cried aloud, it seemed to her, "Too late, too late." Her sick father's large black eyes asked her, "Where were you, daughter, during those long sleepless nights when I prayed God for death? One letter from you, one line, one word, would have meant the world to me then."

And she had tried to deny her parents, had made believe, to Marcella Zembrich, that she had none. Now there was no sacrifice she wouldn't make for them. She wanted to take them with her, but it couldn't be done. Her father was ill, and her mother wouldn't leave him for a day, even if, as she said, you gave her a lapful of gold and the Queen of England's crown in the bargain. So Rosa told herself, "I will provide for them in their old age. I will buy them a house, provide them with an income."

But even this she did more for herself than for them, just as her visit was more for herself than for them. Only one thing, one person, drew her there. Not only didn't she find him, she didn't even find a trace of him or learn a word as to his whereabouts. Of all the big, noisy, happy household there was no one left but an old grandmother in her dotage, an idiot of a brother-in-law, and an ancient dog with one rheumy eye, named Terkish.

The house, she told herself, she would buy for her parents, and she was thinking only of herself. Not because it appealed to her in itself. What on earth would she do with it? No, it was only a caprice. The caprice of a gipsy. Years ago, when she first stepped across the threshold of this house in her torn shoes, she envied these rich people.

237

Why did they deserve all this, while in God's Street they had nothing? She vowed then that some day it would be hers. But perhaps it was dear to her for another reason, because here he was born and grew up.

Be that as it might, she didn't haggle over the price. She bought the whole estate over her mother's protests. "What do we need such a big hat for?" she argued. Naturally Rosa won out. She hired workers to repair the house, clear the land, transplant the garden, to build Pithom and Raamses, like the Hebrews of old.

Meanwhile the whole town looked upon Rosa and her friends as lunatics. They ran around all day and half the night, held picnics in the nearby woods, sang gipsy songs, danced gipsy dances. The local police began to keep an eye on them. The young visitors drove around during the day and went boating at night, while the whole town slept, a town of innocents, with no desires and no ambitions, content with their cornmeal *mameliga*.

Meyer Stellmach had given his partner the gate. Now he was his own master. The wedding was his and the musicians were his. What he did was done and what he said was spoken. That's the way he had established it from the very beginning, that a father is a father and a child is a child. After all, what he had borne on his shoulders and what he had gone through to establish his Grischa, nobody else could have done.

And now this Rosa Spivak, a beauty, and not stupid, either. And what a voice! God knows what would have become of her, if it wasn't for him. He introduced her to Marcella Zembrich, and now she could put in the shade Zembrich and three others like her. Now she sang at the same concerts with Grischa and got almost as much money as he did. And she had him, Meyer Stellmach, to thank for it.

So when he found out about a letter she wrote to his son which fell into his hands by accident—that is, he took it from the mail carrier— he began to burn. The nerve of a girl. He introduces her to Zembrich, he opens a door for her, as they say, into the great world, and that's how she repays him, with a love affair with his son.

And such a fellow as his son. As famous and sought after as he was, that's just how simple and modest he was. And quiet. All he cared about was his fiddle and concerts, concerts and fiddle. Ask him, for instance, how much his last concert grossed. That was not his affair. Do you think he was a stupid boy? He was as bright as they come. But he simply didn't worry his head over such things. And in general, he

238

was not, as the Litvak puts it, "first cousin to the whole world." Why should he be? He had someone else to look out for that. He had a father, and a mother on the side. What then? Go be a prophet and predict that a cantor's daughter will come into the picture, a Rosa Spivak, a nuisance, a "love" affair.

Stellmach sat down and wrote her in plain everyday Yiddish, telling her thus-and-so and how-dare-you and again how-dare-you? Where is common decency, he said, where is justice, where is gratitude? He gave it to her out of both barrels.

He didn't have to wait long for Rosa's reply. First she gave him the devil for that accident. The letter, she said, was not addressed to him. If she wanted to write to him, she knew his address. Second, she said, "Who gave you the idea I have designs on your son? Because all your thoughts revolve about Grischa Stellmach, you are mistaken if you think that's the case with everybody else." And how did he know that her letter to his son wasn't a reply to a letter he wrote to her? And maybe not the first one. But his letters came directly to her hands, while her letters to him had to pass through a censor. In that case, she would see to it that her letters reached their destination and that no more "accidents" happened. "I will do this," she said, "not because my life depends on whether I write to your son or not, but simply because the Bessarabian wench, as you call me, wants to show there's a limit to your despotism. I assure you that if I felt toward your son a tenth part of what he feels toward me, we would go ahead and show you we don't care a rap for your opinion."

The upshot of their correspondence was they became friends. Stellmach and his wife had to get down on their knees to her before she would honor them with a visit. But what wouldn't parents do for a child? And if they had tried to break it up, would it have been any better?

So they became attached to the girl; she was as dear to them as if she were their own. They would have been happy to have the match come off. But no. Neither of the young people was ready for that. Modern children. You couldn't lay down the law to them. They were not just any young man and his girl. They were both celebrities. You couldn't mention the word "marriage" to them. You couldn't even say the word "engagement."

They only ran around London, not on foot, but in a motorcar, and buying and buying. Money meant nothing to them. If not for Stellmach, they would have squandered thousands. They were getting ready to go to America soon. They were both booked for the whole season, and on such terms as you could wish to all your loved ones.

But though Stellmach was kindness itself to Rosa, he still seemed to rub her the wrong way. She didn't like it when he talked about money. She thought he was a tightwad. "Children," Stellmach reflected, "are fools. They don't understand that whatever we do is for their sake."

For Sholom Meyer Muravchik everything was falling buttered side down, and all because of that Holeneshti beauty, Rosa Spivak. He thought he could catch the hare by the tail and all he caught was a cold in the head. Did he earn this by her, that he should run after her like a dog from Paris to London, and from London to Paris, and then to Antwerp, and she shouldn't see him? If not for him, she would never have met Zembrich, and now he could sit three hours by the clock in her *salon* while she blabbered French with a Frenchman and a servant came and told him she wasn't home. Everything turned black before his eyes. He couldn't find the door handle. And when he followed her from Paris to a French resort, he saw her fly by in an automobile with Stellmach's young pipsqueak. But when he grabbed his cap off his head, she looked the other way.

So then he wrote to her, once, twice, and she didn't answer. Finally he sent her another letter, telling her that someone had brought him a package of her letters and asked him to pay through the nose for them. If she wanted Sholom Meyer to buy the letters back, she'd have to send him the money. The little bit she had sent him once was enough to fill one tooth, although if it hadn't been for that, he would have long ago been where horseradish never grows.

This time Rosa answered him, only her letter lay around for months at the Paris Yiddish Theater, where he had told her to send it. Finally the director, Waxman, the cholera take him, turned it over to Sholom Meyer. Money, wrote Rosa, was no object; she wanted the letters back.

Rushing off to London, Sholom Meyer, the *schlimazl*, found that the letters had all melted away like salt in water. Now what could he do? If he could only drag himself to America, he would have nothing to worry about. There he could find that fellow Klammer and get back his satchel with the papers.

To go to America, he needed money. Where could he turn for help? Shchupak! Shchupak owed him plenty. He sat down and wrote the director a long letter, explaining the situation and asking him

240

for a hundred rubles. Shchupak wrote back that money didn't grow on trees and Sholom Meyer wasn't his favorite son, but he sent him fifty. Maybe Sholom Meyer could tear something from that cantor's daughter who had almost ruined Shchupak and insulted him in front of his friend Stellmach, calling him a *"melammed's* helper."

Luckily Shchupak had managed to get to Odessa, his old home, and if not for the competition, he could make out. But still, he couldn't complain. He had a troupe of his own putting on *Essence of the Jew, Hinke Pinke, Velvele Eats Compote,* and other such delicacies, and if it weren't for the other three theaters in the town and for the cholera. . . .

Rosa was gone from Paris, gone from the Grand Opera, on tour with the ex-wonder-child, now violin virtuoso, Grischa Stellmach. But how many people knew that she had run away from Paris? And do you think she ran away because she didn't get enough applause? No, she had plenty of that.

Rosa fled in shame, disillusioned by that Parisian friend, Edmond, a young composer and pianist whom she had idolized. Maybe she should have known better. She was young in years but old enough in experience. But Edmond? The gentle, patrician, reserved, brilliant Edmond, with his beautiful long hands whose golden fingers could draw from the dead instrument such inspired music? How many moments of rapture she had known with him! And now he had failed her.

Compared to him, Salponini was a model of decorum, Ernesto Corrugio, who had driven her from lovely Italy, a seraph. Edmond did not even have their finesse. He offered Rosa a proposition in cold business terms, as though making a deal—a contract in the Grand Opera on such terms as no prima donna had ever dreamed of, if only . . . And here he ran his fingers back and forth over the piano keys and struck a wild jangle of chords.

When he raised his eyes and saw how enraged Rosa was, he tried to appease her. In a practical world everyone, he said, must be practical. Everything was for sale . . . if not for money, then for jewels . . . if not for jewels, then for glory. He reeled off a list of the gay *amours* of famous actresses, singers, and prima donnas, including some whom Rosa knew and for whose honor she would have sworn.

Again he passed his fingers lightly over the piano keys. Looking at her sideways, he spoke in a new tone. "The world," he murmured,

241

each word dipped in poison, "belongs to you Jews. For nobody loves money as you do, and nobody understands the power of wealth as you do."

Suddenly, as Rosa watched, his beautiful hands, lying idle on the keys, swelled to giant proportions. Right in front of her eyes they turned from pure white to steel grey. Hands of steel! Any minute, she thought, they would circle her throat and strangle her. But she must not let go of herself. Hearing him quietly out to the end, she escorted him to the door with courtesy. She even promised him a definite answer by the next day.

After the door closed behind him, she collapsed in a sort of delirium. When she came to, she called her friend Reszko, only to find he had gone out of town. All at once she was overwhelmed by her own insignificance. No one, she thought, is sufficient unto himself. How lonely we are, how utterly lonely. For the first time in many years she felt homesick for her own people, she remembered her origins. How could she have forgotten that she belonged to the wandering folk blessed with the name of Jew? And to be reminded of it in such a manner!

Early the next day she left the hotel. Impulsive as ever, she fled from Paris. And so she came to the tour with Grischa Stellmach.

On the afternoon long ago, when Rosa waited outside the concert hall for another glimpse of Grischa Stellmach and Marcella Zembrich, she had seen a beautiful vision. On one side of Zembrich stood Grischa, and on the other side Rosa herself, suddenly famous and triumphant. And she thought, "This dream must come true!"

So it had. And now, sailing for America with Grischa and his father, booked by their American manager for a tour with all expenses paid and excellent terms, was Rosa happy? Was she contented? She did not know herself. She felt possessed by an evil genius. It seemed to her she could not love anyone, only please herself, do what the whim of the moment dictated. When her prince and magic-worker appeared on the stage, she thought, "How distinguished, handsome, tall, what a noble and radiant face! There's no one like him in the whole world, except . . . Ah, why is he not that other?"

And the older Stellmach never knew what to expect of her. He held no grudge against her. He was willing to let bygones be bygones. When she needled him about setting too low a price for their contract, he wanted to tell her he hadn't gone through Albert Shchupak's

242

school. But was she to blame that Shchupak had led her around like a dancing bear? What's the disgrace in being poor? Hadn't he once roamed from town to town with his Grischa, barefoot and hungry, playing three tunes for a groschen and one thrown in free?

When Rosa was in a good mood, she could match his stories with her own. She knew how to tell them, too. When she impersonated a woman in the market place or a broken-down old cantor with a cracked voice, it was better than an evening at the theater. You could hear them laughing three blocks away.

But sometimes a cloud would gather over her spirits, and she would lock herself in her room, or sit down and write letters for hours. To whom could she be writing like that? Or she asked Grischa to play for her, and he had to play, even in the middle of the night. Could he say no to her? That's love!

So he'd pick up his fiddle and she'd sit down with her chin in her hand, her eyes glued to Grischa. To look at her then—an angel from heaven, a painting. But if you asked *her* to sing, she'd only do it when the mood struck her. Then she'd sing and sing. Arias, concertos? God forbid. Gipsy or Wablachian tunes, ballads, Yiddish songs. You'd come all the way on foot to hear her sing a Chassidic song.

From Chaslavich to Libavich,
Who cares what I do?
From Libavich to Chaslavich,
I only laugh at you.

I take my pack upon my back,
Who cares what you say?
My *tallis 'n t'fillin* in a sack
And I am on my way.

From Chaslavich to Libavich, etc.

To my rabbi in Libavich,
Who cares what I do?
To my rabbi from Chaslavich,
And I laugh at you.

I have a wife and seven children,
Who cares what you say?
I leave my wife and seven children
And I am on my way.

From Chaslavich to Libavich, etc.

243

I have a house with crumbling bricks,
Who cares what I do?
And a *sukkah* made of sticks,
And I laugh at you.

Through the windows beats the rain,
Who cares what you say?
Through the chimney pipes a hard luck strain,
And I am on my way.

From Chaslavich to Libavich, etc.

My thoughts are sad, my heart is heavy,
Who cares what I do?
I am going to the rabbi,
And I laugh at you.

From Chaslavich to Libavich,
Who cares what you say?
From Libavich to Chaslavich
I am on my way.

But Rosa, Stellmach sighed, was a regular imp. The languages that girl could speak—French, German, English! A girl like that, with talent and spirit—how could you dislike her? But she was hard to get along with. You had to watch every word and look. All for Grischa. Thank God, he had at least found his equal. But if you looked at it another way, he could have had any girl he wanted. For the time being he had nothing. Only "Love" . . .

In Holeneshti this year the Cantor would not sing for the High Holidays. Rosa's father was dead, the father who didn't let the name *Reizel* out of his mouth until the last minute. And hadn't his years run out so soon because of her? When she ran away, it was as though the whole world had fallen on top of him. He didn't care if he ate or slept. He kept repeating the parable from the Holy Scriptures about the poor shepherd who had one lamb and God took it; and how many nights his wife Leah saw him get out of bed and tiptoe behind the curtain to kiss the pillow on which Reizel used to sleep.

Well, he had died. And all the honor she had paid him in his last days couldn't save him. It was too late, for the grief had eaten itself into him, gnawed holes in him.

Rosa went into full mourning. Not that she had to. Leah had waited a month after the funeral to let her know, so she would only

need to mourn one hour and could stay on the job. But Rosa threw
off her shoes and sat on the floor to mourn in the old-fashioned pious
way. Stellmach pleaded with her. Not enough that she had refused to
sing for several nights in a row, which cost them double for every
performance. Now this. "For God's sake, Rosa," said Stellmach.
"What are you doing? We are among strangers, among Gentiles, aristocrats, magnates."

She only replied by flying into a rage. Then, on *yomtev* she got
dressed and wanted to go to the synagogue. "I want to say prayers
for the departed," she told Stellmach. "Murderess!" he cried. "What
are you doing? Do you want to slit all our throats? Here, take a knife."
"Don't you go to the synagogue during the holidays?" she threw back
at him. As though she could compare herself to him. He could go to
the synagogue or the Jewish theater, but not she. It would be spread
all over the papers by the next day. And how does she argue with
him? She tells him that Melba and Zembrich and Caruso go to church
on their holy days. So how do you like such examples?

Of course, Stellmach admitted to himself she was right. But what
good did it do? After all, they were still Jews in the world. You could
prattle about right and wrong till you were blue in the face, but the
fact remained that a Jew had to make himself small, stay in the background. He himself loved the Jewish people dearly, was devoted to
Yiddish theater and Yiddish speech, had a good Jewish home and a
pious wife, and brought up his children as Jews. But if he should
once let his Grischa go down to the Jewish quarter, step into a Yiddish stage, or appear in a synagogue, the whole game would be up.
And the same went for Rosa. As long as she moved among Gentiles,
though everyone knew she was Jewish, the wealthiest Jews would run
to hear her sing. But if she made the blunder of mixing with Jews,
then, "Aha, you're one of us—then what's so special about you?"

With Rosa, Stellmach had to guard against saying too much. Such
temperament as she displayed! But he finally prevailed upon her at
least to wear a thick veil over her face when she went to the synagogue.

Meanwhile Stellmach had another headache. Rosa wanted to cable
her mother to come to America. And when she got something like
that into her head, stones could fall from the sky and she wouldn't
budge. And what would happen if her mother did come? What could
you do in New York with a cantor's wife from Holeneshti, Stellmach
asked. He should know as much of evil.

But on the other hand, he thought, the old lady might come to his

245

aid in the romance between Rosa and Grischa. So far it was still a tale without end. Stellmach wished Rosa would decide once for all, yes or no. Now, of course, she had a new excuse. Mourning. Her father died. How much longer could this kind of love go on? Maybe Rosa's mother would make the girl see reason, so they could break plates and announce the engagement. . . .

33 A LITTLE ACCOUNTING

Until he reached America our young hero, Rapalesco, swam along with the current of life, never stopping to reflect or make an accounting. Only then, seeing the enormous distance he had covered since his boyhood, and the point he had finally reached, he stood amazed.

He was amazed not because he had covered such a distance, nor because he had experienced so much. No. Every one of us, when he sums up his past, feels a sense of wonder at what he has lived through. Rapalesco's amazement stemmed from another source. He couldn't understand where he had drawn the strength and endurance, the courage and the faith for such a journey. Who had shown him the way? To what school had he gone? Whose lantern had illumined the dark mazes of the artist's course? And a long procession of figures filed before his eyes . . . His schoolmates with whom he had acted out "shows" on the sly between sunset and evening prayers so the rabbi wouldn't catch them? . . . Or Albert Shchupak's troupe in Hole-neshti . . . Or Hotzmach, his first good friend . . . Or the director of the Lemberg Hereditary Theater, Getzel ben Getzel . . . Or the brothers Shwalb? . . . These were people from whom it was impossible to learn anything. The only people worth listening to, aside from Benny Gorgel, "the man of education," who had opened his eyes a little, were Dr. Levias—Leviathan, the Lemberg Maecenas, who had uncovered new worlds for him, but had fled to where the black pepper grows the minute Hotzmach mentioned money, and the great Zonenthal whose acting had dazzled him. These were all. All alone, through his own blundering efforts, without a teacher, without an alphabet even, he had become what he was.

Looking around him at the other great stars on the Yiddish stage in New York, and asking, "Who are these men and women? Where did they spring from? What had they been once?" he was amazed again. For the incredible biographies he heard could fill volumes.

And at last he understood the riddle of his own life, and many things became clear to him. He learned there were schools in the world where one learned to become an actor, but not for Jews. That there were patrons of art who spent fortunes to help aspiring young artists, but not among Jews. Yet there were Yiddish theaters and Yiddish actors, there were great talents, stars whose light reached as far as the "Nations of the World." Sometimes scouts from these "nations" made forays on the Yiddish theater and lured the stars away. It was difficult for a Yiddish actor to withstand the honeyed voice of the tempter who whispered: "Your place is not here among the Jews. Your talent is lost on this narrow audience. A wide field is open for you, a greater stage awaits you, a new public calls you."

What Yiddish actor doesn't dream of crossing over into this big, wide-open world. And how few who are beckoned succeed. Rapalesco was one of the few, and the opportunity came to him without effort or struggle on his part. And if he broke the enchanted spell, and turned his back on the tempters, it was because of what we will now describe.

The dramatic-musical cooperative, Klammer, Shwalb & Co., whose "Star from Buenos Aires" and whose "Lomzha Nightingale" had won such public acclaim, now gathered its forces for its culminating triumph—the American debut of Leo Rapalesco.

Nissel Shwalb saw to it that the Yiddish papers in New York trumpeted forth the news two weeks in advance. Everyone who could read was made aware that "the great Star from Bucharest whom the Queen of Rumania had crowned with her own hands and over whom the great Zonenthal of Vienna had wept like a small child, when he saw him perform *Uriel Acosta*," was about to appear on the stage of the Nickel Theater in New York.

Mr. Nickel went about with his hands in his pockets, tipping off everybody in the *kibitzarnia* that for the first night performance he expected such guests as Jacob Schiff and Louis Marshall, and "the Governor of the State of New York and certain high officials." He whispered it because he didn't care to have this news spread all over New York, since the performance was sold out.

247

But Nissel Shwalb's mood lacked its usual *élan*. His last and most brilliant combination was not working out too well. The match between Rapalesco and Henrietta still hung fire. When he mentioned it to Henrietta she snapped back, "Don't worry. That's my business." She still had some poses to go in her forty-five photographs with Rapalesco. And Nissel didn't like the looks of "the kid." Since their arrival in New York Rapalesco had not been "all there." He walked around like a man in a dream and asked for letters ten times a day. From whom did he expect letters? And what business did he have with that absurd creature in the red cape who came running in every day "just for a minute" and stayed for three hours? To ask Henrietta was like asking the door-knob. What did that dressed-up marionette know? The applause and her beauty-prize notoriety had turned her head. Say a word and she was ready to heap live coals on you. His brother Isaac had warned him, "Keep away from that heifer; she's almost a cow and she'll butt you with her horns."

His brother Isaac was right. Henrietta was a cow. For if she had a brain in her head, she wouldn't be wasting her time on new clothes and photographs. She'd be speeding up the wedding. Mr. Klammer was of the same opinion. "Bake *bagel* while the oven is hot," or as the Englishman puts it, "Make hay while the sun shines."

Everybody came forth with advice. Everybody. Whoever had God in his heart stuck in his two cents' worth. The Lomzha cantor's wife came every day in her new coat with the fur collar which her husband had bought her in New York, and asked, "When will the Messiah be born?" What did that scarecrow in the red wig mean by that? And why did she, particularly, have to meddle in his sister's affairs? The way that woman strutted about with her nose in the air now that her husband, the Lomzha cantor, had come up in the world! And the cantor himself had changed. In Whitechapel where a loaf of white bread was his dream, he had been so small he could have crawled under your fingernails. But now, as the Lomzha Nightingale, there was no talking to him.

In such gloomy speculations the Master of Combinations went about New York, bickering with his brother and sister, quarreling with his partners. But all of this was, as usual, of little concern to Rapalesco. He went about New York, plunged in his own thoughts and dreams, as though he were strolling in a thick forest, without a thought to his coming debut. Which did not trouble him. He expected to carry off the performance with his usual *éclat*. And what did the triumph mean to him when she, whom he was most anxious to impress, would not be there? And that she would not be there he knew. Madame Cherniak had led him astray. It had turned out that she hadn't set eyes on Rosa. She put the blame on her job. If she could tear herself away for a day and a night, she would run over "uptown" to see Rosa. Next week, when she had a day off, she would surely see her, and everything would be "all right."

But next week she put him off from day to day as before; promising that tomorrow she would get seats in the opera where Rosa was singing or at a concert where she was due to appear with Grischa Stellmach. But you couldn't get tickets to hear Rosa for love or money.

By now Madame Cherniak had become repulsive to Rapalesco. In desperation he went uptown himself to buy tickets, only to find out that Miss Spivak had gone on tour and no one could tell him when she would return. "You've always been a dishrag, and always will be," he berated himself bitterly. Meanwhile his associates kept dinning into his ears that he must prepare for his debut, reporters swarmed about him asking for interviews, harpies with grinning faces approached him with brilliant propositions . . . and on their heels came Henrietta in a new outfit, with a new hat, to drag him off to another studio. . . .

In this state of mind Rapalesco sat down to write a letter to Rosa,

"I want you to know, Reizel, that I, Leibel, Ben Rapalovich's son from Holeneshti, am now in New York, downtown, and that I am an actor in the Yiddish Nickel Theater, and my name is now,

Rapalesco."

This was the letter he intended to write, brief and to the point. What more was there to say? But once he began writing, he couldn't stop. A whole world of thoughts and feelings opened up before him. The words gushed as from a well. And he told her his whole life's story since they had parted on that night of the fire in God's Street, all his dreams and hopes, his sorrows and joys, his longings and aspirations, his achievements and failures.

It was not, properly speaking, a love letter. The word *love* was too hackneyed, too feeble a word. His feeling was subtly disguised, cloaked in mystic allusions, wrapped in allegorical meanings.

Speaking of that night in Holeneshti which had rained stars, he asked her to recall what he had told her, that stars do not fall, they only wander. Then he asked her to recall something much later, the gipsy fortuneteller in a small town in Galicia or Bukovina, who had reminded her of the wandering stars rushing in different orbits that are seldom fated to meet.

His letter was full of such hints and allusions and peppered with question marks and dots . . . long series of dots . . . which left her to draw her own conclusions. . . .

At the end he explained why he was writing instead of seeking a personal interview. First, he had heard that she was inaccessible. One first had to apply to a certain Mr. Bohrman and tell him what "business" he had with her. Furthermore, he didn't want to get in the way of "certain people" now close to her, who appeared on the stage with her. The young diplomat said "certain people," though every child knew that Rosa Spivak appeared on the stage with Grischa Stellmach.

Grischa Stellmach! The name hovered in front of his eyes day and night and wouldn't let him rest or sleep. Who was he? What was he? How did he look and behave? Though he longed to see Reizel with all his heart, he would rather set eyes on this Grischa Stellmach first, even from a distance. Every mention of the name was a stab in his heart. Besides, Madame Cherniak had said that Rosa and Grischa were engaged and the wedding was expected any day.

Braindele had changed tactics again. Her purpose in bringing Henrietta and Rapalesco to America had been to revenge herself on Hotzmach. With that accomplished, what more was there to do? Was she obliged to provide for the weal of the whole world? Where was it written that she must exert herself in behalf of a Rapalesco or a Rosa Spivak? Let them pound their heads against the wall. How many people were there in the world who worried their heads over her, Madame Cherniak? Let her, God forbid, lose her job this day, would anybody stop to look around at her?

Of men folk there was no use talking. The cholera should have taken them off long ago, choked them one by one, so that not a trace of them remained. But take even a girl like Rosa Spivak, with whom she had once been like a sister, Madame Cherniak comes to see her in New York, and she isn't even admitted to the great lady's presence. She writes her a few words, "Rosie darling, my own, my soul, Madame Cherniak would like to see you," and she doesn't answer. She writes her again, and again not a word.

Then Rapalesco arrives in New York; Braindele drops everything and runs to meet him. She takes him in like her own kin, pampers him, smothers him with attentions, and still he's not satisfied. What does he want her to do? Bring Rosa Spivak and Grischa Stellmach down from the sky on one broomstick? Men! Let them all burn in one fire. When they set their minds on something, they want the earth to crack open and the heavens to split wide for them. "Wait a little, have patience, dear Rapalesco. Let's have a friendly little chat first. How is Hotzmach, the evil one take him? And that homely little sister of his, may she sink into the ground? And his mother, the old hag, is that witch still alive?" That's how she spoke to her young friend and couldn't understand why he glowered at her.

When she thought of Spivak, her blood boiled. She couldn't forgive the slut. Not even to answer her letters. Who did she think she was? A cantor's daughter, who not so long ago had one pair of darned stockings to her name. What if luck had come her way and she was famous now? You can be lucky and famous and rich and everything else, but you have to remember the other person isn't dirt under your feet. Fly too high and you will end by falling. Such things had happened.

And not all the lucky ones were so heartless. Look at Henrietta Shwalb, also a prima donna, also famous, the papers make enough noise about her. But how simple and modest she is, how friendly and easy to talk to. Madame Cherniak comes to see her nearly every day and they sit together and talk and talk. Henrietta has no secrets from her. They talk until it grows dark outside, and Madame Cherniak slaps herself over her fat calves, and snatches up her red cape—"Goodness gracious, thunder strike me, it's almost night."

Then Braindele goes forth with her dancing step into the streets of New York, boards a car, and flies to her theater job. And as the car jolts from side to side, and as she sways from her strap, a plan begins to hatch in her brain, a subtle Mephistophelean plan for a quick marriage between Henrietta and Rapalesco. The papers will broadcast the news far and wide; the *kibitzarnia* will talk. She, Madame Cherniak, will be the chief sponsor, both on the bride's and the groom's side. What a celebration! She will hop out on the floor and shake a leg with that son-of-a-gun Nissel Shwalb. They will drink and carouse until the small hours. And that morning she will sit right down and write a letter to Rosa Spivak and offer her a *maz'ltov* on her old flame's marriage. Better still—and here we can see the influence of the serials she has been reading—she will see to it that Rose is invited, that she arrives just when the groom is putting the ring on the bride's finger. Rosa falls in a dead faint. Her fiancé Grischa Stell-

251

mach rushes in, takes a look, and sends a bullet through his heart. Why should poor Stellmach get a bullet through the heart? Don't ask, dear reader. When a person is plotting revenge, he doesn't care who is guilty and who innocent; and blood flows like water.

34 BRAINDELE KOZAK— MATCHMAKER

It was a few days before opening night. Rehearsals were over, costumes and sets were ready, and Mr. Nickel kept in touch with the cooperative every few minutes by telephoning. . . . Now the tickets were nearly sold out, now the public was storming the doors, now they were tearing the theater apart, now he was ready to call the police. . . .

Henrietta and Rapalesco were at a photographer's, and the only members of the cooperative present were the brothers Shwalb, Mr. Klammer, and the Lomzha cantor. There was little accord among the four. In fact, their relationship was at a breaking point. Not because business didn't go well. On the contrary, prospects had never been better. The only one thing lacking, which is lacking, alas, in every human society, was unanimity. Whenever one made a statement, the next one contradicted him. Nissel Shwalb claimed that the success of the whole enterprise was due to his combinations. Mr. Klammer maintained that if it hadn't been for him and his pocketbook, they would all have had to take sacks on their backs and go begging. The cantor retorted sharply that, thanks to the Almighty, they could get along without Klammer's help. He, the Lomzha Nightingale, could certainly administer his own township. Everyone took exception to this last statement, even Isaac Shwalb, who asked if the cantor had forgotten his Whitechapel cellar, where he never saw a full pot of soup from one Sabbath to the next.

Needless to say the cantor did not relish this little reminder. He gave Isaac to understand that his place in the theater was under the roof and his vocation was clapping with his hands and not with his tongue.

252

To which Isaac replied that the time for his hands to start clapping might very well be now, and it would go ill with the cantor's head.

The *dénouement* might have taken place then and there, if news hadn't been brought in that a lady was waiting outside.

The four men came to eager attention. A lady? For whom was she asking?

"The lady wants to see Mr. Nissel Shwalb."

Nissel Shwalb rose majestically, adjusted his tie, smoothed his vest, opened the door, and then called upon all the nightmares of this night and last night and all the nights of his life. For the lady was Madame Cherniak.

Flattered by the look on Nissel Shwalb's face, which she took to be one of pleased delight, Madame Cherniak made him her best curtsy and told him she had something important to communicate to him.

"A business?"

"A business."

"Private?"

"Private."

Since the lady had come on business and private business at that, it behooved him to invite her into a separate room.

Braindele's long preamble took her back to the days when she was still Fraulein Cherniak and hadn't met Shchupak, a plague take him. She hadn't dreamed in those days that she would one day find herself in the land of Columbus. Not that she complained of her lot. She knew very well that many people would like to find themselves in her shoes. She had a good job and she still had a few dollars saved up, not a great deal, but enough, so she didn't have to depend on anyone and didn't need to ask favors, and could earn her own living.

Nissel interrupted her, to say he was very happy to hear she didn't need to ask anyone's favors and could make her own living, may he have everyone's good at heart. But he was a very busy man. In fact, they were all running around in circles. Their leading man, Rapalesco, was about to make his debut and . . .

"He's just the one I came to see you about," said Braindele Kozak. Nissel Shwalb threw a quick look at her sweating face and asked half in earnest and half in jest, "For a sample?"

"What sample?"

"I mean, for example, what can you tell me about Leo Rapalesco?"

"What shall I tell you about Rapalesco? Give me your hand."

"Take both my hands."

Braindele Kozak mopped her sweating face with a handkerchief, then drew her chair up close to his so that Nissal caught a whiff compounded of mint drops, perspiration and onions.

Madame Cherniak told him, in a few words, that she was here as a matchmaker, but a matchmaker without an ulterior motive. Her only interest lay in her friendship for Henrietta. She could wish herself half the good fortune she wished Henrietta. And if Nissel wanted his sister to bear the name of Rapalesco, he must bestir himself or it would be too late.

Nissel pleaded with her to tell him more. He swore secrecy with all the oaths at his command: "As you see me swimming," "May I choke on this table," "As I have everyone's good at heart," and so on. But all he could draw from her was, "Shhh. Not a word to anyone."

At the door she turned, put a finger across her lips. "Remember what I told you. The quicker, the healthier. And—shhhh, not a word to anyone. Goodbye."

35 IN BOX NUMBER THREE

Opening night had come—the night when the "New Star from Bucharest," whom the press had installed in the ranks of the world's great, such as Zonenthal, Schildkraut, Irving, Possart, Rossi, and others, was to undergo his crucial test.

The large Nickel Theater was brilliantly lighted, festively decorated, and packed to the doors. From the directors down to the ushers everyone wore an air of proud confidence. The audience itself looked complacent, if not arrogant. There was the aura of a benefit, a jubilee honoring an established star rather than the trying-out of a comparative unknown. And new faces could be seen in the boxes and orchestra seats, celebrities of the Yiddish-speaking intelligentsia, and some Gentiles over whom Mr. Nickel hovered deferentially. He brought them their programs, escorted them to their seats, and checked their wraps, though this was not his office. Needless to say, Mr. Nickel used their presence in his theater for self-advertising.

About two of these personages he concocted imaginary biographies, though they were recognized as two brothers, managers of a theater on Broadway.

The New York papers had made such a fanfare about "the star from Bucharest" that these theatrical managers had decided to look him over, and see if he were worth "kidnaping." For what do the Jews need a Zonenthal, a Schildkraut, or an Irving for? The Jews themselves won't deny that they are a nation of contractors who have undertaken to supply the world with the finest and best of their talent.

Among the audience were also the ringleaders of the *kibitzarnia*, politicians, poets, publicists and newspaper editors, armed to the teeth and ready to do battle against the new star, who might be an idol to some but an object of ridicule to such cognoscenti.

In a word, the Yiddish theater world of New York was in a state of breathless suspense. Both Nickel's "patriots" and their opponents came with reviews already written. One began: "It is a long time since the walls of the Nickel Theater have resounded with such cheers and applause, and the enthusiasm of the public which reached an unprecedented peak last night should have convinced our venal and time-serving opponents that . . ."

Another began: "Yesterday's debacle in the Nickel Theater should prove a lesson to the two-footed donkeys who will go to all lengths to make a mountain out of a molehill and who for a dollar . . ."

Just as the curtain rose, three well-dressed people stole quietly into the lobby and made their way to box number three. One was a portly older man, the second a young man with a cap pulled low over his eyes, to whose arm clung a slender young woman inconspicuously dressed, with a thick veil over her face. The portly one led the young couple to the box, then turned back and made his way down the long narrow corridor. There he collided with one of the directors, Nissel Shwalb. The two men ran into each other head on, fell back, and exchanged a quick glance. They stepped forward again, fell back again and looked once more. Then they parted and the portly one went down to the orchestra, while Nissel Shwalb looked after him muttering, "Can it be that bird from London? Why did he whistle into his beard?" And he quickly made his way to the box office and sought out his partner, Mr. Nickel.

"Who's that couple in box number three?" he asked Nickel.

Mr. Nickel was a man who didn't like to reflect long.

255

"In box number three? If it isn't Jacob Schiff, then it must be Louis Marshall."

"If you're not a bluffer, then you're an idiot."

Mr. Nickel put both his hands in his pockets and gave his companion a benign look as though he had just received the highest compliment.

"Who can it be then?"

"That's the way to talk, without beating about the bush. If that bird who took them into the box hadn't whistled into his beard, I'd swear it was Stellmach."

Mr. Nickel looked dazed. "What bird? Whose beard? And who's Stellmach?"

"Look here, Nickel, are you really as stupid as you pretend to be? Or are you trying to play the fool? Or are you a stranger in town? Don't tell me you've never heard of Grischa Stellmach."

"Grischa Stellmach!"

Mr. Nickel gave a leap, slapped himself twice on the forehead and uttered something under his breath which would never pass the censor either here or on the other side of the ocean. Then he exclaimed three times at the top of his voice, "I'm an idiot, an idiot, an idiot!"

"Hear, hear! That's what I've told you right along."

Mr. Nickel let this pass, and said in a voice full of jubilation, "Te-te. If that's Grischa Stellmach, then I know who the woman with him is. If not, may I never live to see daylight."

"Amen. Who is she?"

"Miss Rosalie Spivak."

"Rosalie Spivak!"

Now it was Nissel Shwalb's turn to slap himself on the forehead. He left his partner abruptly and ran back into the theater to take another look at his former acquaintance and to assure himself that it was really he who had whistled into his beard.

It is only natural that a "lover of Yiddish theater" such as Stellmach should be among the first to run to see the star from Bucharest. The surprising thing is that he should have taken the risk of bringing along "the children," whom he kept wrapped in cotton wool away from the contamination of Yiddish New York. To account for this slip we must go back a little in our story.

After her father's death, Rosa had announced her intention of bringing her mother to America. With her to think was to act. Tele-

256

grams began to fly back and forth between New York and Holeneshti. The Cantor's wife became truly alarmed when she got the
first cable from her daughter. Reizel must be ill or dying, else why
squander money on telegrams and cables which cost a fortune per
word? Leah later confided to her daughter that it was this fear that
had brought her to New York. "Because in the first place, what would
I see there that I haven't seen already? And in the second place, what
would I do with the bomb?"

"What bomb?" Rosa asked.

"That mansion you hung around our necks in Holeneshti, did you
ever see such a thing? I would try to rent it, but who is there in Holeneshti who can afford such a palace? Unless it's one of the Gentiles,
but they've become such hoodlums in Bessarabia these days I would
sooner a plague took them."

Rosa almost regretted the whole business, for on the day her mother
was to arrive a conflict broke out between her and the older Stellmach.
As a practical man, Stellmach had asked her what she intended to do
with her mother once she arrived? Instead of answering, Rosa gave
him a scathing look out of her black eyes. Poor Stellmach flinched. He
would have preferred a tongue-lashing to one of those looks. He began to justify himself by explaining that he had meant no harm. All
he wanted to ask was where her mother would stay and what her poor
mother would live on, in other words what would she eat.

Rosa saw light. "Oh, that's what you mean." Without thinking
twice she ordered her car brought around and prepared to drive
downtown to find a lodging place for her mother and a kitchen where
she could eat kosher.

Meyer Stellmach leaped up like a man who had been scalded with
boiling vinegar. "Heaven help us! That's all I need." Calling on his
son to back him up, he prevailed on Rosa to stay home. He himself,
Meyer Stellmach, would go downtown to find a suitable lodging for
her mother. He promised faithfully to see to it that everything would
be, as they say in America, "all right."

And everything was indeed all right. But not before Meyer Stellmach had passed through the seven gates of hell. Picture it to yourself. First he had to find a room with the family of a Bessarabian Jew,
a *shochet;* then he had to take her around personally and introduce
her to all the women in the neighborhood; after that he had to buy
her two pairs of brass candlesticks to light the Friday night candles.
He had to drop everything and go chasing over East Broadway look-

ing for second-hand brass candlesticks. Next he had to find a synagogue for her to suit her particular notions. Is that enough for you? After the synagogue had been found, it turned out that in the excitement of leaving, Leah had forgotten her prayer book at the bookbinder's in Holeneshti. So Meyer Stellmach had to go back to East Broadway to find a Jewish bookseller who had just that kind of prayer book. And the agonies he went through before he found her a suitable restaurant. In the first restaurant she went to, they offered her a certain delicacy called "brekfish." She said she would eat fish, but not "brekfish," for who knew if it wasn't lobster? The proprietor assured her that it was not lobster and not fish of any kind, and furthermore it wasn't "brekfish" but "breakfast" which was the same as the morning meal. Said Leah, "You can call it what you like, but I've never eaten such an abomination and I won't start eating it now."

In short, Meyer Stellmach had it both hot and cold from the Cantor's wife. But what sacrifices won't a father make for his child? In the first place, he didn't want Rosa to be seen leading her mother around Hester Street. That was all he needed. In the second place, he hoped to find an ally in Leah to further the match between his son and her daughter.

But that didn't come so easy, either. At first the Cantor's wife wouldn't hear of the match. That the day should come when he, Meyer Stellmach, should grovel in the dust before the Cantor's wife from Holeneshti in behalf of his Grischa. But what won't a father do for his child? Leah Spivak was of the old school. She allowed that his son was a respectable young fellow, and a good provider. Who said he wasn't? The only drawback was his occupation. He was nothing but a fiddler. In vain Stellmach argued that a fiddler who played at weddings in Holeneshti was one thing and a fiddler on the concert stage in New York or London was another. If his son was a fiddler, then he was a rabbi. Said she, "What then does he do? Write books?" Stellmach explained that his son was an artist. She said, "He can be an artist thirty times over, but as long as he plays the fiddle, he's a fiddler. A respectable boy and a good provider, who says no? May God send him his predestined bride, whom he richly deserves, did you ever see such a thing? And may God send my daughter something else, for my husband never in all his days played the fiddle, and his father before him never played the fiddle, and his father's father had never played the fiddle." Try and deal with a woman like that.

However, when she finally came around to his side, he found her a

258

real treasure. Once the Cantor's wife was won over, she decided he suited her daughter as though he had been measured for her. Then she went after Rosa hammer and tongs and heckled her from morning till night. Once for all, how much longer could she dally? It had never happened in their family that a girl should remain an old maid. If her father were living now, he would surely say that Providence had ordained this marriage. But if God had seen fit to call him before his time, she was still here, and as long as her legs supported her sinful body, she would see to it, etc., etc., did you ever see such a thing?

It is a well-established axiom that good news always comes when it is least expected. Meyer Stellmach was seated at the desk in his hotel room one morning writing to his wife in London, bewailing the fact that the children hadn't come to an understanding yet. "What shall I write you, my dear wife, they are just where they started, it's a tale without end, a lingering illness, a dragged out lo—"

He must have meant to write "love," but just then came a knock on the door.

"Come in," Stellmach called out in English, with a singsong accent which made the word sound like *kommein*. The children burst in, both dressed in sports clothes, and both with shining faces, and they cried in one voice, "Papa, you owe us a *maz'ltov*."

Stellmach became paralyzed. His powers of movement and speech failed him. He could only look from one to the other and think, "Has it happened at last?" Then he sighed deeply, leaned back, and said in a scarcely audible voice, "So. I owe you a *maz'ltov*. Then why do you stand there? Why am I sitting like a clay image? Come here and I will give you a *maz'ltov*."

Saying which, he jumped up and began hugging and kissing them both impartially and he didn't notice that tears stood in his eyes. His son, who was no less wrought up than the father, said to him, "Why are you crying, Papa?"

"I? Crying?" said Stellmach, wiping his eyes. "Who told you I'm crying, you foolish child?"

"Nobody said you're crying," laughed Rosa. "Tears are just pouring out of your eyes, the way they pour out of my mother's eyes on *Yom Kippur*. I wonder what she'll say when she finds out? Come, Grischa, let's go to my mother."

Meyer's heart almost melted with joy. "To your mother, to your mother," he repeated, and began running about the room, feeling

259

his pockets and looking for he didn't know what. He had almost forgotten that he must cable the good news to his wife in London. And herding the children before him, he left the hotel. They got into the car and sped downtown to see Leah.

Leah was sitting that morning, as she sat every morning, with her prayer book in her hands intoning the morning devotions. A car is no great novelty in New York, but a luxurious automobile a block long with a liveried chauffeur in front doesn't stop every day in front of a tenement on the East Side. It attracted at once all the small fry in the neighborhood who swarmed over the running boards, climbed on the hood, and would have crawled inside if they had been allowed.

Stellmach leaped out of the car to be the first to give the Cantor's wife *maz'ltov*.

"Good morning to you," he burst in on her. *"Maz'ltov,* do you know we are in-laws now?"

Stellmach was sure that when she heard this news, Leah would drop her prayer book and fall on his neck. But she did no such thing. She calmly pointed to a chair, indicating that he sit down, and she herself stood up and turned her face to the east wall to conclude her prayer. The children, who had followed on his heels, also had to sit down and wait. When she was through at last, she marked the page in her prayer book and said, *"Maz'ltov,* may you always be happy. God grant that it's in a lucky hour. For what has man been created for? When the Almighty has blessed us with children, we hope to have joy from them. Unhappy only is he who lies in the ground. If he, peace be unto him, were here now . . ." And Leah hid her face in her apron.

"Leave the dead lie where they are," Stellmach said jovially. "Let's talk about happier things."

"Happier things? To some it is given to be happy and to some to be sad. Did you ever see such a thing?"

Rosa broke in gaily, "Mother, leave the lamentations for *Rosh Hashono*. Now that you have merited this great joy, as you put it, and don't forget it was you who drove me into it, we have to think of how to spend this day."

"What's there to think about?" Leah declared. "We have to call in some good people, write an engagement contract, break plates. We are still Jews in the world, did you ever see such a thing?"

How great was Leah's disappointment to hear from her daughter's own lips that it wasn't necessary to call people in, or to write a con-

260

tract, or to smash plates. It was all settled; they were engaged, and that was that.

With tear-filled eyes the pious mother regarded the happy young couple and wasn't pleased with what she saw. They were both young and happy and rich and famous. Thanks be to the living God. She had no complaints to lodge with *Him*. But what harm would there be in celebrating the engagement according to custom? What was so wrong with having a few pious men with skullcaps and beards around, among them a rabbi, a cantor and a *shammes*? Let the rabbi bless the young couple, let the cantor read the articles of the contract, and let the *shammes* hurl the first plate to the ground, and let the whole crowd shout, *"Maz'ltov, maz'ltov!"* Where was the beauty of having a bride and groom go about with their arms around each other, the groom without even a hat on his head, and his father—was a hat too heavy for his head, too? A godless country, America.

And the Cantor's wife vented her bitterness on Stellmach. "Well, if the young people have forgotten their piety, that's one thing. It's a modern world—how do you call it—artists? But you, a greybeard going about hatless, did you ever see such a thing?"

This outburst was met with raised eyebrows. Stellmach's beard had recently had a trim from the barber's shears so that hardly a shadow remained. All three burst out laughing. But the Cantor's wife didn't laugh. She raised her pious eyes and saw what was left of Stellmach's beard, and said no more. She only sighed, ruffled the pages of her prayer book, and began to intone quickly in a low voice the words of the prayer: "Thou who art the guardian of Israel, watch over the remnant of Israel and do not overlook those who say, 'Hear O Israel.'"

If there has ever been a truly happy parent in the world, Meyer Stellmach was that parent now. He scarcely felt the ground under his feet. Out of the fullness of his heart, he took the children to one of the biggest jewelry shops in town, asked to be shown the finest diamonds and told Rosa to have her pick. "Forget the cost," he told her with a large gesture, and Rosa did as she was bid and picked her diamonds, forgetting the cost.

Meyer Stellmach had to admit this was the first time in his life that he had squandered money with a light heart. Nothing was too good for Rosa that day. "Dear heart," he told her, in Scriptural language, "even unto the half of my kingdom."

After luncheon Stellmach sat in a large armchair in his son's apartment, comfortably unbuttoned, smoking a Havana cigar, while Grischa walked back and forth improvising on his Stradivarius. Meyer leaned over Rosa and asked her in a whisper if she could guess how much dowry his Grischa had.

Rosa, who sat with her chin in her hand, her eyes glued on Grischa and his fiddle, didn't reply. She was wholly absorbed in the music which the enchanter Grischa Stellmach was drawing so easily and lightly from the strings of his instrument. His fiddle didn't play. It spoke to her, in a heavenly tongue, which only one great artist can speak and another great artist understand. Grischa had never played like this before. Neither the salons of the nobility nor the king's chambers nor concert halls nor theaters had heard the sounds which now issued from his fiddle. He was speaking only to Rosa and to her alone. She, who understood him better than anyone else could, listened, entranced. When he finished, she got up and, forgetting his father's presence, fell into his arms. She would have fallen at his feet, she was so moved by his playing. But she caught herself, ran up to the piano, lifted the lid, struck a few chords, and began to sing without any particular plan or pattern. Only a nightingale alone in a dark wood might have sung like this, pouring out all the longing and pain of its lonely spirit to the still night.

"How many thousands of dollars would these American Yankees pay for such music?" Meyer Stellmach reflected as he sat back with half-shut eyes, and his heart ran over with bliss.

"Do you know what, my children?" said the happy father when the concert was over. "I've just had a brilliant idea."

The happy father stroked the spot where once he had worn a beard and spoke in a voice that had the lilt of a Talmudic chant, "Since we carry such heavy burdens, and since we have a merciful God, and since that God has granted us a day like this, and since our evening is open anyway, why don't we go to the Yiddish theater? I'll manage to shake off that American bird and we'll have the evening all to ourselves. What do you say to this, my doves?"

The doves looked at each other and said with open delight, "All right, let's go to the Yiddish theater."

"And from the theater, my dear canaries, we'll go to a Yiddish restaurant for *gefilte* fish and a roast and stuffed *derma*."

"Bravo, bravo!" the canaries applauded. Then the question came up as to which theater they should go to. There were a number of Yiddish theaters in New York. What was playing today?

"I'll tell you what's playing," said Stellmach. Not for nothing was he such a lover of Yiddish jargon. He bought all the Yiddish papers every day. His room overflowed with papers, books and magazines. It was a crime to throw any of them out. A Yiddish word was sacred to him. But to carry them all from place to place he would need a baggage car.

Meyer Stellmach attacked the mountain of papers which lay piled on chairs and tables. He looked through them hastily, then struck himself on the forehead. "Children, we have a merciful God. This is a great day in the Yiddish theater. Tonight a new artist appears for the first time in the Nickel Theater, a Rapalesco from Bucharest. I may have told you about him. The papers have been full of him."

And Meyer Stellmach proceeded to lay out the evening's program. First to the Nickel Theater, then to Sholom's Restaurant, where they served Rumanian dishes and real Bessarabian wine. Sholom was famous. His picture was in every Yiddish newspaper. You opened a paper and out jumped Sholom and his restaurant.

"I will get a box for the two of you, the best box in the house," said Stellmach, "but for myself I will get a seat in the orchestra. Why? The answer is simple. I mustn't be seen with you at the Yiddish theater. Someone might recognize me, but no one will know you. Grischa, you will do me a favor and wear a big, soft cap and pull it over your eyes. And you, Rosa, will be so good as to wear your biggest brimmed hat so that a person would have to bend down to get a look and then not see your eyes. It's no joking matter. Let those nosy fellows get a whiff of who sat in the box and tomorrow it will be all over New York in big headlines, 'Grischa Stellmach and Rosalie Spivak in a Yiddish Theater.' Ha ha. Those who don't know any better will get the idea that Grischa Stellmach and Rosalie Spivak have joined the Yiddish stage. That's all that I need."

36 A RETURN VISIT

Madame Cherniak's surprise visit and her cryptic warning that "the quicker the better or it will be too late" had left Nissel Shwalb unsatisfied. He decided to return her visit. Clattering up five flights in a Brooklyn tenement and bending his huge bulk almost double, he wriggled into her room.

"Hello. Is this where Mrs. Cherniak lives?"

Mrs. Cherniak was still in slippers and morning dress, a loose robe with flowing sleeves and a low-cut neck, her hair uncombed, her room in disorder, the bed unmade, a pail of refuse at the door, and on the table the remains of last night's supper. Madame Cherniak was taken aback; since she had come to America, Nissel Shwalb was the first male visitor to cross her threshold. She didn't know what to do first—throw a dress over her robe, pull the covers over her bed, carry out the refuse, or clear the table? In her confusion she forgot to offer her guest a chair, but stood mute, with her hands at her sides.

Nissel Shwalb took a chair for himself, brought one for her, and began to put her at her ease with small talk. He told her he had long wanted to become better acquainted with her. Since she had come to see him, he felt he owed her a return visit. He would like to have a heart-to-heart talk with her. He felt he could discuss things with her which he couldn't discuss with anyone else. "And you can feel easy," he assured her. "Everything we say here will remain within these four walls."

Nissel Shwalb gestured at the four walls of the tiny room, complimenting her on its attractiveness. Did she live here all by herself?

"All by myself, alone as a stone," Madame Cherniak answered, sighing deeply and turning red as a beet.

"That's the common lot. I, too, am as alone as a stone," Nissel Shwalb echoed. Madame Cherniak drew her chair up closer to his, arranged her hair with both hands, and asked, "Are you then a single man?"

To the English words "single man" Nissel Shwalb replied also in English, "Sure!" Then he added in Yiddish, "And what a single man! A single man among single men."

At that Madame Cherniak grew cordial. Both sleeves of her dressing gown rolled themselves up above her elbows, and drops of perspiration stood out on her upper lip, shadowed by a black mustache.

"How does this happen?" she asked, with a smirk in which eagerness and compassion mingled.

"I'm on the go all the time. Busy day and night. There are days when I don't have time to stop for a shave or a bite to eat. Of sleep no use asking. Many's the time I catch forty winks while I'm walking, as you see me swimming. You can believe it or not, but sometimes

264

weeks and months pass when I neither eat, drink nor sleep, may I have everyone's good at heart."

Madame Cherniak nodded her head several times, her bare arms crossed over her bodice from which emerged breasts that bore a striking resemblance to overstuffed pillows.

"That isn't good," she admonished him with motherly solicitude. "A person mustn't neglect himself."

"How can I think of myself when I have this burden on my back? I mean my sister, the prima donna. It's in her favor that she's good-looking, the only trouble is she's too good-looking. And what's *too* is an overdose, as they say. If God should help me that my sister got married and my brother found a decent job, then I would be able to think of myself. It's high time, though I'm still . . . how old do you think I am?"

Is it any wonder that after this speech Madame Cherniak's numbed heart melted like butter? Ah, what a man. A true gentleman. It just went to show you couldn't judge by appearances. She would never in her life have believed this burly giant could have such a warm and tender heart.

Nissel Shwalb had no reason to regret his visit to this monkey-face. It had been worth the effort. He had learned a great deal from this intimate tête-à-tête—all about Rapalesco and his secret romance, the amazing tale of the Cantor's daughter now a leading light in the musical world. Everything was clear to him now.

Walking back from Madame Cherniak's, Nissel Shwalb whistled a gay tune. His nimble brain spun out a new combination.

Nissel Shwalb didn't go straight home but first stopped at Mr. Klammer's and informed him that they were going to the Lomzha cantor's for a conference, about what he wouldn't divulge, just asking Mr. Klammer to have patience as he dragged him out of the house by main force. A few doors from the cantor's home Mr. Klammer refused to go any further. He wasn't one to enter into anything blindfold, he said, or as the Englishman puts it, "I don't buy a pig in a poke."

"Talk English, talk Turkish, talk Persian, but come," said Nissel Shwalb seizing Mr. Klammer by the shoulders, and, still protesting, Mr. Klammer went.

They found the Lomzha cantor in his shirt sleeves, directing his orchestra in a new number. When the crowd saw "Uncle Nissel," the rehearsal broke up and the children threw themselves at him, the older ones pumping his hand, and the younger ones climbing on to his back. Laughing, Nissel Shwalb shook off the small fry and shouted, "*Sharrap*. Outside, all of you. And be quick. We have business to talk over. Say, Cantor, where's your missis? Call her in; we're having a conference."

It is safe to say that nobody but Nissel could have got away with such effrontery. What kind of talk was this—"Say, Cantor?" And he would have fared even worse with the cantor's young ones. They'd give him a *sharrap!* But Uncle Nissel was a privileged character, who had earned forbearance. He never came to this house empty-handed, always pre-armed; he brought out some candy, and with their fists full the cantor's offspring cleared out in the blink of an eye. The cantor donned his coat and went to summon his wife from a neighbor's. And a conference took place behind locked doors.

That evening a score of guests were bidden to the cantor's house. In the old country this would have been called "coming in for a glass of tea," and what that denotes we need hardly explain. Everyone knows it is not merely a glass of tea, but a supper. And neither the glass of tea nor the supper is the important thing. The important thing is what comes between tea and supper—to wit, a game of cards.

The gathering at the Lomzha cantor's that evening was a mixed one, most of them the cantor's *landsleit,* fellow townsmen from Lomzha, with a good sprinkling of actors and entertainers.

At first glance it might seem that the guests had little in common. What, for instance, would a "Reverend," that is a rabbi with curled earlocks who specialized in circumcisions, have to say to a peddler with an asthmatic cough? Or what would an up-and-coming typewriter salesman have in common with an elderly Hebrew teacher? Or a haughty druggist who could read Latin prescriptions with a butcher from Essex Street? Or a Bronx landlord, a swarthy man with a bulbous nose and a booming voice, with a pallid tailor from the Bowery whose only possession was a set of false teeth? And what did they have to do with a cantor and a cantor's wife, with actors, actresses, musicians, and theater ushers?

And yet they were all perfectly at home with each other. Each considered himself as good as the next and took pride in the fact that he was in America and made a living. Nobody turned up his nose at his neighbor, as often happens in the old country when people of different stations in life come together for a celebration. The spirit of de-

266

mocracy can be felt wherever you go in America, and our brethren who come to this country in great numbers from all over the world absorb this spirit as quickly as possible.

Besides the cantor and his wife and family, there was present Mr. Klammer in his dinner jacket, with his beard parted in the middle and combed to both sides. He sat next to Mr. Nickel who, this evening, was sporting his gold watch and chain presented by "the President of the United States of America." Their talk was in English and, as any curious eavesdropper would have recognized, it was pure bluff.

Isaac Shwalb and Braindele Kozak hung over a small table at which a heated card game was in progress. One of players was the prima donna, Henrietta Shwalb, in all her diamonds. Luck had been with her all evening, as could be seen by the pile of money before her. All the ladies envied her openly and the men exchanged sallies, winked, and flirted with her. In fact, a certain gentleman with a clean-shaven red face, a long sharp nose, and a diamond ring on his finger, had stepped on her foot more than once, though we know for a positive fact he was married.

In a rocking chair to one side sat Leo Rapalesco, the center of a group of actors exchanging theater anecdotes. Here the life of the party was a certain comedian, a born jester, who could get a laugh before he opened his mouth. And he laughed with them so violently he contorted himself like a pretzel.

"Ladies and gentlemen!" called out the Lomzha cantor, who had reached the halfway stage between raw greenhorn and mellowed American, and whose speech had become half-Yiddish, half-English. "Ladies and gentlemen! To the table, *bitte,* supper is *fartig.*"

The crowd didn't need urging. Those who were doing nothing swarmed to the table at once; and the players had only to score up their accounts. It turned out that the prima donna was the sole winner. Her brother Isaac and Braindele Kozak greedily watched her sweep her winnings into her purse and asked what she intended to buy herself with them—a motorcar, a diamond bracelet, or a shack on Fifth Avenue? Henrietta ignored their pleasantries and the left-handed compliments of her partners who told her she played cards almost as well as she sang.

"Beautiful!" the gentleman with the sharp nose exclaimed in rapture, throwing languishing looks in her direction, and licking himself like a tomcat. He was panting to sit next to her at the table, but his hopes were dashed. Nissel Shwalb, as master of ceremonies, seated the guests at the table, and did it so cunningly that each lady had a gentleman on either side. For instance, the cantor's wife sat between the typewriter salesman and the butcher from Essex Street, and an actress with a huge chignon between the little rabbi with the curled earlocks and the tailor from the Bowery, who must have acquired his teeth second hand, for when he ate they clicked.

It can't be said the ladies and gentlemen were altogether happy with Nissel's arrangements. For what would a cantor's wife have to say to either a typewriter salesman or a butcher? Or an actress to a rabbi or a tailor? But the prima donna had on one side of her Leo Rapalesco and on the other her brother Isaac.

To that only the gentleman with the red nose, who had fallen in love with the prima donna, had any objection. And as if in spite, he had drawn as his table partner Madame Cherniak, who sweated like a locomotive and smelled of laundry soap. May all the kind things he wished her in his heart fall into the sea. And yet he treated her with great courtesy. He pushed her plate closer, offered her bread, poured water into her glass and asked her preference in wine.

At last God, who doesn't overlook his meanest creature, came to this gentleman's aid. Since the tables were small, the guests began shoving, and through this shoving the red-nosed gentleman found himself opposite his lady-love. A gleam came into his eyes, now that he could manipulate his feet under the table. True, it took him a while to find what he sought, encountering first Rapalesco's feet or Isaac Shwalb's clodhoppers. When he discerned a faint smile playing on Henrietta's lips, he knew himself to be "all right."

What a fire burned in his breast against this handsome stranger who sat so close to her. The prima donna kept bending over him, whispering and giggling. The red-nosed gentleman, who had taken a drop before the fish and another drop after the fish, cast such murderous glances at Rapalesco that Henrietta laughed even harder.

"That fresh guy! Betcha he's a greenhorn," thought the lovelorn gentleman resentfully. But he was soon put straight. The toastmaster got to his feet. "Ladies and gentlemen, I would like to announce that the first toast of the evening will be given by our good friend, Mr. Klammer. I will now ask our worthy host and his missis, the worthy hostess, to fill the wineglasses of our worthy guests. Mr. Klammer, you have the floor."

Mr. Klammer stood up, coughed delicately, adjusted his dinner jacket, his shirt and his tie, parted his beard smartly right and left,

268

mopped his dry forehead with a silk kerchief, leaned slightly forward resting his thumbs on the table, swept the whole company with a searching glance, caught his lower lip under his teeth, and after a long pregnant pause, began.

Mr. Klammer had always considered himself something of a public speaker, but since coming to America he had heard so many lectures, sermons and after-dinner speeches that he had been panting to show what he could do. And it cannot be denied—he was an excellent speaker. His speeches may not have been rich in content, but the rhetoric! And the delivery! And his voice! Mr. Klammer, you understand, knew just when to make it thunder and when to let it sink to a whisper. And his posture! And his hands! In speechmaking the hands play nearly as important a part as the tongue. A speaker has to know when to raise them and when to lower them, when to fold them across his chest and to spread them apart, when to hook a thumb into his vest and when to put them in his pants pockets. And sometimes, after an especially telling burst of eloquence, he must step back, drop his hands, incline his head to one side, and pause, to "make a point." This making of points, together with the trick of thrusting his hands in his pockets, Mr. Klammer had picked up from American speakers.

Lack of space compels us to abridge Mr. Klammer's speech.

"The life span of man," he started, "can be divided like the year into four seasons: spring, summer, autumn, and winter. Spring, ladies and gentlemen, is the best, the happiest, or as our teacher Moses has called it, the most poetic time of the year. Spring is the time when everything blooms, when nature, after its long sleep, awakens, when 'the nightingale,' as Heine has said, 'is all right,' when the heart of youth beats faster, when 'a young man's fancy,' as Voltaire has put it, 'lightly turns to thoughts of love.' Which of us, ladies and gentlemen, hasn't sipped of this heady draught, whose name is love? Which of us, as Tolstoi has said, 'hasn't once been young and full of hope and hasn't sought and found her whom he would choose as his companion on life's journey?' What can be more beautiful, more sublime and more sacred than this emotion which our immortal Shakespeare has crowned with the name 'affinity'? According to the greatest scholars of the past, such as Kant, Socrates, Diogenes, Mephistopheles, and our own learned Talmudists, the world rests on three things: on love, on love, and on love. 'Without money,' says Ibsen, 'a man can be all right, but without love our life is empty and stale and unprofitable, as a ship without a rudder,' or as the Englishman puts it, 'like a body without a soul.'

269

"Ladies and gentlemen: Can you not sense this evening at this very table the presence of that sacred emotion of love and affinity which first drew two young hearts together on the other side of the Atlantic? Yes, friends. On the other side of the Atlantic, in the old world, this love was first kindled and burst into flame. Their romance, like all romances, ladies and gentlemen, at first blossomed unseen, and unknown, but 'heaven and earth have sworn,' says Emile Zola, 'that nothing shall remain secret on this earth, that truth shall rise triumphant from the ashes,' or as the Englishman puts it, 'I cannot hide the eel in the sack.'

"Ladies and gentlemen: You know me for what I am, a man of principle. I do not pry into my neighbor's pots to see what is cooking there. It isn't in my nature to give away another's secret. Another man's business is not my business. How does the Englishman put it— 'When friends quarrel, everybody keep away.'

"Ladies and gentlemen: The great poet, Milton, once expressed himself thus: 'Do not think us so foolish as to consider it an impropriety when a boy loves a girl and a girl loves a boy.' I repeat his words and with great pride I hasten to assure you that I and several other of my friends who are present tonight had the good fortune of sharing that exalted moment when the young people plighted their troth on board ship, swearing, as Byron puts it, 'eternal devotion and trust' and when their two souls were 'fused together,' as Zangwill puts it, 'in the common melting pot.'

"Ladies and gentlemen! This was the first act of a glorious romance, of a drama of hearts. A romance which began in the Old World, a drama whose last and final act is destined to take place, as Theodore Herzl puts it, 'in the happy land of the dollar.' Here in this land the final words will be spoken. Here in this land the curtain will fall. Here in this land they will be 'all right,' or as Schiller says, 'Finita la comedia.'

"Ladies and gentlemen! It gives me great honor and pleasure to inform you that aside from the fact that the hero and heroine of this romance are all right—that is, young, healthy and handsome—they are also famous. Both of them are renowned from one end of the world to the other in the spheres of art and Yiddish theater, he as an actor, she as a singer.

"Ladies and gentlemen! Shall I call them by name? This, I think is superfluous, for all of you know them well. Here they sit hand in hand in front of you like two turtle doves. All of you have heard her sing. You have admired her beauty and talent. You have acknowledged her as the Star from Buenos Aires, and her chosen one as the young but well-known Star from Bucharest whom we will all have the pleasure of seeing and applauding no later than tomorrow at this time, when he opens in the famous Nickel Theater.

"Ladies and gentlemen! I gaze at this young pair and I see their faces suffused with a rosy flame. I can understand their emotions at this fateful moment when all our eyes are turned on their happy betrothal. Let us wish them no less success in their life's career than they have already attained in their stage careers. Long live Yiddish Art! Long live its high priests! Long live our Stars! Long live the happy couple! I raise my glass and conclude in the words of King Solomon, 'The voice of the bride and the voice of the groom.' Long live the bride and groom. Hurrah for Mr. Rapalesco! Hurrah for Miss Henrietta Shwalb! Hurrah!!!"

The shouts of "hurrah" and the clinking of glasses after Mr. Klammer's brilliant speech were no more than custom and etiquette called for. The real demonstration started when the Lomzha cantor's wife grabbed a large platter from the table, and sent it crashing to the floor, calling out in a transport of joy, *"Maz'ltov."*

"Maz'ltov! Maz'ltov!" The crowd took up her cry, and the relatives and close friends of the bride and groom crowded about the couple to offer them congratulations. First Nissel Shwalb hugged and kissed them both, then his brother Isaac, and then Mr. Klammer, Mr. Nickel, the cantor, the cantor's wife, and Braindele Kozak. Since no protocol was observed and everyone was kissing and embracing everyone else indiscriminately, the red-nosed gentleman saw his chance, and began kissing the happy couple, addressing himself chiefly to the bride.

"The devil take it!" exclaimed Nissel Shwalb, opening several bottles of wine in quick succession and refilling the glasses all around, not forgetting his own. "The devil take it. I haven't had a drop all evening, as you see me swimming. Mr. Klammer, Mr. Nickel, let's drink *l'chaim* to Columbus who dreamed up this wonderful land. A sweet land, a golden land, this America. Say, Cantor, why are you sitting there like a Lomzha householder at a holy day service? Where are your noisemakers? Why don't you give us a tune? Brother Isaac, get Madame Cherniak up from the table, and give us a dance. Ladies and gentlemen, my brother dances like a ballerina, though he's somewhat heavy on his feet, may I have everyone's good at heart."

At these words Madame Cherniak flushed a brick-red and Isaac, already three sheets to the wind, leaped out on the floor to show

271

what he could do. And the happy couple? The happy couple sat hand in hand, faces shining with bliss as befitted a bride and groom. Nissel Shwalb had reason to rejoice. Of all the combinations his ingenious brain had devised, this "glass of tea" at the cantor's was the most brilliant.

Though he didn't know it, luck had played into Nissel's hands. He had caught Rapalesco at his most susceptible moment, when he was still in a daze. The fanfare about him in the Yiddish papers would have been enough to turn his head, but he was also receiving tempting offers daily from Gentile managers.

Add to this the fact that he had so far received no reply from Rosa to the outpouring of his heart. Looking through the New York papers, he saw her name always coupled with Grischa Stellmach's, a sight that cut him to the heart. "Let her be happy with this Grischa Stellmach," he thought. "Let them grow old together in honor and in riches. But she still could have answered my letter. Either she's so far gone in arrogance she has forgotten her old home, or she doesn't want to remember. She wants to forget. If so, why should I eat my heart out over her? I might as well forget, too."

To make it easier for him to forget, he tried to persuade himself that it was not for her sake that he had come here but for his own career. And, as in happier days, the young dreamer went about in a world of fantasies. He imagined that he had acquitted himself with such brilliance on his first night, that he was given no time for a second performance, but was picked up or, as they called it, "kidnaped" from the Yiddish stage, given fabulous sums, as much as he asked, and won still greater acclaim on the English-speaking stage. Then the name Rapalesco, ringing all over America, reached the ears of the arrogant Spivak and he could even the score with her. He could show her who was older. He could tell her the plain truth, that she was not worthy of him and never had been. That he had once been drunk and now he was sober. That he had been a fool and now he was wise. That he had been sick and now he was cured, entirely cured. . . .

With such thoughts Rapalesco drank toast after toast with the cantor's guests, and laughed and made merry, not acknowledging to himself the significance of the broken plate.

37 THE DEBUT

In all his years of acting Rapalesco had never been so anxious. Never had his heart beat so fast with fear and anticipation. He was like an ambitious student taking his final examination.

When finally the massive curtain of the Nickel Theater went up, the sea of faces in the darkened theater seemed to sway in front of him as though a wave had passed over it. After a rustling and creaking, a hush descended, that blessed hush which lifts up the actor as on wings.

The play that night was again Karl Gutzkow's tragedy, *Uriel Acosta*. From the moment Uriel stepped out on the stage, he drew all eyes. His pale, sensitive face, his large eyes ringed with shadows, his long, fair hair, his newly sprouted blond beard, and his white shirt, open at the throat, combined to personify the Jewish intellectual of an earlier day, fine-grained but with the mettle of tempered steel. He further won the audience with the warmth and richness of his voice and proceeded to astonish them with the mobility of his features, which changed perceptibly with every mood.

Now he stood before you, a young thinker gravely conversing with the learned Dr. De Silva about metaphysical problems: "I do not say that I alone can proclaim the absolute Truth, which none can refute. I only know this—that my ignorance bids me inquire, that my blindness prompts me to look more sharply, that my deafness makes me listen more closely." At the word *blindness* he pointed to his eyes, at the word *deafness* to his ears, with the gestures typical of the Jewish scholar and skeptic, but marked with an incomparable personal charm.

But when the betrothed of his own beloved Judith entered the conversation, a change came over Uriel. Now the thwarted lover stood before you, speaking with the passionate ardor of one who sees his beloved fallen into another's hands. "She had been sent from heaven to this earth. She is a gift from God." Turning to his rival Ben Jochanan, he caught his hand with a gesture of supplication: "Do not touch her with those hands which have been handling gold . . . Approach her with reverence, with humility . . . beg her, beseech her."

And when the Jewish Tribunal entered, with Rabbi De Santos at its head, to try him for heresy, his face and bearing underwent another change. Before you stood a martyr. Here one had only to look at Rapalesco's eyes and at the play of his features, to see reflected the whole tragedy of his life. And all without melodrama, without ranting or posturing, no clutching at the heart, no tearing of the hair, no wringing of hands, no striding up and down the stage, no contortion of the features.

Everyone had to admit, here was no mimic, no posturer, but a true artist, who had wrought something new on the stage. Everyone had to admit that Rapalesco's Acosta was his own creation. Those who had seen Rapalesco in his character roles more than once could have testified that he created a fresh type each time, adding new strokes to the picture, heightening the colors, deepening the shadows, shedding new light on the entire play—the sort of interpretation a dramatist longs for and seldom receives.

At the end of the first act, when Acosta is alone on the stage, Rapalesco changed again; the oppressed martyr gave way to the warrior entering battles of the intellect. "Ah, Ben Jochanan," he cried. "You err greatly. He who is accustomed to fight for the truth will not permit his golden crown to be trampled underfoot."

As Rapalesco raised his arm, it seemed to the audience they saw his head encircled. The crown was not of gold but of affliction, of sorrow and pain. And everyone's heart went out to him. For everyone the curtain descended too soon. A cry went up over the house, "Rapalesco! Rapalesco!" He had to take endless curtain calls.

Hearing the applause, Nickel and the partners of Klammer, Shwalb & Co. were in their seventh heaven. Their enemies, partisans of other theaters and the hard-bitten critics of the *kibitzarnia*, who had been sharpening their teeth for slaughter, chewed their own nails in rage. Hopefully, they said, "Wait, the night isn't over; Karl Gutzkow's tragedy has five acts."

There followed the usual pandemonium which breaks out in every Yiddish theater during intermission. The name *Rapalesco* flew in the air in discussions based on the varied biographies offered in the press. The discrepancies provided matter for argument, as did the varying judgments of the play. Not everyone understood what the play was

274

about; not everyone knew who the author was—Lateiner or Gordon or Lubin or Professor Jacobi. Some waited for a "plot" to develop and maybe a song or two. Which demonstrates how highly developed the taste of the public was. Nevertheless, the play had made a powerful impression even on those who didn't understand it, which they hastened to communicate to their neighbors and friends.

But there was one person in the audience who found himself singularly frustrated. He had no one with whom to share his delight— "the lover of Yiddish theater," Meyer Stellmach. He actually melted like wax on a summer day; and yet he had no one to say a word to. He decided to steal quietly into box number three, first to see how "the children" were getting on, and second to hear their impressions of Rapalesco.

He took three steps, then froze in his tracks. The same giant he had met in the corridor earlier in the evening was blocking his way and looking him straight in the eye.

"*Sholom aleichem,* Mr. Turncoat. Don't you recognize me? That's strange. We used to be great cronies in London. Don't you remember? I even paid you a visit once. That is, I stood outside your door and heard you send word you weren't home. I would have made a scandal then and there, as you see me swimming. But I let it go. 'Never mind,' I told myself, 'let him pass into other hands.' I came to see you not for myself, you remember, but in behalf of the Lomzha cantor and his family. Do you remember that horde of children? Well, you ought to see them now. They don't need your favors—they're doing 'all right.' And how goes it with you these days, my shilly-shallying friend? I'd never have spotted you if your Grischa wasn't sitting in box number three with Rosa Spivak. May I have everyone's good at heart."

If Meyer Stellmach didn't get a stroke on the spot it was a sheer miracle. That remark about Grischa and Rosa! May everything he wished Nissel Shwalb fall into the sea. Still, one thing has nothing to do with another. A man stops you, claims your acquaintance— you can't be a boor and spit in his face. His evening was ruined. He had to put off his visit to "the children" until after the second act, through which he sat, as the saying goes, on pins and needles. It would have been worse for him had he known what was going on in box number three. Had he been there during the intermission, a certain catastrophe might have been averted.

To all appearances nothing unusual was going on in box number three. Grischa and Rosa had sat quietly through the first act, without taking their eyes off Rapalesco. It was a pleasure for them both to see such a talented actor on the Yiddish stage, but particularly gratifying to Rosa. Hadn't she herself once been connected with the Yiddish theater? A rewarding experience like this she hadn't had in a long time, and she was truly grateful to Stellmach for bringing them here.

And her amazement kept growing. She scarcely believed her own eyes. That among Yiddish actors, as she remembered them, there could develop such a sensitive and discerning talent as Rapalesco's! The illusion he created was so strong it carried her back to the Amsterdam of a by-gone century. She lived again in that turbulent age of struggle between free thought and fanaticism, the age of Baruch Spinoza. It was only a pity that in the next box a disturbance was going on. There sat a group of women gossipping in loud whispers like women in a synagogue gallery.

These women were connected with the theater management and with Klammer, Shwalb & Co. Among them was the Lomzha cantor's wife and several others, who, if not actresses themselves, were certainly the wives of actors. What they found to talk about which couldn't be put off until later is hard to say. But it is ever thus: when you are forced to be silent, that's when you are most anxious to talk. As the saying goes, the devil pulls at your tongue.

This minor disturbance could have been put up with if, right in the middle of the first act, the door hadn't opened and a young woman burst in in a hat so large the whole group could have stood under its brim. Now the real hullabaloo started. The newcomer didn't seem to be able to sit still in one place or to keep her mouth shut for an instant, but flitted from chair to chair, rustling her gown, adjusting her hat, jangling her bracelets, chattering and giggling. Rosa and her escort exchanged glances: "Who can this animal be?"

When the curtain fell on the first act and the ovation for Rapalesco began, this creature behaved in the same outrageous manner. As Rapalesco was taking his third curtain call, Rosa saw her lean forward from the box and stick out her tongue at him, sending the whole group into gales of laughter. Unable to restrain her temper any longer, Rosa turned to her and said in Yiddish: "Apparently you were not pleased with this artist's performance?"

"Which artist? Rapalesco?" The girl laughed, merrily displaying two rows of small white teeth. "I'm engaged to him. He's my fiancé."

This was said so simply and with such an unaffected laugh that Rosa took a sudden liking to the strange girl. She moved closer to her. "You're engaged to him? Then you're also an actress?"

276

"Am I an actress?" The girl stopped laughing, "I'm a prima donna," she said with dignity. "My name is Henrietta Shwalb."

"I am happy to know you."

Without giving her own name, Rosa moved so close to the prima donna that they found themselves face to face across the rail between the boxes.

"What I would like you to tell me," said Rosa with a friendly smile, "is whether it's true what they say about this Rapalesco from Bucharest, that the Queen Carmen Silva . . ."

"It's all a lie," Henrietta broke in, with a laugh. "First of all, he's not from Bucharest but from Holeneshti."

"Holeneshti!"

Rosa wasn't aware of having spoken the word. It had torn itself from her heart, and she seized Henrietta's hand in her own. But she quickly recovered herself and pretended to examine Henrietta's bracelets.

"You wear so much jewelry. I like your bracelet."

"It's a gift from my fiancé."

"What did you say was the name of the town?"

"A town? Ha ha. That's a laugh. It's nothing but a village. Holeneshti it's called. It's in Bessarabia, where they eat *mameliga,* a mush fit for pigs." And she laughed again.

Their conversation was brought to an abrupt close as the lights dimmed and the curtain rose on the second act.

Where had her eyes been, thought Rosa? Why hadn't she recognized him at once? She should have known him by his voice. Rosa looked down at her program and read, "Uriel Acosta—Leo Rapalesco."

"Well, Leo . . ."

"What did you say?" asked Grischa Stellmach, noticing the change that had come over Rosa. All during the first act she had sat close to him, her hand in his. Now she had moved apart and was staring at the stage. She seemed to have removed herself from the box.

Looking through her opera glasses she saw a garden, some *papier mâché* trees in the foreground with some figures among the trees, but not his. It seemed to her the figures were like the trees, cardboard, animated mannikins, statues that spoke. One, an old man in elegant dress, was reading a paper in a high, whining voice. Near him stood a serving man in old-fashioned livery with a pigtail down his back. The cardboard figures conversed, but she didn't know what they said, though she saw their lips move. A girl entered, grotesquely made up with crookedly drawn eyebrows, and clumsy hands. Who was this

277

girl? What was she doing here? She spoke in a droning voice, calling the old man "Vater" in German. Their talk was foolish and pointless—about the Amsterdam bourse, Rubens and Van Dyke, Moses and Socrates and Christ, art and religion, all in affected German, all of it meaningless. The servant left. Thank God, one mannikin less. The old man went off, too. The girl remained, aimlessly drifting about the stage. Then she raised her mascara-blackened eyes to the heavens, pressed her hands to her padded bosom, and declaimed in German, "The chains of my despair lie heavy on my breast." Idiotic, pointless words.

But here *he* came. Uriel Acosta. Rosa felt her breath catch in her throat. Her heart pounded against the cage of her ribs. For a moment, thinking Uriel Acosta had looked in her direction, the blood rushed to her face. But she had been mistaken. Uriel was speaking to Judith in a slow, quiet voice. His movements were plastic. Whatever he did carried meaning—not a needless gesture, no wasted nuance. The audience hung on his words as though he were alone. Suddenly his voice rose. A new vibrancy came into it. He took Judith's hands in his. "For the last time, my dearest, farewell."

His eyes, Rosa thought, conveyed his meaning, even better than his words. They were full of love and the pain of parting. Was he leaving the stage? No. The old man had entered again and with him a whole retinue. But Uriel remained. Thank God he remained. Rosa saw Judith take his hand; she saw them leave the stage together. In the distance were heard strains of music.

With a sigh Rosa put down her glasses. Young Stellmach leaned toward her anxiously. What had happened? Why the deep sigh? Rosa didn't return his look. She hadn't seen it. She was completely alone, facing herself. This was the moment she had dreamed of so often. What should she do? Perhaps she was dreaming again. Then she heard a giggle in the next box. No, this was real. Here was the girl who called herself a prima donna and boasted of being his fiancée. Could it be true? She must ask him. This very evening. After the second act she would go backstage and ask to see Rapalesco. What name would she give? None. She would simply say a lady wished to see him. There would be raised eyebrows, but what did it matter? She had to see him. At once. In her eagerness she forgot she wasn't alone, that Grischa Stellmach was with her; she forgot all that had happened between them today.

Suddenly from the stage was heard the sound of a trumpet, startling Rosa from her reverie. The stage swarmed with people, all jabbering

278

she didn't know what. Where was Uriel? Here he was, transformed again. His voice rang with new vigor. Picking up her opera glasses, she watched him through his long monologue, without comprehending its drift. She only heard the voice. How could she have forgotten it? How often in the past years had she heard it with her eyes closed!

"The anguish of my people is my anguish. Their sorrows are my sorrows. You have excommunicated me—but I am still a Jew." His speech ended on a note of triumph, and it was greeted with a sharp burst of applause. This had come from a group of young people, roused to nationalist fervor by his last words, "The anguish of my people is my anguish . . . I am still a Jew." In the wake of the first outburst came another, and soon the entire audience was clapping and cheering. Whatever their beliefs, the people in the audience were stirred. Here was a man who, by the force of his genius, had given life to an outmoded play, with its quaint sentiments, archaic language, and outworn beliefs. He had made it apply to their own lives, their own age; he had translated a dilemma of a period into man's universal dilemma. And he had done it almost without the help of the supporting cast. As he carried the whole play on his own shoulders, so he had the audience in the hollow of his hand. A real star rose in the firmament of the Yiddish theater.

Though the curtain had gone down for the last time, the applause went on, the clapping and stamping, the cries of "Bravo, Bravo, Rapalesco!"

"*Sharrap*. Be still," came from a few querulous voices. But they were lost in another wave of applause. Instead of "Bravo," "Bravo, Rapalesco!" now shouts of "Hurrah, Rapalesco!" were heard.

"The theater has gone crazy!" a lone voice complained.

The speaker was right.

In America everyone, unless born a mute, makes speeches. They are made on every occasion—engagements, weddings, divorces, circumcisions, birthdays, *Bar-Mitzvahs*, anniversaries, housewarmings, funerals, the welcome of a guest and the departure of a pest. Whatever the occasion, merry or sad, it calls for speechmaking. And when it comes to a public occasion, then God Himself has bidden man to speak.

On a guest-artist's opening in a theater it is customary to orate in his honor between acts. This is sometimes done by the guest-artist himself, or by an actor with the gift of gab and a strong voice, or by

279

the manager himself, who steps up to tell the esteemed public what it should know.

On this occasion, after the second act, when the theater had gone crazy, and Rapalesco had grown weary of taking curtain calls the curtain went up once more, but instead of Rapalesco, out stepped the popular Mr. Nickel.

Mr. Nickel, informally dressed, behaved like a host in his own house. He had his hands in his pockets and a smile on his lips, the same ready smile which had made Mr. Nickel known far and wide as a "good guy."

"Ladies and gentlemen," he began. "First of all I wish to express my deep gratitude to the esteemed public for the honor it has accorded me by attending my theater tonight in such great numbers. It is no surprise to me that my theater is packed at a time when in other New York theaters there is room enough to drive an automobile through. I do not mean by this to belittle my competitors—I merely wish to point out that the esteemed public seems to prefer my theater. This is possibly due to the fact that I have always done everything in my power to please the esteemed public. I have never stopped at any expense, no matter how great. And this time, too, I have outdone myself in your behalf by importing from a great distance and at an unbelievable cost, for a few limited performances, the honored guest of the evening. Ladies and gentlemen, he is the king of show people. He is the world-famous dramatic artist, Leo Rapalesco from Bucharest, who has no equal either here in America or on the other side of the ocean. It gives me great pleasure to note that the esteemed public has valued him at his true worth. And I give you my solemn oath that I will not let any sum of money, no matter how great, stand in the way of keeping him with us longer, in order to afford the opportunity to those hundreds and thousands of people who had to go home tonight with heavy hearts, for as you see, there isn't room to squeeze a pin through.

"Ladies and gentlemen. While admitting my debt to the worthy public, I cannot refrain from thanking certain prominent guests who have honored my theater with their illustrious presence tonight. I take special pride in pointing out that these prominent guests have up to this time never graced a Yiddish theater in New York with their presence. Foremost among them are two people who are themselves famous in the theater world on both sides of the ocean. They are sitting, ladies and gentlemen, in a box on my left. I do not believe there is a person among you who hasn't heard the names of Grischa Stellmach or Miss Rosalie Spivak, just as there is not a person who hasn't heard the names of Washington, Lincoln, or Edison . . ."

The rest of Mr. Nickel's speech was drowned out. No one was able to hear a word of it, not even Mr. Nickel himself. At the names Grischa Stellmach and Rosalie Spivak, the theater went crazy all over again. The audience rose to its feet as one man and gave them such an ovation that the famous pair had to get up and flee, driven on by Mr. Stellmach, who had fought his way to their box, whispered something urgently into their ears, and led them out. Once outside, Stellmach helped them into the waiting automobile and left the Nickel Theater with a curse on his lips against the lowbred downtown, New York, Yiddish public which had given them such an ostentatious, almost princely, funeral.

Rapalesco was in his dressing room making up for the third act when he heard the fresh tumult. "What's all the commotion about?" he asked the make-up man, who had run in panting into his dressing room.

"They've gone stark, raving mad," answered the make-up man, a former barber, a free-thinker and socialist, who didn't miss a single Socialist lecture in Clinton Hall if he could possibly get there. "Lunatics, all of them, barbarians without a drop of civilization in their veins. Our manager Mr. Nickel got the itch to make a speech tonight. So make a dignified speech, like any self-respecting person. But no. After all, between you and me, he's a boss, a bourgeois, he has to bow and scrape and lick the boots of the capitalists and their stooges, the uptown artists, who came down to us all the way from Fifth Avenue. A small thing! If Karl Marx were here he'd bury himself alive."

"Who are these actors from Fifth Avenue?" asked Rapalesco, looking into the mirror and striking a pose to fit the third act, when he meets his family and his blind mother.

"Who are they? He's a violinist, he plays the fiddle, Grischa Stellmach, and she's a singer, a prima donna, Rosalie Spivak . . ." If the make-up man had singed him with a hot iron or cut his throat with a razor, Rapalesco couldn't have been more stricken. He stood in a daze, his face pale as death. Then he tore off his wig, ripped the blond beard from his chin, and threw himself at the door. And at that moment Henrietta tore into the room with a swish and a flutter and a burst of high laughter.

"Oh, what a comedy. A regular circus. You should have seen them run as from the plague. A regular comedy, a vaudeville show. Oh, oh."

38 SHOLOM MEYER APPEARS

In the meanwhile the following scene was being enacted in the lobby. Our elegant friend, Mr. Klammer, was standing at the door listening to Mr. Nickel's speech. One of his eyes was shut and a point of his beard caught between his teeth. The expression on his face spoke his disapproval louder than words. How could a raw, uncultivated individual like Mr. Nickel, without a glimmer of history or art or Shakespeare, undertake to make a speech before such a public? If they had only let him, Mr. Klammer, mount the stage, it would have been all right, he would have spread it out for them on tables and benches; or as the Englishman puts it, "I'd fire away for all I am worth."

"Ah, *sholom aleichem,* my dear globe-trotter, and how are you? I've been looking for you with a candle. I came all the way here just to see you, may God grant me fortune and luck!"

Mr. Klammer saw in front of him a little man with shrewd, twinkling eyes, dressed from the top of his derby to the tips of his polished shoes in a spanking new outfit fresh from the needle. His overlong shirt sleeves peeked inquisitively from his coatsleeves, and though he pushed them back, they refused to stay back. This kept his hands constantly occupied. His voice was hoarse and he spoke without stopping to draw breath or hear an answer.

"Tell me, my fine Englishman with the checkered trousers, how goes it with you in this country? How's your health and how's business, and why do you stare at me like a fasting bridegroom on the day of his wedding? Don't you recognize me? Well, I will give you a hint. My name is Muravchik. Sholom Meyer Muravchik. I stayed with you in London one time—perish the memory—I was really on my uppers then. I borrowed a few shillings from you and left a security. Now I've come back to pay my debt and get my satchel out of hock. I hate to owe money, you understand, and the fact of the matter is, I need the papers."

"What papers?"

Apparently Mr. Klammer didn't begin to recognize the speaker. The little man with the twinkling eyes gave a rasping laugh, and his hands didn't stop waging war with his shirt cuffs.

"How do you like that? The man tries to play dead. Did you forget? A small satchel, reddish in color, with a round belly, packed with papers, important papers. For you they may not have any great value, but to me they are a fortune. If you offered me a thousand dollars for them, do you think I would take it? May God grant me fortune and luck!"

"Is that a fact? Think it over, my friend, maybe you've come knocking on the wrong door."

"A fine story, but a short one. Listen to me, I've never made a mistake yet, and I always find what I'm looking for, and I have never knocked down the wrong man. I'll give you proof. You are called Mr. Klammer, you live right in the middle of Whitechapel, and you run a hotel or an inn by the sacred name of 'Café National.' Do you believe me now? If not, I'll give your memory another prod. You took the satchel with my papers right out of my hands, carried it upstairs, and locked it up in a clothes wardrobe. What do you say to this, Mr. Snake-in-the . . . I mean Mr. Klammer?"

Apparently now Mr. Klammer recalled that he had once had such a satchel in his possession. But what he had done with it, he couldn't for the life of him remember, though you chop his head off. He shrewdly decided to play dumb.

"I know nothing of any satchel or of anything else, and if you don't stop annoying me, I'll have you thrown out of the theater right into the street."

At this Sholom Meyer Muravchik drew up to Mr. Klammer; both his fists wrapped themselves about Mr. Klammer's elegant Herzl beard; and who knows what might have transpired next if Mr. Klammer's shouts for help hadn't brought Nissel Shwalb on the scene (how could a scandal be about to break out and Nissel Shwalb not there?) and with him ushers, who took hold of Sholom Meyer's new outfit and his jaunty derby—and once more there was peace in Israel, that is, in the theater lobby.

Sholom Meyer Muravchik had not come to New York merely to wrap his fists around Mr. Klammer's beard. Aside from recovering his papers, he had business with young Rapalesco, pertaining to the Holtzman family.

In a letter to Shchupak from London he had written of his intention to visit the sick Hotzmach. But weeks passed before Sholom Meyer set out to find his friend. Finally, one gloomy day, he pressed on through the crowded and dirty streets of Whitechapel to a tenement which would have done credit to the slums of Vilna or Berdichev.

Sholom Meyer saw two doors in front of him gaping open like the jaws of two hungry beasts. At random he entered one and began to climb up a slippery, dark staircase, through a dense aroma of garlic, onions and fish fried in rancid oil; and through the din of wailing infants and screaming women cursing in every known dialect: "Break your head, you bright angel." "Choke on a bone, you scurvy throat." "Walk on crutches, you dressed-up whore." By such compliments Sholom Meyer knew that he was among his own kind.

Sholom Meyer kept climbing and climbing the twisting steps—hoping to overtake a human being before long. Near the top he met with one—whether human or not he wasn't sure. She had broad bony shoulders and was carrying a large bundle of firewood. She panted and groaned at every step like a leaking windbag.

"Auntie," said Sholom Meyer, catching up with this being, woman or witch, "do you know where I can find a director of a Yiddish theater by the sacred name of Hotzmach—I mean Holtzman?"

The one he called *Auntie* stopped, peered at him in the dark, moaned, and said, "Come, I'll show you."

Having climbed another flight they entered a dwelling which didn't look sumptuous enough to house the director of a theater, even a Yiddish one. In the kitchen the old woman dropped her bundle of wood, straightened her bent shoulders, and examined the newcomer with eyes whose color had long been washed out by tears.

"Whom did you ask for?"

"I asked for the director Hotzmach, I mean Holtzman. Tell him, if you will be so good, that a friend has come to see him."

"To see him?" The old woman raised both arms and dropped them again in a gesture of despair. "To see him is very hard. He is far, far from here."

"Did he leave town?"

The old woman raised her arms again. Then she bent down to the visitor, for she was a full two heads taller than he, and shouted into his ear as though he were stone-deaf, "May he rest in peace."

Sholom Meyer stepped back in horror and began wringing his hands.

"Hotzmach—I mean Holtzman—dead! What are you saying?"

"What am I saying? Woe is me. He was my son. My one and only son." The old woman sank down on a four-legged stool, hid her wrinkled face in her apron, and her shoulders began to shake.

The word *death* is an ugly word, yet it has a curious transforming power. Sholom Meyer stood stricken by the news, forgetting in that instant that the dead man had been his sworn enemy. It seemed to him all at once that he had lost a close friend. Why, he and Holtzman had been like this. Waiting until the old woman calmed down, he sat down close to her on another stool.

"Then you are his mother. My friend's mother. My friend often told me about his mother. He almost always had the word *mother* on his lips. 'As I live to see my mother again.' That was his favorite oath. Do you know what a devoted son you had? Have you any idea what a friend he was? He would share his last bite with another. As for me, we were one in body and soul, may God grant me fortune and luck!"

Sholom Meyer went on with this eulogy of his friend and of the friendship between them, every word of which sounded to him like gospel truth. And it fell like balm on the old woman's ears. At last she had found someone who had a kind word to say of her son, who had gone out like a candle in this miserable London, may all the plagues of Egypt descend on it. For if it weren't for this damp, foggy London air, her son might have coughed and coughed for who knew how many more years.

And Sarah-Brocha told her son's best friend how she had tried to save him, not sparing any cost, for what wouldn't she do for her son? Such a son. And when he had died, how she had refused to believe it. For how could her son die? Such a son. And how they had carried him off, without pallbearers, chants, candles, attendants, without even giving her time to mourn properly. A couple of fellows in black coats had snatched him up and carried him off in a wagon, without even letting her have a good cry.

"Wah, wah, wah." The wailing sound came from an inner room.

Sholom Meyer glanced at the old woman, who had suddenly grown silent. She jumped up, turned this way and that, as though trying to hide, then dropped her head, and stood there looking utterly lost.

Sholom Meyer understood from her stricken face what sort of crying this was. He asked in a hoarse whisper, "A young one?"

Getting no answer, he asked again, "Whose young one?"

Receiving no answer to this either, and seeing the forlorn look on the old woman's face, he asked no more questions. He only remarked, to no one in particular, "A remnant in the bargain."

285

"A big bargain and a small remnant," said the old woman and sat down again. "You put it well. And what a remnant . . . Oh, what a remnant!"

The ordinary words *remnant* and *bargain* proved so apt they unloosened the old woman's tongue. She proceeded to tell him the whole story while Sholom Meyer nodded and clucked with warm understanding. . . . Here at last was a true friend, her son's friend, to whom she could unburden her whole heart.

Who is a man's friend and who is his enemy? If the director, Holtzman, could have risen from his grave and seen his mortal enemy, Sholom Meyer, traveling to America on the same ship with his mother and sister, he wouldn't have believed his own eyes. Sholom Meyer, the sight of whose face used to make his blood boil, cast in the role of benefactor of his family, its guardian angel. If he had seen all this, Holtzman would have died all over again.

Thanks to Sholom Meyer, Sarah-Brocha and her daughter lacked for nothing. They sat all day over a tiny infant, looking up from its pillow for all the world like a large doll, with eyes as blue as pieces of sky. Luckily they had hit on fine weather. The sea was as calm as "Saturday after dinner."

A strange thing about those two women. A remarkable thing. Zlatka's feelings might be taken for granted. As soon as the agonies of childbirth were over and she heard a thin wail in the room, she had asked to see what had been born to her. At first sight of the helpless infant, such a wave of compassion for it had welled up in her that she forgot all the pain she had suffered, the disgrace she had once thought she couldn't live through, forgot her wish to die.

But if there was anyone to marvel at, it was old Sarah-Brocha. For her this had come like a bolt from the blue, like a brick building falling on top of her, like a salvo from a thousand cannons straight through the heart.

As long as her son had been ill and dying, she hadn't given much thought to Zlatka. If the girl looked downcast and ill, she ascribed it to worry about her brother. And the changes in her figure had come about so gradually the old woman, immersed in her other troubles, scarcely noticed it.

It was during the seven-day period of mourning. She and Zlatka were still sitting on low stools in their stockinged feet. Their eyes had long since dried, the wells of their tears exhausted. A strange emptiness had taken possession of their hearts; desolation had settled on their souls.

"Today is the sixth day," the mother said to her daughter. "The day after tomorrow we can get up. What will we do then? Where will we go? To whom will we turn?"

The old woman was working herself up to another outburst of self-pity, when her daughter suddenly fell on her neck and began kissing and hugging her; then she caught at her belly with both hands and screamed, "Mo-ther, save me, I'm dying."

"God be with you, child. Thunder strike me. What's wrong with you?"

Zlatka began wringing her hands, contorting her face, beating her head with her knuckles, and crying at the same time, "Mo-ther, save me, I'm dying."

Then a miracle happened. Or perhaps it was a woman's intuition. Sarah-Brocha understood what was wrong. Without stopping to question or weep, she pulled on her ragged coat, and ran to one neighbor, then to another, until she found a midwife. And after a harrowing night during which her daughter, her treasure, the apple of her eye, wrestled with the Angel of Death, God helped her and toward dawn she became a grandmother.

Wan and exhausted, her face drawn and her pointed nose sharper than ever, her black hair spread on the pillow, Zlatka slept. But the old woman didn't even sit down. She rolled up her sleeves to the elbow, pushed her kerchief behind her ears, tightened her apron strings, dragged out a heavy washtub, and put water on to boil for the child's bath. All the time she did this, she didn't stop cursing and reviling the city of London and its benighted inhabitants.

"A city—may it sink into the earth. A house—may it burn to the ground. Neighbors—may they never stand in a good place. All these Jewish people, and not a single wooden bread trough among them!"

In short, Sarah-Brocha embarked on her new role as though she had been rehearsing for it right along. Mind you, her grief was great enough, and the shame even greater. If a grave had opened in front of her, she would have jumped into it gladly. But things being as they were, what could she do? She wouldn't sit down and give her daughter, who had just gone through such an ordeal, a lecture on morals. That would come later. Let the Almighty help her get on her feet first. Then she'd call the girl to account, she'd rake her over the coals, she'd give her a what-for. "Tell me, my daughter, my fine beauty, how, and when and where and *who?*" Forlorn creatures that they were,

287

where would they go now? To whom would they turn? But all that could wait. Now she had to take care of her daughter, nurse her strength back, cook her broths twice a day. A girl in childbed, and a firstling, too. Thunder strike her! And the baby. How was the baby to blame? An innocent little creature. One of God's living beings. If it had the sense to expire of its own accord. But to strangle it—no. Or to scald it with boiling water—not that, either. After all, they were still Jews in the world. It was lucky a girl had been born and not a boy. They were spared the extra disgrace of a circumcision. And just for spite, it was a healthy girl. A big, lusty infant. And pretty as a picture. All the neighbors admitted they hadn't seen such a beautiful baby in a long time. Whom did she take after?

"Whom does she take after? Her father. He's a good-looking, strapping young fellow. A tailor. He's gone to America." Sarah-Brocha felt her face scalded with blushes. To have lived all these years and become a liar in her old age. Woe to her grey hairs and a curse on her enemies.

In a few days Zlatka was up and tottering about the house. She quickly regained her strength. Yet Sarah-Brocha still didn't find time to scold the girl, and give her what-for. When was there time for reading sermons? First there was the child. You had to swaddle it and unswaddle it, bathe it and feed it and rock it. What did Zlatka know about such things? She was little more than a child herself. And in the second place there was that *schlimazl*, Sholom Meyer, who had wriggled into their graces and had become practically a member of the household. He came twice a day and talked for hours, proposing plans to deliver them from their poverty and disgrace. He himself had nothing to gain by it. He did it only from friendship to her and her son, may he rest in peace, and that was all, may God grant him fortune and luck!

It is quite possible that Sholom Meyer had started out as a disinterested bystander. To stick your nose into another's pot, to find out what it smells of, and to help out with advice—that is a time-honored Jewish custom. But Sholom Meyer's nose had a keener sense of smell than most. What it took another weeks and months to sniff out, he discovered in a day. He could scrape your secrets from under your fingernails. Not only the old woman, but even the shy Zlatka looked him in the mouth and watched fascinated at the words that poured out.

"What shall I tell you two, when you, Auntie, are a woman of the old world, and your daughter is nothing but an innocent lamb? If you ask me, I shall tell you how things stand. I'll read it to you as from

288

a book. I know that breed, you understand, inside out. I'm an actor myself. This young fellow, what I know of him from the old days in Holeneshti—I can still remember him as through a dream—is an excellent young man, none better. It's just that he's thrown off his harness, gone off to America, and forgotten your address. How do we say it? 'Out of sight, out of mind.' But there's a law in America— when a young man gets a girl into a fix like this, he has to answer for it. It's 'one-two-three, get set, go and march under the canopy.' And if he should refuse, there's a remedy for that, too. They put him in jail, the 'jug,' they call it there. I know, though I've never been in America. I'm just planning to go. I have an important piece of business there with a singer, a prima donna. If it goes well, I'll be saying grace over bread and honey. I'll get me a capful of gold this high—'dollars' they call it there. And for a dollar you can get as much as two rubles. So, if we go to America, we'll go together. The young man will listen to me. I'll talk to him, man-to-man, no beating about the bush, as one actor to another. For me, he will tread the straight-and-narrow, I give you my word. And why do you think I am doing this? Only out of pity. I am sorry for your daughter and I want her kid to have a father. That's all I want. May God grant me fortune and luck!"

Sholom Meyer Muravchik didn't content himself with words. When he attached himself to someone, it was heart and body and soul. He couldn't bear to see the old woman staggering under a load of firewood. "Here, Auntie, let me show you how to carry wood so that it doesn't feel like wood but feathers."

In the same way he couldn't bear to see Zlatka wearing herself out with the child, day and night. True, he himself had never had a young one, and didn't expect to have any in the near future, but he had a sister, who though poor in worldly goods was wealthy in offspring. She believed in the two-child system. Every year she gave birth to twins. That was how he had become experienced in such matters. He even knew a trick to stop a child from crying. He grabbed the screaming infant from Zlatka's arms, and tossed it up and down and from side to side. Eventually, the baby stopped crying, but not before Zlatka's heart had almost leaped out of her breast in fright.

In all her life Zlatka hadn't told anyone, not even her brother, the things she told this Sholom Meyer—things she hadn't told her mother. It happened one morning that Sarah-Brocha was out marketing for dinner and Zlatka was alone with Sholom Meyer. She said to him, with a tremor in her voice, "I have a favor to ask of you." The instant she had spoken, she was sorry, but the words couldn't be recalled. Sholom Meyer looked at her intently. "What kind of favor, kitten? Through fire and water."

With trembling hands she took out of her bosom a small packet knotted up in a yellow kerchief. Her brother had entrusted it to her an hour before his death. He told her in a gasping voice to guard it with her life and to show it to no one, not even her mother. Then he had started coughing and the cough had turned to a rattle. . . .

Having handed the kerchief to her new friend, Zlatka felt as though a load had fallen from her chest. She said, "It's all we have in the world. I trust you with it. Take it and do what you want with it, but bring us to him, as you promised."

Sholom Meyer was so touched he didn't even look into the kerchief, but dropped it into his pocket like a magician. At that moment the old woman arrived, and he could only shake Zlatka's hand and whisper, "You can trust me, darling. As my name is Muravchik."

No later than next morning Sholom Meyer walked into their house like a bridegroom, freshly barbered and in a new outfit from head to foot. He called out gaily, "Listen to me, Auntie, here's the story in a few words. My business, thank God, has taken a turn for the better. Everything is ship-shape now. There's only one thing, I am summoned to New York. If you want to forget all your troubles and live to a happy old age, don't waste any more time. Take your pack on your back, as they say, I mean your daughter and her child, and set out with the right foot. I'm running right down to buy ship's tickets. And don't mention money to me. God willing, we'll settle accounts some day."

Sarah-Brocha looked at her daughter. She couldn't make head or tail of it all. A *schlimazl* like that, it seemed, and yet he took so much upon himself. Two round tears, as large as peas, rolled down her wrinkled old face. She was about to thank her son's friend, to bless him as he deserved, but he covered both ears with his hands and said, "Enough, enough, enough. Goodbye, I'm running for tickets, and you start getting ready. We'll be leaving tomorrow."

39 RAPALESCO FACES PROBLEMS

Let us return to Rapalesco as Henrietta burst into the room, giggling about the runaways.

"Who ran away?" he asked her.

At which Henrietta gave him a playful flip on the nose. "You green gooseberry, you. Don't you know what illustrious guests we had at the theater tonight? Grischa Stellmach and Rosa Spivak. They sat in box number three, right next to the director's box. I got to talking to her. She liked my bracelet. I told her it was a gift from you. Then she asked where you came from. . . ."

"And what did you tell her?"

"What do you think? I told her you came from Bucharest. Isn't that rich? The Queen of Rumania. Oh, oh. I almost died. But all that's nothing compared to the way they ran off. You should have seen them. Oh, oh." And she burst out laughing afresh.

Rapalesco wiped the cold sweat from his forehead. As coolly as he could manage he said, "Why did they have to run off?"

"I suppose we weren't good enough for them. Such aristocrats. I watched them while you were on the stage, and they didn't stop laughing."

There had been ups and downs in the lamentable romance between Rapalesco and Henrietta, times when he had despised her for her stupidity, and other times when he had forgiven her for all her giddy whims and caprices. But at this moment she was so repulsive to him he could have strangled her with his bare hands.

Henrietta, on her part, was in excellent spirits. She dropped down on the stool before the mirror, threw her head back, bared her white teeth, and went into gale after gale of laughter.

"Oh, but you missed the best part," she chortled. "If you had seen those two grab each other under the arm and march-march through the theater down to their automobile, and the audience, 'Bravo, Spivak. Bravo, Stellmach.' A regular circus, a vaudeville. Ha ha."

"Get ready. It's time for the third act," shouted the stage manager, shaking his head through the door.

The prima donna jumped off the stool, and Rapalesco sat down, his head bowed. The make-up man went to work with craftsmanlike speed and assurance. On went the wig and the little blond beard. A stroke here, a dab there, and Uriel Acosta was ready to step out before the audience.

As Uriel Acosta appeared, a shiver of anticipation ran over the audience. What new emotion—fear, love, scorn, caprice—would his face and gestures convey? But instead, Rapalesco stared vacantly before him and said in a toneless voice that barely carried across the footlights, "Here I am, De Silva."

"A little louder!" a voice was heard from the gallery, followed by cries of, "Speak up. We can't hear you."

And Rapalesco whispered, "May the condemned man step up to the holy confessor of guiltless souls?"

"Louder. Louder!" the whole gallery shouted.

Rapalesco, unaccustomed to such a reception, looked up. He couldn't understand what the uproar was about. It seemed to him he was speaking at the top of his voice. He became confused and missed his next cue. "Recant?" The actor playing the opposite part looked at him angrily and tried to set him right.

"Good morning to you. I bring you a radish," a derisive voice called out from the gallery, and the whole theater became alive at once. Laughter rolled down from the gallery like thunder. Rapalesco turned to the prompter's box, and tried to catch the words he was mouthing. The stage began to revolve about him and he was afraid he might faint. With a desperate effort he recovered himself—but too late. Led by the lancers of the *kibitzarnia,* who knew when to seize their advantage, the audience went on laughing even though Rapalesco ended the third act with his usual aplomb. It was too late. If he had acted like God Himself, he couldn't have salvaged that disaster. The audience hooted and jeered and whistled.

In the final scene of the last act Rapalesco made a brilliant comeback. His last tortured cry rang through the theater. "Enough. Let me go. Let me go." And supporting his head with both hands, he ran from the stage. In the wings he felt the ground rocking under his feet. He felt blindly for some ropes that supported the scenery and dropped into the arms of a stranger who had run up to him just in time, a short fellow with a crushed derby and shrewd little eyes. He shouted hoarsely to the stagehands, "Why do you stand like clay statues? Water. Bring water, somebody."

292

A few minutes later Rapalesco lay stretched out on the sofa in his dressing room, and beside him sat Sholom Meyer Muravchik.

When Sholom Meyer had been tossed out of the theater by Nissel Shwalb and his bouncers, he had picked himself up, brushed himself off, set the crushed derby on his head, and blithely reconnoitered the alley for the stage door. Once inside, he insinuated himself among the hanging flats and coils of rope. Approaching the man in charge of raising and lowering the curtain, a glum-faced individual with watery eyes who looked as though the whole world had fallen on top of him, he asked, "Which of these actors is Rapalesco?"

"The one with the long hair and the white collar who plays the part of Uriel Acosta."

"You're a real sage from the Talmud. They all have long hair and white collars."

The glum-faced one stared at Sholom Meyer with his pale eyes.

"It's not my fault that you're an ass and they all look the same to you. Can't you tell Menashe from Uriel Acosta?"

"A wise guy, eh? Wait, you're right. I know which one is Acosta." Then Sholom Meyer leaned toward his new acquaintance. "Look here, uncle, have you got a cigarette on you?"

The melancholy one devoured Sholom Meyer with his eyes.

"Greenhorn! Do you want me to pound you into a pulp and throw you down the steps? Here among the decorations you want to smoke?"

"Just look at him, he's ready to snap my head off. I'm not going to set fire to your theater."

And Sholom Meyer tickled the stagehand under the arm and asked him to be so kind as to shove over so he could sit down, too. "I don't want to stand all through the act," he explained. "I haven't had a bite in my mouth all day. Not because I am fasting, and not because I don't have the price of a meal. I'm as well off as the next one. It's just that I've been in such a hustle and bustle all day."

"Busy, we call it," his new friend informed him, giving up part of his seat. Then he asked Sholom Meyer what business he had in New York, when he had arrived from Europe, on what ship, and what kind of crossing he had had.

Sholom Meyer invented a business out of his head, and they became so engrossed in conversation the glum-faced one almost forgot his job. He recalled himself just in time to avert a fresh catastrophe.

When Rapalesco had revived, he said to his rescuer, "Your face looks somehow familiar."

"No wonder. We saw each other often enough in Holeneshti."

At the word "Holeneshti" Rapalesco started, and asked everyone to leave his dressing room. Then he threw himself at Sholom Meyer and demanded who he was, where he came from, and what he was doing here.

"Who am I? I am also an actor in the Yiddish theater. Where do I come from? From London. What am I doing here? I am looking for the day before yesterday. A friend of mine, also an actor, made me swear an oath an hour before his death. Since this friend had a young sister, a pretty little chick, and since a certain actor had fallen in love with this sister, and since as a result of this love, the girl was in nine months' time safely delivered of a child, and since this actor, the father of the child, had carried himself off to America in the meanwhile, my friend made me swear before God, who sits above, and watches all the mischief down below, to take his sister and her child and bring them here to New York, to find this young man and not step away from him until he married the girl according to the law of Israel. Doesn't it sound like the kind of romance you read in books?"

Possibly our hero felt a strange premonition, or else he was curious about the romance, for he asked, "Can you tell me the name of the friend who entrusted this fine piece of business to you?"

"With the greatest pleasure. He was called Hotzmach, though his name was actually Holtzman."

Rapalesco started. "Holtzman, Bernhard Holtzman, you say is . . ."

"Dead. May he rest in peace. And his sister's name is Zlatka. She is here with me in New York. She was eager to come with me to the theater tonight, but she couldn't bear to leave her little one. You know how it is. A mother's devotion. Now do you want to know who the young man is, the father of the child?" Sholom Meyer looked him keenly in the eyes. "He comes all the way from Bucharest. Though between you and me, he's from Bucharest as I am from Jerusalem. God be with you. Why do you turn so pale? You're shaking. Take my word for it, no harm will come to you. I'm only thinking of your good and of the good of my friend in the other world, may God grant me fortune and luck!"

What is a misfortune for some is a boon for others. For Nissel Shwalb and his combinations Rapalesco's failure was a godsend. Now he could tackle his plan with more assurance of success. For a man who has sunk in his own esteem is fair game for anyone. Nissel Shwalb went to work the very next morning after the disastrous performance.

294

What was his astonishment when, upon entering Rapalesco's room, he beheld the same little chap whom he had only last night wrenched away from Mr. Klammer's beard and pitched into the street.

"So you're still alive," Nissel Shwalb remarked with his usual good humor. "Like a weed, you spring up where you haven't been planted."

"What did you think?" the other answered with the same good humor. "Lucky for you that you were so many and I was one, or that gentleman from the London Whitechapel wouldn't have come out of my hands alive. He'd be lying on the ground now, minus a beard, and with a feather under his nose, as my name is Sholom Meyer Muravchik."

"Muravchik you say? A familiar name. Which of the Muravchiks are you?" And Shwalb extended his large, well-padded hand to his new acquaintance.

"Which of the Muravchiks am I? I am one of the original Muravchiks, who never in their lives owed anyone money, for nobody would lend them any, and if they did, it was gone and forgotten, just like the blows I got last night. Believe me, I haven't tasted such blows in a long time, may God grant me fortune and luck. Still, one thing has nothing to do with another. I like your face much better than your fists, may they wither and drop off. Take my word for it, if I had the time, I'd get to know you better. But now I must go. Good luck to you, give my regards to everyone, and drop me a postcard. Goodbye."

Shwalb answered heartily, "You can't imagine how happy I am to have met you. May I have everyone's good at heart."

"I saw it last night," said Sholom Meyer from the door, "and I didn't so much see it with my eyes as I felt it in my bones. May God grant me fortune and luck."

Rapalesco escorted Sholom Meyer out of the door and spoke to him a moment or so in the hall. When he returned, Nissel Shwalb turned to him with a fatherly air. "Who is that *schlimazl*? If I were you, Rapalesco, I'd steer clear of such riff-raff." Then he went on, "Well, let's get down to brass tacks. We have a piece of business to settle. First of all, I came to cheer you up. You don't have to feel so discouraged. It was only a slip. Accidents happen to the best of us."

"Everything is an accident to you. But one accident isn't like another. In all my life, since I've been on the stage, I haven't had to rely on a prompter. No, it was a catastrophe."

"Ridiculous. The day after tomorrow, at the next show, we'll do better. Meanwhile we have a couple of free days. When should we have the wedding?"

295

"What wedding?"

"What do you mean, what wedding?" They stood facing each other as though seeing each other for the first time in their lives.

"Are you joking?" Nissel demanded.

"I, joking?" said Rapalesco. "You're the one who's joking. You've all been playing a practical joke on me."

"What do you mean, all of us?"

"I mean all of you. You and your brother and your sister. That affair at the Lomzha Nightingale's and that speech of Klammer's! Do you think you've got hold of a country yokel whom you'll lead about on a string? God has blessed you with a pretty sister, a stupid little heifer, whom you yourselves call 'dummy' and 'blockhead,' and you are trying to hang her around my neck. I thank you from the bottom of my heart, but I'm afraid I must decline the honor. Find yourself another scapegoat."

The above speech had been delivered with such a fine blend of irony and earnestness, and Rapalesco concluded it with a bow of such mock gallantry, that if it had taken place on the stage, it would have won an ovation. But since it didn't take place on the stage, and since not only his own interests but his family honor was involved, Nissel Shwalb received it quite differently. His face turned white, then scarlet, then blue. On his thick neck a vein stood out and began to throb like an ox's before it is slaughtered. His eyes, bulging like those of a fish when it's being scraped, seemed to say, "Scrape, scrape, but you'll see what'll happen next."

"Tell me something, dear boy," he said. "Do you know what the words 'breach of promise' mean?"

Though Rapalesco was as wrought up as Shwalb, he managed to ask, in his mock-serious tone, "No, what does 'breach of promise' mean?"

"It means that when a young man gives a girl his word before witnesses that he will marry her, and then goes back on it, he gets slapped on the wrists and ends up by marrying her."

Rapalesco came closer to Shwalb. "When did I give your sister such promises? That night at the Lomzha Nightingale's when you got me drunk on sour champagne and all of you, including Braindele Kozak and the cantor's wife, fell on my neck and began smacking me?"

Nissel Shwalb dropped a heavy hand on Rapalesco's shoulder, and said in one breath, "Listen, my boy. You'll have an ugly little lawsuit on your hands. America is a land which doesn't tolerate nonsense. We have witnesses who will swear they saw a certain young man with the girl in his arms. It was on board ship—do you remember? And we'll find others to testify that you bought bracelets and rings from them, and still others who saw you put them on my sister's hand. Fool, take my advice, give in with good grace. If not, may you choke on this table."

With these words Nissel Shwalb left.

Thus ominous clouds gathered on Rapalesco's horizon. Disaster threatened from every direction. Still unnerved by his breakdown in the theater, he staggered under greater miseries.

His failure had actually not been as overwhelming as he had imagined. Only this morning two representatives of an American theater had come to him with a proposition which nearly swept him off his feet.

One of the visitors had a shaven face, a bald skull, gold teeth, and curiously long fingernails. The other was a reporter from a big New York daily, a smiling, astute-looking man with reddish hair, who spoke several languages fluently, Yiddish among them. Though he introduced himself as Archibald Bauerwald, and though his English was faultless, certain intonations in his voice, gestures here and there, a quirk of the eyebrows, a shrug of the shoulders, all seemed to interject: "What Archibald? Who Bauerwald? Call me Artzie Berels and be done with it."

The man with the naked skull talked as though he had just had all his teeth pulled and his mouth stuffed with cotton. The smiling Archibald translated what he said into Yiddish, to wit: Let Rapalesco come right over to the American stage, play his roles in Yiddish first, until he learned the English language. The terms were such they made Rapalesco's head swim. But he retained enough presence of mind to ask for twenty-four hours in which to make up his mind.

"All right," said the one with the naked skull, and got up to leave. The reporter lingered a moment to advise Rapalesco in sharp, idiomatic Yiddish, "Idiot! Don't pass up the chance. It's a fat corpse. Goodbye."

This, too, was a problem. More upsetting was the problem of Rosa Spivak. What had brought her to the Nickel Theater? Pure chance, or had she realized it was his première? If so, why had she run off after the second act? Was it true, as Henrietta had said, that she and Stellmach had mocked him? He would have given years of his life to know the truth. At any other time he wouldn't have rested until he found a way to reach her. But his hands were tied.

Finally, there was Sholom Meyer Muravchik and his glad tidings. The news of Holtzman's death made a profound impression on him. He was almost as stricken as when he had heard from the cashier, "Joy-and-Gladness," of his mother's passing. There awakened in him a sharp feeling of guilt. Hadn't he betrayed Holtzman, deserted him on his deathbed?

Other memories he thought buried rose to haunt him. Zlatka, to whom he had not even had the grace to say goodbye, running off from her like a thief. What had poor Zlatka thought of him when she learned from her sick brother that Rapalesco, her lover and idol, had slunk off to America? What penance was great enough to atone for such a crime? He would punish himself by tearing out of his heart all his youthful dreams, all his foolish fancies, forget there had ever been anyone in the world by the name of Rosa. He must return to Zlatka her tarnished idol; he must go to the poor unhappy girl, fall at her feet, kiss her hands and say, "Zlatka, I am yours, yours forever."

He would have done it at once if Sholom Meyer hadn't held him back. "Zlatka," he said, "is a simple, honest girl (ha, ha, though she has a kid) who has never read any romances. If a young man throws himself at her feet and starts beating his breast and wailing, 'I have sinned, I repent, absolve me!' she will faint with fright. Her mother will come running—we mustn't forget there's an old mother by the name of Sarah-Brocha—and give the young man such a fare-thee-well he won't recover from it for a long time." Better that he, Sholom Meyer, should prepare them. This he would do the opposite way. He wouldn't tell them Rapalesco was beating his breast. Women hated a weakling who went to pieces and spouted apologies and antimonies, philosophy and cabbage. Pfui! Women liked a man who was a man. Muravchik knew. He hadn't as many hairs on his head as he'd had dealings with women, may God grant him fortune and luck.

With that Sholom Meyer went off on his mission. As the young prodigal, after making short work of his next visitor, Nissel Shwalb, was sitting at the window he saw a limousine draw up to the curb. From it a chauffeur in livery stepped and walked into the hotel. "Is he looking for me?" Rapalesco wondered idly. A moment later he heard a knock on the door.

"Come in."

It was the chauffeur with a letter.

With trembling hands Rapalesco took a thin scented envelope, opened it carefully, and glanced down at the signature, which at once made his heart pound so that he had to sit down before he could start reading.

My dear wandering star,

I am still too shaken by the events of the last twelve hours to convey to you a hundredth part of what I would like to tell you in person. It was sheer chance that brought me to your première last night. If my heart didn't burst apart when I learned that Uriel Acosta was you, it must be made of steel. I sat in a daze through the second act. Then something happened which no one could have foreseen. We were recognized, and our identity exposed in such a crude manner we were forced to flee, though every fiber of my being drew me back, back for another look at your face, another chance to hear your voice which hasn't stopped ringing in my ears, all the years of my wandering through the wide, bright world. But wait. This isn't all. Coming home, I found a whole packet of letters which, according to the postmarks, had arrived some time ago, but which had been withheld from me because of a censorship which my manager, though he is an American and calls himself a gentleman, exercised against my will and without my knowledge. I sent for him early today, and without preambles terminated our contract and told him he could go ahead and sue me for damages if he liked. Among those letters was yours which I have read and reread with mingled feelings. Everyone of your dear words has been almost obliterated by tears. Why tears, you ask? I wept over our departed youth, our vanished innocence, our premature love, which though it may now burn with a steadier and a stronger flame, will never again have the early-morning freshness of the old days in Holeneshti.

Ah, Holeneshti. Do you know that I was there not so long ago, looking for my Leibel, for my "rich man's son," like a little Cinderella looking for her prince? Nobody could tell me your whereabouts.

My dearest, in your letter you mention a gipsy who once told me my fortune in a little town in Galicia. How did you know of it? Apparently you looked for me and asked about me as much as I looked for and asked about you. How could you have despaired of me so, you perfidious one, to have allowed another, that prima donna, maybe prettier than I, but far more stupid, to go about boasting she is engaged to you? But what am I saying? How can I reproach you with inconstancy when I myself, through a tangle of circumstances too involved to go into now, was also driven to hang golden chains about my neck? But let us not talk of chains, which we can burst asunder, if it is our wish. Let us talk rather about how we can get together. You will find an address below. Come here between four and five today, and look around; you will find me. Be there without fail, between four and five. I command it. No, that's a lie. Why shouldn't I tell you the whole truth?

299

I do not command, I beseech you. For I love you. Do you hear me?
I love you.

Reizel

Sholom Meyer Muravchik returned to Rapalesco's at the time
agreed upon, but found him gone. A note addressed to him lay on
the table.

My dear Muravchik,

I am going out of New York for a few hours. When I will return I do not know. We shall have to put off our visit for another
time. Please make my apologies to the one we were going to see,
as only you know how to do. You will thereby win my undying
gratitude.

Yours,

L. Rapalesco

"May the nightmares I had last night and the night before and all
the nights of my life, both on sea and on dry land, fall on my enemies.
An actor remains an actor, though he plays the gentleman."

Sholom Meyer turned away in disgust. He was ready to spit on the
whole business, when he heard a rap on the door.

He started joyfully. Rapalesco had returned. "Come in," he sang
out. The knock came again. It couldn't be Rapalesco. To his second
"Come in," Muravchik heard a third knock. In exasperation he
shouted, "Knock your head on the wall!"

Slowly the door opened and in stepped—Braindele Kozak.

If Hotzmach had appeared from the other world, Sholom Meyer
couldn't have been more dumbfounded. But he recovered at once,
stepped forward with an outstretched hand, and said, with a quizzical
smile, "Well, well. Look who's here. An unexpected guest. What's the
good word, Braindele—pfui—I mean, Madame Cherniak?"

But Madame Cherniak wasn't as quick to recover. She had never
dreamed that she would meet her old enemy, Sholom Meyer, here in
New York. And where? At Rapalesco's!

She had just learned from her new friend Nissel Shwalb that Rapalesco had thrown over Nissel's sister. Nissel was on his way to a law-
yer's to start a "breach of promise" suit. Besides the cantor and Mr.
Klammer, who would swear they had seen Henrietta in Rapalesco's
arms on board ship, he was ready to put on the witness stand half of
New York, including Braindele Kozak. He would produce all the
guests at the Lomzha cantor's who had heard the engagement announced, and seen the plate smashed, and kissed and congratulated

300

bride and groom. Madame Cherniak had listened in horror. How could she permit such a thing? A scandal like this would ruin the young star's career. Besides, she had her own axe to grind.

With the arrival in New York of the cooperative, Klammer, Shwalb & Co., there had begun the new Nissel Shwalb chapter in the life of Braindele Kozak. He was her last hope, the last station on her life's journey. Poor Braindele Kozak. She had fallen in love for the last time with the same abandon—perhaps more—with which she had fallen in love for the first time. She was ready to take the most desperate measures to save her final venture from shipwreck.

She knew about Rosa Spivak's visit to the theater. And she put the following two and two together: 1. Why had Rosa suddenly shown up at the Nickel Theater if not to see Rapalesco? 2. Which meant that they had got together by mail and had arranged the meeting. 3. Then why had Rapalesco gone through with the farce at the Lomzha cantor's? Apparently a blind, to throw sand in their eyes. 4. If so, she must pay a visit to this wily young man, first of all, to look him in the eye—that was all she needed. Second, to cajole him into arranging a meeting for her with Rosa. A few words with Rosa alone, and their goose would be cooked. The young man would have to march under the canopy with Henrietta, and she herself would be, as they say in America, "all right."

Imagine her consternation then, on entering Rapalesco's room, to find her old enemy, Sholom Meyer, instead.

"Well, well, you certainly look blooming. America must agree with you," said Sholom Meyer. "You're getting younger and prettier every year. If it wasn't for your red cape, I'd never have recognized you, may God grant me fortune and luck!"

Madame Cherniak, easy prey to such compliments, melted like butter in a frying pan. She was ready to forget all the insults she had ever received from this *schlimazl* with the croaking voice, even the money he still owed her. She undid the strings of her red cape, pulled up a chair close to Sholom Meyer, and the following conversation took place:

Braindele: I never dreamed I would meet you here.
Sholom Meyer: Which shows you've got me six feet underground, while I've been thinking of you day and night and dreaming of you in between.
Braindele: So long may you live.
Sholom Meyer: Amen, to all women.
Braindele: You are the same impudent rascal as always. Tell

me better where is that scoundrel, your old boss, may he burn alive.

Sholom Meyer: Who? Shchupak? He's in Odessa, may the cholera choke him there in the middle of winter.

Braindele: Why not let the plague strangle him tonight?

Sholom Meyer: By me he can drop dead in the middle of the day. And what are you doing here, darling? Did you come to see Rapalesco?

Braindele: Who else? I can't understand it; he's always home this time of day.

Sholom Meyer: Better than that. We made an appointment. We set our watches together. And how goes it with you, kitten?

Braindele: It could be worse. As long as I make a living. And with you?

Sholom Meyer: I can't complain. You work and you sweat and you muddle through. Tell me, sweet soul . . . what was I going to ask you? Oh, yes, what are you doing at this young whippersnapper's? You have business with him?

Braindele: Our business! Have you been long in New York?

Sholom Meyer: If you count the blows I have caught here, then I came with Columbus. Tell me, dear heart, what business have you got, for instance, let us suppose, for example, with my boy?

Braindele: Since when is he yours?

Sholom Meyer: Since when? That's a good one. I've known him since he was a head taller than a cat.

Braindele: Is that a fact? Then you might have some influence with him.

Sholom Meyer: Did you say I *might*?

Braindele: Then why don't you see to it that they have the wedding?

Sholom Meyer: Mind you, it's still a long way from a wedding. . . .

Braindele: Really? What stands in the way?

Sholom Meyer: A mite like this stands in the way.

Braindele: What in the world are you talking about?

Sholom Meyer: I am talking about the "kid."

Braindele: What "kid"?

Sholom Meyer: You ask me what "kid." That shows that you know less than the dead. So what are you yapping about?

Braindele: Never mind, I know very well what I'm talking about. I'm talking about a prima donna, and you drive in with your "kid."

Sholom Meyer: In the first place it isn't my "kid." And in the second place which prima donna are you talking about?

Braindele: Which prima donna? I know two prima donnas.

Sholom Meyer: Where do you get two prima donnas all of a sudden?

Braindele: See, you don't know what's hanging in front of your nose, if you never heard of the prima donnas.

302

Sholom Meyer: Do you know what? You can choke with your two prima donnas.

Braindele: I'll give you the honor of choking first, you're the elder.

Sholom Meyer: Mind you, it's hard to tell who's the elder. I can see there's no use talking to you. You're a worse epilepsy than you ever were.

Braindele: And you were always an apostate, and an apostate you will remain.

Sholom Meyer: With your face you should be a market woman in Vilna in Gitka Taiba's alley.

Braindele: And you are only fit to traipse about with Shchupak, peddling wives.

Sholom Meyer: May you know as much of your mustaches as I know of Shchupak and his wives.

Braindele: Then who snatched the Cantor's girl from Holeneshti if not you and Shchupak?

Sholom Meyer: What do you know about Holeneshti? What do you know about the Cantor's girl?

Braindele: So. You see I know more than you.

Sholom Meyer: Do you know what? Why should we fight in America? America is a land of peace. Let's do it this way. I will tell you the story about the "kid." You can take my word for it that I'll tell the truth. And you tell me the story of the prima donnas. Is it agreed?

Braindele: Will you give your hand on it?

Sholom Meyer: Here is my hand.

The upshot of it was that little by little Braindele Kozak disclosed all she knew about the prima donnas. But when Sholom Meyer's turn came to tell about the "kid," she saw that he was knocking a teakettle. And Braindele Kozak rose to her feet, drew the red cape majestically about her, and burst into a wild laugh, as though a hundred demons had seized her. Sholom Meyer actually got frightened.

"What's come over you?" he asked.

"Everything I told you is a lie," said Braindele. "I made it all up out of my head."

Sholom Meyer gave her a look full of reproach. But in his heart he was thinking, "You can tell that to your grandmother, Braindele." And the strange pair parted, in opposite moods—he elated by the information he had got from her; she angry at herself for having allowed herself once more to be outwitted by those "false, double-dealing men," may a cholera take them all, except one!

40 IN SHOLOM'S RESTAURANT

The story of the two prima donnas which he had wormed out of Braindele Kozak opened Sholom Meyer's eyes. Suddenly he understood Rosa's keen interest in Hotzmach. She had been preoccupied with the Rapalovich boy. "Sholom Meyer," he thought, "you deserve to be laid out here in the middle of America and be given fifty lashes for not making use of this situation before. You could have licked a juicy bone either from the groom's or the bride's side. And when you did get hold of a packet of her letters, you had to go and pawn them for a few shillings with that London dude, may he drop dead in the middle of New York. If I had those papers now, I'd be rolling in wealth. As it is, I can't even show my face before Rosa." Here Sholom Meyer became sunk in thought. Then he started up. "Never fear, may Shchupak in Odessa and Klammer in New York live so long, as I will still put this business to good account. If not, you deserve to chew straw, Sholom Meyer, may God grant me fortune and luck!"

In the meanwhile a certain rumbling in his belly gave him notice that the dinner hour was near. Looking about for a place to eat, he stumbled on the famous restaurant owned by the same Sholom whose picture appeared in the papers every day with the following caption:

DON'T FORGET YOUR FRIEND, SHOLOM, WHO PROVIDES YOU EVERY DAY WITH THE FINEST RUMANIAN DISHES, KOSHER AND FRESH AND TASTY.

No sooner had he found where he could be alone to go over the plans in his head than there appeared before him a sprightly youth, with red hair, and a white napkin over his arm. Like a sleight-of-hand artist he produced a fountain pen and a small book out of the air, fixed the guest with a severe look, as though to say, "Mister, order your dinner, and don't bother me too long. You see how many customers we have waiting. Hurry up."

Unfazed by the youth with the white napkin and the fountain pen,

304

Sholom Meyer sat down leisurely, removed his hat which had been dented by that scoundrel Nissel Shwalb, produced a folding comb from his pocket, and slicked back his hair. Then he ordered a dinner to match his appetite.

"A paprika goulash of gizzards, livers, and chicken wings is not number one. A soup with a good-sized chicken leg is not number two. A laymeout with barley is not three. A carrot *tsimmes* with a piece of stuffed *kishke* is not four. A small glass cognac from a siphon, and a slice radish with chicken fat on the side, and a tall glass lager is not five. And start out on the right foot, step lively, on your toes, and off with you on the double-quick, march."

Sholom Meyer rattled off the last words in one breath, with his usual bravado. The red-haired youth wrote down the dishes he had enumerated with the speed of a stenographer. Then he glanced over the list from top to bottom and back again and asked the guest, "What exactly is a *laymeout* with barley?"

"You've never heard of a *laymeout*? Do you know what a *chokemedown* is? What kind of restaurant servant are you? Why don't you go shine shoes in the street or clean the . . ."

But Sholom Meyer didn't finish what he had started. The sprightly youth with the white napkin gave him a withering look, opened his mouth wide, and addressed him in the language of America:

"Shut your trap, mister. I'm not a servant. I'm a waiter in a Jewish restaurant. I'm a member of a union. I'm a . . ."

It was lucky Sholom, the proprietor, came between them just then and made peace; otherwise one of the two would have fared badly.

The set-to with the waiter hadn't impaired Sholom Meyer's appetite. And while he ate, a plan took shape in his head.

"That this songbird Rapalesco should have fallen for Rosa is all to the good. For what have I got against them, actually? Let them grow old together in honor and in riches. But what will happen to Zlatka? The same thing that happens to all girls who give away their dowry before the wedding. It's a pity, but what's to be done? She will cry until she stops crying. And to be sure I won't let her fall. I'm not Shchupak. I don't have a stable of wives. I don't even have one. It's high time, it seems to me, I had a corner of my own to lay my head down in. Especially since Zlatka is a good, decent girl, modest and quiet, one of God's little lambs. To take a girl like that is an act of piety. To me it's the same difference, with a kid or without a kid. I'll treat her well. I won't throw up past sins to her. And she won't want for a crust of bread, either. I'm not Shchupak, may his name be erased. Naturally, they will have to help us out. It won't be any skin off their noses, they can afford it. Especially she. They say she shovels in gold with both hands here in America. After all, I am taking her just as she is, child and all, with an old mother thrown in for good measure. If he pulls any funny stuff, I'll bring him a gift to his wedding—a baby in a blanket. . . . Oh, Mr. Noodleserver, the check!"

The last words were spoken in a loud voice to the waiter, who pretended not to hear, let the tip go, and sent Sholom, the proprietor, to settle up with the greenhorn.

Rapalesco had started too early for his rendezvous with Rosa. He hadn't even looked at the time. Only when he was in the street and after he had read her letter for the tenth time until he knew it by heart, did he realize that it was only noon and his appointment was between four and five. He stopped in a barbershop for a shave and then in a café for a bite to eat, and still had hours to spare. Never had time dragged so. He walked along slowly, stopping to read the signs jutting out from every shop window and pasted across house fronts, clamoring to the passersby to stop, look, listen, and buy. Hardly noticing what he did, he descended some steps to the subway. A train pulled in and Rapalesco found himself sucked into the current which was being absorbed into the train, when suddenly there flashed before his eyes, among the descending passengers, a familiar figure—a little man with a dented hat—could it be Muravchik? Rapalesco tore himself loose and let the train leave without him.

Sholom Meyer had also seen Rapalesco. It seemed almost uncanny to meet him here just when he had been thinking how best to approach him, to carry out his plan.

He stood still, trying to conceal his joy at meeting Rapalesco. Rapalesco, on the other hand, frankly showed his pleasure at this unexpected encounter. "Hello, how do you do," he greeted Sholom Meyer, in the American manner. "It's a good thing we met. God Himself must have sent you here. I want to talk to you."

"The pleasure is all mine," said Sholom Meyer. "Where shall we go?"

"Nowhere," said Rapalesco, looking about for a place to sit. "Here's a bench. We can talk right here."

"Here under the ground?"

"Here under the ground."

"If you're happy, then I'm willing."

There on a subway station bench they began talking. That is, Rapa-

306

lesco talked, while Sholom Meyer looked and listened. A strange man, that Sholom Meyer. He has the faculty of understanding you at a glance. It was a joy to deal with a man like that.

"You don't have to put a finger in my mouth," Sholom Meyer murmured, close to Rapalesco's ear, in a voice that had a rasp in it, but was at the same time as soothing as syrup. "Believe me, I understand perfectly. I can read it to you as from a prayer book. May we be spared the evil eye, these things happen to the best of us. We're only human and a pretty girl is a temptation. A man isn't to blame if the devil gives him a push. And how can you be an oracle and foresee it will end up with a kid? Let's face it. She's not meant for you, and you're not meant for her. Do you think she doesn't understand it? She understands it better than any of us, may God grant me fortune and luck!"

At these words a tremendous weight rolled off Rapalesco's chest. Plainly Sholom Meyer implied that the girl wasn't so anxious for the match either. To reassure him further, Sholom Meyer went on.

"Where do you think I'm coming from, now? From Zlatka herself. I gave her your message and she starts weeping, 'Am I his equal?' she says. 'He's got such a name in the world! Why should I feel that I forced myself on him?' "

Rapalesco was touched. "Did she really say that?"

"What then? Would I be making it up out of thin air?"

"I don't mean that. I mean, did she say it in those words?"

"May God grant me fortune and luck! Do you have any notion of what a loyal soul she is? She's worth eighteen prima donnas."

In Rapalesco's eyes tears appeared. But he hid them from his new friend. And Sholom Meyer went on.

"So it went, back and forth. I saw the girl talked sense. I thought to myself, 'Maybe you're right,' and I said to her, 'Listen, my little soul, here's the story. The young man meant it all for your good and for the good of your little one. But nobody will drag you to the canopy by force. And the kid? You don't have to lose any sleep on that score. Rapalesco will see that you're taken care of, and your child, too, and even your mother doesn't have to fall back on strangers. And I'm not dead yet, either. Who brought you here if not Muravchik? Who,' I said, 'registered you under his name when we left the ship if not Muravchik? Just imagine you're already mine and I am yours and that's all there is to it. And for that matter, we can find four sticks for a canopy in America.' And as you see me here before you, I'm not averse to it. First, because I'm sorry for her. A friendless orphan. And second, she's a good, decent girl, quiet as a dove. The question is only how we'll get along. Well, God is a father, and as I said before, you won't forget us either."

"Forget you?" Rapalesco pressed Sholom Meyer's hand with his. "I will put it in writing, if you like."

"What do we need writing for? You will sign a couple of notes, made out to myself. I will come to you tonight and bring everything. And now, were you on your way somewhere?"

Rapalesco had become so absorbed in their conversation that he hadn't noticed how the hands of the clock had crept up to three. He shook hands with Sholom Meyer cordially and jumped on the next train.

"Sholom Meyer, you're all right," Sholom Meyer said to himself. "It's a great land, America. Oi, what an America!"

41   AMONG THE CAGES

The spot Rosa had chosen for their rendezvous was the park of the large Zoological Gardens, which was less frequented by people in winter than in summer. One could walk about without seeing anyone except the animals in their cages.

Rapalesco arrived at the designated spot almost an hour early. And what he lived through in that short hour, while pacing from cage to cage, he hadn't lived through in all his years of wandering over the wide world. All kinds of dark thoughts and forebodings came to plague him. What if Rosa didn't come? And if she did, would she bring with her the "golden chains?" What sort of scene had taken place between her and Grischa Stellmach at the last moment? His heart tightened with foreboding. Try as he might, he couldn't dispel the gloomy thoughts crowding into his head. He thought of the bargain he had just struck with Sholom Meyer. No use glossing it over with fine words. He had bartered poor Zlatka away like a piece of goods. And a few hours before he had been ready to fall at her feet in atonement.

If he could only lose himself here, escape from himself! If he could only blot out his past life and start afresh! That past rose before him, with all its failings, all his sins, all his aspirations and dreams. As in an open ledger, he saw the two columns of debits and credits. Totalling them, he pronounced his own verdict: As a man he was a sinner; as an artist, he was insignificant, surrounded by petty people, a minuscule blown up by false notoriety, all bluff. Much water would flow, many sacrifices be offered up, many altars overthrown, and still he would stand as he did now, at the outer door of that holy temple toward which this young but pain-burdened heart had yearned since childhood. But wait. Someone was coming down the path. His heart nearly stopped, his eyes grew wide. A young woman, lovely and self-possessed, was approaching. To his fevered imagination she seemed to be floating, not walking.

Seldom do we meet a person whom we have long awaited and find what we expected. Rosa was not the person Rapalesco had imagined, not the Reizel he had known in Holeneshti, nor the Rosa he had built up out of his own fancy. He saw a different woman, taller, older, graver than the girl he had remembered. At first glance she appeared aloof, her face too pale, her features too regular, her bearing too stiff. Only her eyes were the dark, lustrous gipsy eyes he remembered.

And to Rosa he was not the Rapalesco she had seen in her dreams, not the Leibel, the "rich man's boy," she remembered from her father's *cheder*. Only his eyes had not changed. They were the same, pensive dreamer's eyes. For a moment they stood facing each other without movement or speech, as though trying to read in each other's faces the whole story of their self-imposed exile. But only for a moment. A slow smile appeared on her face; his heart gave a leap, and he felt himself drawn toward her as by a magnet. . . .

If this were a melodrama, the hero and the heroine would have fallen into each other's arms. He would have called out "Reizel!" in broken accents; she would have cried "Leibel!" in a strangled voice; and tears would have flowed like water. But since this is not a melodrama, we shall refrain from giving the particulars of their meeting. The moment was too exalted, their emotions too sacred to be put into words. Let us leave these two wandering stars who had gravitated toward each other at last, in this curious trysting place among the animal cages. Let them go from cage to cage; let them sit down now and then on the benches to look into each other's eyes. Let them talk; let them pour their hearts out to each other until night falls and the stars appear. And if they talk to each other with candor, if they are

309

honest with themselves in their own thoughts, they will overlook each other's foibles, their mistakes, both great and small; and they will find in each other the ideal they have sought.

Dear reader, let us wish them good fortune and fulfillment of their dreams. And now let us come to the end. We will let excerpts from some letters finish our tale.

From Rosa Spivak Rapalovich to Marcella Zembrich

. . . you ask if I am happy in my marriage. If there can be a happy person in this world, there are two such, my Rapalesco and I. But no. That isn't quite true. Everything in this world is relative. And we are relatively happy. If I wanted to explain myself truly, I would have to write you not a letter, but a book. And that I am not competent to do, nor do I have the time. But since we are back in our old Europe and I have engagements in London, Paris, Berlin, Vienna, and Budapest, we are certain to meet and I will introduce you to my husband. He's a big, simple-hearted child with very little education, but with so much talent and divine fire in him we may all hide our heads in shame. His ideal is the stage, and his goal is to reform the Yiddish theater and place it on as high a plane as possible. Will he succeed? I do not know. I only know that he won't stop halfway. As much as it lies in my power, I will help him. In the meanwhile he is still shockingly green and raw and untamed, more untamed even than I, your eternal gipsy, who sends you much love,

Rosa Spivak Rapalovich

From Meyer Stellmach to his Good Friend

. . . that's how it is, brother, and don't ask any questions. It's—how do they say—a big world with little worlds revolving around it. If they had only made a clean break, I wouldn't complain. It happens sometimes that a match doesn't come off. But here the match fell through, and they're still friends. And what kind of friends do you think? There are friends and friends. These two write each other every week, and he writes not only to her, but to her husband, Rapalesco. Since my Grischa and this Rapalesco met, they've become bosom friends. Soulmates, no less. When you talk about "love" . . . But if that was all, I could put up with it. How do they say it, "If you're eager, then I am willing." But the disgrace of it! After I spread the news of their engagement all over town. So be a prophet and guess that she'll marry an artist in the Yiddish theater. And who's to blame for it, if not I? If I hadn't taken them to the Yiddish theater that night, it wouldn't have happened. And now I have to fill my mouth with water, and clamp my teeth down. I can't say a word against them. Any little thing and my Grischa flares up like a match. And the world doesn't sleep. Our Jews know everyone's heartaches. Whenever I meet anybody, it's, "I am surprised, Mr. Stellmach. How could you have allowed it? You a practical man, and a father." And so on and so forth. Forgive me for boring you with my troubles. When you pour your heart out to a good friend, you imagine you feel easier. . . .

From your confused and unhappy friend who is at odds with the whole world, Meyer Stellmach.

From Sholom Meyer Muravchik to Albert Shchupak

. . . here is your fifty and be damned to you I am now thank God able to advance you a fifty myself if you need money and I am writing to tell you that I got married to Hotzmach's young sister Zlatka a decent little woman I mean a girl and she has a child I mean we have a child and I love the child with all my heart it's one in a million and I have no business as yet but I am looking around for a little theater that is not a theater but a vaudeville house if I can get something cheap I will buy it and do good business though to be truthful with you the Yiddish theater is going to the dogs here in America they have started to bring down the best German actors from Berlin and they pay them a fortune and I hear that this Rapalesco I wrote you about is coming here with your Rosa and they are bringing new actors and writers and plays from Russia that's America for you woe to Columbus but in the meantime before they get going you can set up shop here with your troupe so take my advice and spit on Russia and come here and we'll go into partnership and if not bury yourself six feet underground and bake bagel.

Sholom Meyer Muravchik

From Braindele Kozak to Henrietta Shwalb

. . . and write me of everything, dear soul, how goes it with you in your new home in Johannesburg? May the evil eye spare you, they say he's a millionaire several times over and that he bought you so many diamonds and jewels that only a Rockefeller could afford it. You can't imagine how happy that made me. For who knows as well as I do the kind of life your brothers led you? And even lately when you began earning good money, they tried to botch up your life. I don't want to speak ill of them, they are your brothers, and I'm not trying to flatter you, but believe me, they aren't worth your fingernail. And especially Nissel with his honeyed words and his oaths. May God repay him a thousand-fold for the way he treated me. Though, mind you, he's getting his share. I understand he's fallen on evil days, I mean your

311

brother Nissel. Since the cooperative fell apart, he's tried every kind of combination. Now he has something new, a paper model of the Jerusalem Temple, and he's running around pasting notices all over New York, and he will no doubt be buried with this combination as with all the others. May God pay him back for you and for me and for all of Israel.

Now your brother Isaac is a lamb next to Nissel. Though he has earned his. May everything he says about you fall into the sea. He goes around telling everybody that you sold yourself for money. I won't soil my lips by repeating his words. I advise you to stuff up his mouth with a few dollars. He could stretch himself out in the middle of New York and nobody would give him a hand. Who would look around at him? The Lomzha Nightingale? So long may she live, that red-haired wife of his. She has thrown off her carroty wig and she's a regular "missis" now. A small thing! Her children, they say, are shoveling in gold with both hands. This land is like a fever—some catch it. Who would ever have guessed that a Lomzha cantor would come here with a kindergarten and strike gold? And he has as much conscience as a Russian Cossack. What more do you want? Mr. Klammer, who sacrificed everything to bring him and his family here and set up the cooperative, barely scraped up enough money for a passage back to London. And do you know who loaned him the few dollars? You'll never guess. That *schlimazl* Sholom Meyer Muravchik who married your Rapalesco's first sweetheart and adopted her child. It's a regular comedy with them. They say Rosa herself sends them money and writes letters and begs Sholom Meyer to look after the child. May all my troubles fall on their heads.

The two of them, Rapalesco and Rosa, are now in Europe. They got married and are doing all right—what do you think? But you don't have to envy her, darling, you've got them both you know where. You are richer and have more jewels. You needn't hanker after the stage, either. If you forgive me for saying so, I think it's foolishness on your part to be homesick for the theater. Enjoy yourself and have a good time and don't forget your family. I mean your brothers. Rather than let them fall back on strangers, you ought to send them something.

And don't forget, my dear, about your friend who is devoted to you body and soul. Write me, and whatever you want to know I will tell you. And if you want anything done, I'll be glad to do it. And if you hear of a decent job for me, write, and I will come to Johannesburg. I'm getting good and tired of Columbus's land and its people, especially the men, and in particular our actors, may a plague choke them all in one day. Amen. Amen. Amen.

I send you a thousand kisses.
Your loving friend,
Braina Cherniak

From Leah the Cantor's Wife to Her Daughter:

. . . and I want you to know, my child, I am waiting for you and
your Leibel to come to us in Holeneshti for a visit, as you promised. I pray God that you both stay in good health and earn a lot
of money and come to us, God willing. If it wasn't for that I
would have sold the house long ago, for what do I need a mansion
like that with so many rooms and I one woman alone? But if you
think there are buyers here, you're mistaken. A town full of
paupers and beggars, nobody has any money. And whoever had
a little has long since gone to America. There's only one prospect,
Henich the Vintner's son-in-law. A new *nogid* in Holeneshti. He
has his eyes on the house, but he's afraid to come out as a buyer
so I won't set the price too high. And I won't let him know I'm
selling, so he won't try to snatch a bargain. Meanwhile, I am
neither here nor there, and I am waiting for you to come.

May I hope that God has blessed me and that you are coming
to your mother for a certain event? Foolish child, don't be
ashamed to tell me. It's a natural thing for Jews, did you ever see
such a thing? I want you to tell me just when and what and I
will get everything ready. And if God sees fit, we may have a
namesake for your father, may he enjoy his paradise. He deserves
the honor. He had enough troubles from you while he was alive.
He wasn't fated, apparently because of my sins, to live to enjoy
so many blessings as I have, that I should live in Rapalovich's
house, one woman alone in so many rooms, and that Ben Rapalovich's son, the best of all his children, should be my son-in-law.
May God grant us long life and much joy, for his brothers and
sisters have no luck at all. The whole family has gone to wrack
and ruin. They are scattered over the seven seas. Only Anshel is
left. He comes to me sometimes for help and I give him what I
can. But how can you fill a sack full of holes? If Beilka, may she
rest in peace, were to rise from her grave and see what has become
of her home and her children and husband, poor man. He's gone
out of his mind and he's been put away in some madhouse or
hospital somewhere and sits there and waits for his son-in-law,
"Joy-and-Gladness," to bring him a pound of tea or a cone of
sugar. He comes to see me, too, this "Joy-and-Gladness," and sits
all day and all night and talks and talks.

And can you believe it, the old grandmother, the blind one,
still lives. Do you suppose the Almighty has forgotten about her?
The people who go on living! As we say on *Rosh Hashono*, "He
who lives and he who lies in the ground." Wouldn't it have been
a thousand times better if your father were alive and living here
with me, so I wouldn't be one woman alone in such a big house?
But you can't question God's ways. For instance, Yechiel the
Musician—do you remember him—up and dies just the other
day. Still a young man. And Henich the Vintner passed away,
too, though it's no great loss, he was full of years and a rich

man. If you saw the funeral they gave him! For what, I would like to know. For his piety, or his charities? It was different with your father, but Henich the Vintner! How did he earn such an honor? Just because a man is rich, do you have to flatter him after he's dead? But I don't begrudge him the honor. He left a widow and four children, though with a good business and plenty of money. Still, they are orphans. They will never have a father again. But the one to be pitied is the musician's wife. She was left without anything. They took up a collection for her in town. I also gave what I could, though the deacons grumbled, they said it wasn't enough. "You're a rich woman now," they told me, "with a daughter like that and a house with so many rooms." So go tell them the house is a dead weight on my shoulders. May the Almighty help us that I see you soon in good health and then I will take counsel with you and your Leibel about what to do with the house, for what do I need a house with so many rooms for, one woman alone? Do you think that I'm the only one who says so? Everybody in Holeneshti says so. And everybody is waiting for your coming. Even the widow Necha and her two sisters (they aren't married yet, a plague on them). They keep calling me, "Leah, my darling, my life, when are your children coming to see you?" She must have forgotten the shame she brought on me that time you ran away and they dragged me before the police chief, may his name be erased, he's long since gone from this world.

And stay in good health, my child, and write me if it's true that you and Leibel are planning to go back to America? I don't like this plan at all. It's not a bad country and the people are decent enough, but I don't like their language. When a neighbor is a "nexdorige" and a fowl is a "chicken" and everybody is "all right," even when he's dying on his feet. But before you do it, come to Holeneshti first, God willing. The whole town sends you regards, and Chaim Shaye's son Nochem, who is writing this letter, sends you special regards.

Your mother who prays for you day and night,

Leah Spivak